WHITE RABBIT

An American Satire

Also by the author:

The Boy in Mitchell Bay

(as Trevor Chittick)

WHITE RABBIT

An American Satire

TC SCOTT

TSC BOOKS
Nova Scotia, Canada

White Rabbit: An American Satire

Cover Design by: Miblart

First Trade Paperback edition: September 2024

ISBN 978-1-0688155-1-5 (ebook)

ISBN 978-1-0688155-0-8 (paperback)

www.tscbooks.ca

contact@tscbooks.ca

This book was entirely written by a real person.

For progressives,

and to the conservatives, for the endless material.

ONE

Max!" she screamed, her mouth open so wide, her perfect teeth lit the room.

Martha Molder stood at the bottom of the staircase and angularly peered to the second floor. Her blue eyes turned crimson as she rhythmically tapped a high-heeled shoe on the white porcelain tile floor. She gripped the banister so tight; she could have easily ripped it from its anchors.

"Max... Max... Max," she seethed as she unintentionally tried to grind her flawlessly capped teeth into dust.

Martha's professionally lacquered, cream-colored nails drummed on the wooden banister in unison with her high heel. Finally, with no response from the second floor, a flustered Martha turned on her heel and marched toward the kitchen like a general on her way to give the order to bomb the enemy. Her arms mechanically swung by her sides, and her heels clicked on the tiles.

"Jack!" she commanded as she entered the dining area, "do something about your son will you!"

Seated at the dining table, Jack Molder hid behind a newspaper. A steaming cup of coffee, and a half-finished bowl of cereal sat on the table in front of his paper. Martha stopped at the table and rhythmically tapped her heel on the floor again.

"Jack, did you hear me?!" she loudly enunciated.

Martha neatly rearranged the three already-perfectly squared table settings. She adjusted spoons, centered bowls, and smoothed imaginary wrinkles from the placemats.

"Hmmmm?" Jack blindly answered.

"Jack, Max isn't awake yet!"

"Leave him be..." Jack muttered.

"Leave him...?" Martha sputtered as she shot a glance to the clock on the wall.

She glanced to Jack, and back at the clock as she made exaggerated, panicked little noises. The tension on her face indicated she was nearing a stroke.

"But... but... but he'll be late for school. I have things planned. He'll upset my whole day! Chaos will reign!"

"Calm down," Jack said, "give him time."

Martha threw her hands in the air. "No wonder he has no direction," she snapped.

She walked to the kitchen window and fussed with the ruffled curtains.

"I have big plans for him. He won't be a slacker let me tell you. When he comes home for a visit with his perfect wife and three kids in the newest BMW, the whole block shall look at him and say, 'ah yes, that's his mother's work, what a great job.' Not, 'it's so sad, such a promise, now a disappointment, a failed single writer who drives home in a 1982 K car.'"

Martha peered out the window.

"Jack, why aren't the sprinklers on? Did the gardener forget... ahhhhhh!" she screamed.

Jack shook and softly crumpled the newspaper in his hands.

"My sign! My sign!"

Martha whirled around, twitter pated, and paced back and forth by the window like a dog demanding to go outside.

"He took it down and didn't put it back up when he mowed the lawn! That stupid, stupid man," Martha fumed as she ran into the kitchen, and wrenched open a drawer.

She pulled out a hammer and an oversized ruler, slammed the drawer, and marched to Jack. She brandished the tools at him.

"That's it! I'm calling immigration!"

"On me or Enrique?"

"On Rick! On Rick!"

"You think it's a good idea?" Jack asked calmly. "After all, you yourself said he might have been illegal when you hired him off a street corner."

"Yes, well..." Martha stammered, "once I get into office, I'll promote this country's real values, stop illegal immigration from Mexico, and this country will be great again!" she announced as the tools she brandished made a crude hammer and sickle sign.

"Ummm, Enrique is from Canada," Jack said calmly.

"Yes, well..." Martha stammered again, "those Canadians aren't any more welcome... stealing our jobs... importing their maple syrup... and Anne Murray..." she mumbled.

Martha marched to the front door, flung it open, stepped out onto the doorstep, and slammed the door shut. Jack shrugged and resumed reading the newspaper.

Outside, Martha tromped along the meticulously patterned stone footpath to the front lawn. A thin wispy dew coated the lawn, making it look like wet silver dust. The pathway was precisely cut and even. Martha was so obsessed with her misplaced sign, she clearly didn't notice a blade of grass higher than the rest.

Martha's sign leaned against a white stone bird bath with a cherub angel in the middle. She grabbed the four-by-six feet wooden sign and marched to the edge of the lawn. She plopped the stakes into the existing holes. She raised the hammer like an executioner and pounded the sign into the lawn. She measured the height at each end with her ruler, and made sure it stood straight and level.

Martha stood back, her legs apart in a wide stance, her hands on her hips, and stared at her sign with pride. A pristine white background contained bold, all-caps red lettering: YOUR PROVEN CONSERVATIVE CHOICE! PTA PRESIDENT! GUNS 'N GOD GALS PRESIDENT! MARTHA MOLDER FOR STATE REP. GOD BLESS YOU... A large picture of Martha overwhelmed the sign. It showed her dressed in white in an angelic pose, looking skyward, beaming widely, hands clasped, in a wispy, pastoral setting.

She peered to the street, and around the neighborhood to see if anyone watched her. As she gathered her tools, she saw her neighbors exit their house.

Connie Frame, dressed casually in a sweatshirt and jeans, and Sally, her sixteen-year-old daughter, stepped out onto their doorstep. Sally, dressed in a lacrosse uniform, carried a medium-sized sports bag and a lacrosse stick. As Connie locked the door, Sally saw Martha on the lawn.

"Oh no Mom, it's Mrs. Molder," Sally warned.

Connie quickly turned her head, grimaced, and fumbled with the keys in the lock.

"Oh God," Connie whispered. "Hurry Sal. Get in the car. Quick!" she urged.

Too late. Martha thrusted an arm out and waved at them.

"Yoo hoo Connie! Yoo hoo!" she warbled in a high-pitched demented songbird voice.

Sally and Connie almost jumped off the steps and ran to the car.

"Hurry Sal," Connie said as she followed Sally closely.

"Mom... Mom! You're stepping on my heels!"

Connie and Sally managed to reach their mini van, but Martha had stealthily moved from her front lawn to Connie's driveway like The Flash. Martha lunged at Connie and Sally, who stopped to avoid running into her.

"Oh Connie, I'm so glad I saw you."

"Well actually... we're leaving..." Connie said.

"Oh good," Martha interrupted. "I wanted to get your opinion about my sign."

Martha swept an arm back to motion towards her sign, and almost clipped Sally with the ruler in her hand.

"Well... I... errr..."

"Rick forgot to install it after he cut the grass, and I wanted a second opinion to make sure people could see it from the street at the right angle."

Martha spread her arms wide, and almost clunked Sally in the head with the hammer in her other hand.

"Rick?" Connie said puzzled. "Oh, you mean Enrique."

"Shhhhhhh," Martha shushed Connie, and nervously laughed.

Sally leaned back against her mother and clutched her athletic bag tight to her chest.

"No, Rick. Our gardener Rick!" Martha broadcasted to the neighborhood. "We call him Rick. It's easier."

Sally covertly reached behind her, grasped her mother's hand, and held on tight.

"So, about my sign..." Martha said as she threw her arm back, causing Sally to flinch.

Connie briefly glanced behind Martha. "Well, actually Martha... I was surprised..."

"Surprised? What's wrong with my sign?"

"No, I was surprised to see you as a candidate."

"Dear, someone had to be the conservative choice on the ballot, what with that old Communist Norman Gaines running again."

"True, since your homophobic evangelical conservative Christian candidate dropped out after being caught for soliciting sex in a Walmart men's washroom."

Martha dropped her tools and laughed uproariously. "Oh Connie, no he wasn't."

She reached out and covered Sally's ears with both hands as she leaned past her to Connie. "Where did you hear that?" she asked seriously.

"Facebook... Instagram... TikTok... the news..."

"It was a set up, I tell you, a set up!"

"Yes, a man willingly solicits gay sex in a public washroom, and it's a set up."

Martha withdrew her hands from Sally's ears and laughed again.

"What a fairy-tale Connie. Fake news! Fake news!" she announced to the neighborhood.

Sally glanced around to see who Martha was shouting at.

"So, Connie," Martha said, "will you be at the next PTA meeting?"

"Well, I..."

"You were the one who blocked my motion for ten minutes of prayer before class..."

"Well, the school is non-secular... and actually the vote came in at twenty-four to one, so I technically wasn't the one..."

"Oh, but the children," Martha moaned as she reached behind Sally to grasp Connie's arm. "They need guidance and direction from above," she said as she glanced skyward. "We need to think about the children..."

"We were thinking about the children."

"Oh Connie, I know you're doing your best, being a single mother after your husband dumped you, and having to take a grubby, grimy night job to make ends meet, but you drop the ball and Sally here is at risk of being raped or murdered or enslaved in a child sex ring by sex Marxists who work out of a Democratic pizza parlour, so you aren't the best example for our precious children."

As Connie's blood boiled and Martha's hand cut off her circulation, Connie wrenched herself free.

"Martha, I work nights because I'm the early morning news director at the radio station."

"Oh, I know dear, the one with all the fake news."

Connie fumed. "Furthermore, Sally is a straight-A student and athlete, and she knows self-defence and how to use her lacrosse stick..."

Connie nudged Sally forward. Sally's athletic bag bumped into Martha and her lacrosse stick gently clocked her in the head. Martha let out a little yelp.

"Oh, I'm so sorry Mrs. Molder," Sally said sincerely.

"Oh, it's okay dear. I'm sure you'll grow out of your clumsiness soon."

"Well Martha, we must be going," Connie announced as she ran around to the driver's side. "Sally has an early lacrosse practice..."

Connie jumped in the driver's seat and started the van. As Sally opened the sliding door and tossed her bag and stick inside, Martha hovered over her like an ominous storm cloud.

"Lacrosse?!" Martha yelped. "Now you be careful Sally," she said as she waggled a finger at her. "That's an awful lot of lesbians to hang around with. Use your stick to beat them off if you must."

"Mrs. Molder," Sally groaned as she rolled her eyes.

"To be on the safe side, you should come over and visit Max, Sally dear. You're the perfect girl for him – smart, pretty, golden blonde hair, perfect blue eyes, clear, shiny skin, presents well heterosexually... and athletic too!"

"And White," Connie added as she leaned over toward the open passenger window.

"That too."

"But we're just friends Mrs. Molder," Sally said as she slammed the sliding door, and leered away from Martha.

"You are? Well, I'll have to have a talk with that boy – again."

Sally struggled to open the passenger door because Martha pushed her against it. Finally, Sally wrenched the door open and hopped in the front seat.

"Well, goodbye Mrs. Molder," Sally said as she shut the door in her face and quickly raised the window.

"Goodbye dear," Martha said loudly against the glass.

As Connie backed out of the driveway, Martha motioned toward her sign.

"Take a look at my sign," Martha blared.

Connie nodded and fake smiled. The tires squealed as she made her getaway past Martha's sign she didn't look at.

"Oh my God, that woman," Connie grumbled. "She's like a cold. You don't want it around you, and when you have it, you can't get rid of it."

"Mom, you should run for state representative," Sally said.

"Me?"

"Yeah. You were on the community association board..."

"I don't know the first thing about politics."

"Maybe it's an advantage."

"Maybe, but there's already a progressive candidate. Martha would get elected for sure."

"Scary."

Connie glanced at her. "Sally, you and Max aren't...?" she asked discreetly as she encouraged Sally to answer her half question.

"Mom, no! Max is gay. He told me. He has a boyfriend even."

"And Martha doesn't know?"

"I don't think so..."

Connie laughed. "Or she does but she's conveniently blocked it from her mind and tries to marry Max off to any girl she meets, thinking it'll cure him."

"Mom, you're terrible."

"Oh, come on Sally, I'm talking about Martha Molder, the woman who passes off her husband as Italian so no one will find out he's actually Puerto Rican."

They both laughed as Connie drove away.

Martha marched into her yard. She stopped and eyed the lawn. She bent over and measured the grass with her ruler. She frowned a bit, then plucked a few blades from the lawn. She strode into the house.

"Well," she said as she slammed the door behind her, "another fire put out."

Jack ignored her. Martha marched into the kitchen and put her tools away.

"I ran into Connie and Sally Frame. I don't get it. Sally is perfect for Max... comes from a broken home mind you, but otherwise, perfect. And Max has no interest. I don't get it."

Jack bit his lip behind his newspaper.

"Has he made an appearance yet?" Martha asked as she pointed to the ceiling.

"No. Martha, leave him be..." Jack said, annoyed.

Martha growled at Jack's perceived reprimand. Her entire body convulsed in mild, quick little shakes, and she almost stamped her feet like she was having an adult temper tantrum.

The modern, gleaming kitchen appeared as sterile as an operating room. White cabinets with glass doors, a spotless white and grey granite countertop, and stainless-steel appliances made the room look like a laboratory where dissections were completed. A trendy mixer, an old-fashioned toaster, and a set of cannisters were neatly placed on the counter.

Martha picked non-existent dirt from her white dress before she grabbed a ruffled, flowered apron neatly laid out on the counter. She put the apron over her head, careful not to mess with her perfectly coifed, brilliant-blonde hair pulled back in a ponytail so tight it appeared to be a sports helmet. Martha aggressively tied the apron strings behind her and elicited a sharp wince because she tied them too tight.

"I always said you were too soft on him," Martha said as she attached beaters to an electric mixer. "I'm a traditional woman Jack. I come from a traditional family. I've always believed a boy should have a strong male influence in their life. Without it, he'll turn homosexual and sing show tunes in the shower. Instead of putting up a poster of Farrah Fawcett on his wall, he'll put one up of Angela Lansbury. But I let you raise him too..."

Jack peered over his newspaper at Martha. His thick black hair was perfectly sculpted in place. His black-rimmed glasses framed his dark brown eyes. He wore a lavender colored shirt with a shiny grey tie.

"And once he became our only child," she continued, "it was too late to save him. You filled his head with sacrilegious progressive nonsense and let him run wild like a free-range chicken." She quickly raised her hands. "But I didn't interfere..."

Jack rolled his eyes so hard, the sound almost jiggled the cutlery on the table.

"He needs direction and discipline!" Martha announced as she grabbed a rolling pin and slammed it on the counter.

Jack jumped in his chair.

Martha put the beaters into a bowl and turned on the mixer. As she continued to ramble on about Max, Jack couldn't hear a word she said. Her mouth moved with dramatic flair though, as if she were in a silent movie. Jack sank behind his newspaper.

TWO

In Max Molder's bedroom, Max writhed under the covers on his bed, tortured by a disturbing nightmare. He thrashed his head back and forth on his pillow, causing his thick black hair to become wild and unkempt. He tightly clutched his bed sheets between his fingers. Bare chested, he pulled the sheets tight around his waist, then thrust his arms in the air as if he were trying to ward off a demon. His right leg drooped off the bed, while the left twitched beneath the sheets.

"No... no... Mom," he moaned.

Then he muttered a woman's name.

"Miss Tutley..."

Naked tree branches swayed in the dark as the wind groaned to a crescendo and fell. The bright, full moon weaved between fast-flying clouds and intermittently bathed the baseball diamond in light. Fog swept through the trees that surrounded the field, embraced the chain link fence that circled the diamond, and lazily tumbled through the field.

Lit spotlights, perched on tall poles, surrounded the diamond. Instead of lighting the entire field, each intense light was trained on a group of teens lined up along the first base line as if the lights deliberately tried to hypnotise, blind, or torture them.

The teens were tethered together by nylon rope and dressed in white robes with hoods pulled over their heads. They looked like cult members in line to drink mind-altering Kool-Aid before being told they were going to be whisked away on an imaginary spaceship to some fake planet.

A small group of adults gathered at the pitcher's mound. All were dressed in black robes, except for one adult dressed in a blazing red robe. A folding table covered with a black satin cloth was set up beside them. Black bibles with fake gold embellishments, and small white Styrofoam containers of red liquid sat on the table.

Max stood amongst the teens and fidgeted as the adults mumbled gibberish. He nervously glanced around and shuffled from one foot to the other. He nudged the boy next to him with his elbow.

"Hey," he whispered, "when is this gonna end?"

Without glancing at Max, the boy whispered, "I think they're waiting for another pastor."

"Another one?"

"Yeah, didn't you hear? He was arrested for having child porn on his computer."

"Another one?"

"Quiet!" one of the black robes shouted from the pitcher's mound.

One of the folding table legs buckled, and that corner of the table collapsed to the ground. The bibles tumbled off the table, and the Styrofoam cups with the blood-red liquid spilled onto the dirt. The black robes and the red robe shrieked with alarm, then bumped into each other like Keystone Cops as they attempted to save the bibles and salvage the red liquid before it seeped into the soil.

"You idiot! Didn't you lock the leg?... Save Jesus' blood! Save him!... Watch it! Those bibles were $100 each for my Senator's racketeering defence fund! ... No, some of them go back to the motel rooms I stole them from!... You stepped on my hand!... Ow! Well don't head butt me!"

Max nudged his neighbor. "Can't we just make a run for it?"

"We're all tethered," the boy said as he wobbled his wrist at him.

"I know but look at them – they're idiots."

"Silence!" the woman in the red robe announced.

She grabbed a half empty cup of the red liquid, swiped a bible from the ground, accidentally bonked a black robe in the head with it, and marched toward Max.

"Martha," the black robe announced, "we have to wait for the high priest of sexual perversion so he can perform the conversion."

"Martha?" Max asked. "Mom?"

Before she could answer, she stumbled in the grass, her red hood fell off her head, she lost control of the cup, and the red liquid splashed over the front of Max's pristine, angelic white robe. Max licked a drop from his lips.

"This is melted cherry popsicle."

"Hey, we're on a budget!" one of the black robes shouted.

"Max!" Martha exclaimed. "Now look what you've made me do! I'll never get that stain out!"

"St-stain? Stain?!" Max sputtered. "The hell with this stain! Mom, what the hell are you doing?" he asked as he wobbled his tethered hands at her.

"Max, your mom is in a cult?" his neighbor asked.

"Yeah, the church."

"Oh Maxxxx..." Martha moaned as she plopped the bible on his head. "I can't wait for the high priest of sexual perversion. We must rid the evil gay sex Marxist from you right now... from all of you!" she shrieked as she waved an arm down the line of teens.

"Max, I'm scared," the girl next to him moaned.

"Don't worry, she's just drunk – again. I hope."

Martha put both hands on the bible, closed her eyes, swayed back and forth, and recited phony religious proverbs mixed with 'Martha-isms'

"Dear God, save this wayward son of mine from a life of sin by casting out the gay sex Marxist within! He rang the devil's doorbell, and the devil let him in! Drive out his sin like Jesus drove the tellers out of the Bank of Israel!"

"Mom, would you knock it off!" Max yelled as he attempted to wiggle the bible off his head. "I'm gay Mom, and your nutso conversion therapy crap isn't going to change me."

"Oh, this boy must be inoculated with Jesus! They all must be inoculated! Bring me more of Jesus' blood!"

The Keystone Cops in the black robes bumped into each other again as they tried to assemble a full cup of melted cherry popsicle.

Martha made an unimpressed noise and rolled her eyes. "Bring it! Now!"

The teens grew restless.

"You're not going to 'cure' us with melted popsicle Mom. Listen to me!" Max shouted.

Martha covered one ear with her hand and spoke in tongues as she tried to drown him out. "La la la la la la la la la..."

As the teens' protests and Martha's psychotic chants took over the field, a huge thunderclap sounded in the sky. Everyone screamed.

From the dark corner in left field, a figure slowly emerged dressed in a long red cloak with a white hood, like a Handmaid. The figure wore a bizarre Halloween mask – a demure white rabbit with wild spiked orange hair. Wisps of blonde hair snaked out from under the hood and fluttered in the wind.

The Halloween Handmaid raised their arms out, expanding the cloak to appear more intimidating. The glint off a butcher knife in their hand caught the light, and they ran full tilt toward Max and Martha. As they ran past the pitcher's mound, the black robes chaotically attempted to take cover behind the broken table. The Halloween Handmaid screamed an unearthly sound and waved the butcher knife at them.

"This must be the high priest of sexual perversion they were waiting for," the boy next to Max quipped.

The Halloween Handmaid ran straight to Martha, stopped dead in front of her, waved the butcher knife around, and let out a piercing scream. Martha fainted.

The crazed Handmaid turned to Max, raised the knife in the air, and deftly cut both his tethers, freeing him. The Halloween Handmaid stared at Max for an uncomfortable moment, then screamed in his face.

"RUN!!"

Max turned, bolted towards the forest, and vanished into the fog. Each group of tethered teens fled in opposite directions. The Halloween Handmaid twisted their head almost 180 degrees and peered menacingly at the black robes. They yelped and bumped into each other as they fled in different directions. The Halloween Handmaid turned to where Max disappeared and raced after him.

As Max ran, he pulled his white robe off, ditched it in the woods, and continued in his street clothes. He emerged from the fog into a creepy cemetery. As he glanced behind him, he tripped over an exposed tree root and landed spread-eagled on the ground. He shook his head and spit out bits of grass and dirt.

Max apprehensively peered behind him again, then sprang to his feet. He gasped, and his breath hung in the night air. He stood still and darted his head from side to side. A twig broke behind him. He whirled around. He scanned the dark and the fog, and heard a low, continuous, guttural moan.

"Maaaaaaxxxxx... It's me Maaaaaaxxxx," a woman's voice spookily moaned.

Max peered into the dark at the familiar voice. "Miss Tutley?!"

"Maaaaaxxxxx... you kkkkkilled me Max..."

Max covered his ears. "Stop it! I can't take it anymore!"

"You killed me Max... me and our unborn baby..."

"No, no, no! They made me do it!"

A perplexed expression consumed his face, and he uncovered his ears.

"Wait... what? Baby? We never... You're my teacher. This isn't Florida..."

The woman's voice changed tone from unnervingly ghostly, to sincerely fragile.

"Oh Max, I'm crushed you don't remember... your car... your stick shift..."

Max palmed his forehead.

"Oh... my... God..." he enunciated. "That wasn't me. It was one of the men you cocooned after you seduced them. Miss Tutley, I told you. I'm gay. I like boys. How could you possibly misinterpret that?"

"I don't know," Miss Tutley said, frustrated, "I thought you were trying to tell me you weren't Jewish..."

Max moaned as he threw his hands in the air. "Not goy, you twit! Gay!"

Miss Tutley, the Halloween Handmaid, emerged from the dark behind Max, and wobbled unsteadily toward him like a zombie. Unable to see properly through the Halloween mask, she walked into a tall gravestone.

"Owww!" she cried out.

Max whirled around and stifled a laugh.

"Miss Tutley, why are you wearing that stupid mask? And what was up with that screwy performance at the baseball field? Don't get me wrong, I appreciate being saved from a half-assed conversion therapy clown show put on by a bunch of fake Christian nutbars whose leader is so far in the closet himself, a search and rescue team couldn't find him."

Miss Tutley slowly removed the mask.

"I had to scare everyone to save you."

"You didn't have to wear a mask. Having you as a teacher is scary enough."

Miss Tutley stepped toward Max, and theatrically slumped her head in defeat, her face hidden by the Handmaid's hood. She softly wept and sniffled.

"Oh Max, how can you say that?"

"How can I say that? Miss Tutley, you put the biology dummy at the front of the class one Friday and skipped off with the principal for a weekender in Vegas."

"I had to!" she whined. "It was the weekend before his wife's first cancer treatment, and he simply wouldn't have been able to get away the next week..."

"You're an immoral nitwit."

"Max, my favorite student turns on me..." she wept.

"Miss Tutley, you made all our lives a living hell. You made my life..."

Max cocked his head, considered her words, and smiled.

"Favorite student? Really...?"

Miss Tutley dramatically leaned against a grave marker.

"Oh Max, it's all my fault," she wept. "I didn't mean to be a stupid, senseless, sinful, sexually psychotic sociopath... from Sioux City..."

As she wept louder, Max took a step toward her.

"Oh Miss Tutley, I didn't mean it..." he said as he reached out to touch her arm.

In one swift movement, she dropped the rabbit mask and lunged at him. The hood fell back, revealing her ghostly-pale skin, and demonic red eyes. As her long, gnarly fingernails gouged at Max's stomach, he screamed...

"Ahhhhhhh!" Max screamed as he leaned forward in bed.

He whipped his head wildly around the room as he gasped for air. Sweat beaded his forehead. His eyes settled on a stuffed animal on a shelf – a white, fluffy rabbit with floppy ears. He glanced to his desk in the corner, and at the live rabbit in a cage on the desk.

"Oh, Mr. Fluffy Puffy..." he moaned with relief.

Loud footsteps pounded in the hallway outside his closed bedroom door. Martha swung the door open, and stood in the doorway, her hands on her hips.

"Max, what is going on?! I've been calling you for the past twenty minutes!"

Max tried to shake himself awake.

"Mmmm... mmmmbbbb..." he incomprehensibly babbled.

"What?!" Martha snapped. "Get up. You'll be late for school."

Martha marched into the room with military authority. She grabbed his discarded clothes from the floor beside his bed and threw them at him.

"Get dressed," she ordered.

She swiftly marched to the window and thrust open the curtains. The glaring sunlight flooded the room, and hit Max full force, almost making him hiss as if he were the undead.

"I have breakfast waiting Max!" Martha snapped as she strode toward the door. "Move it. Move it!"

Martha left the room and slammed the door behind her. Her whirlwind appearance was a bizarre combination of devastating, catastrophic hurricane, and Tasmanian Devil.

Max stared at the door. A stray sock lay on his head and dangled in his face. He shook the sock from his head, swung his legs from the bed, and stood. He only wore white briefs. He absently scratched himself and performed a full-body stretch. He stumbled to his desk where the fluffy white rabbit sat in a cage. The rabbit wiggled his nose at Max.

"Awww Mr. Fluffy Puffy, I won't let anyone hurt you..."

Max put his hand on the cage. The bedroom door swung open again, and Martha leaned into the room.

"Max! Move it!"

Max tried to cover himself with his hands and almost stood with his legs crossed.

"Mom, I'm like half-naked..."

"Oh please, I'm your mother – not one of your vacuous, giggling girlfriends."

Max shifted his eyes and frowned.

Martha groaned. She grabbed a shirt from the floor and popped it over Max's head.

"There! Now hustle!"

Martha turned on her heel and breezed from the room again. Max trundled to the door, peered around the corner, and watched as his mother marched along the hallway, her arms swinging by her sides.

THREE

In the kitchen, Martha operated like a worker bee in a hive. She wore her flowered apron as she ambidextrously buttered toast, poured milk into glasses, put a cereal box away, wiped the countertop, and moved a stray hair away from her face. In the dining area, Jack simultaneously glanced at the paper on the table, and at the television fixed to the wall in the kitchen, tuned to the morning news.

"...which is why the President keeps pushing the gun control bill..." the announcer said.

Martha glanced at the television. "Hmmmpf," she mused, offended, "she might as well try and ban apple pie. The nerve. We might as well open the front doors to all our homes, and let the criminals walk in and kill us all!"

"You mean like the school shooting last week?" Jack said. "What's it now – forty so far this year?"

"Those liberal schools didn't have safety pods Jack! And those weak liberal teachers refused to take AK-47 training! So unpatriotic!"

"How about not having automatic assault weapons on the street in the first place?"

Martha turned around, and wielded the butter knife like a bayonet, her eyes bulging.

"It's an American's right to live in peace!"

"And how do you know it was a liberal school?"

"It happened in Massachusetts Jack, a state known as a hotbed for radical left-wing give-everyone-a-free-ride-in-a-fancy-car socialist sex crime atheist-loving gay marriage pushers."

Martha slapped the knife on the counter with a clang, walked into the dining area, and set a bowl of fruit on the table.

"Jack dear," she said sweetly, "all I want is to be able to murder intruders with a semi-automatic rifle like the constitution says."

"The constitution does not say that," he said tersely as he read the paper.

"Hmmmpf," Martha gasped, "well, we'll see who has the last laugh lady," she said as she turned and chuckled at the television. "Once I get into the legislature, there'll be another Madame President to be reckoned with – one who will put a stop to the liberal fascists who are selling out our country to the highest bidder!"

Martha slapped a palm on the dining table.

"Tell me Martha, what exactly is a liberal fascist?"

"You know," she stumbled, "those sex Marxists... those communist democrats... those pedophile multi-sex organ gay atheist drag performers who want to unleash perverted public sex performances in front of our pure and saintly children. People like me in the legislature will put a stop to it."

"Weren't you and your Guns 'n God Gals banned from being anywhere near the legislature when one of your... Gals shot a small child while his class attended a field trip?"

"She thought she saw a suspect who fit the description of the refugee hoodlum who just robbed a convenience store!"

"The refugee hoodlum turned out to be their bus driver."

"And the clumsy child should have remembered to tuck and roll, as our great Secretary of Education said. We were forced to limit our charity appearances to gun shows and street corner Jesus rallies because of that clumsy child."

"So close to a maniacal grip on power."

"It's a start Jack!" Martha said hysterically, her eyes bugging out a bit. "I'll get there, I'll get there," she whispered as she turned to the television and nodded with an evil grin on her face.

Max entered the dining area, dressed in jeans and the shirt Martha pulled over his head – backwards. He slumped into his chair at the table. Martha set a bowl of cereal under his nose.

"Eat," she commanded emphatically as she leaned close to his face.

Max leaned away from her in mock fear. He dipped his spoon into the bowl, then played with the cereal. Martha took off her apron and neatly folded it before she placed it on the counter. She sat in her chair, between Jack and Max, who sat at either end of the table. She eyed them both with contempt – Jack as he ate some fruit, and Max with his spoon in his mouth.

"Ahem... ahem..." Martha exaggeratedly coughed.

Jack and Max regarded her with expectant wide eyes.

"The grace..." she announced as she plopped her hands on the table and wiggled her fingers.

Jack and Max exchanged glances. "But we've already started..." Max mumbled with his spoon in his mouth.

"The grace!" she commanded again, then groaned loudly. "You two are pushing a very fine line. I think it's time we resumed weekday church services to correct your blasphemous behavior."

"For whose benefit Martha?" Jack asked. "Ours or yours? Last Sunday, your campaign manager made sure a camera crew was there to document your perfect family's attendance."

"It wasn't just a camera crew Jack. It was the local Fox and Friends morning show! After their story, the donations rolled in from even more stupid hicks... I mean, supporters – like those poor people whose mobile home park was destroyed by a tornado."

"I guess flushing their money down the toilet was more important than having a toilet."

Max swallowed the spoonful of cereal and boldly dipped his spoon in the bowl for another. "Mom, I'm not going to your First Self-righteous Church of the Unredeemed Grifters in the middle of the week. That place is scary. The woman who sat in front of us last time stood up and offered her son as a sacrifice because she found a bag of Skittles in his backpack."

"Oh my! The insolence from both of you!" Martha gasped. "We do need the grace!"

Jack rolled his eyes, and Max slowly lowered his spoon into the bowl. As they tentatively reached their hands out to her, she grabbed them, and Jack and Max fell forward into the table. They eyed her almost fearfully.

"Dear God," Martha said, "we thank you for your bounty, which I prepared," she emphasized, "and for keeping us safe from terrorists, sexual interlopers, and the endless fake news from the liberal media which threatens our freedom. In your name, we pray for their forgiveness. Amen."

Martha squeezed their hands, then let them drop to the table with a thud. Jack and Max each shared pained expressions as they tried to massage the kinks from their hands. Martha neatly ladled fruit from the bowl to her plate.

"Max," she ordered, "I want you to remove that filthy beast from your room today. It's probably swimming with disease."

"But it's my turn to take care of it. We need it for biology class," Max said as he played with his cereal.

"Then take it to school," Martha said as she dismissively waved a hand at him.

"But I can't. Miss Tutley is allergic to rabbits."

"Why on earth are you studying rabbits if she's allergic to them?"

"Because she's a moron," Max said, and ate his cereal.

"Max!" Martha said as she whacked him on the back of the head.

Max gurgled out milk and cereal into his bowl. Martha immediately spat on a napkin and wiped his chin. Max squirmed away.

"Mommmmmm!"

"Can't you use your stuffed rabbit? Do you have to have a live one?"

"I've had Mr. Fluffy Puffy for ten years. It was fate when we started studying rabbits and reproduction, the one we got looked exactly like him. That's why we called him Mr. Fluffy Puffy."

"Reproduction!" Martha exclaimed, horrified. "I don't remember signing any permission slip to allow it to be taught."

"'Cause you didn't Mom. It's part of the schoolwork. It's part of life. When a male and a female..."

Martha covered her ears with her hands. "La la la la la la la la la la..."

Max waggled his hands at Jack in frustration. Jack nodded, set the paper on the table, reached over, and took her hands away. He continued reading.

"Ugghh," Martha groaned, "I can only imagine what other ridiculous socialist propaganda they're forcing on my sweet innocent baby at that alleged place of learning... the benefits of ripping stem cells from pregnant mothers... man evolving from plankton and bacteria... the earth being millions of years old and so on... Right Jack?"

"Huh?" Jack said as he read the newspaper.

"Oh Jack, I wanted to send him to a good, sensible school..."

"You mean Reverend Joel's Give-Me-All-Your-Money-I-Need-A-New-Gold-Plated-Beach-House-And-Escalade-To-Minister-To-The-Perpetually-Stupid School?"

"...but as usual," Martha continued, oblivious to his comment, "you got your way again," she emphasized, "and we sent him to Den of Vipers High."

"Ummm Mom," Max interrupted, "I think it's called Daniel Volpers High..."

Jack peered over his paper, and he and Max shared mischievous grins.

"So, Dad, anything exciting happening at the bank today? Max asked.

"Well, the young man who's replacing Mrs. Horgenstefler starts today."

"Hmmm, how nice," Martha said. "It's a shame she's retiring. You two are so close. She always gave you the most... interesting Christmas gifts. Like last year wasn't it..."

"Thong underwear," Max finished.

"It was a joke," Jack explained.

"Mmmmm... yes..." Martha glowered as she dabbed at her mouth with her napkin. "Such a shame she's retiring..."

"Martha, she's been with the bank for sixty-five years..."

Jack folded the newspaper and set it on the table.

"Oh, by the way, I'll be working late with them tonight."

Martha tapped her mug with her fingernails so hard, Max grimaced and almost plugged his ears at the noise.

"How cozy," she snapped. "So, dear, do you think you'll be rushing over to her house almost every night like you've been doing the past several months to 'fix things'" she said as she made air quotations, "after the old bird retires? Or is her family finally going to stick her in an old folks home?"

"Mom, Mrs. Horgenstefler is a nice old lady," Max said.

"She's had a husband every decade she's been alive. She probably has more stacked like firewood in her basement we don't know about. Once a manhunter, always a manhunter."

"Is that from the bible Martha?" Jack asked.

"Actually," she emphasized, "I'm going to be late tonight too. The Guns 'n God Gals want me to plan a rally at that awful abortion clinic..." She cocked her head and put a finger to her lips. "Which reminds me, I have to go to WalMart and get a few dozen plastic fetuses..."

Jack gaped at her. "Martha, you know you and your nuts... I mean, your group isn't allowed within a two-mile radius of any women's health center."

"Women's health centre?" Martha scoffed. "Come now Jack, let's call it what it actually is – a baby killing assembly line!"

"Come now Dad," Max said sarcastically, "if I was a young pregnant girl, I'd want someone like Mom to tell me what I could and couldn't do with my own body..."

Martha reached over and captured Max's arm in a loving death grip. "Thank you Max. One doesn't have to wonder where you get your compassion and thoughtfulness..."

Max and his father shared a smirk.

"I'm also visiting a lovely new church group who moved into the old, abandoned farmhouse on the edge of town. Later, there's an emergency PTA meeting. Apparently, the more sensitive members are against my proposal to add creationism in the curriculum. And don't forget," she wagged a finger at Jack, "tonight we have our weekly session cataloguing all the gratuitous sex, nudity and foul language on HBO."

Martha pursed her lips, grabbed Max's left cheek between her thumb and forefinger, and gave it a few shakes. Max's teeth rattled.

"We don't want our little Maxie Waxie to be an over-sexed pervert with out-of-control hormones, do we?" she said sweetly.

Max lurched away.

"And don't forget Jack, tomorrow night is parent/teacher night, so you'll have to put off any little meetings you have with that old woman."

"I haven't forgotten. It shouldn't take too long anyway. Max is a great student."

"Yes, our Maxie is a perfect little angel..."

Martha reached over to Max again, who leaned away from her.

"And you have wonderful teachers... although..." She dramatically stroked her mouth with her thumb and forefinger. "I think your English teacher... how do I put this... likes his pizza delivered to the back door..."

Max dropped his spoon into his bowl. "Mom!"

"Martha, it's none of your business," Jack carefully enunciated.

Martha leaned into the table. "It is when my innocent son's virtue is in danger of being soiled by a gay sex heathen and his sex Marxists coven!"

"It is not Mom!" Max implored. "I'm... I mean I've already..."

Max stopped himself and appealed to Jack for approval. Jack nodded his head. Max hesitated and reluctantly shook his head.

"Martha," Jack said, "what about your campaign manager Leslie? Why is he not on your radar?"

"What about him?"

"Mom, the man's as gay as a raspberry torte," Max quipped.

"Max! Do you want me to wash your mouth out with soap again?"

"You mean like ten years ago when I said penis?"

"Max! I have another one on standby young man!"

Max rolled his eyes and slumped in his chair.

"Jack, Leslie is not a homosexual. He's a strong-minded, loyal, caring Republican."

"You mean a self-hating log cabin Republican. He supports a political party that hates him and would rather see him invisible or dead."

"Oh Jack, where are you getting this nonsense – the Communist Broadcasting System?"

"Martha, if Leslie had been a Jew in World War II, he would have supported Hitler."

Martha made an irritated noise, then smoothed her placemat.

"Mom," Max said, "Mr. Riley is the best teacher I've ever had. Even if he is gay, what's the problem?"

Martha stared at Max. "The problem!?... The problem!?... If!?... If!?... He drives a Miata."

She tapped a finger hard on the table.

"He's from Canada."

She tapped her finger on the table again.

"And I've seen him buy Spumoni ice cream at Safeway. Case closed."

She slapped both palms on the table. Jack and Max jumped simultaneously. Martha lifted her coffee cup to her lips and took a quick sip. She stole an impish glance at Max.

"It'll be nice to talk to your new teacher Miss Tutley. I think you have a crush on her..."

Max froze his spoon in mid-air, then dropped it into his bowl.

"Tutley?!" he asked, incredulously. "Mom, are you nuts?!"

Martha grabbed Max's cheek again and squeezed it.

"Awwww, my little Maxie Waxie is blushing..."

Max lurched away from her again.

"No, your little Maxie Waxie threw up in his mouth a little bit."

"Awwww," she cooed, "there's no need to be embarrassed honey. You're a handsome boy, like your father, attracted to and popular with all the ladies...young... and old," she emphasized at Jack.

Max appealed to his father again. Jack acknowledged his son's frustration with an accepting smile.

"I saw Miss Tutley last week," Martha continued, "outside an awful sex shop I've petitioned to have closed. You know the ones with all the neon SEX SEX SEX signs in the windows," she emphasized by dramatically blinking with her fingers as if they were traffic lights. "Male and female sex mannequins dressed in sex clothing, hands on their sex parts and holding sex devices for all the sex perverts to see. These sex shops, that's where all the sex criminals go to have live sex in their sex dungeons and their back sex alleys where the worst sleazy sex fiends hang out looking for sex."

"Sexy," Max quipped.

"And Miss Tutley was there?" Jack asked demurely.

"Yes, the poor thing. She must have happened upon that sordid Sodom and Gomorrah shop, and became so upset she turned and ran the other way when she saw me approach her..."

Jack played with his tie as if it became too tight. He gulped his coffee.

"I wonder why I haven't seen her in church? She seems like a sweet, innocent girl..." Martha mused.

"She's a floozy and an airhead," Max muttered before he ate more cereal.

Jack sputtered his coffee.

"Max!" Martha exclaimed, then whacked him on the back of the head again.

Max spat out more cereal and milk.

"Oh my! I think it's off to school with you Mr. Potty Mouth!" Martha ordered.

She immediately stood, grabbed him by the arm, and pulled him from his chair. Max stumbled as if he were drunk as Martha dragged him across the room to the front door.

"Here's your backpack," she said as she grabbed it from the floor, and thrust it against his chest. Max let out a pained, little cry.

"Don't forget your jacket." Martha yanked it from the closet and draped it over his shoulders.

"And put something on your feet," she commanded as she forced him into his sneakers.

She opened the door and pushed him out onto the doorstep. "Out you go."

Max flailed on the steps like a duck on ice. The door slammed shut behind him. As he collected himself, the door opened again, and Martha popped her head out.

"And fix your shirt," she barked. "It's on backwards."

Martha shut the door in Max's open-mouthed face.

FOUR

Students and teachers murmuring from behind closed classroom doors leaked into the quiet high school hallways. Shiny and new, the modern building had a lot of glass and metal but was mainly constructed of concrete in hopes it would not burn to the ground like the previous school in a chemistry lab explosion.

In one lonely, cavernous hallway lined with red and blue lockers, a janitor mopped water next to a fountain. The floors gleamed. The hallway was lit by bright, natural light, creating a kaleidoscope pattern in the corridor.

As the janitor wrung his mop out, the bell rang. Chaos. Students spilled into the hallway from the classrooms like ants from a hill set on fire. All at once, loud voices, laughter, and cell phone notifications filled the corridor. The janitor backed against the wall, almost in fear for his life as the students threatened to overwhelm him.

Max and two of his classmates emerged from a classroom. They chatted as they walked along the hallway among the other students.

"Next, T and A Tutley," Alex, an athletic-looking, jock-type boy said as he sensually curved his hands through the air to mimic Miss Tutley's alleged voluptuous form.

"Yeah, you got that right," Max said, "tart and airhead."

"Come on Max," Alex implored, "I know you're gay, but you gotta admit the woman's babe-a-licious."

"The woman's a black widow in a cocktail dress. Tell him Robin," Max said as he turned to their bookish-looking friend who trailed behind them.

Robin cradled a few books in his arms. With his plaid shirt buttoned to his neck, and his black hair neatly combed to the side, except for a protruding cowlick in front, he looked like a boy ready for his first day of school. Robin thought for a moment and shook his head.

"Poor old Mr. Mullally. Heart attack. Two days from retirement."

"See!" Max exclaimed. "Be careful Alex, or you'll become a Mr. Mullally – screwed to death by a man leech and found with your underwear stuffed in your mouth."

"Silk boxers, I heard..." Robin said.

"Lay off guys. If I don't get an A with her, I'm toast. Besides, it's only harmless flirting."

"Alex," Max stated, "flirting to Tutley is like you're already naked and tied to her bed."

"Maxwell, I gotta do what I gotta do. Besides, the woman's hot!" Alex implored.

"Okay, now pay attention Alex because this is where you can get a genuine objective opinion," Max said as he pointed to his own chest.

Max grasped his shoulders and stared into his eyes.

"Alex," Max said in a measured tone, almost trying to hypnotize him, "Miss Tutley is a complete and total idiot. No one should find that hot. The only reason she's a teacher is because that's the degree the mechanical claw grabbed."

Alex put his hands on Max's shoulders and stared into his eyes.

"Max, those hips... those thighs..."

As the two boys stared into each other's eyes, a tall, lean, Black teen with wild, short dreds appeared in the hallway – towering over the other students. As he approached the trio, Robin attempted to get Max and Alex's attention.

"Ummmm, guys, you might... want to break... you know... your thing... guys..."

The tall boy stood beside Max and Alex, and folded his long arms across his chest before they could break their death stare contest.

"Well, well, well, what do we have here?"

Max and Alex gazed at him.

"Marc," Max exclaimed as he and Alex quickly disengaged from each other.

Max and Marc affectionately embraced as Alex stood awkwardly beside them. With an arm around Max, Marc stared at Alex with a smirk.

"Tryin' to start somethin' again with my man are you Lopez?"

"Start... something?" Alex sputtered. "Again?!... Screw off Johnston," he said to Marc.

Both Marc and Max erupted in laughter. Marc punched Alex in the arm.

"I know, I know Mr. Ladies Man blah blah blah. But I could forgive you. Look at this face," he said as he held Max's chin between his fingertips.

As Max blushed, Marc leaned forward, and the two boys kissed.

"Oh God," Alex cried as he feigned indignation, "get a room you two."

"Ummm, I don't think they'd allow that here," Robin said seriously.

Max, Marc and Alex shook their heads at Robin.

"So, what were you two going on about before I arrived?" Marc asked Max. "Lopez telling you about another conquest?"

"Hey!" Alex exclaimed, "you know my heart belongs only to Fiona."

"Uh huh," Max said sarcastically, "except when a certain grade is at stake."

"Uh oh, lemme guess," Marc said. "Tutley."

"Yup. Tutley's sexy bombshell schtick is a dud. One day Alex'll realize when there's nothing upstairs except cobwebs and sawdust, nothing anywhere else has any substance either."

"Max is right Lopez. Tutley's a moron."

"Awww guys, how can you say things like that about her?" Robin implored.

"How can we say that?!" Max exclaimed. "If Miss Tutley ever got fired... or run over by a cement truck... or hit by a meteor..." Max clasped his hands together, closed his eyes, and made a silent wish. "... the plastic Biology dummy in class could replace her."

"I think she's misunderstood," Robin said innocently.

Max, Marc and Alex glanced at each other with raised eyebrows.

"Binster," Marc said, "you need to get a clue. Tutley puts the ho in homeroom."

"Fuck that," Alex said bluntly, "dude needs to get laid."

As Marc, Max and Alex laughed, a larger-built teen pushed his way through the crowd to the four boys. He wore frame-less glasses he constantly pushed to his face. His shirt was tucked in clumsily at various points around his chinos. He struggled to carry several binders as he waved a piece of paper at the boys.

"Hey guys!" he exclaimed. "Look at this!"

The four boys stood back as the excited teen shoved the paper in their faces – a test with a blood-red 59 scrawled at the top.

"Ohhhh," Max fake-knowingly said, and seriously, "what is it Elliott?"

Elliott beamed. "It's my best mark of the year!"

"What is it, a gym test?" Alex deadpanned.

Alex laughed, and punched Elliott in the arm.

Elliott giggled. "No silly. Chemistry. It's my worst subject."

Elliott frowned, glanced at his arm where Alex hit him, and rubbed it.

"Elliott, you should be proud," Marc said.

The bell rang. The students in the hallway scattered in different directions. Robin tried to corral his friends.

"Come on guys. Let's go or we'll be late."

"Yeah, Tutley might punish us... Owwww!" Alex yelped and laughed.

Max rolled his eyes, and the boys joined the other students as they made their way to their next class.

FIVE

Alex opened the door to the biology lab, and the five boys entered the room. They stumbled into each other as Alex stopped and scanned the room for any empty seats. Their classmates stared at the boys as they bumbled their way amongst the counters. Max and Marc sat together, while the other boys scattered to empty seats.

A pristine blackboard and a blank whiteboard lined the entire front wall. Cabinets containing glass beakers, microscopes, and other equipment lined another wall. Tables sat beneath the cabinets and contained on-going experiments.

Behind the students, a life-like, full-size, pliable plastic and rubber biology demonstration model on wheels stood guard. The model's skin and hair were removed to reveal veins, tendons, blood vessels and arteries. Its chest cavity was exposed to show all the organs. Its face, with eyes bulging, had a terrifyingly sedate expression. Its lips were pursed as if it were about to say something or sing a song.

Windows lined another wall and overlooked the parking lot. Beneath the windows sat a large aquarium with fish and plants. Miss Tutley stood at an open window. Her carefully tousled long blonde hair blew softly in the breeze. Her eyes were closed. A faint satisfied smile enveloped her face. She cooed and moaned – lost in her own world of unknown pleasure, and completely unaware students sat behind her. Her makeup – perfect. Her little black dress – smooth and tight, as if she were about to depart for a cocktail party. Her heels – high and fashionable.

The bell rang again. Miss Tutley remained rooted in place. After a few moments, the students glanced at each other and murmured amongst themselves. Miss Tutley emitted short, sexual moans as she ran her lacquered fingernails sensually along her thighs – clearly enjoying her morning siesta.

Sarah, a neat, studious-looking girl in perfectly entwined pigtails, dressed in a plaid, official-looking school uniform (although the school had no dress code), seated in the front row with her hands folded on the countertop, turned her head, and glanced briefly in Miss Tutley's direction. She grimaced and turned around to face the front. She tapped her fingertips on the countertop. Her pen, notebook and other utensils were laid out in perfect angles on the counter. Sarah turned again and glared at Miss Tutley.

"Ummm, Miss Tutley...?"

Miss Tutley moaned an acknowledgement, still lost in herself.

"Miss Tutley!" Sarah shouted.

Miss Tutley opened her eyes, shook herself from her haze, and turned to look at the students who stared at her with open mouths and 'what the hell is this woman doing?' expressions. Miss Tutley manufactured a fractured smile and walked to her desk at the front.

"Right, so today..." she said before she tripped over a power cord and cut the power to the aquarium.

She screamed, then fell to the floor. All the students leaned from their chairs and peered over their lab counters at her. Miss Tutley quickly rose, smoothed her dress, and ran a hand through her tousled hair. She brandished the power cord in her other hand.

"What is a power cord..." she said.

Before she could continue, Sarah immediately thrusted an arm in the air, turned to Miss Tutley, and wiggled her hand ferociously at her.

"Oh! A power cord sends an electric current from a power outlet to appliances that need electricity to work."

Miss Tutley eyed Sarah with muted venom as she bent over and plugged the cord into the outlet. Some of the boys, including Alex, gladly watched her semi-exhibitionist display with bulging eyes and pubescent leers. When she caught them staring at her, they turned away. As she gave her hair a toss and giggled, the girls collectively rolled their eyes so hard, it sounded like a convoy of cement mixers in symphony.

Miss Tutley strode to her desk, grabbed some papers, and shook it at the class.

"Okay now, books away. Time for the test."

The students' mouths dropped open simultaneously as they stared incredulously at each other. Moans, groans, and whines commenced.

"Test? What's she talking about?... I didn't know about any test... Test?... Did you know about a test?... She's insane... I would've studied... There's no test!... Her hair dye's eaten away at her brain."

"Okay, okay. You should know this stuff..."

Miss Tutley passed out the papers.

Max scanned his test. "Marsh Ecosystems?! We haven't even covered this yet! What the hell?!..."

As his fellow students echoed his sentiments, Max slammed the paper on the countertop.

"This seals it! She's dumber than a fence post, and twice as stupid."

Marc laid a hand on Max's arm. "Calm down Max..."

"Calm down?! I haven't seen someone this incompetent in a position of power since 2016."

Robin leaned over toward Max. "She made a mistake..."

"Yeah, when she decided to be a teacher..."

As the class continued to moan, Sarah attempted to get Miss Tutley's attention by waving her tablet at her.

"Miss Tutley... Miss Tutley... I have it noted on my tablet we're to discuss the reproductive system today."

As Miss Tutley loomed over her, Sarah shoved her tablet at Miss Tutley, who lurched backward, and squinted at the screen.

"It sayyyyys," Sarah said exasperated, "reproductive system. I've already done the report, and a video presentation interviewing a top researcher at the Mayo Clinic."

Miss Tutley pushed the tablet away.

"Okay, okay! Alright, hand your papers back in..."

More moans and groans from the students as they thrusted the papers at her.

"Holy fuck," Max whispered, "half her brain doesn't know what the other side is doing."

"Yeah, like there's a wall separating the two," Marc whispered back.

Miss Tutley gathered the papers and placed them on her desk. She drummed her fingernails nervously on the desk, darted her eyes around the room, and bit her lip.

"Sooooo..." she drawled. 'Reproduction..."

Sarah turned and gawked at her fellow classmates with a 'do you believe this woman?' expression. She turned and stared at Miss Tutley expectantly.

"Perhaps the model could help...?" she offered.

Miss Tutley stared blankly at Sarah, who pointed to the dummy behind them.

"The model...?"

"The model!" Miss Tutley shrieked, startling the class. "Yes!"

Miss Tutley ran to the back, her heels skipping across the tiles. The students stared at her as she grabbed the model. As she quickly rolled it to the front, the wheels squeaked cartoonishly. When the wheels hit the power cord she had strewn across the floor to plug into another outlet, the dummy came to an abrupt stop, and she struggled to wheel it over the cord.

Jenny, a quiet, unassuming student who constantly swept her long, straight sandy brown hair from her face was seated next to Miss Tutley's dilemma. She instinctively rose from her seat to assist Miss Tutley, but not in a 'look at me, I'm helping the teacher' way.

"Here Miss Tutley, let me help you," Jenny said.

She attempted to help Miss Tutley lift the dummy over the power cord. Miss Tutley tried to wrestle the dummy from her.

"No... I can do it... by myself... leave it..." she spat out in frustration.

"But if we lift it a little more..." Jenny said.

"I don't need... your help..." Miss Tutley hissed as the class watched the power struggle between the two people who were complete opposites.

"But we're almost there Miss Tutley," Jenny pleaded.

"Back in your seat Plain Jane!" Miss Tutley ordered.

Jenny relinquished her hold on the dummy and dejectedly sat in her seat. Miss Tutley successfully negotiated the model over the power cord and ran to the front. As she banged the dummy into her desk, the head popped off and became a projectile as it shot across the room into the first row. Marc caught it. The students screamed.

"Nice reflexes," Alex said, and held out his hands. "Pass it here."

Marc smiled widely and deftly passed the head to Alex.

"Hey, over here!" another boy said.

Before Alex could toss it to him, Miss Tutley moved into his row, and blocked Alex. She placed both hands on the head, leaned into him, and whispered seductively in his ear.

"If you wanted some head so badly, why didn't you ask me?"

Miss Tutley giggled and smiled demurely at him as she took the head. His mouth fell open as she walked away, gyrating her hips. She glanced back at him and pursed her lips until she stumbled over the power cord. She smoothed her dress and walked back to her desk.

She clumsily plopped the head on the dummy. The right eye fell out, bounced on her desk, and to the floor where it rolled until it came to a dramatic stop under a table.

"Now, let's start with the male reproductive system..." she announced.

"She would, wouldn't she," Max whispered to Marc, who stifled a laugh.

Miss Tutley stroked her throat with her fingertips.

"...so powerful... filled with life... a magnificent monument of masculinity... such a pulsing powerful stallion... ready to erupt with enormous passion!"

She faced the model, then grasped it by the shoulders. She glanced to the class and smiled weakly. The students stared at her in complete bewilderment, turned to each other, and raised their eyebrows in unison.

"Are you okay Miss Tutley?" Jenny asked.

"Why yes, yes I am Jane," she replied as she removed her hands from the model and smoothed her dress. "It's a little hot in here. Would someone open a window?"

"It is open," Robin said.

"Oh, is it? Oh my," she fretted as she grabbed a folder from her desk and fanned herself.

Papers from the folder flew out and cascaded across the room. Miss Tutley set the folder on her desk and pointed to the model.

"As I said, this part is the..."

Her finger lightly touched the groin area. Instantly, the entire contents of the model's chest cavity emptied out onto the floor with a clatter. When the last kidney stopped spinning, she turned to the class.

"Let's take some notes," she said as she tactlessly kicked the plastic body organs across the floor.

She stepped to the overhead projector that sat on a table beside her desk. She put a piece of blank cellophane on the glass. She glanced to the whiteboard on the wall and waited.

"You have to turn it on," Robin offered.

The students stifled giggles. Miss Tutley turned and leered at him with an evil gaze.

"Yes, thank you Gavin."

"It's Robin, Miss Tutley. Robin."

"Gavin... Robin... whatever," she said, and waved her hand dismissively at him. "They're both names for lonely, sexually deprived bookworms."

Robin sank into his seat. Miss Tutley fumbled for the 'on' switch, flipped it, and the intense light instantly blinded her. She squinted, stumbled back a bit, and pawed at the utensils on her desk. She blindly grabbed something and attempted to write on the cellophane.

"Okay... 'male repro'..."

"Ummm, Miss Tutley," Sarah interrupted, "that's not a marker, it's an eyedropper."

Miss Tutley stared at it wide-eyed, set in on her desk, grabbed another utensil, and attempted to write with it.

"Right... 'male repro'..."

"Miss Tutley," Sarah interrupted again, "that's a test tube."

Miss Tutley flung it across the room where it shattered against the wall.

"All I need is a damn marker!" she wailed.

Sarah thrust a collection at her. "What color would you like?"

Miss Tutley eyed her venomously and snapped one from her hand. She stood aggressively in front of Sarah with her legs planted apart, and both hands on her hips.

"You know Sarah dear," she snapped, "your brain's only going to take you so far. When you have a body like mine, that men would step on their mother's neck to get at, you can write your own ticket. Your ticket," she paused before she uncapped the marker, "is only one... way."

Everyone in the room gasped as Miss Tutley deliberately drew a red X on Sarah's forehead. Sarah, mouth agape, crossed her eyes as she tried to eyeball the X. Miss Tutley, with a self-satisfied grin, turned on her heel, and walked to the whiteboard. She turned to the class.

"Let's do something more important, instead of this silly biology stuff. I have some very exciting news to share..."

"You're leaving," Marc said.

"No..."

"You're dying," Max said.

"No..."

"You're going back to kindergarten for retraining," Jenny said.

"No. This!"

She turned around and excitedly scrawled on the whiteboard with the red marker: SHELLEY TUTLEY – THE ONLY CHOICE FOR THE STATE LEGISLATURE! She dramatically underlined the exclamation point, turned, and put her hands on her hips.

"Well..." Miss Tutley said, exasperated.

"Well, what?" Jenny asked.

Miss Tutley gestured to the whiteboard. "I'm running in the election to be a state representative," she said excitedly.

Silence overwhelmed the room. The students gawked at the whiteboard, at Miss Tutley, then at each other. The room erupted in exhaustive laughter. As she gazed at her teenage audience, they attempted to tell her how they felt amid their hilarity.

"Are you kidding me?... You're an idiot... That's exactly what we need – another stupid politician... She doesn't even know her ABCs... This is a joke, right?... Are you feeling okay Miss Tutley?... Did she fall and bump her head?... Who did she sleep with?"

Miss Tutley waved her hands at the class. "Okay, okay. I know you're all excited for me, but I do need your help."

"Help? How could she think we'd help her get elected?" Max hissed at Marc. "I thought there was a system in place to keep morons like her far away from public office?"

"Max, you know that's not true. Look at Congress..."

Max nodded his head in agreement. The class quieted.

"Everyone," Miss Tutley announced, "this is your chance to participate in democracy. Now I know this isn't civics class..."

"No, it's biology," Sarah said. "You know, what you're supposed to be teaching?"

"But this is a teachable moment about democracy," she said as she eyed Sarah evilly.

She grabbed papers from her desk, and handed them to Sarah, who regarded them with maximum derision. She frowned, took a paper, and passed the stack along the row.

"Tonight's assignment is to think about a good slogan for my campaign – something punchy, upbeat, and memorable. I have some examples on the handout."

"Has she lost her fucking mind?" Max asked Marc as he received the stack.

"Max, you have to have a mind to lose one."

The class groaned and muttered to their partners when they received the handout.

"Now, along with a slogan, I need an eye-catching logo. Let's think about some now, shall we?" Miss Tutley said as she moved to the whiteboard.

She froze as if the greatest idea in history came to her.

"I know. We'll have a contest. Whoever gives me the best logo, can be my old people vote coordinator, working with me to brainwash... errr convince the old people to vote for me."

"Are we in some kind of bad dream?" Jenny asked her lab partner, who shook his head. "This is ridiculous."

"Now, here's one I thought about," Miss Tutley said as she drew an image on the whiteboard.

"A snake with something caught in it's throat?" Robin asked.

She frowned slightly, scribbled through the image, and drew another one.

"A used condom?" Jenny asked.

Miss Tutley fumed, furiously scrawled through the image, and drew another.

"Oh! Oh!" Max said as he raised his hand, "a blob of Silly Putty?"

His classmates laughed.

"Yay!" Elliott said gleefully. "Pictionary!"

There were a few giggles and coughs. Miss Tutley dropped the marker, deliberately releasing it from her grasp as if her hand were robotically controlled. The marker clattered to the floor as she walked slowly and devastatingly to Elliott, the sharp click of her heels on the tile floor the only sound in the room. She loomed over him and gave her head a slight shake.

"What... Elephant?" she snapped.

She leaned toward him, then drummed her blood-red nails on the countertop.

Elliott slowly pointed to the whiteboard. "Pictionary... hee hee..." he said softly with an innocent giggle.

"Pictionary?!" she shouted. "Pictionary?!! Here I am trying to make a difference in the world, putting myself out there to help society..."

Max offered a quick, high-pitched chuckle.

"... and I get no respect from the generation I'm trying to help!"

Miss Tutley threw her arms in the air and rested her hands on her hips. She walked back and forth in front of Elliott – stalking him.

"You overgrown, overripe blueberry! There's too much fat here..." she shouted as she reached out and jiggled his stomach. "And there's too much fat here!" she yelled as she thumped his head as if it were a melon.

The entire class stared in silence, mouths opened, shocked.

"Your parents must be proud," Miss Tutley continued. "Tell me Elephant, for entertainment, do they tie you up out back, so they can watch you chase a half-eaten rib roast around a tether ball pole as they sit on their porch and knock back the Mountain Dew?!"

Elliott sobbed.

Marc stood. “Now wait a minute Tutley...”

“Yeah, how dare you! You can’t put your hands on him, and say things like that to him,” Max chimed in.

The girl who sat beside Elliott put an arm around him. “You’re mean Tutley...”

The door flung open, and a girl with shocking red hair burst into the classroom. She stomped militarily across the floor, and sat next to Alex, who gave her a kiss on the cheek.

“Fiona, finally...”

“Quiet!” Miss Tutley shouted.

She angrily walked to where Fiona sat, stood behind her like a cold, deathly presence, and rhythmically tapped her heel on the floor.

“Do you know what time it is?”

Fiona slowly turned and glared at Miss Tutley with contempt.

“Time for you to slip your filthy hands into another old man’s pants?”

“How dare you...”

Fiona put a hand to her chest. “How dare I? How dare I?! You sick, twisted, gold digging tramp!” Fiona spat. She turned to Alex. “You’re not going to believe this. Daddy’s lawyer told me that this...” she gestured, disgusted, at Miss Tutley, “thing inherits all his estate!”

Miss Tutley smirked and casually looked away.

“Look!” Fiona said as she pointed at her, “she already knows!”

Miss Tutley’s Cheshire grin grew.

“You scheming, manipulating maneater!” Fiona shrieked. “She sleeps with my father, like she’s slept with half the town, worms her way into his life, and steals his money. I get screwed and get nothing except an old poetry book. She gets screwed and gets everything!”

“A perfect way to fund my campaign,” Miss Tutley said demurely.

“Campaign? For what – town whore? You’ve already clinched it.”

Miss Tutley smiled sweetly at Fiona. “Calm down dear. All this stress you’re putting on yourself will do even more damage to your scaly, blanched Irish skin.”

Fiona turned three shades of red. “You psychotic slut!”

Fiona lunged at Miss Tutley, tackled her, and they both fell to the floor with Fiona on top. The students surrounded them and recorded the event on their cell phones. With one hand on Miss Tutley's head, Fiona grabbed at some petri dishes stacked under the counter.

"Here!" she shouted, "have some paramecium!"

As Fiona tried to stuff the contents of the dishes into Miss Tutley's mouth, the students hooted and hollered and caused the commotion to leak into the hallway. Miss Tutley twisted her head from side to side and tried to keep her mouth shut to avoid the microorganisms. A persistent Fiona forcefully mashed the goo on her face.

"Here! Have some bacterial culture!" Fiona screamed as she grabbed at more petri dishes and haphazardly squashed the contents onto Miss Tutley's face.

The classroom door swung open, and two men rushed into the room – Carter Riley, a young, well-dressed teacher, and the principal Mr. Douglas, an older, tall man with greying hair. They peeled their way through the students and pulled Fiona off Miss Tutley.

"Enough! Enough!" Mr. Douglas shouted.

Carter held Fiona by the shoulders as he backed her away from Miss Tutley. Mr. Douglas helped Miss Tutley to her feet.

"Fiona, what's gotten into you?" Carter asked.

Like a wildcat, Fiona tried to claw at Miss Tutley.

"You're dead Tutley! Dead!"

Miss Tutley wiped the goo from her mouth. "Keep her away from me Carson!"

"It's Carter, Shelley. Carter. We've worked together for almost a year..."

Carter rolled his eyes, shook his head, and dragged Fiona from the classroom. Mr. Douglas put a reassuring arm around Miss Tutley's shoulders. He took a handkerchief from his jacket pocket and wiped the paramecium and bacterial culture from her mouth.

"Are you alright Shelley?"

"I think so Phillip," Miss Tutley skilfully whined. "It was such an unprovoked attack..."

Max scoffed hard.

As Miss Tutley sobbed, Mr. Douglas gave her a tight squeeze.

"Don't worry Shelley, she'll be dealt with severely."

"But Mr. Douglas," Marc interjected, "Fiona didn't start this..."

"Yeah… Miss Tutley did… You should have heard what she said… She screwed Fiona's father and rubbed it in her face… Yeah…" a few students chimed in.

"Okay, enough," Mr. Douglas said. "We'll deal with this. Everybody back to your seats."

"But Mr. Douglas…" Max said.

"Now."

Max and his fellow students mumbled, grumbled, and returned to their seats. Mr. Douglas wrapped an arm inappropriately around Miss Tutley's waist.

"Come to my office Shelley," he leered. "We'll have to… have a chat," he whispered devilishly into her ear as he squeezed her again.

Miss Tutley gazed at him with a conniving smile. He pulled away from her.

"Sarah, you're in charge for the rest of the period," he announced before he marched from the room.

Sarah, disinterested, dismissively waved a hand at him. "Yeah, whatever."

Miss Tutley leaned provocatively against Alex and whispered in his ear. "We'll work on your A later."

As her hand casually drifted to his backside, he squirmed as if an eel crawled into his pants. Miss Tutley and Mr. Douglas exited the classroom. On cue, every student stared at Sarah expectantly. She glanced around the room, disgusted.

"Class fucking dismissed."

SIX

From her spot at a table outside a brand name coffee shop, Martha enjoyed an ideal view of the bank where Jack worked. She couldn't see inside the bank but glared at the entrance with hawk-like precision whenever someone arrived or exited.

Martha appeared to have stepped from the 1970s. She wore a wide-brimmed, white sun hat with a gold ribbon wrapped around it. Large, oversized, dark sunglasses tried to hide her face. She wore a flower-print dress with an exaggerated wide white belt, pearls and white gloves.

She attempted to peer at the bank entrance, but the person seated across from her at the table constantly poked his head in her sight line. An immaculately dressed, trim young man with flawless skin, bright blue eyes, and perfectly styled, highlighted blonde hair tried to capture her attention.

"Mrs. Molderrrrrr," the young man crowed as he waved at her, "am I boring you?"

"What Leslie?" she asked, ignoring him.

"Mrs. Molder," he announced, "you asked me here to go over your itinerary for this week, and now you completely ignore me. I took time from managing all your social media and adding to your archive of conspiracy theories on your website to meet you."

"Huh?" She finally met his gaze and patted his hand – hard.

"Owww!" he squealed with a high-pitched yelp.

"I'm sorry Leslie. I should have cancelled. I'm going through a marriage infidelity crisis right now, and it requires my full attention."

"But what about your campaign? You said yourself it was the most important thing in your life... wait, infidelity?" He leaned in closer. "Are you having an affair? Oh Mrs. Molder, the optics for your campaign... bad bad bad."

"Not me you idiot. I would never soil the vows I made before God."

She let out a brief cry, sniffed, took off her sunglasses, and wiped at her eyes.

"It's Jack. He's the one who has soiled our marriage with... with that old woman he works with."

"Jack? Your gorgeous, swarthy, sexy man?"

"Yes Jack... wait, what?"

"I mean, oh my how horrible. Mrs. Molder you must do something. If this gets out to the public..."

"I know! I know!" she shrieked, drawing looks from nearby tables. "I haven't come this far, within a grasp on power, to let some blue-haired hussy destroy my plans," she seethed.

"Mrs. Molder, you're the only right-leaning candidate in the race. This is your shot. You can't afford a scandal to ruin your chances like the indiscreet fool who tapped his foot one too many times in the Walmart washroom."

"You're right and... wait, how many times is too many?"

"Well, it's... well never mind. We need to keep your image clean, and your opponent's dirty. I'll have everyone believing Norman Gaines, the socialist communist as you call him, is a pedophile who sex traffics children from a pizza parlour before you can say Fox News."

"Very good Leslie. Very good. But don't let the merchandise side of my website slide. I got a shipment of me and Jesus holding hands toothbrush holders in yesterday from China. Pennies to make. Mark the crap up to $24.99."

"Don't you think that's a bit high?"

"Leslie, remember, I had a bunch of idiots buy watered down hand sanitizer that was 'proven' to cleanse their sinful flesh for $99.99. That bought me prime time TV spots!"

"Your campaign donation merchandise is selling well, but I still think your scam... errr scheme 1-900-MarthaM prayer line is your best fund raising opportunity."

"I knew my three-pronged approach would be a sure-fire campaign funding winner – cheap crap from China, a sit-back-and-watch-the money-roll-in telephone scam, and a few well-placed GoFundMe campaigns. Don't let up Leslie. All these rubes are buying more advertising!"

"You leave everything to me Mrs. Molder."

"And you leave my dear, sweet husband and his floozy granny to me. I'll fix her hash."

Martha slapped her sunglasses on, stood, and faced the bank.

"You go and keep making those outraged videos about our Godless, depraved, sex-obsessed, socialist Hell world dominated by gun-hating homosexual immigrant terrorists, and I'll continue to be the only choice for America's soul."

She walked away from the table. Leslie turned to her.

"But Mrs. Molder, what about your itinerary for this week?" he whined.

She wrenched her head at him. "Oh, just e-mail it to me Leslie!" she barked, and strode toward the bank.

Leslie pursed his lips, and sipped his Grande jade citrus mint, honey, vanilla bean, hazelnut, caramel, skinny mocha, soy matcha blend, with a hint of hibiscus coffee.

The busiest time for the bank happened mid-morning. Customers queued at all the tellers. All the ATMs were in use. Meetings between employees and customers were in progress in cubicles and offices. Throughout the cavernous, expensive-looking granite and wood structure, work sounds filled the space – chatter, telephones, office equipment, and the building itself.

Jack stood beside a desk in the center of the bank, behind the public counter, surrounded by other similar desks and cubicles. He wore a gold-colored, metal name plate on his chest that read JACK MOLDER – MANAGER. Mrs. Harriet Horgenstefler, an older woman well past mandatory retirement age, sat at the desk. She had been the personal assistant to all the bank managers since the mid-Twentieth Century.

Mrs. Horgenstefler's long white hair was pulled back in a tiered, weighty bun. She wore bright, pink lipstick, and chunky, garish, candy-looking jewelry. Eyeglasses, with dainty chains drooping from them, sat on her nose as she closely peered at the computer screen on the desk.

Beside her sat a young man who appeared to be recently graduated – from junior high school. Two years removed from his commerce degree, Stevie's new job as Jack's assistant was his big break. Neatly dressed in a brown sweater vest, shirt, tie and pants, he was well groomed with straight, combed brown hair. The oversized eyeglasses he wore made his already impossibly young face even younger.

Stevie listened intently as Mrs. Horgenstefler carefully, and painstakingly, explained the computer program they worked on, though if the truth were known, Stevie could have easily designed the program. He patiently entertained her as she torturously explained it to him.

As the threesome engaged in conversation at the desk, Martha's shadowy figure passed in front of the tinted windows beside the bank's main entrance. She stopped at the window and peered into the bank.

Martha stepped into an adjacent flower bed and tried to get a better look inside the bank, her big hat pressed against the glass. A postal worker, who re-painted a street mailbox on the sidewalk, stopped her work, paint roller in mid-air, and watched Martha. Similarly, visitors to the bank eyed her oddly as she bobbed her head back and forth in front of the window.

Martha awkwardly stepped from the flower bed as if she were trying to avoid a lava flow, barged ahead of a couple customers at the front door, and entered the bank.

Inside, Martha peeled off her sunglasses and peered around the bank. She stopped her laser-like scan when she saw Jack, Mrs. Horgenstefler and Stevie gathered around the desk behind the counter. Mrs. Horgenstefler laughed uproariously and put a hand on Jack's chest.

"Oh Jack, if only you weren't married," she tutted as her hand lingered on his chest.

Martha's eyes bugged. Mrs. Horgenstefler placed both hands on Jack's face and kissed him on the lips – long and hard. Martha's eyes almost burst from their sockets as she deliberately ripped her sunglasses off. Utter disgust filled her face.

When Mrs. Horgenstefler released Jack from her gnarly clutches, Jack put an arm around Stevie's shoulder and lightly manhandled him.

"Don't be nervous Stevie," Jack said. "You'll do just fine – just fine."

"I only hope I can give you the same service Mrs. Horgenstefler has," he said sheepishly.

Martha gasped, covered her mouth with one hand, reached back, and fell against a velvet rope that queued customers to the counter. The rope's pedestals slowly fell to the floor like dominoes with an embarrassing crash. Patrons in the queue all turned and stared at Martha.

As Jack, Mrs. Horgenstefler, and Stevie moved from behind the counter to the public area, Martha clumsily put on her sunglasses and slunk behind a tall potted plant. She pulled leaves from her face and watched as they walked to the front door.

"So, Stevie, how about a little Greek?" Jack asked.

"I'll try anything once," Stevie said innocently.

Martha contorted her face in disbelief. Jack held the door open for Mrs. Horgenstefler and Stevie. As they exited the bank, Mrs. Horgenstefler put an arm around Jack's waist. Martha gasped again.

A security guard approached Martha and peered at her. Martha quickly let the large leaves go, attempted to stand still, and be invisible. The guard slowly pulled the leaves away and gawked at Martha.

"Ma'am?" he asked.

Martha jumped back a little.

"Ma'am, what are you doing?"

Martha impulsively smoothed the leaves and played with her pearls.

"Me?"

The guard put his hands on his hips and cocked his head. "No, the leprechaun hiding in the air vent..." he said as he nodded toward the ceiling.

Martha glanced to the air vent.

"Ma'am?" the guard asked again.

"Oh me? Well, I'm... I'm a little concerned..."

Martha stepped out from behind the plant.

"Concerned," she said loudly to anyone in the bank, "about this lovely plant. I mean, look at this!" She brandished the leaves and shook them. "Doesn't anyone here know how to care for these gentle, fragile creatures?!"

The leaves she gripped tore from the stem and into her hand. She stared at them, discreetly threw them to the floor, and wiped her hands together. She peered around the bank, then smoothed her dress.

"Well, good day," she said to the guard and walked toward the exit. She stumbled over her feet as she glanced around.

The security guard folded his arms across his chest. Martha looked back at him, then opened the front door.

Two tellers who sat beside one another leaned toward each other, and whispered as Martha left the bank.

"Did you see Mrs. Molder?" one asked.

"Yeah," the other said. "What's up with her?"

"Back on the sauce probably."

"Uh huh..."

Martha scurried from the bank. She bumped into people on the sidewalk as she desperately twirled around. In the parking lot beside the bank, she saw Jack, Mrs. Horgenstefler and Stevie at Jack's car. Jack's arm wrapped around Mrs. Horgenstefler's waist.

"Oh Jack," Mrs. Horgenstefler laughed, "if only I was sixty years younger..."

"Harriet, you're like a fine wine."

Jack opened the passenger door. Mrs. Horgenstefler giggled and cooed as he helped her in the car. Her dress hiked up, and Jack touched her bare leg as he pulled her dress back down.

Martha drew in a long, exaggerated breath.

Jack put a hand on Stevie's shoulder and gave it a squeeze as Stevie sat in the back seat. Jack ran around to the driver's side, jumped in the car, and drove away.

Before the car passed Martha, she hid behind a street mailbox on the sidewalk and pressed her back flat against it. As the car passed, Martha stood, and watched it disappear around a corner. She sobbed dramatically and wiped a manufactured tear or two away from her face.

"Oh Jack, what have I done to deserve this?" she quietly wailed.

She steadied herself and narrowed her eyes as she glared at the street.

"I'm a public figure and I won't be made into a fool!" she said determinedly.

Martha turned on her heel and stomped away, her arms swinging by her sides. Onlookers turned and watched as she brushed past them, then they pointed at the strip of bright blue wet paint on the back of her dress.

SEVEN

The school office buzzed with activity during the lunch hour. The phone rang constantly, couriers arrived, parents collected students, teachers arrived and disappeared, and all interacted with the secretary, who tried her best to multitask her way through the hour of complete insanity.

Comfortable chairs circled the front desk. The principal's office was to the right of the secretary's desk. Carter Riley and Fiona silently sat beside each other in the chairs next to the closed office door. Fiona fidgeted in her seat. She tapped her foot on the floor, played with her cell phone, and occasionally burned holes in the door as she glared at it.

In the wall beside the door, a frosted glass pane allowed anyone to see silhouetted movement in the office. Unexplained noises – thumps, chairs being moved, moans, giggling, and heavy breathing – emanated from the room.

When Mr. Douglas cried out 'Oh Lordy be!', Carter and Fiona turned to each other. Carter smiled uncomfortably, and Fiona grimaced. A high-pitched giggle followed from Miss Tutley. Fiona drummed her fingertips on the chair's arm.

"Hmmmm," she pondered, "I wonder whose story he's going to believe..."

Carter nodded and smiled reassuringly.

"Maybe if I gave him a..." she said.

Carter raised a hand to stop her. "No. No, I don't think it's a wise decision Fiona."

"I'm kidding Mr. Riley."

Furniture moved inside the office. Behind the frosted window, two people stood facing each other, and buttoned buttons and zippered zippers – though they could have been picking lint from each other's clothes.

The two blurred figures walked to the door. Mr. Douglas opened the door, and Miss Tutley exited. She pulled at her dress and attempted to tame her tousled hair as she tried to slink from the room with some dignity. Mr. Douglas leaned against the door frame, straightened his tie, and pulled the knot back to his throat.

"Okay Fiona," he said as he waved her into his office.

Fiona and Carter stood. As Fiona and Miss Tutley passed each other, Fiona sneered hatefully, and Miss Tutley grinned satisfactorily.

"Tart," Fiona said.

"Disinherited," Miss Tutley snapped back.

"Wow, five syllables, a new record," Fiona said as she disappeared into the office.

As Miss Tutley stopped to compute the insult levelled at her, Mr. Douglas shut the door.

Miss Tutley turned around. "Yeah, well..." she said childishly to a closed door.

She shrugged indifferently, turned, and walked past Carter, who tapped her on the shoulder.

"Ummmm Shelley, could I talk to you for a minute?"

Miss Tutley turned and groaned. "If it's about that horrible girl and her lost estate, I earned it the old-fashioned way, okay?" she barked.

"No, no, I've been meaning to talk to you about something... personal," Carter said as he gently pulled her aside.

She stared at him, puzzled, flashed a suggestive smile, grazed his face with her fingertips, and gave him an exaggerated wink.

"Yes Parker..."

Carter sighed and stepped back. "No, no, it's about our neighborhood, since we live on the same street... and again it's Carter... I hoped you could shed some light on something."

Miss Tutley, disinterested, opened a compact and examined her face. "Oh, what about?" she asked as she dabbed at her makeup.

"Well, someone complained to the city about the solar panels and the windmill Christian and I installed. We paid a hefty fine and removed them."

"Oh, that was me," she said matter-of-factly.

"What?" Carter said, flabbergasted.

"Yes, the glare from those silly panels and the noise from the windmill interrupted my beauty sleep."

"But... but we borrowed on our mortgage to pay for those things... and now the fines. We're broke. What are we going to do?"

"I don't know," she snapped, "unless..." she drawled.

Miss Tutley slowly eased to Carter again and violently pressed her bosom against him. Carter stared at her, shocked. She put a hand on his chest, then twirled her fingers through his hair. She regarded him seductively.

"You do a favor for me... and I'll do a favor for you..."

Carter lurched back.

"Shelley, I told you, I'm married... to a man! How much clearer could I have been?"

Miss Tutley eased off, rolled her eyes, and tapped her heel repeatedly on the floor.

"I don't know!" she said. "I just thought you went to church a lot!"

"I can't believe you did this!" Carter said. "Please, let us put them up again..."

"I don't know," she mused, "unless..." she drawled again.

Miss Tutley moved in again, popped a button loose from Carter's shirt, and twirled a finger in his chest hair. Carter backed off again.

"No!"

"Then I can't help you Keifer!" she announced. "My stunning beauty is much more important than your silly flagpole."

"It's a windmill, Shelley. A windmill. And for the last time, my name is Carter!"

"Maybe you can talk to your elected official about your water wheel Arthur... oh wait, it's going to be me!" she exclaimed, and laughed maniacally.

"You?"

"Oh yes. Haven't you heard? I'm running in the election for state representative."

Carter's mouth fell open so far, and stayed open for so long, chipmunks could have relocated their home and hibernated there all winter. He shook himself from his shock.

"Ummmm, Shelley, you have to get elected first."

"Oh, I have this in the bag Harper."

"Don't you mean in the sack?" Carter muttered.

Miss Tutley shrugged her shoulders, turned on her heel, uninterested, and walked away. Carter watched her, his mouth agape again.

#

The public park opposite the high school teemed with activity during the lunch hour. Two people threw a frisbee; another couple tossed a football; three girls kicked a soccer ball back and forth; a few older people did tai chi; mothers walked with strollers; senior citizens sat on benches; and various people sat under trees and ate their lunch – all peaceful and serene.

But across the park, under a gnarly, withered oak tree, an evil plot hatched around a picnic table. Miss Tutley's biology class huddled around the table, the site of many children's birthday parties, family get-togethers, friendly chess matches, and declarations of undying and perpetual love. Now it hosted a plot to kill or maim or make disappear or publicly humiliate the worst teacher in the world.

"I don't know about you guys, but it's time we did something about her," Max said as he leaned forward.

"Yeah! Get her… get her good!" Sarah spat out.

The group regarded Sarah as she intensely carved skull and crossbones on the picnic table with a switchblade. Miss Tutley's red X still marked her forehead.

"Ummmm Sarah, where did you get the knife?" Jenny asked.

"From those old grannies."

She waved the knife dismissively at two female senior citizens who sat on a nearby bench. They gave Sarah a friendly wave with white mesh-gloved hands. Sarah returned a 'rock on' fist pump.

"Okay..." Jenny drawled. "So, I thought about poisoning her lunch everyday so she'd have perpetual diarrhea and wouldn't come back to school."

"I thought about publicly humiliating her..." Max said.

"Yeah, well I thought more about publicly beheading her," Sarah said.

"We can always get the mob to take her down," Elliott chimed in.

"Wait, wait wait..." Robin cried. "Beheading? Take her down? What is this, 'The Sopranos'?

Sarah jabbed her knife at the group. "She's a cancer who needs to be removed."

She forcefully stuck the blade into the table and flicked it with a finger to make it move like a metronome. "Anyone got a joint?"

Elliott innocently patted himself, then shook his head.

"It's okay Sarah," Jenny said as she patted Sarah on the shoulder. "Take it easy."

Sarah leaped off the bench and stood defiantly in front of her friends.

"Take it easy?! Are you flippin' kidding me?! I will not take it easy and neither should you! The woman's a disgrace to teachers everywhere! Isn't it bad enough she separated the boys from the girls on the first day and told the boys to write an essay on what a dream date with her would be like, while she gave all us girls make-up tips?! Like I want to know how to put on make-up with a trowel. She's supposed to be a biology teacher for fuck's sake – not some kinda lame brain Instagram queen who takes pictures of her ass all day."

Sarah threw her arms in the air as she paced in front of the picnic table.

"Now she demeans me and degrades everything I've worked so hard for. And Elliott," she said as she gave him a hug. "Humiliating him... I'll do anything to make her disappear!"

Elliott stood, then slammed his palms on the table. "Yeah! Roll her ass!"

Everyone stared at Elliott.

"Make her disappear? Roll her ass?" Robin disbelievingly repeated. "Listen to yourselves! This isn't who we are. We're all human beings. Where is our humanity?"

Everyone regarded each other, frowned, and silently bowed their heads in silence and embarrassment over their bloodlust until Sarah quickly broke the quiet.

"Shut up Ghandi."

"But," Robin continued, "who have we become – a blood thirsty mob?"

"Yes!" Sarah shouted.

"Alright, I think we're all agreed we have to do something," Max said.

"Max is right," Marc said. "Miss Tutley must be stopped, especially after she dropped the bomb about running for office. Can you imagine her in politics?"

"Yeah," Jenny said. "Congress already has two braindead bimbos. We don't need a third."

"Max, isn't your mom running in the election?" Robin asked.

"Yesssss," Max moaned, and tried to hide his face in his hands.

"Sooooo, what if they run for the same side?"

"I dunno. Maybe they'll cancel each other out."

"What does your mom think?"

"Ummmm, I don't think she knows yet. If she did, her head would've exploded by now."

"And another thing," Sarah said. "Who the hell does Tutley think she is, having us work on her campaign? The balls. The balls!"

"I know," Jenny said. "The next thing you know, she'll have us making buttons with her ugly face on 'em like in a sweatshop factory."

"Then it's settled. Tutley is a goner!" Sarah shouted.

The two senior citizens raised their arms and clenched their fists in solidarity.

"I don't know about this man," Alex wavered.

"Oh, what a surprise," Marc sarcastically announced. "Mr. Sex Machine who's only using the teach to get a good grade doesn't want to upset his sick little plan. Lopez, would you forget about getting Tutley's A for one stinking second and think about your friends for once."

"But I have her hooked..." Alex whined.

Jenny slammed her hands on the table. "Keep it zipped Romeo! This is serious shit!"

"Okay, let's think about this," Max said. "We can't go to Mr. Douglas. It's obvious she has her claws in him. She has her claws in everyone. It's what she does to get what she wants."

"Tutley's a horrible, incompetent, manipulating parasite who can't be fixed. No matter who we turn to for help, she'll cast her spell on them like the sociopath she is."

"What's a sociopath?" Elliott asked frightened. "A sex addict?"

Max laughed. "You're not far off Elliott. A sociopath is a person who has no morals or conscience. So, yes, Miss Tutley."

"Keep her away from me!" Elliott whined as he cowered against Jenny. "I'm saving myself for my wedding night!"

"But why do we have to do something about her?" Robin asked.

"Because we're all her victims," Marc said. "We've all been on the receiving end of her crazy nastiness. She's insulted everyone based on our weight, our looks, our personalities, our sexuality, our race... me more than you – the big gay Black guy with the White boyfriend. If I hear one more stupid comment about me and Max being an Oreo, I swear I'll choke the life from her myself."

"And don't forget her biggest fault – she's an imbecile pretending to be a teacher," Sarah said.

"I know guys," Jenny said. "I've had it with her innocent, dumb little sex kitten act."

"I know!" Max said, exasperated. "I don't get it. What is this hold she has over men – taken in by her damsel in distress attitude, teased blonde hair, pounds of make-up, mounds of implants, and tight, barely-there clothes? Are all men this shallow?"

"Yes!" cried out all the girls.

In the distance, Fiona ran toward the group.

"Hey, here comes Fiona," Alex said. "I wonder what punishment she got..."

"In a perfect world, she wouldn't get any," Marc said.

"Well, she did try to choke Miss Tutley with bacteria," Robin said.

"Robin, whose side are you on anyway?" Marc said. "Remember, she practically called you a future 40-year-old virgin."

"Ya know Binster," Sarah said, "I'm gettin' reallllly tired of you defending the amoeba. She wipes the floor with you, and you still defend her."

"But I didn't..."

"Yeah right. I'm surprised you didn't whip out an oversized novelty hand with 'Miss Tutley is #1' on it and waved it in class."

"But I..."

"Okay, okay," Max said. "Let's not trash each other. The common enemy is Tutley."

Fiona ran to the picnic table and threw her backpack on the ground.

"Tutley the psychopath is dead!"

"Yay!" Elliott shouted as he threw his arms in the air. "Now we don't have to kill her!"

"No... I mean I want her dead."

"We were just talking about getting rid of her," Jenny said.

"Yeah, so Max, what's with meeting here in the park? No witnesses?"

"Exactly."

"Max, we could hold a 'Kill Miss Tutley' rally at the school, and no one would blink."

"Screw that," Marc said. "We could have it in the football stadium, invite the whole town, and still no one would blink."

Alex gave Fiona a hug. "So, babe, what happened to you?"

"Suspension."

"Oh no..."

"I don't care. What ticks me off is Tutley got off again – after getting Mr. Douglas off..."

The group murmured in agreement.

"After getting him off what?" Elliott asked.

Everyone groaned and giggled.

"Oh Elliott, we love you," Jenny said as she gave him a hug.

"So, what's the plan?" Fiona asked. "Drive her out to the woods and leave her? Put her in a bag and throw her off a bridge? Hire a hit man?"

"Wait, wait," Alex said. "We weren't actually talking about killing her... were we?"

Fiona turned to Alex, pressed against him, stared into his eyes, burning holes deep into his skull.

"You're not choosing her over me are you... honey?"

Alex swallowed hard. "Ummmm no... sweet pea." He half-smiled.

"Good."

In the distance, the school bell rang.

"Oh shit, we gotta get back," Marc said.

"But we're not finished with our plan man," Sarah said.

"Let's meet later after school at the mall," Max said.

"In public?" Robin asked.

"We're teens hangin' out at the mall. We're not planning a coup."

"Well, we kinda are," Marc said. Max nodded.

The teens gathered their things.

"I don't think I can," Alex wavered. "I have wrestling practice..."

"Wait a minute Lopez," Marc said. "My basketball team's practice was cancelled today because they're using the gym for a play. So, how could you possibly have practice today?"

"Ummm, it's in the auxiliary gym, Johnston!" Alex snapped back.

Fiona patted Alex's face. "You wouldn't be meeting a certain whore after school today would you, honey?"

"No... no," Alex protested.

"Cause if you are..."

Fiona made a fist in his face.

"It's a knuckle sandwich," Elliott said.

"It's okay if you lead the brainless tart on because she deserves it. But if you even try something physical with her, it'll be worse than a knuckle sandwich ten times over."

Jenny leaned over to Alex so she and Fiona were both in his face.

"Like I said, keep it zipped Romeo. Fiona'll fix it so you and her won't have kids."

Jenny pointed to Sarah's knife stuck in the picnic table. Sarah fingered it again to make it wobble menacingly.

Alex gulped.

Fiona broke away from Alex, and stood resolutely in front of her friends, her hands firmly planted on her hips again.

"So, we're all in agreement... right? We make her go away."

"Yeah," Max said as he made air quotations, "make her go away."

EIGHT

Martha, still dressed in her 1970s, spy-extraordinaire outfit, drove her BMW SUV along a winding rural highway. If she would have been driving a sports car, the long, sheer white scarf around her neck would have been breezily blowing behind her – giving her an aura of a Hollywood actress who played a princess of some Mediterranean kingdom.

She passed suburban subdivisions one moment, and cornfields and hayfields the next. Long dirt roads led to old farmhouses in the fields. She carefully scanned the rural address markers placed beside the mailboxes. She quickly looked at the map on her GPS, then jerked her head back to stare at the narrow roadway.

Martha encountered few vehicles on the road. Various livestock manure smells almost overcame her, and she closed her windows – and locked her doors, the area being so rural, and so not Martha.

As she drove on, she encountered a huge billboard with her name and picture on it placed in a farmer's field. Like the sign on her front lawn, it showed her dressed in white, with her hands clasped as she gazed skyward. Unlike her urban sign, this rural sign said: HEATHENS ARE THE DEVIL'S WORK. VOTE MARTHA MOLDER TO SAVE OUR UNBORN CHILDREN FROM THE TERRORISTS AMONG US. PRAISE JESUS. She smiled.

At a bend in the road, Martha slowed the car to read an address next to a mailbox. The old, rusty mailbox hung by a wire on a post on a severe lean. An old, rusty wire mesh gate leaned into the ditch. To complete the old and rusty theme, a decrepit sign sat beside the driveway obscured by the tall grass. It might have read 'Fairweather Farms' at some point in its youth.

Martha tightened her grip on the wheel, then turned off the highway. She slowly drove along the overgrown gravel driveway. She darted her eyes from one side of the road to the other as she hunched over the steering wheel – trying to see into the thick, tall, weathered grass. She said silent prayers, and not-so-silent prayers.

"Please Jesus... please God... please Jesus... please God..."

As she drove into a clearing, no one or entity attacked her. The driveway ended in the yard of a dilapidated farmhouse, partially on a lean. She parked her car in the grass and scrutinized the old house. The wood shingles were weathered and grey. The windows were either cracked or broken, and the shutters beside them sagged at a sad angle. Moss grew on the roof, and grass grew in the eavestroughs.

The yard existed as a wild jungle. Untamed bushes grew unchecked beside the house. Gnarly, weather-damaged old oak trees surrounded the property. Branches and broken tree limbs littered the yard. Tire tracks through the tall grass disappeared behind the house.

As Martha opened her car door, a couple dozen plastic fetuses fell out onto the ground. She scrambled from the car, scooped them into her arms, and threw them back into the car. As she slammed the door, a fetus got caught in the door frame and made a high-pitched wheezing sound as the air expelled from it.

Martha adjusted her sunglasses and hat and apprehensively walked the overgrown pathway to the house. She fought her way through tall grass, prickly bushes, and fallen tree branches to stand on rickety wooden steps. She picked the prickles from her dress.

Two large Rottweilers bounded around the corners of the house – one on Martha's left, and the other on her right. They barked ferociously. Martha screamed and ran to the steps. Halfway up the wobbly steps, her right foot broke through the rotten wood. She desperately yanked her foot free, and fell to the front door, which was solid steel, and in infinitely better condition than the house.

As Martha pounded a fist on the door, bolts unlocked from the inside, and the door opened. A man's heavily tattooed arm reached out. His large hand grabbed her by the arm and yanked her inside. Martha yelped, and the door slammed shut. The dogs leapt at the door, sniffed it, and whined as they prowled on the porch.

Inside the dark, dank, and gloomy farmhouse, the only light source was an old dim sconce on the wall. Martha couldn't see the man who rescued her – or held her captive. She sniffed the air and immediately contorted her face – at the mustiness of the house, and at her captor who smelled like extra cheesy Doritos and Brut.

The unknown man dragged her by the arm along a confined passageway. Martha stumbled after him. As she steadied herself, she tried to wrench away from him.

"Who are you?!" she breathlessly questioned. "I demand to know. I'm a prominent woman in this town. I know people... the police... the military... I know the mayor!"

The man stopped, and Martha fell into him. He quickly moved behind her and pulled her hands behind her back. He turned on a flashlight and shone it in her face. Martha yelped.

"Quiat!" he shouted.

"But... but I'm here to help!" Martha whined.

The man gripped her hands tighter and leered over her shoulder.

"Quiat," he drawled.

Martha smelled anchovies on his breath. Combined with the aged Doritos and failing Brut, she almost retched. The man pushed her forward, holding her hands tight. He pointed the flashlight down rickety steps. Martha's eyes widened. The man nudged her forward, and they descended the steps with reckless abandon. Martha tried not to trip and fall or snag her expensive dress on the loose nails poking out from the wall.

At the bottom, the man quickly opened a door, unhanded Martha, and pushed her inside a dank, musty room with a concrete floor. Martha stumbled and flailed into the center of the room to stand under an intense, bright, overhead light. As the man slammed the door behind him, Martha tugged at her dress and assembled herself back together.

Martha tried to gauge her surroundings, but with the bright light, she could only see within the spotlight. A figure rushed past her in the dark.

Martha raised a hand to shield the light from her eyes. A diminutive woman rushed to the gangly, tall man who had accosted her. He stood a foot taller than the petite woman. She swatted him in the arm. He flinched.

"Who is this doofus?!" the woman asked the man.

Martha put a hand on her hip. "I am no doofus."

"I wuz talkin' ta him, Miss Hoity Toity Fancy Hat!"

"Caught me a trespasser Arlene!" the man said proudly.

Arlene swatted him in the arm again. "Don't say my name doofus!"

The man flinched again and recoiled from Arlene. Accustomed to her surroundings, Martha peered into the shadiness and tried to determine who the two people were.

"I am no trespasser," she said. "I want to help you..."

The man sniggered and casually stepped into the light. The twenty-something man's smooth baby face, and his buzzed hair made him appear much younger. Both arms were sleeve tattoos. He wore a white tank top, and tight blue jeans.

"Helps us?" he drawled. "You? If that ain't the most comically thang I ever heard, my name isn't Jimmy Joe Johnson."

Arlene groaned in frustration, stepped into the light, and swatted Jimmy Joe in the arm again. Also in her twenties, her streaked blonde hair was pulled back in a hastily arranged ponytail. She too wore a tank top and jeans. Her aggressive demeanor more than made up for her lack of height. A tattoo of a cobra wrapped around a gas can adorned her left shoulder. On her right, a tattoo of an angel in a heart, with the inscription 'Daddy's Little Angel.'

"Now you've dun done it dummy!" Arlene beaked. "She knows our names and wut we look like!"

"Ummm, I think there's a misunderstanding," Martha said. "I'm here to welcome you to town and... oh wait..."

Martha glanced at her purse, then reached into it. Arlene snatched it away.

"It's the Welcome Wagon, Leeny!" Jimmy Joe said excitedly as he stretched out his arm to shake Martha's hand. "I'm Jimmy Joe... well, ya already know that... and this is ma wife Arlene... well, ya already know that too," he chuckled loudly.

Martha hesitantly reached a hand out and offered her fingertips. Instead, Jimmy Joe grabbed her hand and shook it uncouthly and clumsily. Martha stumbled forward.

"So, whatcha got for us?" he asked. "A big basket a fruit? Free dancin' lessons? Bowlin' membership? Huh? Huh?"

Arlene aggressively swatted their handshake apart, and clocked Jimmy Joe across the head with Martha's purse.

"She ain't no Welcome Wagon lady dum dum..." Arlene slowly circled Martha, regarding her with disdain. "I know her kind. I seen this get up lots 'a times. I got her pegged from her million-dollar hairdo to those fancy pointy toed shoes."

Arlene leaned into Martha, glared at her, and smirked.

"She's a spy for the government."

"A spy?" Martha said. "Oh no..."

"Oh yes!" Arlene screeched. "That's some disguise... big floppy hat, big floppy pearly thangs," she said as she fingered Martha's pearls, "fancy dress – and the blue stripe up the back... it's Hot Cotter right?"

Martha strained to see over her shoulder. "I think you mean Haute Couture..." she said in an exaggerated French accent.

"Ohhh, excuse me Krystle Carrington," Arlene said as she bowed deeply before Martha. "We'll let ya go so yous can make ur hairdo appointment before ya have lunch with ur richy-rich lady friends at sum swanky restaurant with fancy finger sandwiches with the crusts cut off!"

Jimmy Joe massaged his stomach. "Ohhhh Leeny, I'm gettin' awful hungry..."

Arlene groaned. "Hungry?! Ya just had a big plate a sardines and Doritos..."

"Please," Martha pleaded, "in my purse you'll see your pamphlet I obtained at Walmart."

Arlene eyed Martha suspiciously, opened her purse, and picked through it.

"Compact... lipstick... eyeliner... lip balm... mascara... moisture goo... Good grief it's a flippin' Mary Kay convention in this thang. You sure you're not sellin' these here doo dads?"

"No, the pamphlet... it should be there..."

"Mace... miniature bible... steak knife... crucifix... flask... Focus on the Family membership card... a plastic baby head... oh, here it is..."

Arlene pulled out a folded flyer. She walked to the door and flipped a light switch. The main lights turned on. She flipped another switch, and the interrogation light turned off. Arlene glanced at the brochure.

"You see," Martha said, "your message resonates with me... and others too."

"Reznates? Meanin' it gives her the runs or she likes it?" Jimmy Joe asked Arlene.

"Yes!" Martha said. "You'd be surprised what people think after I tell them what to think. I regularly accost customers at my husband's bank with my opinions. Why, last week at my monthly book burning of gay terrorist books, the crowd grew tenfold from the previous month. I want to spread your message..."

"Like manure?" Arlene asked.

"Yes! Your church group is exactly what I'm looking for."

"Church gro...?" Jimmy Joe said before Arlene slapped him in the stomach.

"So, your husband owns a bank?" she asked, genuinely interested.

"Oh no. He manages it."

Arlene and Jimmy Joe exchanged sly smiles.

"I can see you're good Christians," Martha said as she peered around the room at the small-time military operation. "Why, the fertilizer stacked along the wall tells me you only want to cultivate the earth..."

Martha pointed casually to a wall lined from top to bottom with bags of fertilizer.

"And your armor..."

She pointed to another wall lined with pistols, assault rifles, grenades, and surface-to-air missile launchers.

"...tells me you only want to protect your family and your country from socialist immigrant criminals and terrorist sex Marxists. So do I!"

Arlene considered Martha, then offered a toothy smile. She gave Martha back her purse.

"Jimmy Joe, why don't you git Miss..." Arlene cocked her head, and encouraged Martha to offer her name.

"Martha."

Arlene smiled. "Git Miss Martha a box a those new fancy flyers. I've a feelin' Miss Martha wud do a good job... ministerin' for our... church."

Jimmy Joe gawked at Arlene, puzzled. "What chur...?"

She slapped him in the stomach again. "Git dem flyers!"

He frowned, massaged his stomach, and sauntered to a dark corner of the basement.

"I knew we were going to be kindred spirits," Martha said. "We have to stick together. I mean, you and your husband are obviously on the lowest rung of society, but our common bond to destroy liberal demons and sinners is stronger than our social breeding."

"Ummm... yeah, okay..." Arlene said.

"Oh, I will do a great job spreading your word."

"Ummm... yeah, yeah, our word..." Arlene said.

Arlene put an arm around Martha's shoulder. Martha eyed her arm, as if it were a snake.

"I like ya Miss Martha. But before ya go out ministerin', how 'bout a nice tall glass a Kool-Aid...?"

"Well, that sounds lovely," Martha lied.

Arlene led Martha upstairs. She glanced behind her and shared an evil grin with Jimmy Joe.

NINE

Outside the main entrance to a massive mall complex, Miss Tutley's students congregated beside an experimental bronze art sculpture. Max, Marc, Sarah, Jenny, Fiona, Robin and their fellow biology classmates either sat on the sculpture's concrete ledge or sat on the art in the shade to shield themselves from the hot afternoon sun. Alex and Elliott were missing. Fiona furiously tapped on her cell phone.

"The two-timing little rat," she spat. "I warned him. You all heard me."

"Come on Fiona," Jenny said. "Alex would never cheat on you with Tutley."

"Yeah, especially after you threatened to castrate him," Robin said.

"Jenny's right," Marc said. "Alex's 'big stud on campus' act is just an act. It's part of his... what's the word...?"

"Persona," Max said. "We all know Alex, and despite him sometimes being a self-absorbed, preening... well..."

"Asshole," Marc said.

"Thank you. Despite all that, he's a good guy," Max said as he put a hand on Fiona's shoulder and squeezed it.

"Oh, I know. I know!" Fiona relented. "I trust him. I do. It's Tutley I don't trust, the man-eating leech."

Sarah casually leaned against the sculpture. Her once perfectly braided hair fell loose around her shoulders. A plaid headband pushed her hair into a spike in front. She fashioned the headband from her skirt she had ripped to a length above the knee. The arms of her blouse were rolled to her biceps. The red X remained emblazoned on her forehead.

"Tutley's scum," she snorted as she jumped off the sculpture.

"Ummm, Sarah, you know the red X is still on your forehead, right?" Robin asked.

"Yes, thank you Binster," she snapped.

"You're welcome."

"Look guys, we have to do this Tutley thing tonight!" Sarah said as she jabbed a finger at her friends.

"Wow, don't you think it's a little short notice Sarah?" Max said. "We need to make plans, get on the same page, make sure we all know what's going on..."

"Oh my God Max! We're not planning to invade Canada! We're knocking off our moronic biology teacher!" Sarah shouted.

"Shhhhhh!" her friends hissed at her, as customers passed.

"What?!" she asked, exasperated, her hands in the air. "If they knew what a twit she was, they'd want in on it too!"

"Look," Max said, "I know we're all pissed at her for one reason or another, but we have to think this through. We have to be rational about this."

"Rational? We're talking about..." Robin lowered his voice, "killing our teacher."

"Look Binster," Sarah said, "you knew this meeting involved murder, so even you have a little bloodlust."

"Hey, I only want to do something easy, like put glue in her hair gel."

"Oooooohh, how horrible!"

"Robin's right," Marc said. "We all have ideas. Some are... out there," he said as he glanced at Sarah. "And some are... cute," he said as he peered at Robin. "The point is to meet somewhere in the middle."

"And we will, but we should wait for Alex and Elliott," Fiona said. "They hate her just as much as we do."

"Where is Elliott? He said he'd be here," Jenny said.

"He said he'd try," Robin said. "You know his parents. If he's not home on time, they think he's been kidnapped."

"I know. Remember when he followed a butterfly downtown on his bike," Marc said.

"Yeah. They turned it into the next Lindbergh baby kidnapping," Sarah said.

"Poor Elliott," Max said as he shook his head. "He's so sheltered. If my folks tracked me by GPS twenty-four/seven like his do..."

"You mean your mother doesn't now?" Sarah quipped.

"No! And shhhhh! Don't give her any ideas either."

"Why are you shushing me? Did she bug your underwear Max?"

"Probably."

"Uh oh..." Marc said.

"I gotta hand it to you Max," Sarah said. "You turned out reasonably okay, even with the mother from hell."

"Reasonably? Gee thanks Sarah."

"You know what I mean. Anyone else would have been carted off to a mental hospital. She showed up at our house the other day selling mugs and back scratchers with her picture on them. She wedged a back scratcher in the door and wouldn't leave until dad shooed her off with a copy of Mother Jones. What the hell was that all about?"

Max tried to shrink into a little ball as he shook his head. "She's trying to fund her stupid campaign."

"What kind of a moron would vote for her? She's nuts."

"Sarah, you're talking about Max's mom," Robin said defensively.

"Oh, please Robin! Everyone knows she's off her head. Even Max says so."

"She is Robin," Max nodded to him. "Our garage is filled with boxes of expired cookies she got cheap from Russia with her face imprinted on them to sell for her next grift... err, marketing campaign. She wants me to go out dressed in a boy scout uniform to sell them. I won't do it!"

"Remember the time she forced you to dye your hair blonde so people wouldn't know your dad is Puerto Rican?" Jenny said.

"I don't know how you do it babe," Marc said. "I would've had a meltdown by now."

"I don't know either. Listening to her whine every day about the 'perfect girl' she wants me to marry brings me to the edge."

"You still haven't told her you're gay?" Jenny said.

"I've tried!" Max said as he jumped off the sculpture. "Every time I try, she starts talking about shock therapy and 'gay conversion' clinics – you know, like the one she sent her alleged straight campaign manager to, to stop him from being so gay so he wouldn't ruin her campaign."

"Riiiiiight," Marc said. "It worked well, didn't it?"

"She gives me nightmares. I can't even tell her about Marc!"

"But she's met him, right?" Jenny asked.

"Oh yeah, I've met her," Marc said as he rolled his eyes.

"She thinks he's my token Black friend," Max said, "as if he's a charity case and 'good for me' I'm hanging out with him. I swear I'm this close," Max said as he ground his thumb and forefinger together, "from telling her to fuck off."

"Make out with each other in front of her," Sarah said. "It'll blow her mind."

"She'll explode," Marc said.

"Well, I know why Max turned out alright," Sarah said. "His dad."

"I know!" Marc exclaimed. "He's so cool with everything: Max and me, staying at Max's house – when his mother isn't there – Max staying at my house, and lying for him, saying he's at a 'friend's' house. He's so... cool!"

"Guys, can we wait for Alex and Elliott inside. It's freaking hot out here," Sarah said.

"We could," Max said, "but if we're not exactly where we told Elliott we'd be, he'd think we deserted him – again."

"I know," Jenny said. "Remember when he forgot English moved to another classroom. He stayed there and cried until the janitor found him in the evening."

"Yessss," Max moaned as he shook his head.

"Let's go inside the entrance. We can see the sculpture fine from there," Marc said.

"I'll text Alex and Elliot, and tell them where we are," Fiona said.

The teens gathered their belongings and walked toward the mall entrance.

"I'm surprised Elliot has a cell phone," Max said.

"Oh, he has two," Jenny said. "One in case criminals kidnapped him, and another one in case he lost the first one."

As the group made their way across the parking lot to the entrance, a brown Audi sedan drove toward them. Max saw it first.

"Tutley!" he screamed.

The teens froze.

"Run! Run!" Robin yelled.

The teens scattered amongst the parked cars like ants in an underground maze. Miss Tutley almost clipped an elderly woman with a walker, almost pinned her to a lamp post, and almost side-swiped the car next to her as she haphazardly parked her car. The Audi screeched to a stop and belched a cloud of black smoke from the tailpipe.

As the teens peered over parked cars like rabbits who poked their heads from their holes, Miss Tutley swept her door open and lightly dinged the car beside her. She carefully stepped from the car, pulled at her short skirt, slammed the door, clicked it locked, and skipped toward the entrance. When she disappeared inside, the teens emerged from their hiding spots.

Sarah swatted Robin in the arm. "Why did you yell 'run'? Now we look like guilty idiots."

"But... but we're plotting to kill her..."

"No one knows that!"

The group walked toward Miss Tutley's car.

"Maybe we should meet somewhere else," Marc said.

"Are you kidding?" Fiona said. "This is perfect. We plot to kill her right under her nose, and she's too stupid to realize it. I love it!" she laughed.

"Maybe we should let her in on it – she still wouldn't get it," Sarah said.

"You guys..." Robin said as he shook his head.

Max surveyed the car.

"Wow, look at all these dents in the bumper. What the hell has she been doing?"

"Max, she meets men by rear ending them," Fiona said. "It's how she met my father."

Jenny peered into the windows.

"Guys! Guys! There's something moving in the backseat!"

"Probably one of the guys she rear ended," Max said.

"Naw, he'd be tied to the roof," Fiona said.

As they gathered around Jenny to peer into the car, Elliott rolled over in the backseat and pressed his round face against the window.

"Ahhhh!" the teens screamed as they lurched away.

"Elliott!" Jenny yelled at him and pressed her hands against the window.

"Elliott, what are you doing in there?" Max shouted.

"Following her."

"What?! Why?!"

"To try and get some dirt on her."

"Dirt?"

"Yes. You know, evidence."

"Elliott, we have all the evidence we need," Marc said. "She's a racist, lying, conniving, incompetent, sociopathic sex addict."

"But... but I know things... about her and... Max... and..." Elliott faltered and wiped at his forehead. "Oh my, it's hot in here..."

"Holy shit, it must be a hundred degrees in there," Fiona said. "Elliott, get out!" she yelled as she tried to open the door.

Elliott tried the handle and tried to push the door open.

"I can't... get out..." he said faintly.

"It's probably a child-proof lock," Sarah said.

"Elliott! Is there a button next to the door handle?!" Max yelled.

Elliott scanned the door. "Nooooo..."

"Oh my God, the dumb twit locked him in!" Fiona said.

"She didn't know about him in there," Robin said.

"Oh, what a surprise, a word from the Tutley fan club president."

"We have to do something!" Marc said. "Break the window!"

"With what, another car?" Sarah said. "There's nothing around here to smash it with."

"I'm calling 9-1-1," Jenny said as she pulled out her phone and dialed.

"Come on Marc," Max said as he pulled him by the arm, "let's go in the mall and find someone to help."

"Alright."

The two boys ran toward the entrance. Max turned and yelled at Fiona.

"Call me if you get him out!"

"Okay."

As Max and Marc disappeared into the mall, Alex approached the group.

"What the hell is going on guys?!"

Fiona grabbed his arm. "Oh God Alex, Elliott is locked inside Tutley's car."

"What?! How? Why?"

"Don't... don't ask..."

"Did she try to kidnap him? His parents will be pissed."

"No. He hid in the backseat playing detective. She locked him inside."

Alex pounded on the window with his fist. "Elliott!"

"I'm a big Black boy in a little brown box..." he faintly wailed against the glass.

"I think he's hallucinating," Fiona said.

"The police are on the way," Jenny said.

Inside the mall, Max and Marc ran to the glass railing that circled the atrium one level below them. Max scanned the large open space.

"We should go to the information booth and have them page security. It's on the first level near the north entrance, right?"

"Yeah, I think so."

"Okay, let's go," Max said as he pulled on Marc's arm.

Marc didn't budge, and Max sprang back into him like a rubber band.

"Oh... my... God..." Marc slowly said.

"What?" Max said, slightly irritated.

Marc regarded him sympathetically. "Max, I'm so sorry..."

"What!?"

Marc frowned, then pointed to a store on the lower level. Max followed his direction.

"Tutley..." Marc said.

Miss Tutley, and Max's father Jack exited Emmanuelle's Erotic Emporium & Oxygen Renewal. She hooked her arm through the crook in his arm and wrapped herself around him like a warm tortilla. She giggled as Jack furtively scanned the mall. She carried a large gold-colored bag with the store logo. As they walked through the mall toward the exit, Max's jaw dropped with every step. When they disappeared, Max circled the railing to keep an eye on them.

"Max... Max!" Marc tried to discreetly yell as he ran after him. He grabbed Max's arm. "What do you think you're doing?"

"Lemme go! I gotta go after them!"

"No, it's the worst thing you can do."

"But... but Tutley," he said as he waved a hand at her, defeated.

Marc put an arm around Max. "I know. I know."

"Why Marc?" Max moaned.

"Tutley," Marc said simply.

The two boys stood and watched as Jack and Miss Tutley hurried toward the exit. As they disappeared out the door, Max shook his head.

"Of all the women in town, he has an affair with her?" A dark pall cast over his face. "Tutley, the scheming leech," he spat. "Like, what is her fucking problem?! Is she going through the phone book alphabetically? It's pretty clear she's made it to the M's."

"Max, you can't let this get to you, man. Come on, let's find someone to help Elliott."

Max slumped his shoulders, and they walked to the escalator to take it to the lower level.

Outside the mall, a crowd gathered around Miss Tutley's car. The police arrived. Curious onlookers guessed wildly at the commotion.

"There's a baby in the car!... Pretty big baby... The poor thing... The parents should be ashamed!... They should be in jail!... It's no baby, it's a big dog... The ones that look like little horses... Break the window!... Please, won't somebody think of the children!"

Miss Tutley and Jack exited the mall and saw the fracas. She shooed him away. He disappeared into the parking lot. Miss Tutley ran to her car as quickly as she could in her high heels. As a police officer raised his baton to bash the window, she reached out to stop him.

"No! Wait! It's my car!"

The officer stopped in mid-swing as Miss Tutley pushed her way through the crowd to stand between him and her car.

"What is going on here?!" she yelled, as she spread her arms, and leaned against her car.

"Ma'am," the officer said, "this is your car?"

"Yes!"

"Oh, she's no ma'am," Fiona spat. "More like a madam."

"Madam... errr ma'am, there's a child in distress in your car."

"What?!" Miss Tutley said as she wheeled around to see Elliott innocently wave at her. "What are you doing in there Elephant?!"

"Oh my God!" Sarah exclaimed. "You ignorant cow! He's dying in there! Let him out! Where are your keys?!"

Sarah snatched Miss Tutley's purse and searched it. Miss Tutley slapped her hands.

"This my private purse Sara Lee!"

A chant grew in the crowd, amplified by the teens.

"Let him out! Let him out! Let him out!"

As a flustered Miss Tutley fumbled for her keys, she dropped her shopping bag. A slinky corset, a thong, an odd-shaped sex toy, and a tub of hot body oil tumbled out onto the pavement.

"She's a sex worker!" a woman in the crowd gasped as she pointed to Miss Tutley's purchases.

Robin turned to her. "No, she's not. She's our teacher," he said proudly.

Miss Tutley finally retrieved her keys from her purse amidst the growing chants from the crowd. She attempted to unlock her car, but only succeeded in making the car alarm sound, which drowned out the chants. People screamed and covered their ears. Miss Tutley pressed another button, and the trunk popped open.

A frustrated Jenny swiped the keys from her hand.

"Oh, give me those, you twit!" she snapped.

Jenny pressed a button, and the doors unlocked. She pressed another, and the car alarm stopped. A cheer arose from the crowd. Jenny pushed Miss Tutley away and flung the door open. She reached in and helped Elliott out.

"Are you okay son?" the officer asked.

"I think so," Elliott said as he wiped his brow. "I'm just a little overcooked..."

Miss Tutley put her hands on her hips. "Yeah, like a baked ham."

"Shut up Tutley!" Jenny sneered. "Does anyone have any water?"

"Water?! Don't reward this little heifer. He accessed my car illegally. Arrest him!"

"Arrest yourself Tutley!" Sarah said. "He could've died."

"You haven't answered my question Elephant. What were you doing in my car?"

"Research," Sarah said. "To find out if your backseat really does have a point of sale terminal."

"But I..." Elliott said.

"Yes, yes," Sarah said as she put an arm around him, and clamped a hand over his mouth. "He knows he did wrong, but we were forced to do it for science's sake."

"Mmmmhhmmmfffmm..." Elliott mumbled.

Someone from the crowd handed him a water bottle. Jenny took the bottle from him and unscrewed the cap. Sarah uncovered his mouth.

"Max is gonna kill her," he blurted before Jenny popped the bottle in his mouth.

Sarah held his head like a baby as Elliott gurgled the water.

"There, there," Sarah cooed as she rocked him a bit, "just drinky winky..."

"Okay," the officer said to the crowd, "everything's fine now. Let's all move along."

As the officer ushered the crowd away, the teens quickly moved away from the car.

"But officer," Miss Tutley protested, "that oversized child invaded my car!"

"Look miss, there's no harm done here – only kids playing a harmless prank. And if you want to know the truth, you're lucky the kid's okay."

"But... but... but Officer," Miss Tutley said huskily as she brushed against him. "Can't you do anything?" she said as she danced her fingertips on his arm.

Fiona rolled her eyes. "Uugghh, the woman is disgusting."

"Look, lady..." the officer said.

"Lady? Ha!" Fiona scoffed. "What a stretch."

As she and her friends walked away, Miss Tutley shot her a vile look.

"I've got five kids at home," the officer continued, "a wife about to drop number six, a mother-in-law climbin' inside my ass every day, angina through the roof, and a half-a-million-dollar mortgage poundin' on my head every night. So, keep your hands to yourself and let this go. We have more important things to deal with."

The teens almost stopped and applauded the officer, who scoffed at Miss Tutley, and walked to his vehicle. Miss Tutley tapped her heel on the ground and suspiciously glared at her students. She gathered her erotic belongings back into the bag, then tossed it in her car. The teens ran into Max and Marc who exited the mall with a security guard.

"Elliott!" Max exclaimed, then ran to him.

"He's okay," Alex said.

"Okay, I guess we don't need you," Marc said to the security guard. "Sorry."

The guard nodded, turned, and walked back to the mall. Elliott tried to wrestle the water bottle from his mouth.

"Max! Max!" he sputtered. "I have to tell you something..."

"Elliott, you need more water," Jenny said as she tilted the bottle back into his mouth.

"No!" he yelled as he swiped it away. "Max, Miss Tutley, she said... she said..."

"What? What?!" Alex asked.

"My dad is fucking Tutley," Max said flatly.

"What?!" Fiona screamed.

Max nodded.

"Oh my God, Tutley has less morals than a televangelist registered under a fake name at a sleazy motel," Sarah said.

"We saw them in the mall," Marc said. "She was all over him like a cop on a Black dude for driving the speed limit."

"Max, we're so sorry," Jenny said as she put an arm around him.

"Well, that seals it," Sarah said as she slapped her hands together. "I don't know what straw this is for anyone else, but for me, it's the last one. Tutley has to go."

The group nodded in agreement as Miss Tutley drove away.

"Elliott, is that what you heard – she and Max's dad are having an affair?" Alex asked.

"No!" Elliott exclaimed. "She said this is her chance to get a stud."

Elliott stood in front of Max and put a comforting hand on his shoulder.

"Max, your dad and Miss Tutley... they bought a racehorse."
Max stared at Elliott, then offered a sympathetic smile.
"Elliott, I'm so glad you're okay," Max said as he hugged him.

TEN

In the late afternoon, Martha marched along the sidewalk in a suburban neighborhood. She carried some brochures on a clipboard. A large designer purse was slung over her shoulder. She stopped to catch her breath and seek shade from the blistering sun under a large oak tree. She unflatteringly stuffed the clipboard between her knees.

Martha pulled a water bottle from her purse and took a long swig. She popped the bottle back into her purse and furtively removed a silver flask. She glanced around, unscrewed the cap, and took a swift drink. She smacked her lips, capped the flask, and put it in her purse.

Martha straightened her dress, took out her compact, and scrutinized herself in the mirror. Satisfied, she dropped the compact into her purse, retrieved the clipboard and flyers from between her legs, and continued her journey along the sidewalk.

She randomly stopped people she encountered, and thrusted a brochure, followed by a personalized box of cookies or pen or miniature bible at them before they refused, and quickly escaped her aggressive electioneering. Unfazed by the thorough rejection of her platform, Martha merrily stopped to smell some flowers growing in flower beds beside the sidewalk. People regarded her strangely as they passed. Some stopped dead when they saw her, and either tried to sneak by, turn around, or run away onto another street to avoid her.

Mrs. Richards, an older PTA member, pushed a stroller along the sidewalk. When she saw Martha bent over a flower bed, she froze. Before she could dive into a bush with the stroller, Martha stood, saw her, and reeled her in with her invisible tractor beam.

"Mrs. Richards!" she screamed as she thrusted an arm toward her.

Mrs. Richards glanced to her left and to her right, hoping she could leap into a time travel portal. No such luck. Martha freight-trained her way toward them.

"Mrs. Richards, I'm so glad I bumped into you," Martha said as she strode toward the stroller. She shook her brochures at her. "I've been ministering to the heathens and securing votes, and I remembered I forgot to say thank you for your support at the last PTA meeting."

"Support?" Mrs. Richards asked, puzzled.

"Yes! When I brought forth the motion that there should be a partition built in the gym to separate the boys and girls, and the ones who have been brainwashed by the liberal left that they aren't a boy or a girl, when they have gym class."

"Well, I..."

"You know how it is. All those hormones popping and crackling in the same room," Martha said as she animatedly wiggled her fingers in Mrs. Richards' face. "And you know I don't approve of those skimpy uniforms..."

"Sweatpants and t-shirts?"

"Yes! The girls blossoming out and the boys... leering at them."

"But I..."

Martha clutched Mrs. Richards' arm. "Anyway, thank you. You raising your hand and seconding my motion is a big step forward."

"But... but I was only trying to shoo a fly away..."

"And I hope to see you tonight at the emergency PTA meeting. I've learned my motions have caused quite the stir amongst the faithful..."

"Well, not in a good way..."

"... I think we're finally going to see genuine pushback against all these scandalous liberal ideals that have been bulldozing their way into the school system in recent years like intersex Marxist clubs, indoctrination seances, Communist flag cults, left-wing teachers..."

"Well, actually Mrs. Molder..."

"Oh!" Martha yelped, then thrust a brochure at Mrs. Richards. "Where is my head. Please take a flyer Mrs. Richards. It's why I'm out here ministering in our community."

"Well, I..."

Martha pressed it against Mrs. Richards, crumpling it a bit, and leaned into her.

"We must be on the lookout for the socialist sinners among us," Martha said as scanned around them furtively. "It's why the Tomorrow People's Liberation Army's arrival in our city is so important."

"Oh, is that the name of the party you're running for?"

"Oh no, it's a lovely new church group who just moved into our community. And by the way, here's my campaign brochure. Take several. Give them to your friends..." Martha said as she thrusted a handful in Mrs. Richards' hand.

"But you already gave me a bundle..."

"Oh!" Martha screeched as she dipped a hand into her purse. "I keep forgetting to ask if you are interested in one of my mugs..."

She whipped out her flask. Mrs. Richards eyed the flask and raised an eyebrow. Martha held the flask in the air for a moment as she regarded it, her eyes bulging, then she casually laughed, and dropped it in her purse.

"Well, that's not a mug, is it?" she laughed. "I-I picked that up as I was ministering. Can you imagine, some inebriated lowlife wandering around the neighborhood, drinking in public in front of children. Why won't somebody please think of the children?!"

She continued to laugh uneasily as she searched through her purse, then brought out a mug embossed with an American flag and her picture emblazoned across it.

"Here we are. Only $19.95. But for you Mrs. Richards, a true friend and supporter, only $14.95. All proceeds go to my campaign to bring freedom and justice back to our wayward nation, and to end the tyranny of socialist sex Marxism!"

As Mrs. Richards' mouth fell open, Martha waved the mug in her face.

"Okay, $9.99." Martha searched her purse. "I also have some high-quality back scratchers, spoon holders, trucker hats and non-rainbow-colored highlighters. I could give you a cut if you wanted to become one of my authorized sellers..."

Mrs. Richards stifled a gasp and gripped the stroller's handle. "We really must be going Martha. It's time for our nap."

"We? Ooohhhh, and who do we have here," Martha squealed as she stooped to leer into the stroller.

"This is Danny," Mrs. Richards said proudly.

"Oh, a boy. You must be careful Mrs. Richards and not let the parents continue to dress the child in frilly pink things with flowers, lest the feminine rubs off..."

Mrs. Richards raised her eyebrows. "It's a red onesie with a sunflower on the chest..."

"Best not take a chance..." Martha admonished her.

Mrs. Richards scowled at Martha.

"Awwww, what a little angel," Martha cooed. "A prime example of what those pro-abortionists are against. Gooo gooo naaa naaa mama..."

As Martha leered closer and continued to make goo goo noises, the baby spat onto her face. Mrs. Richards bit her lip, tried not to laugh, and reached into the stroller for a wipe.

"Oh Martha, I'm so sorry," she said as she handed Martha the wipe.

"Oh, it's quite alright dear," Martha said as she wiped the goo from her face. "Sometimes even an innocent child regurgitates the devil."

She finished cleaning her face, then plopped the soiled wipe in Mrs. Richards' hand.

"Well Mrs. Richards, so nice talking to you," Martha said as she tried to maintain her dignity, "but I must continue with my important work. I'll see you tonight at the PTA."

Martha clutched her clipboard and strode purposefully along the sidewalk. Mrs. Richards reached into the stroller and stroked the baby's face.

"Good job Danny. Good job."

She regarded Martha's pamphlets, located a nearby garbage can, and tossed them inside. She turned her head at Martha and quickly made her getaway.

Martha methodically turned from the sidewalk and marched along a walkway to a well-kept house. She climbed the few steps to the door and rang the doorbell. She casually wiped at her face, then glanced with concern at her fingers. As she waited for someone to answer the door, Martha experimented with various facial expressions to greet them. In between a pained look of concern and hilarity, the door opened. A thirty-something, well-dressed man with perfectly coiffed dark hair, and a trimmed beard appeared. He wore a plain white apron that read: KISS MY COOKIES.

Martha thrusted a hand at the man. He reticently shook it.

"Oh, hello sir. My name is Martha Molder. May I speak with you a moment?"

"Well, I do have something in the oven," he hesitated as he glanced over his shoulder.

"Oh, thank you!" Martha said, ignoring him. "An extremely important group has moved into our town, and I'm here to announce their arrival and ask for your support!"

"I don't give money to religious..."

"Oh, I'm not asking for donations," Martha said as she waved a hand to allay his fears. "I'm here as a messenger, a disciple, a courier conveying decency and goodness."

Martha shoved a brochure at the man.

"The Tomorrow People's Liberation Army is here to save us from evil Mr....?"

She leaned into him expectantly, eyebrows raised and encouraged him to offer his name.

"Riley. Christian Riley."

"Oh!" Martha twittered. "A Christian! I know we'll be kindred spirits if your name is Christian!"

Christian offered an uneasy smile.

"My son's teacher is also a Mr. Riley. Isn't it a coincidence?!"

"Yes..."

He stopped when he peered at the brochure. His eyes widened. The organization's name, written in large Nazi Germany-era block letters, overwhelmed the flyer. Their symbol resembled a swastika. The members featured were all White. In the photo on the front page, they stood on a seaside dock and enthusiastically waved goodbye to a large ship filled with people of different ethnicities, and men holding hands with the Democratic Party flag.

"Y-yes, it is quite a coincidence," he said slowly.

Martha leaned in and touched his forearm. "The world needs saving," she whispered.

He recoiled from her, but she clutched his arm like a hawk choking the life from its victim. He audibly winced.

"There's so much sin in the world Mr. Christian," Martha announced, her voice rising to a crescendo. "Men with men, murdering unborn stem cells, illicit affairs, shoe bomb terrorists, marijuana pushers, liberal media fake sex news, pre-marital teen sex, pro-abortionists, Mexican aliens, gay underwear, Canadian health care, sex Marxists... Pray with me Carrie!"

"Christian."

"Christian."

"Look, Mrs. White... I mean, Mrs. Molder," Christian said as he flung his arm back to release her death grip. "Have you seen this?" He waggled the brochure in the air. "I mean, have you actually read it? It's exceptionally disturbing."

Martha glanced at the flyer. "Well, no. Jimmy Joe and Arlene just gave it to me, so I haven't had time to read it."

"Perhaps you should. I don't think these people are who they say they are."

"Oh, but they seem like a lovely couple. After the initial interrogation in their windowless basement under the bright light, and being chased by their guard dogs, Jimmy Joe showed me their collection of military weapons, and Arlene kindly gave me some Kool-Aid, which gave me a funny headache. Fine Christian people Christian."

"Well, Mrs. Molder..."

His attention diverted to a delivery van that stopped in front of the house. A woman stepped from the van, opened the sliding side door, and pulled out a tall, large cardboard box with air holes. The woman awkwardly carried the box to the doorstep, peering around the box to see where she stepped. At the doorstep, she set the box on the ground.

"Excuse me, I'm sorry to interrupt, but I have a package for you."

"Oh no, you're not interrupting," Christian said quickly. "I think Mrs. Molder is... leaving?" he offered.

"Oh, no I'm not," Martha said frankly.

Christian smiled ostentatiously. "I didn't order anything," he said to the courier.

The woman glanced at the label. "This is for Carter Riley," she said.

"Oh, he's my..." Christian eyed Martha. "Yes, he lives here."

"Great," the woman said as she scanned the package, and offered the hand-held computer to Christian. "Sign where the X is please."

Christian glanced at Martha as he signed the computer, then returned it to the courier.

"Thank you," she said. "You have a nice day."

As the courier walked away, Martha snooped at the box labelled: CAUTION: LIVE PLANT.

"My, what an intriguing box. Maybe your brother bought a tree or something..."

Martha poked a finger into an air hole.

"My brother?" Christian asked.

"Yes, Carter."

Christian grimaced. "Mrs. Molder, Carter is not my brother. He's my..."

Martha shrieked and quickly withdrew her finger from the box.

"Ahhhhh! Whatever's inside the box attacked me!"

"What?"

"Yes! Oh, my expensive professional manicure..." Martha cried as she shook her hand.

"I'm sure you only pricked yourself on something Mrs. Molder."

"No, it's alive. It's alive!"

"Well sure it is – it's a live plant. Are you bleeding? Would you like a bandage?"

Martha examined her finger. "No, no," she dramatically moaned. "I'll live. I hope I don't pass out later, and have to have my arm amputated..."

Christian raised an eyebrow.

"There should be a warning on the box... or it shouldn't have air holes," Martha said as she wagged a finger at him. "Any idiot could stick their fingers in there..."

Christian bit his lip.

"Then the plant would die," Christian said as if he were explaining it to a child.

Martha sucked on her finger and pointed to the box.

"It's a deviant devil-seeded aberration – like gay people, terrorists and atheists."

Christian raised his other eyebrow.

"Your brother Carter should know better."

"Mrs. Molder, Carter is not my brother," Christian insisted.

"He's not? But you have the same last name..."

Christian shook his head and tried to smile.

"Mrs. Molder, I should get back to my oven..." he said as he nodded inside. He fingered the racist, homophobic flyer in his hand. "And I think I'll hang on to this..."

"Please do, and oh, take one of my election brochures," she said as she retrieved one from her purse, and shoved it at him.

"Oh yes, I've seen these before," Christian said with contempt.

"Perhaps you'd also like a Martha Molder stress ball – for a nominal campaign contribution of only $29.95."

She blindly rooted around in her purse and pulled out a plastic fetus head. Alarmed, Christian tried to take a step back inside the house, but Martha reached out and established another death-like grip on his arm. She leaned in and smiled widely.

"Perhaps your wife would be interested in my book 'I'm Keeping My Apron On – For America's Sake' – only $49.95."

Christian smiled uneasily. "No, my husband wouldn't be."

Martha anxiously laughed. "You mean, your wife..."

"No, I mean my husband, Carter."

Martha dropped the plastic fetus head. It hit the doorstep and bounced down the stairs. Martha put a hand to her mouth and repeatedly gasped, as if she were choking on a fish bone or air was being forcibly removed from her lungs with a vacuum cleaner. She released her hold on Christian, backed against the metal railing, and clutched at it desperately to keep from collapsing. As her embellished fake hyperventilation seizure continued, Christian stepped forward to offer some assistance.

"Mrs. Molder are you okay?"

Too traumatized to offer a coherent response, Martha desperately looked skyward as she clung to the railing.

"Jesus... Help... Me... Jesus... Save... Us!"

#

A short distance away at another house, the front door opened. Jack warily peered outside and darted his eyes back and forth, before craning his neck to the street. He tentatively stepped onto the doorstep. He carried his suit jacket in his hand. A woman's bare arm snaked from the house, grabbed his shirt collar, and tried to pull him inside. He peeled himself away, then rushed to the sidewalk. The door closed.

Jack ran to his car parked on the street. He glanced at his watch and jumped in the car. He searched his jacket pocket and pulled out a package of breath mints. He popped a couple in his mouth. He peered in the rear-view mirror, and ran a hand through his hair, trying to tidy its unruliness. He did a double take, and his eyes bulged as he saw Martha stumble from the Riley's house. She turned and rushed along the sidewalk in his direction.

Jack sank low in the front seat and watched from an obtuse angle as Martha walked by his car. He slowly gripped the steering wheel, and peered over it to see Martha ascend the steps of the house he had exited, and ring the doorbell. Sweat appeared on his forehead.

On the doorstep, Martha smoothed her dress and glanced around – at the miniature naked stone garden ornaments placed conspicuously around the property, at the phallic-looking ornamental doorknocker, and to the street. She turned around when the door swept open.

"Back for more you wild stallion!?" Miss Tutley blurted as she stood in the doorway with her eyes closed and her arms flung wide.

Dressed in a provocative corset, with stockings and high heels, her wild and teased hair envied any hair style from the 1980s. Martha screamed and drew a hand over her eyes. Miss Tutley screamed and drew her arms across her chest. Martha put her other hand to her throat as she peeked at Miss Tutley.

"You're Miss Tutley, right? My son's teacher?"

"Y-yes," Miss Tutley faltered as she hunched over with her legs crossed. "And you are?"

"I'm Martha Molder, Max's mother," she said as she lowered her hand from her eyes.

"Molder!?" Miss Tutley shrieked, then laughed loudly, and awkwardly.

Martha leaned away from Miss Tutley's bizarre outburst. Miss Tutley tried to cover herself further but only succeeded in clumsily caressing herself with her hands.

"Ummm, am I interrupting something?" Martha slowly asked.

"Oh this?" Miss Tutley gestured to her attire. "I... I was ummm... rehearsing... for... for a play..."

"For school!?" Martha asked, shocked.

"Oh no! It's for an... off... off... off community theater... benefit... for the homeless."

"Oh, thank goodness! That attire might be okay for demonstrating perverse sexual sins, performing benefits for the homeless, and rousing a marriage from the ashes, but certainly not for virtuous, innocent children made in his image!"

An uncomfortable silence fell between the two women.

"Amen?" Miss Tutley asked hopefully.

Martha smiled at her sweetly. "So... what play are you performing?"

Miss Tutley's eyes widened. "Ummm... an old Shakespeare play..."

"Oh, what one? I remember Shakespeare from college."

Miss Tutley's eyes widened further and darted from Martha's face to Jack's car parked on the street.

"What one?... Ummm... a really old one... Hamlet... and Juliet... Make... Much Ado About... Worcestershire... Sauce..."

"I don't think I've ever heard of that one..."

Jack's car started, then moved from its parking spot.

"They recently found it... at a castle... in a turret... behind some drapes..."

"What role are you playing?"

"Ummm... Worcestershire's wench."

"Oh yes," Martha said knowingly, "I remember her. Shakespeare created some unforgettable characters."

As Jack drove away, his tires squealed. Martha turned at the sound. Miss Tutley abruptly reached out, grabbed her by the shoulders, and turned Martha to face her.

"Mrs. Molder, you must come to my performance!" Miss Tutley insisted, almost peering into Martha's soul.

"Well, sure. When is it?"

Jack's tires squealed again as the car turned a corner.

"When is what?" Miss Tutley asked absently as she watched the car disappear.

"Your performance?"

Miss Tutley removed her hands from Martha's shoulders. "Oh, it's late... late, late, late."

"But you told me to come..."

"I'll have to get back to you," she said quickly. "The space rented for the performances is condemned for... mice droppings... diphtheria... and... asbestos."

"Oh my. Well, maybe some other time."

"Yes, well, goodbye Mary Ann," Miss Tutley said as she attempted to shut the door.

"Miss Tutley, the reason why I'm here..."

"Oh right, where are my manners? Here I am rambling on about my charity performances for the homeless..."

"Miss Tutley, I'm on a recruitment drive to save our country."

"Oh, I'm not joining the army," Miss Tutley said flatly. "Beige is not my color."

"No, I'm selling something wonderful, and it will leave you hungry for more..."

"Oh, okay. Let me grab my purse," Miss Tutley said as she moved inside. "I'll take one vanilla, and one chocolate mint..."

Martha waved at her. "Oh no, I'm not selling cookies... although..." Martha rooted around in her large purse. "I may have a box or two in here... Your generous contribution to my campaign is only $9.99 a box."

Miss Tutley stopped, then turned around. “$9.99 for a lousy box of cookies?!” Her eyes bulged as she spied Jack’s striped tie on the floor next to the door.

“I have a back scratcher if you prefer – only $5.99...”

“Ahhhh!” Miss Tutley screamed as she awkwardly ran to the door.

“I’m sorry but the lowest priced item I have is a bumper sticker – $4.99”.

Miss Tutley clumsily attempted to kick Jack’s tie into the corner and almost closed the door on Martha. “No, I just realized how late it is.”

Martha glanced at her watch. “Oh my, you’re right.”

“I am?” Miss Tutley asked as she peered around the door at Martha.

“Yes. Trying to heal the sinners, and condemn the adulterers takes time...”

Miss Tutley forced an exaggerated laugh.

Martha raised an eyebrow, smiled sweetly, and cocked her head to Miss Tutley. “Will you be at the parent-teacher interviews tomorrow night?”

“Yes. I bought a new outfit...”

“You’re wearing that?”

Miss Tutley laughed. “Well, not only this. I’d look pretty silly wouldn’t I? Well, goodbye Margaret,” Miss Tutley said as she attempted to quickly close the door.

Martha put a palm on the door to hold it open.

“Before I go, and it’s Martha by the way, would you take a Tomorrow People’s Liberation Army brochure? It’s the reason I stopped by.”

Martha pushed a flyer into Miss Tutley’s face.

Miss Tutley leered at the obscene flyer. “Okay. Well, goodbye Margot,” she said sweetly as she attempted to close the door again.

“Oh, and one of my election flyers too,” Martha said as she waved one at her. “It has a similar, but more personal message.”

“Oh yes, you’re running in the election, aren’t you?” Miss Tutley coyly asked. “Have you heard who your opponents are?” she asked with a sly smile.

Martha groaned. "Yes. Norman Gaines the old Communist, and some drugged-out hippies who have no chance. It'll be a cakewalk to the finish line."

Miss Tutley bit her lip, as she tried to conceal the world's biggest grin. She tried to close the door again, but Martha put a foot inside and poked her face into the house.

"We must stop them," she said coldly and calculatingly. "The evil dwellers. The sinners. The godless sex-crazed heathens who terrorize us with their Communist ways and loose morals. Only if we band together as a united front will be banish these gay sex Marxists, pro-abortionists, and drag-loving liberal gun-hating unpatriots to the Lake of Fire!"

Miss Tutley attempted a concerned, uneasy smile.

"Well, see you tomorrow!" Martha said brightly as she stepped back, turned, and descended the stairs.

Miss Tutley shut the door, then leaned against it.

"Wow. And I thought my mother was an unhinged religious nutcase. Jack was right. What a wacko..."

She regarded the Tomorrow People's Liberation Army flyer.

"So, little Miss Muffet thinks she's spreading a righteous church's good word, does she? Hmmmm..." she schemed. "Getting little Jackie all to myself might be easier than I thought. I'll finally have a real family..."

She played with the flyer between her fingers and crumpled it in her hand. She laughed manically.

"Who's the wacko now Mommy? Huh? Huh?!" she yelled at no one.

She grabbed Jack's tie and twirled it in the air as she strode into her living room.

#

When Carter entered his house, he immediately noticed the large, boxed plant in the entryway. He closed the front door and smiled deviously. He ran his fingertips around the airholes, then jumped back as a plant stem poked itself from the box and curiously searched the air. He smiled at the plant's shrewdness.

He walked into the kitchen, glanced around, and sniffed the air.

"Christian?" he called.

"In the living room," Christian announced.

Carter walked through the kitchen, and into the spacious, modern living area. Large windows overlooked a lush, green backyard. Metal posts, which had supported several solar panels, remained in the ground. A barren square of gravel, which had housed the windmill, sat in the corner. The lot backed onto a pond with an excellent view of Miss Tutley's house a short distance away.

Christian faced the windows and performed awkward, comical martial arts moves. Carter stopped when he saw him.

"What... are you doing?"

Christian did not turn around. "I'm doing the Miss Tutley workout," he said as he brandished an imaginary sword, and swung it around his head.

"Oh no, not again."

Carter approached him and peered over his shoulder. His eyes bulged as he stared at Miss Tutley's large picture window. In full view, she stood in her living room and performed crude, wild, aerobic-style exercises while she wielded a large medieval sword. She continued to wear her corset, but added thigh-high red boots, and a gold-colored tiara-like crown.

"You're recording this right?" Carter asked.

"No."

Carter pulled out his cell phone and pointed it at the window. "Well, I will. She'll be the next YouTube sensation. Hell, it might even get her fired..."

Christian reached out and lowered Carter's phone. "Best not. She'll find out."

"I want her to find out. I've had enough of her – everyone has, the students, the teachers, the parents, our neighbors... Last week, the Andersons, you know the retired couple who live beside her, asked me if we saw her nude sunbathing..."

"You mean the time she waxed her car, and wore a string bikini while she sang 'Pour Some Sugar on Me'?"

"No, the week before. Remember, Mr. Anderson went outside to mow the lawn, and two hours later Mrs. Anderson wondered what happened to him. She found him in Tutley's yard fanning her with an oversized palm leaf."

"Right, right."

"She uses people like tissues and throws them away. Look at her," Carter motioned in disgust. "She looks like a Fredericks's of Hollywood superhero reject, Xena the Wonder Tart. Whose benefit is she doing this for?"

"Certainly not ours..."

"Her M.O. is 'what can I get from the people I use'."

"Look," Christian said as he put an arm around Carter's shoulder, and turned him away from the window, "dinner should be almost ready. Don't think about Tutley anymore."

"I'll try, except I'll probably bump into the twit tomorrow night at school."

Carter and Christian walked into the kitchen. Christian wagged a finger at him. "Ah ah ah, no more about Tutley."

"Sorry."

Christian opened the oven and peered inside. "Hey, a parcel came for you today."

Carter approached the box by the front door. "Yes, I saw. You didn't open it did you?"

"No, I didn't want to disturb it, besides, it attacks people."

"Good."

"What?"

"I mean, good you didn't open it."

"It's not for the house, is it?"

"No, I'm taking it to school."

A vine poked from an air hole and surveyed its surroundings.

"For what, show and tell? You're an English teacher."

"It's something... to brighten someone's classroom..."

Christian removed a pot from the oven and set it on the countertop.

"Carter, what are you scheming?"

"Nothing."

Carter lurched away from the box as the stem aggressively lunged at him. He smiled and walked into the kitchen. His eyes landed on Martha's brochures on the dining table. He grabbed the Tomorrow People's Liberation Army flyer and shook it in the air.

"What the hell is this?"

Christian glanced at him as he dished food from the pot into a bowl. "Oh, Martha Molder stopped by earlier..."

"Oh Godddd..." Carter moaned and crumpled the flyer. "She and Tutley should have their own 'American Horror Story' series. What did she want?" He held a hand in the air. "Wait, don't tell me. She either wanted to convert you or condemn you to eternity in a lake of fire."

"It didn't go there, not after she found out we were married. Then, she short circuited."

"What a surprise. Every time I see her, she insinuates teachers who are gay make their students gay – the idiot."

"Try not to let her bother you."

"I think I'll get drunk tonight before the PTA meeting, so I can get through her craziness. It appears to work for her."

ELEVEN

Twelve PTA members were gathered in the school library. They sat on chairs in a circle and faced each other. Among the parents were Connie Frame, and Mrs. Richards, who sat beside an empty chair. Carter Riley and a few other teachers attended.

Everyone quietly talked amongst themselves until Martha breezed in through the open library door. She wore a brilliant white pant suit, accentuated by a large, loud red flower in the right lapel, making it appear as if she were fatally wounded. A large 'VOTE MARTHA' button adorned her left chest. A bird-like fascinator perched in her hair. Oversized pearls concealed her neckline.

Martha awkwardly squeezed between two chairs, grunting as she entered the circle, and made her way to the empty chair beside Mrs. Richards. She sat, then heaved a sigh as if she had completed a marathon.

"Now that Mrs. Molder has finally arrived, I suggest we complete this meeting as quickly as possible," a teacher said, irritated. "We have to finish preparing for the interviews tomorrow night."

Martha plopped two sets of flyers into Mrs. Richards' lap – her election flyer, and a handout listing all the merchandise she offered on her website with a campaign 'donation'. She leaned over toward Mrs. Richards.

"Could you pass these along dear?" she whispered. "This is a perfect opportunity to drive more traffic to my website."

Mrs. Richards smiled uncomfortably. Martha dropped her purse on the floor beside her chair. When the purse made a muffled thud as it hit the floor, Mrs. Richards glanced at it and stared wide-eyed at a metal flask in the open purse.

She smiled uneasily again, and when she awkwardly attempted to pass the handouts along, the irritated teacher interrupted her.

"Mrs. Molder, this is neither the time nor the place for politicking, so please put your election propaganda away so we can get on with this meeting."

Martha eyed her evilly as she dramatically swiped the handouts from Mrs. Richards and aggressively shoved them in her purse.

"Oh my, what a trying day," Martha announced as she straightened her lapels. "Beating back the wickedness nipping at our heels everyday is..."

"Mrs. Molder," the irritated teacher announced, "would you please get on with it. You're the one who called this 'emergency' meeting'," she said as she made quotation marks with her fingers, "on one of the busiest days of the year for us teachers."

"Pardon me Mrs... it's Mrs. Bradley, right?" Martha asked the woman. "The same Mrs. Bradley who ignored the curriculum for a month to selfishly teach students about her own life."

"It was Black History Month Mrs. Molder."

"And unapproved by the board..."

"Pardon me, but the board approved..."

"But I heard stories it went on for eight hours a day non-stop for a month..."

"Pardon me, but that is exactly what you heard – stories. I'm a history teacher Mrs. Molder. I deal with facts, not ludicrous assumptions."

"Which brings me to my point..."

"Finally..."

Martha stood. "I know there has been some grumbling about my proposal to introduce creationism into the curriculum..."

"Well, it's a little more than grumbling dear," Mrs. Richards said.

"I'm sorry, but if Mrs. Bradley can teach urban issues for a whole month," Martha said as she spread her arms wide, "someone can teach our children about the beautiful, peaceful, natural way God created our world."

Mrs. Bradley folded her arms, waggled her head, and eyed Martha. "Urban issues?"

"Martha, who would teach this class?" Connie asked.

"A revered minister from the community, or even a famous, inspirational teacher from a critically acclaimed televised ministry..."

"So, our choices are," a parent said, "a pastor who might have been charged with sex abuse or the televangelist who funneled donations to his secret porn star wife and children."

"Noooo," Martha emphasized, "the priest who wasn't charged with sex abuse, and the telepastor who didn't send money to his secret porn star wife and children."

"Are you kidding me with this?" the parent asked. "Why are we even discussing this? This isn't a church. This is a public school."

"He's right Mrs. Molder," Carter said. "These issues belong with the school board, and even further, with the state. We have no power to set curriculum."

"But we should!" Martha implored.

"No, we shouldn't," another parent said. "It stops crackpots from making ridiculous, reckless decisions."

"Martha dear," Mrs. Richards said as she put a hand on Martha's arm, "you should discuss this with the school board."

"Yeah, and see how far she gets," Mrs. Bradley said.

"But... but... but... I need your support. Won't somebody please think of the children!"

"We are thinking of the children," another parent said.

"But as PTA chair, president and CEO, it's my duty..."

"To protect and nurture the children while they are in the school's care," Carter said.

"Exactly," Martha said as she stepped toward Carter and splayed out her arms, causing him to lean back. "We must protect the children. We must inoculate them with God's word because they're being poisoned by the sinful world around them!"

Mrs. Bradley rolled her eyes, dramatically crossed her leg, tapped her foot on the floor, and rhythmically drummed her fingertips on her knee as Martha paced around the circle.

"Oh, at times I feel like I'm in my own little world..."

"You are," Mrs. Bradley whispered.

"... I'm the only one against sex Marxists, communist Democrats, foreign terrorists, and homosexual socialists," she said as she stared directly at Carter, who raised his eyebrows. "At first, when you elected me PTA Queen..."

"Barged into is more like it," Connie whispered to her seatmate.

"... I thought I had found a few kindred spirits, like dear Mrs. Richards."

Martha wheeled around and presented her with an outstretched arm. Mrs. Richards smiled meekly and tried to avoid everyone's eyes. Martha turned around again.

"Who voted with me to segregate the girls and boys, and their sexual hormones..."

Mrs. Richards shook her head vigorously.

"And my dear neighbor Connie..." Martha presented, as Connie opened her mouth to bad-mouth Martha again, "...who is with me one hundred percent in introducing ten minutes of power prayer and reflection before school each day."

A shocked Connie stared at Martha. As Martha turned away from her, Connie shook her head more vigorously than Mrs. Richards.

"But who is going to stand with me against evil?" Martha continued as she stalked the room. "Who is going to stand with me to arm our teachers with not only knowledge from above, but with guns and ammunition from God? Who is going to be counted as the one who stood for every-other-Thursday Communist propaganda book burnings? Who is with me to heal our broken, weak children who have been indoctrinated by homosexuals and their agenda, by shocking the devil from them? Who is going to join me in replacing the school washroom condom machines with bible verse fortune cookies? The insidious liberal causes threatening to turn our precious pre-teens into pizza parlor pickings preyed upon by pedophiles is upon us!"

When Martha finished her tongue twisting rant, behind her, Mrs. Richards reached into Martha's purse, lifted the flask, and wiggled it in the air with one hand, while she tipped back an imaginary highball with the other, and crossed her eyes. Everyone glanced at Mrs. Richards, and stifled laughter.

"Well, Mrs. Molder," Carter said as he stood, "thank you so much for presenting your... opinions."

He gently took her by the arm to usher her from the room.

"So, you'll think about them?"

"Oh sure," Mrs. Bradley lied, "how could we not?"

"Should we vote now, or should we vote at our next meeting? I'm sorry I'm so pressed for time right now, but the election..."

"You leave it with us Martha," Connie said.

Everyone stood, and the chairs parted so Martha could easily leave. Mrs. Richards touched her arm and handed Martha her purse.

"Why thank you Mrs. Richards."

Everyone smiled at Martha uneasily.

"I knew God would open your hearts," she exclaimed.

"He sure did," one parent said.

"I shall eagerly await your thoughts. Goodnight all," Martha announced as she offered a wave to the group not unlike Queen Elizabeth's.

She strode from the circle, then breezed from the room. Connie turned to the group.

"So, does anyone know how to get an exorcist for our next meeting?"

Carter rubbed his temples. "Alright, let's get this over with. All in favour of Martha's harebrained proposals?"

No one said a word or raised their hands.

"Opposed?"

Everyone raised their hands.

"Unanimously defeated."

Everyone sighed, then murmured amongst themselves.

"I'd like to propose another vote," Mrs. Bradley said, "and we can get on with our real purpose here – helping our students."

The room quieted.

"I would like to propose Martha Molder be banned forever from the PTA."

Everyone nodded and smiled.

"All in favour of Betty's proposal?" Carter asked.

Everyone raised their hands.

"Opposed?"

No one said a word.

"Motion carried."

The dark, oppressing cloud that hung over the room lifted, angels sang 'Hallelujah', and a warm, bright rainbow shone through the windows.

"Coffee break time!" Mrs. Bradley said enthusiastically.

As everyone mingled, Connie approached Carter.

"Excuse me Mr. Riley... Carter, could I talk to you for a moment?"

"Sure Connie. Is it about Martha?" he cringed.

"Oh no... well, yes. You see, Sally and I were talking this morning, after Martha accosted us in our driveway..."

"Oh no, what did she do now?"

"Nothing. Just Martha being Martha. As I drove away, Sally made a casual remark about me running in the election. I laughed at first, but I thought about it later. When I stopped by the Norman Gaines campaign office to volunteer, I talked to him, and he told me he's having health problems and is going to step aside."

Carter pulled at his hair. "No! Martha will win for sure."

"Well, no. I've decided to run in his place."

"Connie that's great! You'll be a great candidate."

"Norman said I could use his resources, but I have no idea what I'm doing, so I thought maybe you could help me because you have experience with student government, and Sally admires you..."

"I'd love to. Nothing would give me more pleasure than taking down Martha Molder."

"Except we must keep it quiet for now. Norman hasn't made his announcement, and neither have I."

"Oh sure. But promise me one thing. When you do, please announce it with Martha in the room. I'd love to see her head explode."

Connie and Carter laughed.

#

Outside the school, Martha quickly skipped to her car. She pulled her phone from her purse, speed-dialed a number, and slapped the phone to her ear. She unlocked her car, jumped in, and started the engine.

"Leslie! Finally! Where have you been? I've been trying to contact you! We have a busy schedule tomorrow. I have a sunrise rally outside the baby killing center at eight thirty, followed by tea and refreshments sponsored by the generous dry cleaning store 'No Wire Hangers."

"Mrs. Molder..." Leslie tried to interrupt.

He sat at a table next to a stage/runway in an establishment called The Screwdriver. Younger and older men filled the place. They laughed, danced, caroused, and generally enjoyed a good time. Leslie wore a tight, multi-colored vest, black hot pants, and army boots. Loud, thumping music shook the venue. Three young male dancers dressed as couriers in ball caps, boots, carrying small cardboard boxes, and wearing matching metallic bow ties and g-strings with plastic water guns stuffed into the waistbands, gyrated their hips, sensuously stroked each others' bodies, and jiggled their exposed derrieres to the patrons.

"At ten o'clock, we have a public book burning outside the main library, followed by a prayer and pancake brunch..." Martha continued.

A dancer flexed his pecs, slowly undid his bow tie, and dangled it in Leslie's face, as Leslie gawked at him.

"Ummmm, Mrs. Molder..."

"In the afternoon, my Guns 'n God Gals group is having a public prayer for the teenager who is unjustly being held in prison for defending himself with an AK-47 from a woke socialist mob screaming about big sea turtles or something..."

The dancer dropped the bow tie in Leslie's lap, pulled the water gun from his g-string, and showered Leslie with water.

"I have an interview with Fox News going on their supper-hour newscast..."

Leslie wiped the water from his face as the two other dancers made out on the stage.

"And finally, before the parent/teacher interviews at the school, I have a 'Don't Say Gay' rally in the parking lot where you are the guest speaker because you successfully completed the gay conversion therapy camp last summer..."

Leslie enthusiastically waved a twenty-dollar bill at the two men, who stopped kissing, and gyrated their pelvis' in Leslie's face. Leslie toyed with the two men, playfully-undecided about which g-string to stuff his money into. Finally, he provocatively slipped the bill into the g-string of the dancer with the biggest box.

As Martha drove from the parking lot, she screamed into the phone.

"Leslie! Are you there?! Answer me! What is going on? Where are you?"

As the dancers moved away, Leslie sat back in his chair and plugged an ear as he attempted to hear Martha.

"I'm sorry Mrs. Molder, it's so loud here... there's... there's a children's birthday party here at Chuck E. Cheese..."

"What? Have you heard a word I've said? Tomorrow is an extremely important day for me Leslie, and I need you to... ahhhhh!"

Martha simultaneously screamed and slammed on her brakes. She dropped the phone. The car skidded to a stop on the street. Martha gripped the steering wheel, and leaned forward until her face touched the windshield. Her mouth dropped open, and her eyes bulged. On the corner, two men finished assembling a huge billboard. The sign showed a picture of Miss Tutley, dressed in a white robe a cult member would wear. She beamed angelically toward the heavens. The slogan, in blood-red said: THE ONLY CONSERVATIVE CHOICE FOR BUXTON COUNTY. SHELLEY TUTLEY: SAVING YOU FROM FAKE NEWS, FAKE CANDIDATES AND MARXIST COMMUNISTS. GOD BLESS US ALL!

"Mrs. Molder?" Leslie asked, concerned. "Mrs. Molder?"

Martha, on the verge of a stroke, gaped at the billboard, and tried to find her phone on the floor. She grasped it, bobbled it, and robotically put it to her ear.

"Leslie, there's a buh... a buh... a buh... a billboard," she sputtered.

"A what?"

"A billboard! Shelley Tutley! She's running in the election!"

Leslie closed his eyes and palmed his forehead. "Oh right," he murmured.

"Right?! You knew about this?!"

"Mrs. Molder, I found out about it on Facebook not too long ago, but a friend dragged me to this strip... errr birthday party. I planned to call you after the strippers... errr revelers stopped being so loud, I swear."

"Leslie! I want this fixed. Now!" she enunciated.

"There's nothing I can do to stop her from running. She's already filed the proper paperwork. This is a free country Mrs. Molder."

"Oh no, it's not free. We aren't free Leslie. We're being held hostage by an unjust system that won't let me win! What does she think she's doing?! With two conservative candidates on the ballot, that old Communist Norman Gaines will win for sure!"

"I know what it means Mrs. Molder."

"Then fix it," Martha hissed. "I don't care what you have to do. Find some dirt, throw some dirt, bury her in dirt, make her eat dirt. I don't care. Get her off the ballot!"

Martha violently ended the call by mashing her palm into the phone. She threw it on the passenger seat.

"Mrs. Molder... Mrs. Molder..."

Leslie shrugged, and put his phone away as a beefy, bronzed waiter dressed as a construction worker in boots, skimpy cut-offs and a yellow safety helmet approached his table.

"Another one sir?" the waiter asked, then nodded to Leslie's empty glass.

Leslie leered at the waiter and smiled. "Please."

Martha gripped the steering wheel as she stared at the billboard. The two men mimicked squeezing Miss Tutley's ample bosom and laughed. Martha narrowed her eyes as rage threatened to pop the blood vessels on her temple. Her hands shaking, she swiped her phone from the seat and quickly dialed a number.

TWELVE

Max bounded down the stairs and walked into the kitchen. He stopped when he saw Jack at the counter making coffee.

"Dad, what are you doing? Mom usually has breakfast on the go and ready before you have a chance to make a mess." He peered around the room. "Where is she?"

"Your mother got in late last night. I think she fell asleep in her war room."

"I guess planning world domination tires her out... oh no! Dad!" Max yelped as he ran to his father, grabbed a dish cloth, and wiped spilled coffee grounds from the counter. "Mom'll have a fit if she finds these all over the counter."

Jack shooed him away. "Never mind Max..."

"Dad! She'll think they're mouse droppings, call an exterminator, and force them to tent the house for a week."

"Well, you do have a point," he said as he swept the remaining grounds with his hand and tossed them into the sink.

"Dad, can I talk to you?"

"Well sure you can. What is it?"

Max nervously shook the dish cloth over the sink. "Well, it's about Mom, I guess..."

"I know. She's deeply involved in this stupid election, and it's made her kinda crazy..."

"No... well, yes it has, but I'm talkin' about..."

Max tossed the dish cloth between his hands like a bean bag and shuffled his feet.

"I wanted to talk to you last night, but I didn't know how."

"Max, what is it?"

Max walked across the kitchen, listened at the basement door, and tip toed back to Jack, who eyed him strangely.

"Max, what is going on?"

Max lowered his voice. "Dad, I saw you yesterday with her... that trollop."

Jack scanned his son's face, then lowered his eyes. "You mean Miss Tutley?"

"No Dad, I mean Mrs. Horgenstefler. Yes Dad, Tutley. Dad, are you nuts?"

Jack pulled Max further away from the basement door to the window.

"Son, I know what you must be thinking, but there's a reason..."

"A reason?! Dad, if you were desperate for a fling, there are women who do that kind of thing professionally."

"Max, you see, your mother and this election, well, it's reached a point, and Tutley..."

The basement door opened dramatically, interrupting Jack's confession. Jack and Max clutched each other. Martha stepped into the kitchen. She wore a shiny silver dress bulging at her hips as if she wore a hoop skirt from the Civil War era. Topped by a bowl-shaped silver hat, she looked like the Liberty Bell. A garish red, white, and blue sash, like one found at a county fair, adorned her waist. With a briefcase in her left hand, and her election signs tucked under her right arm, she clicked her heels.

"Well, I'm off," Martha announced.

"You sure are," Max murmured.

"Martha, what about breakfast?" Jack asked.

"Oh, I don't have the time," Martha said as she struggled to close the basement door without wedging her dress in the frame. "I have a sunrise Life for Jesus rally at the baby killing factory, and the local news is going to be at my book burning at the library!"

"Martha, you seem awfully calm despite the fact you learned Shelley Tutley is running in the election against you."

Martha's right eye twitched. "Oh, I welcome her challenge," she said brightly, and turned to the front door. "She doesn't know who she's dealing with," she snarled under her breath. She turned her head and wiggled her fingers at Max. "Come on Max, I'll drive you to school."

"Dressed like that? You look like a science fair experiment," Max mumbled.

"What Max?"

"I said, I'm not dressed yet. Besides, it's only seven-fifty-eight."

Martha turned and opened the door. "Suit yourself." She stopped and turned again. "Oh, and Jack, I won't see you until the parent-teacher interviews tonight, but we have something incredibly important to talk about, so don't be late – like you've been the past few weeks every night," she enunciated with venom.

She bored holes into him with her demented, wide, crazed animal-like eyes, and waggled her head at him.

"If it's so important, why don't we talk about it now," Jack said.

She sputtered, whined, and showed him her election signs and briefcase.

"Oh right, the election is much, much more important," Jack said.

"Well, I'm sorry, but it is," Martha snapped. "Our world is at stake Jack."

"It sure is," Max mumbled.

"But make no mistake," Martha said as she pointed at him. "We will talk about this."

She regarded him smugly, turned, and left the house as she struggled to fit her liberty bell outfit out the door. She popped onto the doorstep like a finished bonbon on a conveyor belt at a candy factory. She reached in, grasped the doorknob, laughed maniacally, and closed the door.

"Dad, do you think she knows about you and Tutley?" Max asked.

"I don't know how she would, unless she saw us too."

"Oh Dad," Max moaned, "why? Why did you get involved with Tutley? She's a moronic man-leech. Don't you see? Don't you get it?"

Jack put a hand on Max's shoulder and guided him to the table.

"Have a seat Max. We have to have a talk."

Max regarded his father with uncertainty.

Outside, Martha wobbled to her car. As she opened the hatch and threw her signs inside, she casually glanced at Connie Frame's house. On the front lawn, a man finished hammering a small, neat, square sign into the ground. In humble blue letters, it succinctly read: CONNIE FRAME FOR STATE REPRESENTATIVE.

Like the previous night when she saw Shelley Tutley's election sign, Martha's blood pressure soared to previously unknown heights. Her brain synapses failed to fire, and she stood by her car, paralysed by anger. She opened her mouth to scream some high-pitched howl, but no sound came from her pinched vocal cords.

Finally, she moved her legs, and marched to Connie's yard, hindered by her liberty bell dress. Every step was like a dramatic, thunderous clang of the clapper against the bell's waist – an insidious, slow-paced version of Tubular Bells from the Exorcist.

The man on Connie's lawn walked to his truck as Martha clanged her way into the driveway. She pointed at the sign, her arm convulsing in quick spasms and contractions.

"What is that?" she asked the world.

The man shrugged, uninterested, and hopped in his truck.

"I only install 'em lady."

The man started his truck, then put it in gear. Martha wobbled to his door and clutched the open window.

"Is this a joke?" she asked as she lunged her head into the cab.

"A joke? Do I look like I sell lumpy pillows? If you'll excuse me, I have dozens more..."

The man crept the truck forward in a more-than-obvious way to escape.

"Dozens? Dozens?!"

"Right. You have a good day now," the man said as he deliberately reached over and pressed the button to raise the window.

Martha held on to the window until her fingers were almost crushed. The man smiled and waved as he drove away, leaving Martha in the street.

In Connie's house, she stood at the front window, behind a curtain, and watched the scene on the street. Sally stood behind her with her hand over her mouth as she tried not to laugh.

"She looks like a lab rat caught in a maze," Sally whispered.

Connie provided running commentary on Martha's movements, as she paced back and forth in the street, beside herself, sputtering, and talking to herself.

"Right turn. Left turn. Stop. Mutter. Must find the cheese. Look to the sky. Pray a little bit. Right turn. Mutter. Left turn. Moan. Must find the cheese... must find the cheese..."

Finally, Sally couldn't take anymore, ran across the room, threw herself on the sofa, buried her face in a pillow, and howled with laughter.

"Stop it Mom!" she screamed into the pillow.

Connie discreetly moved away from the window, and joined Sally on the sofa, where they both laughed uproariously.

"I told you she'd blow a gasket," Connie said.

"A gasket? Mom, you broke her brain."

"What brain?"

They both fell against each other, laughing.

Outside, Martha clanged her way to her car, this time with a sped-up version of Tubular Bells. She grabbed her cell phone from her briefcase, twitterpated, and mashed her fingers against the screen. She smacked the phone to her face so hard, it almost gave her a concussion.

"Leslie! Leslie! Leslie!" she screamed into the phone.

At Leslie's apartment, he bolted upright in his bed, his cell phone smouched to his face, and the bedsheets crumpled around him. He clutched as his already-messy hair as he glanced at the clock on the bedside table.

"Mrs. Molder, I'm sorry, I'm sorry. I'm awake..."

"What?! You're still in bed?! Get up! Get up! Get up!"

"I'm sorry, I had a late night."

A hand slithered from under the sheets and tickled him. Leslie giggled.

"This is no laughing matter Leslie!"

A stripper from the club crawled out from under the sheets and casually leaned back against a couple pillows beside Leslie.

"I know, I know Mrs. Molder," Leslie said seriously, and emitted a high-pitched squeal as the stripper reached over and pinched him.

Martha fumed and lowered her voice. "Leslie, if you've experienced another relapse from your conversion therapy again, I swear..."

"I haven't. I haven't. I swear," he lied.

"Remember Leslie, I paid for it. I simply won't have any homosexual outbursts on my campaign. My image is at stake Leslie. My image!"

"I know. I know," Leslie said as he rolled his eyes, and the stripper blew into his ear.

"Anyway, do you know what I've seen Leslie? A campaign sign for Connie Frame. My neighbor. She's running in the election! What is going on?!"

"Oh right..."

"Right? Right?!"

"I found out last night Norman Gaines is withdrawing from the race, and Connie Frame is taking his place."

"What?! Why didn't you tell me? Why am I always the last to know about what is going on in my campaign?"

"I'm sorry Mrs. Molder. I was so consumed in the erection... election, I didn't have a chance to contact you."

"Now you listen to me Leslie. I want obedience and loyalty. Remember, I'm the one who saved you from the clutches of homosexuality and put you on the right path."

The stripper put his arms around Leslie and squeezed him.

"I'm grateful Mrs. Molder," he groaned.

"Leslie, I want you by my side at my first event today, the life rally at the baby killing assembly line office in fifteen minutes. Fifteen!" Martha shrieked.

She threw her phone into her briefcase, closed her eyes, and attempted to practice some deep, stress-relieving chanting.

"Praise Jesus... praise Jesus... praise Jesus..."

THIRTEEN

At the high school, Miss Tutley's biology class sat in the biology lab at their stations and awaited their pseudo-teacher. Loud laughter, talking, and carousing filled the room. The life-size biology dummy stood at Miss Tutley's desk. It wore a black shag wig, and Sarah's previous conservative attire. Max glanced at his cell phone.

"It's almost nine-thirty. Why are we still here?"

"Someone should go to the office and tell them Miss Tutley isn't here," Robin said.

"You mean like you?" Alex said.

"You're almost right Max," Sarah said.

The once staid, steady, and proper student continued her transformation into an indifferent bad ass with an attitude. The red X Miss Tutley had drawn on her forehead remained there, enhanced with more red ink. She wore a tattered jean jacket with a faded image of Che Guevara on the back, black tights, and army boots. Her hair stood out in many directions.

"Why are we here in her class period?" Sarah spat. "The woman knows as much about biology as a traffic cone."

"Sarah's right. We should all be given an A for being tortured by her," Fiona said.

"Sounds good to me," Alex said.

"Is everybody excited about tonight?!" Elliott exclaimed.

"Shhhhhh, Elliott," Max said. "We all have our jobs to do. Let's not brag about it ok?"

"But I've never tried to kill anyone before," he whispered.

"Shhhhhh! Elliott!" Marc hissed. "Put a lid on it."

Jenny put an arm around Elliott. "It's okay Elliott. We hate her as much as you do."

Fiona gathered her things. "Alright, enough. I'm leaving. If the stupid woman doesn't have the courtesy to come to class like we did..."

The door opened, and Miss Tutley entered, dressed in a 'sexy Handmaid' outfit she possibly purchased at a Halloween/Adult costume shop. The white bonnet resembled the traditional style, but the similarities ended there. A sheer red cape replaced the usual red cloak. She wore a shiny red corset, black fishnet leggings, and thigh-high red boots.

Her students, silent, stared at her as she rushed into the room with a large box in her arms. She set it on the counter beside Sarah, who gaped at her.

"What in the actual fuck are you wearing?" Sarah asked.

"Sarah! Our Lord is not amused with your language," Miss Tutley said.

"How do you know?"

"Sarah, he knows all and sees all. He's in this room right now. Praise be."

She curtsied, glanced around the room, and clasped her hands together.

Fiona leaned over at Marc. "Okay, the twit has totally lost it now."

"She looks like a Handmaid who got lost shopping at Frederick's of Hollywood," he said.

"Believe me, this is only an act," Max said.

Jenny timidly raised her hand and motioned toward Miss Tutley's get-up.

"Ummmm, Miss Tutley, what's going on with your... costume?"

"Jane, since I am now a candidate standing for election, it is my duty to be the ultimate conservative woman, and be a symbol of tradition, selfishness, patriotism, and liberty," she said proudly, and added, "praise be."

"You nitwit," Fiona said. "A Handmaid doesn't represent that garbage. A Handmaid symbolizes oppression, tyranny, and totalitarianism."

Miss Tutley stared at her.

"Okay, I think you made her brain malfunction," Sarah said.

"Or totalitarianism has way too many syllables," Max said.

Miss Tutley stood proud. "I am the conservative Americans will vote for."

Fiona scoffed. "Probably. You are a fraud in cheap lingerie."

Elliott waved his hand in the air. "Is this going to be on the test?"

Robin raised his hands in defeat, shook his head, and surveyed his fellow students. "Aren't we supposed to be learning biology? This is biology class, isn't it? Isn't it?"

"Children, children, I would love to answer all your questions about God and the resurrection, but I must leave to campaign for... Him..." Miss Tutley eyed the ceiling.

"Leave?" Marc said. "You just got here."

"I only dropped by to leave you some work."

She reached into the box, and brought out a pin stamping machine, a plastic bag filled with her campaign pins, and bundles of her campaign flyers and envelopes.

"I thought the boys could do the more manual labour job, and assemble my campaign buttons, and the girls could stuff envelopes with my flyers, the way God intended."

Sarah violently waggled her head. "What?!"

"Tomorrow I'm starting a new tradition with a morning prayer, so I'll get you ready with one now before I go."

She entwined her fingers, closed her eyes, and gazed skyward.

"These boots are made for walkin' Lord. Cause that's what Jesus would do. One of these days my saviour and I will walk to heaven with you. Amen."

She curtsied, then turned to exit the class. At the door, she turned and bowed.

"Blessed be the vegetables!" she proudly announced, then left the room.

Her students gawked at each other, dumbfounded.

"What the fuck is she on?" Alex asked.

"I say we kill her now before she gets out there among the people and brainwashes the weak, the stupid, and the unwell – for America's sake," Jenny said.

"She's here for two minutes, doesn't teach, and leaves. I learned more this year from the biology dummy," Fiona said.

"Well, I guess we'd better start on these buttons," Robin said, as he stood and made a move toward the box.

Alex grabbed him. "Are you nuts? Fuck that shit."

"Do you believe her?" Jenny asked, "thinking we'd actually work on her campaign to get her crazy ass elected?"

"Well, there is a method to her madness," Max said.

"What do you mean Max?" Fiona asked.

"She's running on purpose as another right-wing candidate to cancel out my mother – who's even worse. My dad convinced her to."

"Why?"

"Because my mom has to be stopped and having her and Tutley out-crazy each other is easier than my dad trying to have mom committed to a mental institution or convince her to go to a cult deprogramming program."

Marc rested a hand on Max's shoulder. "Max, I'm sorry it has to be this way for you cause you're caught in the middle now."

"Sooooo, does this mean we're not killing Tutley tonight?" Elliott asked.

"No way, the plan's still on" Max said.

"And this is what I think of this bullshit," Sarah said.

She grabbed the flyers and envelopes, threw them into the sink beside her, and turned on the water. She tossed the buttons into the garbage can. She snatched the pin stamping machine, walked to the open window, and hurled it out. It landed in the parking lot with a clatter as Miss Tutley drove away.

FOURTEEN

Martha zoomed along an expressway in the city. Leslie sat in the passenger seat and furiously took notes on a clipboard as she rambled off unhinged idea after irrational idea.

"And I need a balloon," she demanded. "Not a cartoon balloon like Snoopy. I mean a big hot air balloon-shaped cross with my name on it as it floats across the city during rush hour..."

"Hot air balloon," Leslie mumbled as he wrote on his pad.

"And I want prime time television spots on all the networks, especially during that cop show where guns are our saviour against the liberal criminals..."

"Guns on prime time..." Leslie stopped writing. "Mrs. Molder, this is going to cost money. Your website merchandise and 1-900 prayer line are paying for your current promotional material, but prime time television... that's expensive."

"Ah Leslie, you've forgotten about the dumb white hicks from across the country who send me money because I've convinced them the leftist sex Marxists are a threat to their children's lives, and their survival as a race depends on the complete and utter annihilation of communist anarchists. You get me on prime time, and their cash will roll in tenfold."

"Mrs. Molder, by the way, I'm still waiting on my first paycheque..."

"You'll get it Leslie. You'll get it. All you have to do is keep making those YouTube videos where I keep repeating 'guns guns guns, God God God, 9/11, transexual rapists, immigrant terrorists, homosexual perversion pizza parlour rings, her e-mails, his laptop, communist

Democrats, sex predators, Jewish space lasers causing forest fires, and government microchips in fake vaccines', and you'll see big bucks."

Martha put a finger to her lips and pondered.

"If I wasn't running for office, I could be an influencer and be a millionaire!"

Martha exited the expressway onto a city street.

"The baby killing center certainly received my message, didn't they?" she asked.

"Well, you were kinda outnumbered by a hundred or so counter protestors..."

"I know!" she exclaimed. "It's as if they knew my schedule, and all their keyboard warrior woke baby killer supporters were there to try and shame me for doing God's work!"

Leslie shifted uncomfortably in his seat.

"And what about that liberal TV station? They totally ignored me when they did their live report. I missed my chance to speak directly to the people – live!"

Leslie cleared his throat and nervously tapped his pen on the clipboard.

"Mrs. Molder, aren't you a bit nervous about going back to the library today?"

"Why?"

"Well, after your protest of the Drag Queen Storytime they had last month, they banned you from ever stepping foot inside the library."

"Leslie, I don't intend on going into the library – it's filled with shameful socialist sex Marxist books, and a haven for sleazy sex perverted pornography pushers! Besides, I was having a perfectly legal protest outside, authorized by our saviour when..."

One Month Earlier:

On the sidewalk in front of the library, six protestors carried homemade cardboard signs attached to wooden posts and marched back and forth as parents with children slipped by them and entered the library. The messages on the signs varied from HONK FOR OUR CHILDREN to SEX MARXISTS GO HOME to JESUS SAVE MY BOOKS! and JACK AND JILL, NOT ED AND PHIL.

One protestor had their two young school-aged children with them, not in school. The children wore oversized misspelled sandwich boards that read I DON'T WANT TO BE ENDOCTORAINATED and SAVE ME FROM SOSHALLIZM.

Most of the protestors were conservatively dressed except Martha, who looked like a mashup of Dorothy from The Wizard of Oz, and Mary Poppins. She wore a gingham dress with white sleeves, fashioned into an exaggerated late-19th century corset, plastered with large gold lamé stars with free-flowing ribbons of red, white, and blue. She wore sparkly red sequined high heels, and her hair in long pigtails. Her makeup was garishly applied to highlight her long eye lashes, her cheekbones, and her lips.

Martha and her fellow protesters made snide comments to the parents – 'shame shame shame', 'think of the children', 'child abuse', and 'God have mercy on your Communist souls', while they made inappropriate comments to the children – 'don't look under the dresses kids', 'Mommy and Daddy are sinners', 'go in and you'll have bad dreams', and 'Jesus doesn't love you anymore'.

When it appeared the last of the parents and children had entered the building, the chain gang stopped their monotonous shuffling.

"Where are those draggies anyway?" a protestor asked. "We've been here for an hour."

"They must have circumvented our wall of shame, and snuck in the back way," Martha said.

"Hmmmpf," a protestor grumbled, "they would, wouldn't they."

"Well, we made our point to those poor deluded parents and their brainwashed children," Martha said, and scanned the street. "But where is Fox News? I specifically told them we'd be here..."

"Look," a protester said, and pointed at the entrance of the parking lot where a large mini van drove toward the library. "That must be them now."

The unmarked silver mini van parked in one of the spots marked RESERVED close to the entrance. Martha and her crew resumed their enthusiastic picketing. When the van doors opened, four drag queens emerged, dressed in colorful, glittery attire, expertly applied makeup, and coiffures that could have won hairstyling competitions.

When Martha saw them, she stopped, and her mouth dropped open so far, her chin rebounded off the sidewalk. One of the drag queens spied her, and instantly reached out a long, white-gloved arm toward her.

"Jerry! Jerry! Jerry!" he exclaimed as he rushed toward Martha. "Where have you been? We've been trying to get a hold of you! We thought we'd be doing this without you."

Martha recoiled as the other drag queens followed their fellow performer and descended upon Martha like fans of a major celebrity seeking their priceless autograph.

"Oh Jerry," one of the drag queens announced as they fingered the ribbons on Martha's dress, "you really nailed the Judy Julie collaboration."

"And that hair," another one said, "it's Judy to a T."

"I don't know how you fit into that dress Jerry," another one said. "But corsets are a wonder, aren't they?"

"Come on now guys, enough," the first drag queen said. "We're late as it is. The kids are waiting. We found Jerry, so let's go in."

As he put a hand on Martha's arm to guide her, she looked at his gloved hand, horrified, and shook her head vigorously.

"I'm not Jerry!"

"Of course you aren't," the second drag queen said, "you're Dorothy Dictionary. I'm Carol Chapters, Doug is Bette Books, and Charlie is Liza Learning – at least for today."

"So, let's go Dorothy," Charlie said as he pulled Martha toward the entrance, "our audience awaits."

A stunned Martha shook her head as if she were having a seizure.

"No! No! No!"

"Come on Jerry. Now's not the time for your first bout of stage fright," Doug said.

As the four drag queens dragged her to the front door, her fellow protestors stood in shock, then recoiled in fright, ready to flee as if the drag queens were going to hiss bright florescent green radioactive fluid at them.

Martha struggled for her freedom and amplified her protestations.

"Help me! I'm being dominated by homosexuals!"

"Careful Jerry," Charlie said, "this is my wife's dress. She'll kill me if I get one snag in it."

Before the drag queens and Martha disappeared inside, Doug turned to the protestors and hissed at them. Instantly frightened, they grabbed the two children with them and bumped into each other like Minions as they attempted to escape, dropping their protest signs, and stumbling into the parking lot to their vehicles.

Back in Martha's car:

"It wasn't my fault Leslie," Martha protested. "I was kidnapped!"

"Well, maybe they won't recognize you today since you don't look like Dorothy Gale on her way to a cocktail party."

"How was I to know the Judy Garland look was a favorite of those crossdressers?"

Martha simmered as she gripped the steering wheel. Leslie consulted her itinerary.

"Mrs. Molder, I think your itinerary is a bit too full today. You still have your Guns 'n God Gals prayer meeting... your Don't Say Gay rally... Maybe that's why your protest at the women's health center wasn't the success you thought it would be."

"Well at least I managed to pass out a few dozen plastic fetuses with my campaign information heat stamped on them. You watch and see how the liberal media comes crawling to me after I do my interview later today with Fox News. It will be my pleasure to tell them all... ahhhhhhh!!"

Martha screamed as they approached the main city library. Along with an ample parking lot, a generous green space with trees and park benches surrounded the building. In the parking lot next to the entrance, a large wooden sign with big, red letters read: 'STOP THE LIES! STOP THE HERESY! STOP THE PROFANITY! THINK OF THE CHILDREN! Underneath, in even bigger letters read: 'VOTE SHELLEY TUTLEY FOR STATE REPRESENTATIVE.'

Martha hyperventilated. "What... is... going... on... here?!" she choked out. "This is my event!" she whined.

Miss Tutley, still dressed in her sexy Handmaid outfit, stood beside the great big sign, and what looked like a huge witch's cauldron. Smoke wafted from the container. A skid of books sat beside the cauldron. She casually tossed a book from the pile into the smoking pot. A long table covered with a white tablecloth sat nearby. Clear plastic glasses filled with red liquid lined the table, equally spaced apart.

Martha quickly stopped the car, throwing Leslie forward. She jumped out, and marched to Miss Tutley's area, her arms and liberty bell dress swinging wildly back and forth like crazed, sped-up bells from multiple cathedrals in the Austrian alps.

Library patrons initially regarded Miss Tutley's setup with curiosity, and ultimately with derision and ridicule, though she did manage to rope a rube or two into her farcical scheme. Miss Tutley motioned for a patron to choose a book from the pile, toss it into the cauldron, and raise their arms in praise as flames consumed the book. She motioned to a large pickle jar on the table crudely labelled DONATIONS, and finally to the mysterious blood-red refreshments on the table.

Martha barged past a few patrons to Miss Tutley as Leslie hopped from her car. Martha stood at the cauldron with her hands on her silver bell hips.

"Shelley Tutley! What is going on here?!"

"Oh, hello kind supporter. Care to offer a sacrifice to God, and help me rid blasphemous literature from the world?"

Miss Tutley gestured to the books on the skid. A large neon yellow RETURN TO PUBLISHER – NO SALE sign adorned the pile. All the books were in mint condition with $5, $1 or CLEARANCE stickers on them. Martha elbowed her way to the books and frantically did a quick search through them.

"Donald Trump: Mein Fetter Arsch... Ann Coulter: Off My Rocker... Scott Baio: Life on the Z List... Tucker Carlson: A Brief History of Me & Other Useful Idiots... Kari Lake: I Hear Voices... Susan Sarandon: How to Elect Monsters... Laura Loomer: Political Stunts 101... Rudy Giuliani: Has Anyone Seen My Scruples?... What are you doing burning all these fine examples of conservative triumph?"

Miss Tutley reached out and put a hand on Martha's shoulder.

"Mrs. Molder, won't you join me and incinerate the sins written by communist leftists who threaten to pollute our children's minds?"

"But all these books are from American patriots! I will not!"

"So, you won't help me?"

"No!"

"There you have it ladies and gentlemen," Miss Tutley announced to the small, but growing crowd as they stopped to witness the spectacle. "Martha Molder is a Russian agent, probably a communist herself who is okay with your children being exposed to sex traffickers who lurk within these liberal walls," she said as she gestured to the library.

"I am not!"

"Then join me Martha Molder," Miss Tutley said in an almost staccato, computerized voice as she grabbed Ann Coulter's book, and thrust it into Martha's hand.

As she attempted to force Martha to toss it into the cauldron, Martha grabbed her arm, and they wrestled.

"No! I have the books you should be burning in my car. The gay penguin book, the Judy Blume monthly visitor book, all Oprah's book club books, Carrie, The Handmaid's Tale..."

Miss Tutley gasped. "What did you say Martha Molder? You want to burn me in effigy?! Blasphemous! This woman is a blasphemer!" she shouted as she pointed at Martha.

"I'm not! I'm not!" Martha shouted as they continued to struggle.

Miss Tutley managed to make Martha toss Ann Coulter's book into the cauldron. It burst into flames, causing a minor explosion, and evil ghostly smoke to erupt from the container. Leslie ran to the scene and attempted to break the two women apart.

A short distance away, in the corner of the parking lot, Arlene and Jimmy Joe Johnson sat in their slightly rusted, oversized, early-model Ford F-150, and observed the spectacle.

Jimmy Joe sat in the driver's seat. He wore an old ball cap, a bright white athletic shirt, and faded jeans. Thin stubble sprouted on his face. Arlene leaned as inconspicuously as possible out the passenger window and pointed a small camcorder at Miss Tutley and Martha. She wore tight ripped jeans, and a tight blue t-shirt that read 'Sugar 'n Spice' in gold glitter surrounded by a red devil's tail.

As the two women continued to wrestle, insult each other, and fight for control over the public book burning, Jimmy Joe sat back in his seat and noisily ate roasted peanuts. Arlene glanced at him.

"Would you stop that there crunchin'," she snapped. "I want this video ta be clean as a whistle, so's I can post it on YouTube."

"But I'm hungry Leeny," Jimmy Joe whined.

"You hold yer horses mister. We'll git sum I Hop after we finish this here video tapin'."

"How much longer are we gonna halfta stay here?"

"Now you listen ta me buster. We're gettin' paid lotsa dough ta sit here and do this here documentin'. We have two crazy ladies danglin' on the 'ol fishin' line, and a bank vault a money waitin' fer us, sayin' 'take me, take me!" she said in a high-pitched cartoon voice.

"Ya got that right Leeny. We kinda stumbly stumbled inta good fortune in this here crazy town. Who woulda thunk, us gettin' outta tha jug and findin' a pot a gold so soon."

Arlene laughed. "Funny ain't it. Two screwy broads in the same town out ta get each other, and we get tangled up with 'em. When the catfish are bitin', they're a bitin."

Jimmy Joe fluttered his hands in the air. "Those two 'lil fishies swam right to us."

"And Miss Martha's husband ownin' the bank – the cherry on top a the sundae."

"That's some getup the sexy 'lil schoolteacher has on innit?" Jimmy Joe said as he leaned closer to the windshield and leered at Miss Tutley.

Arlene peered from the viewfinder to eye him contemptuously.

"Sexy 'lil schoolteacher?"

"Ya know... the crazy, sexy, bouncy 'lil thing with the..."

Jimmy Joe mimicked cupping breasts.

"And the..."

He made sensuous curves with his hands.

Arlene continued to eye him, held the camcorder steady, reached over, and slapped him across the head.

"I know who ya mean dummy."

Jimmy Joe frowned and massaged his head. Arlene pointed at him directly.

"You keep yer peepers to yourself Mr. Hot Pants. I ain't been through hell 'n back with ya over the past few years ta have ya go wanderin' along some other girl's path. So you keep dem trousers zipped Valentino," she enunciated.

"Awww shucks Leeny. I didn't mean anythin'. I'm only pointin' out her... better qualities."

"Yeah, well, yer right there hun. She's all glim glam and shimmy sham on the outside, but on the inside, she's nuttier than a squirrel in matin' season."

"Just like Miss Martha."

"Uh huh."

"Can you believe she thought we were a church group?" Jimmy Joe laughed. "Last time I sat in church, I got caught stealin' from the collection plate."

"After talkin' to her, yes I can. Miss Martha done got her brain wires fried by watchin' too much Fox News."

"We watch Fox News Leeny..."

"Yeah, fer the entertainment darlin'. Crazy middle class White folks like Miss Martha watch it cause they want someone ta tell them ta be afeared the Black folks are gonna kill 'em, the Mexicans are gonna steal their money, and the gays are gonna touch their damn kids." Arlene shook her head. "Stupid, stupid White folks."

As Arlene continued to film Miss Tutley, Martha, and Leslie, who inserted himself between the two women as they clawed at each other, a television news truck arrived in the parking lot. It lurched to a stop, and a camera operator and reporter jumped out. Arlene stopped filming and recoiled back inside the truck cab.

"What's wrong Leeny?" Jimmy Joe asked. "The sexy Tutley gal wanted us ta film the whole thing..."

She slowly glared at him, then backhanded him in the shoulder. He flinched.

"It's the TV people dum dum. We can't be seen... anywhere. If we wanna pull off this little 'ol bank heist, we gotta keep outta the glare a peoples' peepers. And as fer the 'sexy' Tutley gal, we got enough material to make her happy. Now, let's go."

"But... but... but I think they're about ta start throwin' drinks at each other. Maybe we should stay and record the whole thang, ya know, in case the sexy Miss Tutley gets wet, and soaks her sexy outfit in the cat fight."

Arlene grabbed him by the ear. "You start the truck, now," she ordered, and sensually stroked his neck. "Maybe after we git home and put this screwball video on the net, I can dress like crazy Miss Tutley, and git the horny toad outta ya."

"How? Ya don't have anythin' like she's wearin'."

"I still have the nun's outfit from the time we pulled that charity scam."

Jimmy Joe licked his lips. "Oh yeah..."

He giggled, she squeezed his thigh, and he started the engine. He drove as inconspicuously as possible from the parking lot as the TV crew quickly assembled their gear to capture the melee.

Martha, unable to stop Miss Tutley from tossing books onto the fire, grabbed a glass of the blood-red liquid in each hand, and attempted to throw the contents on the fire. Leslie, who stood between the two women, unexpectedly received both glasses in his face.

"Mrs. Molder!" he exclaimed, as he wiped the liquid from his face, stopped, and smacked his lips. "Is this Chateau La Mission Haut-Brion?"

Miss Tutley stopped tossing books onto the fire. "Why yes, it is?"

"This is expensive Miss Tutley. How can you afford to give this away?"

"I have the most generous benefactors," she said, and laughed maniacally.

"I'll bet you do!" Martha shouted.

She ripped the white bonnet from Miss Tutley's head and threw it into the fire. Miss Tutley's blond locks whirled about her head like strands of wheat in a hurricane. She clutched at her head, and pointed at Martha, making sure she stared at the camera.

"Sacrilege! Martha Molder is an unholy devil's spawn! And she wants to hold public office and do God's work?! Never!" Miss Tutley thundered as she dramatically swept an arm out, her cloak waving behind her.

Martha yanked on the cloak from behind, choking Miss Tutley, and forcing her to stumble backwards. They both staggered into the refreshment table, knocking over the glasses, and spilling the wine onto the spotless white tablecloth. As they grabbed at glasses and tossed wine on each other, Leslie tore at his hair.

"Mrs. Molder, the press! The press!" he shouted as he pointed at the camera operator and reporter, who stood beside the camera, shocked, but delighted.

"You're getting this right?" she asked. "Tell me you're getting this."

The crowd around the scene grew. People held their cellphones out and recorded the event as if it wasn't going to air on the six o'clock news.

FIFTEEN

At six-thirty in the evening, Max's house sat quiet and in darkness. The front door opened, and a shrouded figure dressed entirely in black entered the house. They softly closed the door and switched on a flashlight. They pointed the light around the kitchen, then silently tip-toed through the room. The person inadvertently bumped into the kitchen table, causing it to squeak across the floor. The person abruptly stopped and shushed themselves.

The shrouded figure pointed the light at the staircase and walked to the stairs. They shone the light upstairs and silently crept to the second floor. At the top, the person shone the light around the hallway, then settled on Max's closed bedroom door. The figure opened the door and slipped inside.

They shone the light around the room until it fell on the table with Mr. Fluffy Puffy in his cage. The rabbit blinked and wiggled its nose at the sudden bright light. The shrouded figure grabbed a blanket off Max's bed and threw it over the cage. Deftly handling the cage and the flashlight, the mysterious person walked from Max's room, then disappeared into the hallway.

#

The high school buzzed with activity. While teachers and parents met in classrooms, the hallways hummed with chatter between parents, teachers and students. TV screens were mounted on the walls at various points around the school. They alternately broadcast events at the school, and a local evening news telecast.

To lighten the atmosphere, Mr. Douglas hired circus performers to entertain everyone. Jugglers, mimes, acrobats, contortionists, cartoonists, card players, dancers and strongmen roamed the hallways.

Though they were not required to attend, some students arrived with their parents. Miss Tutley's entire biology class attended.

Max and Marc sat in the atrium near the front doors. A strongman dressed in fake animal furs acted as the doorman. When their classmates walked in with their parents, the pair nodded silently to their friends in a pre-arranged secret code, and they scattered off around the school.

Someone who forgot about the clandestine evening or anything related to a secret code was Elliott. He entered the school with his parents and immediately announced his presence and association with the people who he plotted with to eliminate their biology teacher.

"Hi guys!" he said sunnily and waved enthusiastically at Max and Marc.

Max raised his hands in a 'what do you think you're doing Elliott?' manner.

"Hello Mr. and Mrs. Hanover," Marc said politely. "How are you this evening?"

"We're well, thank you Marcus," Mr. Hanover said as Mrs. Hanover smiled and nodded at the boys.

"Mom, can I go hang out with Max and Marc?" he pleaded.

"Hang out?" his father asked, almost offended at Elliott's slang.

Mr. and Mrs. Hanover were well dressed, neat and tidy, well spoken, and clearly not the low brow, slovenly, irresponsible, abusive, barefoot hicks Miss Tutley claimed them to be. Mr. Hanover consulted his wife, and after a moment, they collectively nodded.

"Yes Elliott," Mrs. Hanover said, "you may go and visit your friends."

She reached out and picked lint from his shirt.

"Thanks Mom! Thanks Dad!" Elliott said excitedly as he bounded to Max and Marc like a happy puppy.

"But only for a few moments," Mr. Hanover said. "We'll be upstairs... waiting..."

As Mr. and Mrs. Hanover ascended the staircase to the second floor, a mime dressed in a fluorescent green leotard joined them, and mimicked walking an imaginary staircase. The Hanovers regarded the mime strangely and occasionally glanced back at their son.

"So, guys," Elliott said energetically, "gonna be quite the night huh?!"

Max grabbed Elliott's shirt sleeve and yanked him closer.

"Would you put a lid on it!" he hissed. "This is supposed to be a secret!"

"Oh right," Elliott said as he exaggeratedly winked.

Marc rolled his eyes. "This isn't a party, Elliott. This is serious stuff."

"I know. I know. But this is the most exciting thing that's ever happened to me!"

"What about the time you accidentally drank glue?" Max said.

"Hee hee," Elliott giggled. "Yeah... but this... being in a gang with you guys, you know, for the first time, makes me feel... wanted."

"This isn't a gang," Marc said. "We're not knocking people off to control the drug trade."

"No, but we're going to kil..."

"Shhhhhh!" Max angrily shushed him.

"Oh right," Elliott remembered. He put a finger to his lips and winked again.

Max and Marc eyed each other.

"So, where is everyone else?" Elliott loudly whispered.

"They're around... they're around," Marc tried to explain without going into detail. "Just go to your assigned location like we discussed."

Elliott quickly saluted Marc. "Roger Commander."

Mr. and Mrs. Hanover stood next to a railing on the second floor and stared at the boys in the atrium.

"Elliott?" Mrs. Hanover said.

She beckoned him to come upstairs with a polite wave. The mime in the green leotard stood beside Mr. Hanover, and mimicked staring at Elliott through binoculars. Mr. Hanover turned and glared at him.

"Do you mind?"

The mime slinked away as if he were paddling a canoe.

"Okay, gotta go guys." Elliott stood motionless, still saluting Marc.

"Elliott, I think your mother's waiting..." Max said.

"You have to dismiss me first."

Marc reluctantly and discreetly dismissed Elliott.

"Wish me luck!" he said excitedly.

"Good luck Elliott," Max deadpanned.

Elliott ran upstairs to join his parents. He enthusiastically waved to Max and Marc.

Max grimaced. "He's gonna screw this up, I know it."

"Maybe we should've chloroformed him for the night like we discussed."

Max nodded, stood, and held out a hand to Marc. "Come on, let's go."

Marc took his hand, and they disappeared around a corner.

SIXTEEN

In a classroom on the second floor, Martha and Jack sat at the front in the student desks and faced Carter Riley. Jack wore a dark suit with no tie. Martha changed from her wine-stained liberty bell dress, and wore a royal blue pantsuit with a garish, oversized, red, white, and blue flower in her lapel, and pearls around her neck. A plastic bird's nest fascinator filled with fake fruit sat on her head.

Carter sat behind his desk. Casually dressed in jeans, and a shirt with the sleeves folded to his elbows, he also wore a tie, loose around his neck. He passed a sheet of paper to Jack. Martha snatched it away. Carter eyed her spitefully.

"I have no complaints about Max" he said. "His marks so far this year have been excellent. He completes all his assignments on time and with effort. He is a well-rounded, thoughtful, gifted student who obviously has a supportive team around him including his parents, his friends and his..." Carter eyed Martha again. "His best friend Marc."

Jack nodded and smiled, while Martha stared at the paper with a frozen grimace. Jack snatched the paper from her.

"These grades are fantastic," Jack said enthusiastically. "Aren't they dear?" he vehemently enunciated.

"Well, I guess..." Martha allowed.

"Is there a problem Mrs. Molder?" Carter asked.

Jack gripped his desk, his knuckles ghost white, and peered at the ceiling.

"It's not the marks. I agree, Max is brilliant. He is my son after all."

Jack closed his eyes.

"I'm concerned with how he's being taught..."

"Okay..." Carter said slowly. "Am I doing something that is causing you some concern?"

"Oh no, no, no, I don't think so... yet."

Jack moved in his seat, causing the chair to loudly squeak.

"If there is anything..." Carter tried again.

"Well," Martha said as she put a finger to her chin and thought for an extended moment. "Max does come home with some wild ideas I can't help but think come from this place..."

Carter's left eye twitched, and he shifted in his chair. "Oh, like what?"

Jack eyed Carter, tried to covertly shake his head, and converse with him telepathically to say, 'don't engage, don't engage, don't engage'.

"Oh, I don't know, let's say... gay marriage."

Jack lowered his head and massaged his forehead with his fingertips.

"Mrs. Molder," Carter carefully explained, "I teach English. Sometimes, social issues arise in English literature. Sometimes, the kids want to engage in a discussion about real-world issues. I'm here to facilitate the discussion and help grow their reasoning and cognitive skills. Me being gay has nothing to do..."

"Oh, you're gay?" Martha asked innocently.

Jack sighed heavily.

"Yes Mrs. Molder."

Martha's right eye twitched. "Y-yes. Yes, I remember now," she sputtered.

Jack glared at her and scowled.

"But what about all this pseudo-science mumbo jumbo he brings home like climate change, the moon controlling the tides, electric car fuel cells, dinosaur fossils, plankton re-birth, and our God-created world being a million years old..."

"Billions," Jack said quickly.

"And don't get me started on the Canadian metric system..."

"He... doesn't... teach... science!" Jack slowly shouted.

Martha glanced at Jack innocently, while Carter bit his lip.

"But he's associated with the liberal school system that's brainwashing our babies and..."

Jack slammed his palms on the desk and stood.

"I think we've more than abused your time Mr. Riley," Jack said. He reached a hand to Carter, who shook it.

"But I..." Martha tried.

"Mr. Riley has other parents to see, I'm sure," Jack said as he pulled Martha from her seat. "Don't you Mr. Riley?"

"Why yes, I do," he said quickly.

"But... but the plankton," Martha tried again.

Jack pulled her toward the door. "Come along... dear."

"But my innocent baby," Martha whined. "All the innocent babies..."

At the door, Jack turned to Carter and nodded, who in turn mouthed 'thank you'. As the Molders disappeared into the hallway, Carter performed deep breathing exercises.

#

Jack and Martha walked side by side as they rounded a corner in the hallway. His hand clutched her elbow. Jack walked at a brisk pace, causing Martha to stutter-step in her high heels beside him. Students, teachers, circus folk, and other parents watched them.

"Would you slow down!" Martha wailed.

"No," Jack announced.

"What is your hurry?!"

"We're going home. I... I am so embarrassed..."

"About what?" Martha asked innocently.

Jack glanced at her incredulously. "Ummmm, where do you want me to start? You made a complete fool of yourself earlier today by handing out those damn plastic fetuses at the abortion clinic, and you practically get into a fist fight and throw wine at a teacher at a ridiculous book burning event, and get on the six o'clock news..."

"I did not."

"Oh yeah? What is that?" Jack asked as he pointed to a TV screen mounted on the wall outside the cafeteria.

A local news station showcased their TOP STORY: STATE ELECTORAL CANDIDATES GET INTO PUBLIC FIGHT. Even with the sound muted, the video said it all as the report showcased Martha and Miss Tutley's spat. People in the hallway stopped and laughed at the TV. Martha whirled around, scanned the crowd, and turned back to the TV.

"They weren't supposed to show this!" she hissed. "I gave an interview to our national state television station Fox News, talking about my campaign and..." Martha peered at the screen more closely. "That's not Fox News! It's the Communist Broadcasting System!"

Jack closed his eyes. "Please, shut up Martha," he muttered.

"You'd know they'd air this sensationalist left-wing smear campaign."

"Martha," Jack said, on the verge of rage, "the only smear campaign tonight is yours in our meeting with Mr. Riley. You turned it into a crazy right-wing interrogation."

"I did not," Martha said, offended. "I simply offered my opinion on the crumbling state of today's public school system. I'm the one who should be embarrassed."

"What?"

"Look at you," Martha motioned to him. "Tie-less. I can't believe you misplaced the red-striped tie I gave you. You look sloppy."

Jack laughed. "Are you kidding me? A tie? You're embarrassed about me not wearing a tie? This isn't a White House party hosted by your former Moron-In-Chief."

Martha gasped and contorted her face in anguish. She raised a hand to the ceiling.

"He didn't mean it." She turned to the audience in the hallway who gave the couple only a passing interest. "He didn't mean it. Here, take my election flyer," Martha said as she reached into her purse, and passed out her flyers to random people. "Patriotic mugs, freedom cookies, righteous mini bibles, liberty back scratchers – all free with your generous donation..."

"Would you stop forcing your bullshit down everyone's throats!" Jack shouted.

"Oh... oh, that is so traitorous!" Martha whispered to him. "This is America! The land of freedom! These people are Americans," she said as she waved an arm around the hallway. "You insulted everyone here. Apologise to them," she commanded.

"What? Give me a break. I don't have time for your fake patriotism. Let's go," Jack said as he tightened his grip on her arm.

"Oh my... oh my," Martha wailed. She tried to bow and curtsy to everyone as she handed out more flyers. "I'm so sorry... I'm so sorry for my husband... Vote Molder...I'm so sorry... Call my prayer line... I'm so sorry... Vote Molder... Genuine cork coasters now fifty percent off with your donation... Vote Molder... I'm so sorry..."

A man dressed as a jester approached them and waved a bell-laden scepter.

"There's no need to apologize mi 'lady. Tonight, I am the fool!"

"No, she is," Jack said as he yanked a thumb at Martha. "Let's go Martha!"

She frowned childishly, as if Jack said she wasn't getting any more ice cream.

"But we haven't seen Miss Tutley yet. I cancelled my Guns 'N God Gals rally and my Don't Say Gay rally because of her antics. She needs to know she's ruining my campaign!"

They were only steps away from the biology lab. Jack swallowed hard.

"I-I'm sure Max does well in her class... Let's go."

Jack attempted to pull her along. Martha yanked her arm free.

"No! I told her we'd see her tonight!"

Jack stopped. "You did?"

The jester waved his noisy scepter between them.

"Did you hear the one about the food in the cafeteria?" he asked.

Jack grabbed the scepter and hurled it down the hallway like an axe in a lumberjack competition.

"My scepter!" the jester cried as he scampered off.

"Look Martha, tonight is about Max, not your ridiculous campaign. I don't want another scene like the one today."

"Oh Jack, there won't be a scene. We happen to be engaged in a political battle. We're two grown adults who can act civilly toward each other..."

"Right..." Jack said as he eyed another TV screen showing the two women throwing wine at each other.

Martha groomed him. "Now, now, don't be embarrassed to see her because you're not wearing a tie. Even without one, it's possible to make a good first impression."

"Right... a first impression."

Jack recoiled when she brushed stray hairs away from his face. As she straightened his jacket, she eyed a long hair sitting precariously on his shoulder. It could have been a blonde hair. It could have been a white hair. To Martha, it was as white as her heaven. With her thumb and forefinger, she reached out and deliberately plucked it from his jacket. Her eyes grew as big as crop circles, and she brandished it at Jack.

"Evidence!" she shouted.

"What?"

"You know what," Martha accused. "I saw you yesterday with that... harlot!"

"You... what?"

A young woman carrying a lute, and dressed as a medieval minstrel, sauntered toward them. She plucked the lute strings.

"You've been a cheatin' on meeeee..." she sang in a country drawl and slowly crept away.

"Please Jack. The eyes God gave me recorded your shameful behaviour."

"I think your recording device is on the fritz."

She leaned in close to him. "We'll talk about this later – in private," she hissed.

Jack bent away from her as she breathed fumes into his face.

"Have you been drinking – again?"

"What?" Martha heartily laughed. "Of course not!"

Jack attempted to grab her purse. "What's in here besides your election propaganda?"

"This is my personal property!" she yelled as she whipped her purse away from him.

When everyone in the hallway stared at her, Martha's demeanor changed from hostile drunk to pleasant wife. She smiled luminously at

Jack and delicately took him by the arm to lead him away. When Jack didn't move, Martha banged back into him.

The minstrel returned and theatrically strummed her lute. "You're my boomerang, baby! My boomerang, bayyy-beeee!" she wailed, and wandered away.

"Come on Jack, this is embarrassing," Martha whispered to him. "I am a pillar of this community, an advocate..."

She abruptly reached out to a woman and forced an election pamphlet in her hand.

"Vote Molder. Heavenly-white prayer crystals free with donation."

The woman raised her eyebrows at Martha when she touched the woman's forehead as if Martha was attempting to heal her.

"I'm a healer, and a shining example of what American conservatives are today."

The woman lurched away from Martha.

"You sure are," Jack said. "You've lost your mind, and you've tried to make everyone afraid for your own personal gain."

"Well, I'm sorry!" Martha irrationally blurted as she shook her arms and stamped her feet. "I haven't been able to think straight after what you did, and after the trauma Mr. and Mrs. Riley caused this afternoon," she sneered.

"What are you talking about?"

Martha leaned into him, glanced around furtively, clutched his arm so tight her fingers turned ghostly white, and peered at him irrationally disturbed.

"Max's teacher Mr. Riley," she whispered, "he's married to another ma..." She choked a bit. "Another ma... man."

The minstrel returned, enthusiastically strummed her lute, and wildly gyrated her hips as she sang, "I need a man! Yeah! Yeah! Gimme a man! Yeah! Yee-yahh!" and disappeared again.

Jack shrugged his shoulders. "And? Who cares? He's in a committed relationship..."

Martha abruptly released her hold on Jack and stumbled backwards like a robot that had short circuited. Her eyes grew large, and shock seized her face. She clunked a hand to her head, moaned, clutched her pearls, looked around for a couch to faint on, then dramatically crumpled against a man who ate peanuts from a paper bag. She grabbed the bag and breathed into it to prevent herself from hyperventilating.

Jack regarded her with utter contempt.

Eventually, Martha regained control of her breathing and stood, with some help from the man she fell against. She shoved the paper bag, and an election flyer at him. He glanced at the flyer, then crumpled it together with the bag, and threw them into a garbage can.

Martha put a hand to her chest and gasped. "A committed relationship?! They have you quoting their homosexual propaganda!"

"What? You're being ridiculous," Jack said.

Martha stepped toward him and tightly grasped his arm again. "You know what's ridiculous? My poor little Max caught in a sordid web of gay marriage. God knows what they've tried to do to him," Martha said as her eyes bugged out. "Convert him to their side, brainwash him with Lady Gaga music, lure him into their harem with rainbow Skittles..."

Two male contortionists, dressed entirely in black spandex, approached the couple, twisted themselves together, and leaned back on their hands with their crotches touching. The newly formed crab scuttled around beside Jack and Martha.

"Ummmm, what's gotten into you?" he slowly asked her.

Jack winced as Martha grasped his arm tighter. She peered furtively around them.

"9/11 Jack... 9/11."

"What does 9/11 have to do with gay people?"

"National security Jack. They're all around us, destroying America one piece of apple pie at a time – the homosexuals, those Muslim terrorists, the atheists, the pro-abortionists, the Democrats, the drugged-out marijuana addicts, the stem cell pushers... the 5G Canadians!"

Jack clutched at his face with his hand to resemble the face hugger from Alien.

"I'm leaving," he said bluntly as he tried to yank his arm free from her.

"No!" she cried. "We have to show we're a happily married couple... for America's sake." Martha stared at the ceiling, shook her head proudly, and beamed psychotically.

The minstrel returned. "Aaaaamerica! You're my apple pie! Aaaa! Merica!" she sang passionately, then slunk away again.

Jack shook off Martha's grasp. "You mean for your sake." He turned from her. "I can't look at you anymore. Your touch disgusts me."

"But you touch that harlot! You haven't touched me in months!"

Jack turned and grasped her shoulders. His voice echoed off the cinder block walls.

"Because you fucking scare me! Because you've turned into a psychotic, deluded, right-wing bible-beating menace! And because you've locked up your pussy in a creepy Puritan chastity belt!"

The ambient chatter in the hallway ceased as everyone stared at the Molders. The minstrel strummed her lute quietly in a corner, and softly sang, "silence is a sledgehammer..."

The biology lab door swung open, and Miss Tutley appeared in the doorway, dressed conservatively as an 1800s school marm. She wore a floor-length brown skirt, and a tasteful white ruffled blouse buttoned to her neck, fastened with an antique cameo. Her hair was pulled back into a small, tight, sophisticated bun, and frameless spectacles sat on her nose. She stepped aside, and a man and a woman exited the classroom.

"We'll see you again," she said breathlessly to the man as he passed, then pressed her election flyer against his chest.

The man glanced back at her as she pursed her lips and waved to him with her fingertips. His wife narrowed her eyes, glared at Miss Tutley, and yanked on the man's arm. He fell in behind her as she dragged him away.

"Who's next?" Miss Tutley asked huskily.

She attempted to lean sexily against the door frame, but her constricting attire forced her into an awkward position as if she were experiencing back spasms.

Jack shielded his eyes from her and walked away. "I'm outta here."

"Jack!" Martha and Miss Tutley exclaimed.

Martha peered at Miss Tutley curiously. Miss Tutley gawked at Martha with abject terror. She stood straight, then took a couple steps along the hallway as she called out to Jack.

"I-I mean... Jerk!" Miss Tutley blurted. "What a jerk for leaving your wife here! Sheesh! Jerk!" She put her hands on her hips and shook her head in faux disgust.

Jack disappeared around a corner.

SEVENTEEN

Miss Tutley spun around in the hallway, fixed her spectacles, forced a fake smile, and waved an arm wide toward the biology lab.

"Won't you come in Margaret?" she said sugary sweetly to Martha.

"I don't know what's wrong with my husband," Martha said as she walked past Miss Tutley and into the classroom. "He's been a little off since I found out he's having an affair."

Miss Tutley forced a piercing laugh. "Oh, men, men, men. They're strange creatures..."

She closed the door and followed Martha. She tripped over a power cord, stutter-stepped behind Martha, and almost ran into her.

Martha turned around, and scrutinised Miss Tutley. "You have quite a... diverse wardrobe Miss Tutley. From Sodom and Gomorrah to Little House on the Prairie."

"Oh this," Miss Tutley said as she pulled at her skirt. "My campaign manager said I should wear something less..."

"Tasteless?"

Miss Tutley glared at her. "Well yes."

"Miss Tutley, I didn't mean to say anything about my cheating rat of a husband. I'm just so gosh darn mad at the harlot he's been seeing..."

Miss Tutley offered another uncomfortable high-pitched laugh. "Dear, I know all about men and their carnal, animalistic ways."

Her eyes grew as big as petri dishes as she knew she had said too much, and she immediately put a hand on Martha's arm in a friendly manner. Martha eyed her, and her hand warily. She attempted a fake smile.

"You know Miss Tutley, perhaps we should focus on our own campaigns, even though mine is better," she said under her breath, "stop attacking each other since we have similar platforms, even though mine is better," she said under her breath again, "and may the best woman win."

"Why Margaret, that's so big of you, and I'm not talking about your kindness," Miss Tutley muttered under her breath as she glanced around at Martha's rear end. "We should each put our unpleasantness behind us, if you can fit anything else back there," she muttered.

The two women guardedly sneered/smiled as they fake kissed each other on both cheeks.

"I'm so glad," Martha said. "As a politician and community leader, I need to be completely open and honest about my life. The voters should see all the sins and warts every candidate has, especially the wart on your neck," she said under her breath, "and especially if the sins are not my fault." She leaned into Miss Tutley. "It's the backstabbing harlot's fault."

Miss Tutley let out another high-pitched nervous laugh. "Please," she motioned toward the front, "have a seat at the front counter."

"Oh, thank you."

Martha walked to the front counter where she sat at an empty station and faced the whiteboard. Miss Tutley swallowed hard, and followed Martha, being careful not to trip over any rogue power cords. She awkwardly sat on a stool at the counter and faced Martha. She consulted some paperwork, glanced at Martha, and smiled anxiously.

"Your daughter Morgan, is a wonderful student..."

Martha stared at her, confused. "No, it's Max."

Miss Tutley glanced at her notes. "No... I'm quite sure it's Morgan."

"But I'm here for Max..."

"Oh, I'm so sorry. Parents and their nicknames for their children...Your daughter Max is a wonderful student..."

"No, Max is my son."

"So, Morgan is not your daughter?"

"I don't have a daughter."

"So, Morgan is your other son?"

"I don't know who Morgan is."

Miss Tutley reached out a hand and sympathetically patted Martha's arm. "Oh, I'm so sorry. Perhaps if you spent more time with him..."

Martha shook her head. "No, you have this Morgan confused with my son, Max Molder."

"Max. Max Molder."

Miss Tutley shuffled her notes so hard, they slid across the slick, shiny countertop, and fell off the end to the floor. As she attempted to reach for them, she swiveled herself off her stool and fell to the floor. She shrieked. Martha stood and peered over the counter.

"Oh my goodness! Are you okay?"

Miss Tutley clutched the countertop with her fingertips and slowly stood.

"Thank you, I'm fine," she said, a dazed look on her face.

As she smoothed her blouse and skirt, Jack's red-striped tie peeked out from under her skirt. Miss Tutley's eyes grew large. She tried to cross her legs as if she needed to pee. She leaned over the lab counter at Martha.

"Perhaps you'd like to see the experiments the class has done," she said.

Miss Tutley put an elbow on the counter, rested her chin in her hand, smiled, and pointed to the back of the classroom where four tables contained biology experiments. The plastic biology dummy stood guard over them.

"Oh my, yes."

Martha turned, eagerly walked to the tables, and inspected the experiments with her back to Miss Tutley. She eyed the biology dummy, its missing eye, and the organs in the chest cavity in the wrong places.

"You know," Martha said as her gaze shifted from the dummy to the projects, "I enjoyed biology in high school, especially the field trips..."

Miss Tutley stood behind the counter, spread her legs as wide as she could, and awkwardly tried to stuff Jack's tie back under her skirt.

"...going to the seashore," Martha continued, "and learning about the push and the pull of the tides..."

Miss Tutley hiked up her skirt, stretched a leg out onto the counter like a clumsy ballet dancer, and tried to pull the tie out.

"...going deep into the forest and pulling plants out to examine their roots..."

Miss Tutley clambered onto the counter and reached under her skirt to try and wrench the tie out.

"...watching the tall trees sway in the wind..."

Miss Tutley sat on the counter and waved her legs wildly in the air.

"...trekking through marshes and stomping the mud off our boots..."

Miss Tutley jumped off the counter and hopped in place, with the tie waving wildly between her legs.

"...such hard work. We were all exhausted at the end of the day..."

Miss Tutley did a wild hula dance, then leaned back against the counter, exhausted. Jack's tie fell out from under her skirt and landed on the floor in a soft crumple.

Martha turned around to face Miss Tutley, who immediately tried to pose in a ladylike manner, and offered Martha a psychotic, clownish grin.

"This is all extremely interesting," Martha said. "I'm so proud of the work I've done to make him a success. You are happy with him, aren't you?"

"Oh yes!" Miss Tutley blurted as she tried to kick Jack's tie under the counter. "I'm happy. Happy happy happy!"

Martha walked back toward the counter. "I'm so glad."

Miss Tutley quickly stepped forward. She grabbed Martha's arm and haphazardly swung her around to face the door.

"Well Margaret, thank you for coming..."

Martha stumbled forward. "Again, it's Martha. And I must apologize for Jack..."

Miss Tutley abruptly stopped. "Why?!"

"Because he ran out on me..."

Miss Tutley swung Martha around to face her. "This time, it's not my fault! It was all his idea!" she implored.

"I know dear. Now don't you pay any more attention to him," Martha said as she playfully wagged a finger at her.

"I'll try," Miss Tutley said sweetly.

She walked Martha to the door, with Jack's tie snagged on her heel. Martha opened the door, then turned to Miss Tutley.

"I hope you will remember our understanding to play fair during the election, since we both want the same things..."

"How could I not? Goodbye Margaret," Miss Tutley said sweetly.

Miss Tutley smiled and waved congenially as Martha left the room. Miss Tutley took a few steps outside the classroom, and watched Martha disappear around a corner. Her fake cordial visage swiftly faded. She sneered cunningly. A man and a woman approached her.

"Miss Tutley?" the woman asked. "I think we're next..."

Miss Tutley regarded her as if the woman cut her off in traffic.

"We're closed," she snapped.

Miss Tutley turned on her red-striped tie heel and marched into the classroom. She slammed the door and locked it. The parents glanced at each other, shrugged, and walked away.

Miss Tutley stood at her desk and tapped her heel as she searched through her purse. She brought out Arlene and Jimmy Joe's flyer and fingered it.

"Oh, I'll remember you, Margaret!" she shouted. "But no one else will!"

She laughed manically as she stuffed the flyer in her purse, then pulled out her phone. She regarded the time.

"Oh no, I'd better get ready for my meeting with that stupid horny boy..."

She threw her phone into her purse, then removed her fake spectacles. She quickly undid her hair and shook it out until it grew into a teased mess. She ripped off the antique cameo, the ruffles on her blouse, and undid the three top buttons. She wrenched her floor-length skirt off as if it were fastened by Velcro to reveal a black leather miniskirt, stockings, and high heels. Wonder Woman couldn't have performed a quicker costume change.

She stuffed her school marm outfit under her desk, and stood provocatively, but awkwardly against the front lab counter. She faced the door and awaited her prey.

EIGHTEEN

The school hallways were dark except for the automatic security lights illuminating dark corners and doorways. The only noise in the building came from the vending machine motors. The school, filled with life during the day, felt like an abandoned hospital from a horror film.

All the classrooms were dark, except for Miss Tutley's. Both doors to the lab were closed, but light flooded through the windows, and into the hallway. A person dressed in black crept through the darkened hallway to the rear lab door. They carried a large cage draped with a blanket. The stranger set it on the floor and peered into the classroom. Another person dressed in black arrived at the front lab door.

The new stranger carried a large, tall cardboard box, and set it on the floor beside the door. The two strangers casually waved at each other. They carefully peered through the windows, and into the classroom.

At the front, Alex lay on Miss Tutley's desk, on his back, shirtless, with his jeans undone. Miss Tutley kneeled over him. Her hands pinned his arms to the desk. Her unbuttoned blouse flapped in his face. She kicked off her heels, and they fell to the floor.

She released her grip on him and sensually pulled her blouse from her shoulders to reveal a satiny push-up bra. Alex gulped. She aggressively pinned him again, and he tried to wriggle his way out from under her.

"Miss Tutley," he wailed, "we can't do this. It's not right..."

"Oh Alex, of course it's not right," she breathed, "that's what makes it so wrong..."

"Ummm, isn't that the same thing?"

"Oh, I don't know," she said sensually, "I don't teach philosophy..."

Beneath the desk, another phantom figure reached out, grabbed Miss Tutley's shoes, and retrieved them as if the desk came to life, and ate them for a snack.

"But I am a biology teacher," Miss Tutley continued, "and I know a thing or two about chrome zones and gnomes. I know hot-bodied homosaplings must conjugate themselves."

"That wasn't in my textbook..."

"It's in the teacher's edition."

She leaned forward, ground into him, stuck her tongue out, and almost licked his chest. Alex shut his eyes.

"But... but... Fiona..." he wailed.

Miss Tutley groaned, leaned back, and plopped herself onto Alex's legs.

"But but Fiona!" she imitated in a high-pitched voice. "Oh my God! I am so tired of hearing about that irritating girl!"

"But she's my girlfriend..."

"Exactly! A girl..." she drawled as she thrust her bosom toward him and closed her eyes.

Alex gulped, stared at her, and shook himself from her spell. He quickly leaned forward. As he did, she clumsily rolled backwards and tumbled to the floor in a heap.

Alex leaped from the desk, adjusted himself, and buttoned his jeans. He glanced around wildly for his shirt as Miss Tutley groaned on the floor. He grabbed his shirt from the desk and put it on as he raced to the back door. Miss Tutley unsteadily rose to her feet.

"Alex! Alex, come back here!" she moaned. "I'm a woman. You're... almost a man... we were meant to do this!"

The stranger outside the rear classroom door grabbed the cage, turned, and hid in a dark corner as Alex opened the door, and ran into the hallway.

Miss Tutley grabbed her blouse and fought with it as she tried to put it on and chase Alex. As she ran from the classroom, she put her arms through the wrong sleeves, and it looked like she wore a straight jacket.

"Alex, come back here!" she wailed.

But Alex had disappeared. Miss Tutley stood in the hallway and flailed her arms.

"You can kiss your A goodbye!" she screamed.

"No, I'm kissing your A goodbye," he echoed.

As the front door of the school slammed, the stranger emerged from the dark corner with the cage and slipped into the classroom. At the opposite end, the other stranger opened the front classroom door and slipped inside with the large box.

"Alex! Alex!" Miss Tutley shouted.

She turned and stomped into the lab. She sneezed. She took off her straight jacket blouse, and put it on the right way, buttoning it as she grumbled.

"This never happened at my last high school. Stupid, stupid moral students."

The stranger at the front placed the box next to her desk, slipped out into the hallway, and softly closed the door. The stranger at the back slipped out behind Miss Tutley and closed the door. She turned, regarded the door, and sneezed again.

Miss Tutley walked to her desk and scanned the floor for her shoes. She wheeled around and put her hands on her hips.

"Where are my damn shoes?"

Instantaneously, an arm appeared from under her desk, plopped her shoes on the desk, and disappeared again. Miss Tutley turned and saw her high heels on her desk. She shook her head, sat on the desk, and slipped her shoes on.

"I'm so glad this damn night is over," she moaned. "Stupid crazy Molder woman... Hot, horny ethical jock tease... Whiny entitled ungrateful parents and their stupid kids... babysitting their half-wits while they pull in the big bucks and force me to raise them... stupid stupid people..."

As she reached for her long, black trench coat draped over a chair, she noticed the tall cardboard box beside her desk. A large, red bow decorated the top, with CAUTION: LIVE PLANT written on the side. She cocked her head and furrowed her brow.

"Where did that come from?" She wheeled around. "Jack?" she said hopefully.

Miss Tutley eyeballed the box when it moved. Two long, green vines snaked their way from the air holes and waved to her. Intrigued, she walked to the table and held out a hand as the vines played with her fingers. She twirled her other fingers through the red bow.

"Oh, how thoughtful," she giggled, "a present from one of my many, many, many, many acquaintances." She searched the red bow. "No card... oh well, this makes up for tonight with all those horrible people."

Miss Tutley ripped the bow off and peeled the tape from the box. When she opened the flaps, a large, beautiful, magenta-colored flower slowly rose from the box.

"Ohhhhh," she gasped, fascinated by the flower's beauty and its surprising life-like state.

When she leaned in toward the flower to smell it, the bloom unexpectedly spat yellow dust in her face. At the same time, the once gentle, wispy vines bolted from the air holes and wrapped themselves around her neck.

Miss Tutley coughed, wheezed and choked. She tried to wrench herself away from the now-vicious plant, but the flower from hell pulled her towards it. She grasped the evil vines with both hands, and tried to pry them from her throat, but the harder she pulled, the tighter they secured themselves. She gasped for air and wrestled with the plant still inside the box.

Miss Tutley and her new dancing partner smashed into the desk, and into the overhead projector – sending it crashing to the floor. She body slammed the box into the white board, but the plant remained tenacious. She glanced wildly around the room for a solution. Her bulging eyes narrowed, and she awkwardly slow-danced the plant to the first row where propane gas outlets were located at every station.

Miss Tutley removed her hands from the vines. She turned a valve on, grabbed a flint with her other hand, and lit the gas. A flame shot from the valve. Her eyes bulged again, and she leaned dangerously close to the flame until it scorched the vines. The killer plant appeared to scream as it released the vines from Miss Tutley's throat, then fell harmlessly to the floor.

Miss Tutley collapsed on the counter, lay there for a moment, and massaged her throat. She turned off the gas and stared at the weakened demon plant. When the flower twitched and rose again, she screamed. She lurched off the counter and ran to a supply cabinet. She grabbed a portable torch and turned it on high. She lit the torch and advanced on the demented plant like a crazed assassin.

"Die! Die! Die!"

While she murdered her attacker, she also set the box on fire. The flames grew.

"Uh oh," she said.

Miss Tutley switched off the torch and threw it on the counter. At a lab station, she turned on the tap and tried to cup the water in both hands. She ran to the growing inferno, losing water from the gaps in her makeshift hand vessel, and sprinkled the remaining water over the flames. The fire grew.

Miss Tutley ran to the cabinet again and grabbed the fire extinguisher. She pointed the nozzle at the escalating blaze and squeezed the trigger. Nothing. She stared at it, shook it, and pointed the hose at the flames again. Nothing. She glared at it, and her eyes glazed over at the instructions on the tube.

"I don't have time to read all this!" she exclaimed.

She scanned the room and found another water source: the aquarium. Fire extinguisher in hand, she marched to the aquarium, then stood beside it menacingly.

"Sorry little fishies," she barked as she brandished the extinguisher, "but my life is more important than your pathetic little lives!"

As if she stood in a batter's box, Miss Tutley drew back the extinguisher and swung it against the aquarium. It shattered instantaneously. The sudden tidal wave upended Miss Tutley and carried her and the fish into the fire. The flames hissed and were drowned as water cascaded over them.

Miss Tutley sat amongst the wet, gooey, blackened cardboard and dead killer flower parts. She spit out aquarium plants, and a few fish flopped around in her matted hair. She crawled to her knees, and warily stood as she picked charred, wet cardboard pieces from her once-pristine white blouse.

She turned, glanced at the smoldering apocalypse, and waved at it. "Ah, the janitor can deal with this in the morning. He owes me several favors anyway..."

Miss Tutley reached for her coat and briefcase. She sneezed. As she put on her coat, the biology model at the back moved toward the door. Miss Tutley sneezed again. The model disappeared out the door. A gloved hand reached inside, turned the lock on the doorknob, and closed the door.

Miss Tutley whirled around and stared at the door until her eyes watered. She blinked repeatedly and wiped at her eyes until she sneezed again. She bent over, continuously wheezing and sneezing. Max's rabbit Mr. Fluffy Puffy appeared from under her desk and brushed against her ankle. She gawked at him in horror and tried to scream between sneezes.

"Get... away... you... horrible... beast!"

Miss Tutley stood, and backed away from him, still sneezing, as if she encountered the devil. She grabbed her water bottle from her desk and took a generous gulp. Her eyes bulged, and she performed a huge spit take, spitting out the offensive liquid inside the bottle. Along with her sneezing, she coughed and gasped for air. The skin around her lips turned bright red. She ran to a lab station, turned on the water, and held her face under the faucet, simultaneously drinking and spitting out water.

Miss Tutley turned off the tap and stumbled to a nearby eye wash station where she gazed in the mirror. Her lips were puffy as if she had received several botched botox treatments.

"What dis habbening do be?" she garbled.

She sniffed at her water bottle. In the mirror behind her, Mr. Fluffy Puffy peeked around her desk, stared at her, and hopped toward her. Miss Tutley whirled around and sneezed again.

"Geb daway fum be!" she screamed, then threw her water bottle haphazardly at the gentle rabbit.

Mr. Fluffy Puffy scattered under the counter. Miss Tutley ran to the back door. She briefly glanced behind her and tripped over an electrical cord strung across the aisle. She sailed through the air and crashed head-first into the table filled with biology experiments.

Miss Tutley writhed and groaned on the floor. One experiment, manufactured intestines from a fetal pig, fell from the table, and plopped onto her back. She screamed as an intestine drooped into her face.

Miss Tutley leapt to her feet and ran to the door. The fake intestines dangled off her shoulders like fresh deli sausages, and wrapped around her neck like a warm, comforting, meaty scarf. She wrenched on the doorknob, simultaneously sneezing, coughing and screaming.

"Helbd me! Helbd me! Helbd me!"

She opened her mouth wide and stretched her newfound big lips into various positions to try and get her regular speaking voice back, adding in strange sounds as if she were a professional singer warming up for a concert.

"Owwwwwww… whaaaaaaa…eeeeeeiiiiii… oooooooo… yayayayaya… dooooo… ewewewewew… nininininini…whawhawhahwahwa… mimimimi… hiyahhiyahhiyah…" She felt her lips with her fingers. "Dat feels a bit better."

Mr. Fluffy Puffy peeked out from under the counter, and advanced upon her again. He stopped a few feet from her and wiggled his nose. Miss Tutley quickly turned around. She backed flat against the door, her body tense, and her eyes wild with fright. Her fingers danced kinetically around the doorknob. In between sneezes, she whined and cried.

"Pleeeeeese…" she wailed, "I'm toob young and pretty to die!"

Her mascara cascaded down her cheeks like a televangelist's wife as she wept in defeat. Summoning invisible strength from deep within and gathering the courage to escape the horrible creature that wiggled its nose at her, Miss Tutley resolutely slapped her hands against the door.

"No!" she shouted. "Dis isn't da way Shelley Tutley is going out!"

She turned around and wrenched on the doorknob. The fake fetal pig intestines swung wildly about, and her damp, limp hair dramatically whipped about her head.

"Lemme out! Lemme out! Lemme out!"

Her fingers finally tripped the simple lock, and the door unlocked. She stared at the doorknob in amazement, wrenched open the door, and fled into the hallway.

Miss Tutley glanced back at the classroom and laughed victoriously. "Ha ha, I escaped you crazy rabbit!"

She turned and instantly ran into a tall potted fern. She wrapped herself around it and gave it a big hug. She and the fern fell to the floor.

Miss Tutley detached herself from the fern, then spat out greenery bits. She disentangled the fake pig intestines from around her neck and gaped at a broken fingernail.

"Damn it! Back to Catwoman's Esthetics for a repair job," she said, and bit the broken nail. "She charges a bundle too..."

As she sat on the floor amongst the broken fern leaves and fake pig intestines, and pined for perfect cuticles, Mr. Fluffy Puffy poked his face around the door frame, stared at her. His eyes appeared to glow in the dim light.

Miss Tutley tried to crabwalk backwards. "Get back! Get back!"

She grabbed at the fern leaves and threw them at him. He nibbled them contentedly. She rolled her eyes, struggled to stand, and tried to run away. Her right high heel broke off, however, and she clip-clopped at an abbreviated pace.

At the staircase to the front door, she stopped and glanced behind her. Mr. Fluffy Puffy hopped toward her. She yelped and recklessly descended the stairs. Her other high heel broke off, and she wobbled along the stairs like a drunk puppet. At the landing, her broken shoes caught the mat at the front door. In a unique re-enactment of The Matrix, Miss Tutley catapulted through the air in slow motion – her appendages flailing about her.

"Noooooooooooooooo..." she screamed as she landed headfirst into a food bank donation bin near the front door.

Canned goods, pasta, juice packs, flour, and powdered milk exploded from the bin. As the cans clattered to the floor, and rolled endlessly along the hallway, Miss Tutley struggled not to drown in the donated food. She attempted to swim against the canned tomato soup and sweet green peas but only succeeded in denting them.

She grabbed onto the bin, and draped her arms over the side, exhausted from her late-night swim. Dry pasta tangled in her hair, powdered milk dusted her face, and pasta sauce splattered her white blouse. She glanced at her hands. Another broken nail. She hung her head and groaned.

Mr. Fluffy Puffy appeared on the staircase. Miss Tutley slowly turned her head and glared at him. He wiggled his nose at her.

"No... no... no..." she wailed.

Miss Tutley pulled herself from the bin. She fell to the floor amongst the canned goods and pasta. She clumsily stood, then made her way to the front door. She stumbled over canned baked beans and slipped on crushed cookies and rigatoni. She threw herself at the door, and fell out into the night, where it lightly rained.

She staggered onto the concrete landing and sucked in as much fresh air as her lungs could handle. She wheeled around, ran back to the door, and pushed on it until it slammed shut. She leaned against the door.

"There!" she shouted. "You can't get me now you crazy rabbit!"

Miss Tutley walked across the landing and stumbled to the parking lot. Her car was the only one left in the lot, parked under a bright lamp. She fell against her car, spread her arms wide, and hugged it. She lifted her head to the night sky. She closed her eyes as rain fell on her face, causing the powdered milk to congeal and blotch her skin.

"What is going on?!" she cried out. "I don't deserve this. I only tried to be myself. I'm a good girl... I am. Daddy told me so... he did... all the time..."

She squeezed a hand into her skirt pocket.

"...so did Mommy," she continued. "All those beauty pageants... pretty dresses... perfect little angel... I tried to keep them together... tried to make them happy... did it for them... not me... made them so proud..."

She fumbled in her coat pocket.

"... tried to get good grades... be the best... at everything... gotta be better than them... I showed them... I showed them all... Where the hell are my keys?!!" she screamed.

Miss Tutley shoved a hand in her other coat pocket. Instantly, she let out an ear-splitting scream and flung her hand from her pocket. A small scorpion latched onto her hand.

She shrieked continuously as she whirled around the parking lot in the rain. She danced under the lamp as she tried to shake the scorpion from her hand. Anyone who watched her performance from a distance would think she performed a highly choreographed dance sequence for a 1980s music video.

Miss Tutley knelt on the wet pavement and took off her right high heel. She placed her palm flat on the pavement, raised her shoe in the air with her other hand, and repeatedly bashed the scorpion and her hand as if she were beating dough.

"Die! Ow! Die! Ow! Die! Ow! Die! Ow!"

The scorpion finally let go. She hung her head, let out a huge sigh, and stood. She put on her mangled shoe and menacingly stood over the fatally wounded scorpion like a giant about to destroy a tiny village. She lifted her foot and stomped on the scorpion, grinding it into oblivion as if she were trying to put out an eternal flame.

Miss Tutley took in several long breaths and exhaled them theatrically. She thrusted her arms into the air, shook her hands, and closed her eyes as the rain pelted her face.

"Where are my keyyyyyyyyyys?!" she cried out, exasperated.

She glanced at the school and pointed at the front door. "I am not going back in there," she said resolutely.

She turned to her car, grasped the driver's door handle with both hands, and gave it a mighty yank. Surprisingly, the door opened, and she soared backwards toward a mud puddle like an Olympic swimmer off the blocks to do the backstroke, screaming as she reached for the water.

Miss Tutley splash-landed in the puddle. Dazed, she softly wept. She drew her knees to her chest and rocked back and forth in the dirty water. She bowed her head to her knees and wept harder. The rain plastered her hair to her face.

A familiar sound echoed from her car – a continuous, high-pitched beep signaled that car keys were in the ignition with the door open.

Miss Tutley slowly peered through her wet hair. She smiled and laughed. She slapped the puddle repeatedly with her hands like a little girl playing in a mud puddle. She tossed her head back, and released a full, throaty laugh.

She gleefully rose from the puddle. Dirty water dripped off her, and mud clung to her clothes. She spied a pool of clear water nearby and happily skipped to the puddle. She kneeled, and splashed the cold, clear water on her face.

She spat water from her lips like a baby who learned to gurgle. She wiped at the grime on her face and smeared it around even worse. She brushed her matted hair away from her eyes and smiled satisfactorily. She stood and hobbled to her car.

As she approached her car, the beep grew louder. She stuck her head in the open door and stared at the keys in the ignition. She stamped her feet, threw her head back, and laughed hysterically.

"I'm going crazy crazy crazy crazy crazy..." she howled as she sang the melody to some long-forgotten pop song.

Miss Tutley plopped herself in the front seat and shut the door. The beep stopped.

"Good little beep," she told her car as she patted the dashboard.

She regarded herself in the rear-view mirror, and brushed the matted, wet hair from her forehead. She attempted to wipe the mascara from her face but only succeeded in smearing it further. She giggled as she played with the black goo, then drew cat whiskers on her upper lip.

"Rowwwwrrr," she purred, and pawed at the mirror. "This kitty has claws."

Miss Tutley smiled, satisfied with her new look. She buckled her seatbelt, started the car, put it in reverse, and happily drummed her fingers on the wheel as if she didn't have a care in the world. She made a sharp turn, hit the lamp post, and sheared off the front bumper.

She stopped, casually glanced out the window, and shrugged her shoulders.

"Meh."

She drove away as she bopped along to a song in her head. Her fingers tapped the steering wheel, and she silently mouthed the words. She turned on the radio. 'Touch Me' by Samantha Fox played. Her eyes brightened, and she excitedly cranked the volume. She waggled her head to the beat and sang along.

"This is the night! This is the time we've got to get it right. This is the night! Touch me, touch me, I want to feel your body..."

As Miss Tutley sharply turned the steering wheel to the left, the dummy biology model rose in the backseat.

"Your heartbeat next to mine! This is the night!"

High beam headlights from an oncoming car blinded Miss Tutley. As she jerked the wheel violently to the right, and touched her brakes, the dummy slammed against her seat.

"Touch me! Touch me now!"

The dummy's right arm flew over her shoulder. She screamed as she stared at the arm draped over her chest with its missing skin and exposed tendons. She glanced in her rear-view mirror. The dummy stared back with its terrifyingly benign facial expression, missing skin, one bulging eyeball, and blonde wig.

Miss Tutley screamed louder.

She jerked the steering wheel back and forth as she tried to get the dummy off her but only succeeded in wrapping it further around her. She panicked, and her foot flubbed the brake pedal as she attempted to stop the car. Ultimately, she lost control and screamed again.

The car careened off the highway, sailed majestically through the air, almost in slow motion, and smashed through a Martha Molder roadside election billboard. On the sign, a beaming Martha waved, with the slogan: GOOD RIDDANCE – TO SOCIALIST HELL! The car crashed through the 'to socialist hell' and left the 'Good riddance.'

The car swept through bushes and severed the tops off several trees before it eventually landed in a heap in a ravine. Serene silence followed for a moment before the car burst into flames, and exploded, lighting the night sky like a fireworks celebration.

NINETEEN

Max and Marc were asleep in Max's bed. The blinds were closed but the sun filtered through the cracks and shone thin lines of light on the two boys. Marc's arms were spread wide as he soundly slept on his stomach. Restless, Max twitched and rolled over onto his back. A moment later, he rolled to his side and wrapped his arms around himself.

Finally, Max's tormented sleep caused him to violently roll toward Marc and crash into him, almost pushing him off the bed. Max immediately woke. Marc stirred, and groaned as his long limbs came to life.

"What the hell?" he questioned. He propped himself on his arms, and stared at Max. "What is the problem? Was I hogging the sheets or something?"

"No... no," Max said. "I had the horrible Tutley dream again..."

Marc turned onto his side to face Max. "Oh no. Did she attack and murder you again?"

"No! This time, I killed her," Max said. "Do you think it means something... you know... now that we've... done something about her?"

"Maybe. The mind does crazy things when you're in la la land."

Marc reached over and stroked Max's arm.

"Did you scream?" he asked.

"When?"

"Now, after your nightmare."

"I dunno. Probably. It always feels like I do."

Marc rolled onto his back and put his hands over his face. "Oh no. No no no no..."

"What?"

"What?! Are you kidding me?" he whispered. "Your crazy mama's gonna be wondering what all the noise is... if she didn't hear us last night..."

"Awww, we were quiet..."

"I'm not even supposed to be here!" Marc hissed.

He drew back the sheets and leapt from the bed. Max lay back, and watched Marc as he quickly collected his clothes, and put them on. Max smiled.

"You're beautiful..." he mused.

Marc stood beside the bed, shirtless, and shook his hands at Max.

"I can't believe you're taking this so casually. Your mom... your mom!" he whispered sharply as he pointed to the door.

"You're right, she'd be here in a flash, but she's not. I know her. Something's wrong."

"Anyway, it's late," Marc said as he moved to the window, and peered out the blinds. "We gotta go..."

"Okay, okay..."

Max tumbled from the bed and put on his clothes. Marc popped his shirt over his head and slipped into his runners.

"What do you think is gonna happen today?" Marc asked.

"You mean with Tutley?"

"Yeah."

"Hopefully she's gone forever, and we can get a real teacher."

"They might be worse."

"Ha! Impossible."

Max frowned as he stared past Marc to the empty table where Mr. Fluffy Puffy's cage usually sat.

"Hey, Mr. Fluffy Puffy is gone!"

Marc turned around. "Wasn't he here when we came in last night?"

"I don't know. It was dark and late..."

"Well, he couldn't have hopped far."

Max peered at Marc and playfully hit him.

"Shut up. If she's done something with him, I'll..."

"Your mom?"

"Yeah. She hates him. Something about him spreading disease or something..."

Marc stifled a laugh, then pointed to the bookcase against the wall.

"Hey," he said as he walked to bookcase, "if you ever need a replacement Mr. Fluffy Puffy, you always have this one."

Marc reached out and took the stuffed animal from the shelf.

"Ewwww," he moaned as he passed the stuffed rabbit from one hand to the other, "what is in this thing?"

"Gel," Max said.

"Gel?"

"Yeah, to make it feel more life-like."

Max took the stuffed animal from Marc. He held it tight against him.

"When you hold it for a little while, the gel warms, and it feels like a real rabbit."

"Max... that's sick man."

Max offered the rabbit to Marc. "Here, try it."

"No way man," Marc said as he waved his hands. "It's way too disgusting. It feels like I'm holding a corpse."

"How many corpses have you held?"

"Shut up. You know what I mean."

Max put the rabbit back on the shelf. "Okay. You don't know what you're missing."

"Yeah, I do. What happens if you puncture him and he... bleeds?"

"Well, I don't have knife fights with him. He's a cuddle bunny."

"I thought I was your cuddle bunny?"

Max raised his eyebrows. "What?"

Marc laughed.

"Come on, let's go," Max said as he pulled Marc by the arm to the door.

Marc pulled back. "Ummmm, maybe you should go first... to make sure the coast is clear. Remember, I'm not supposed to be here – at all, let alone in your bedroom overnight."

"Okay, I'll go first. Stay here until I give you the all clear to follow."

"Right."

Max placed a hand on the doorknob. He tried to take a deep breath. He peered at Marc, then they smiled and shared a brief kiss. Max slowly opened the door. He poked his head out, glanced both ways, and slipped from the bedroom.

A radio played in the kitchen. Max tiptoed on the soft carpet. At the staircase, he peered over the edge, turned, and waved for Marc to join him.

Marc exited the bedroom and quietly walked along the hallway to join Max. Max crept down the stairs. At the landing, he peered into the kitchen. Jack sat at the table, drank coffee, and read the newspaper. Max leaned as far as he could over the banister to peer further into the kitchen. He hoisted himself onto the railing like a gymnast, using it like parallel bars.

Jack glanced at Max's performance over his newspaper. He half-smiled.

"Morning son..."

Max awkwardly held his position. "Morning Dad..."

"Don't worry, she's in her war room, asleep... or something..." Jack said as he continued to read the newspaper.

Max ended his unexpected gymnastics routine. "Oh... great."

Max glanced at Marc and waved at him to follow. Marc quickly trundled down the staircase and followed Max into the kitchen.

"Good morning Marcus," Jack said as he read his newspaper.

Max sheepishly peered at Marc.

"Good morning Mr. Molder," Marc said politely, and nodded at him.

Jack set his newspaper on the table. He sipped his coffee. "When did you boys get in?"

"Ummmm, late... way late," Max said.

"Max, you should tell me what you're doing," Jack calmly scolded him. "You do have a curfew on a school night. And this is an... unconventional household," he carefully said, "with another parent who is not as... understanding as I am."

"I know. But..."

"It's my fault sir," Marc interrupted. "I never should've stayed in the first place without your permission."

"Do your parents know you're here Marcus?"

"Yes sir."

"Well, it's two more than zero."

Max stared at his runners.

"Max, I don't mind you having friends over," Jack said as he stood. "I don't care if you have your boyfriend over... I don't care if you have a boyfriend!" he shouted, then shushed himself. "Shhhhhhhh!"

Max and Marc exchanged glances.

"Anyway," Jack continued more calmly, "it's breakfast time, so have something..."

"Sorry Mr. Molder," Marc said as he moved past Max to the door, "but I don't wanna see Max's crazy mama... I mean, I have early b-ball practice. Thanks anyway."

"There's some bagels, fruit and juice boxes on the counter," Jack said. He pointed into the kitchen. "You're more than welcome to take some with you..."

Marc stopped, walked into the kitchen, and took a juice box, an apple and two bagels.

"Thanks," he said, and put a bagel in his mouth.

"I'll see you at school," Max said as he came forward and showed Marc to the door.

"You bet," he garbled.

At the door, Marc took the bagel from his mouth, and he and Max shared a shy kiss. Max brushed a few sesame seeds from his lips. They both giggled, then Marc stuffed the bagel back into his mouth and opened the door. He waved to Jack, who smiled and waved back.

"'Bye Marcus."

As Marc left the house, Max held the door open and watched him leave. Max closed the door and walked into the kitchen.

"You really like him, don't you?" Jack asked.

Max walked to the kitchen counter. "Yeah, I do."

"And he likes you."

"Yeah, he does."

Jack sipped his coffee. "Good."

The doorbell rang the first two lines of the refrain of the hymn Bringing in the Sheaves.

"Goddamn I hate that tune," Jack muttered.

"We could always disconnect it Dad."

"Yeah, and your mother would have something twice as annoying installed, like Onward Christian Soldiers."

"True," Max said as he walked to the door. "Maybe Marc forgot something."

Max opened the door to Connie and Sally on the doorstep.

"Oh hi Connie. Hi Sally."

"Hi Max," Sally said, and waved.

"Hello Max," Connie said. "Is your mother home?"

"Ummmm... Dad..."

Jack came to the door. "Hi Connie. Hi Sally. Martha is... sleeping it off... I mean asleep in the basement. I can get her..."

"No!" Connie abruptly said, then grabbed Jack's arm.

"It's great isn't it Mom?" Sally said. "You were worried you'd have to talk to the crazy..." She bit her lip.

"No, please continue Sal," Max said. "It's the truth."

"Well, I wanted to let Martha know I've removed her election sign she installed on my lawn," Connie said.

Jack groaned. "She did what?"

"I put it beside your garage."

"You should have tossed it in a dumpster Mom, like I said," Sally said.

"Connie, I'm so sorry," Jack said.

"Oh, it's not your fault Jack. I plan on running a clean campaign."

"Mom, I told you, you have to get down in the dirt with people like Mrs. Molder otherwise, they'll run over you with their craziness," Sally said.

"Sally..." Connie admonished.

"No Connie, Sally is right," Jack said. "You need to fight fire with fire. But in this case, you keep being the sensible candidate." He leaned in close and lowered his voice. "I have a plan in motion to ensure she never gets elected." He winked.

"Jack, what are you up to?"

A deathly, guttural moan wailed from the basement. Connie and Sally eyed each other.

"Connie," Jack said, pretending he didn't hear the ghastly moan, "you continue with your campaign as you have been. I'm behind you one hundred percent."

"Traitor... adulterer..." Martha moaned from the basement.

Sally grabbed Connie's arm. "Come on Mom before she rises from her crypt..."

"And tries to marry me and Sally again," Max said.

"Exactly," Sally laughed as she pulled on Connie's arm.

"Okay, okay," Connie said as she and Sally stepped off the doorstep.

"Don't worry about anything Connie," Jack said. "Trust me."

Jack and Max waved at them, then Jack closed the door. Max walked into the kitchen and popped two pieces of bread into the toaster. He unscrewed a jar of strawberry jam.

"Dad, Mr. Fluffy Puffy is missing."

"What? No, he's probably around here somewhere..." Jack said, and quickly glanced under the table.

"But his cage is missing too."

"Well, maybe your mother..."

"No, she wouldn't... Would she?" Max opened the refrigerator and grabbed a container of milk. "Why did she sleep in the basement again?"

"We had a little... argument last night."

Max poured the milk into a glass. "And Mom slept in her command center voluntarily?"

"Well, I kinda carried her there. She had a bit too much to drink."

"Oh no, not again. What were you fighting about?"

Jack sipped his coffee and drummed his fingertips on the table.

"Max, I think your mother knows about me and Miss Tutley."

"Oh no... Ummmm Dad, about Miss Tutley, I think your plan to not get mom elected may hit a snag because me and my friends..."

"What Max?"

Max swigged his milk.

Martha flung open the basement door and aggressively pointed at Jack.

"Adulterer!!"

Max did a huge spit take with his milk, and Jack spilled his hot coffee on himself.

"Goddamn it!" he swore.

"Blasphemer!!" Martha screamed, then pointed at him again.

Jack grabbed some napkins, and tried to mop the coffee from his shirt, tie and trousers. Martha stumbled across the floor and stood by the table. She pointed at Jack again and waved around a half-empty vodka bottle with her other hand.

Martha wore the same clothes as the previous night, however, they were completely dishevelled: her blue pant suit was wrinkled and stained with wine; the large flower in her lapel missed most of its petals; her pearls hung backwards around her neck; her bird's nest fascinator was crushed and missing its fruit; her hair was piled high and messy on her head; and her usually perfect makeup was smeared over her face.

"You thought you were so careful..." she sneered at Jack. "But you took it out in public so... so deliberately to embarrass me and my campaign!"

Martha stumbled into the kitchen.

"Ummmm Mom... are you okay?" Max asked.

Martha stared at Max and torturously smiled at him. She walked uneasily toward him with her arms outstretched like a happy zombie.

"My little Maxie Waxie... the innocent... the pure and saintly..."

She grabbed a dish towel, clumsily wiped the milk from his face, turned her head, and stared evilly at Jack.

"... unlike others in this house who are clearly the Satan's spawn."

Jack grimaced and stood. "Okay, enough with the drama. Give me the bottle," he said as he reached a hand to her.

Martha whirled around and clutched the bottle to her chest. "No! This is my knight in shining armour now, not you!"

Martha dramatically moved behind Max and tried to hide. Jack walked into the kitchen, while Max tried not to get caught between them.

Jack waggled his fingers at her. "Give it to me."

Martha popped from behind Max. "Ho ho! Is that what she said Jack?"

"No, it's not," Jack said calmly. "And for the last time, my name is not Jack, it's Juan!" he shouted. "And my last name is Martinez! And so is his!"

Jack wheeled Max around to face his mother.

"I'm Puerto Rican, not Italian, like you explain to everybody! You whitewashed me and Max to fit your ridiculous white bread world. Why I ever agreed to take your name and go along with all this bullshit is beyond me!"

Martha wheeled Max around to face his father.

"To give our son the best opportunities. He can't get ahead with a last name like Martinez. And neither can you!"

Jack wheeled Max around to face his mother.

"I was already a success when you met me. Your last name had nothing to do with it. Admit it Martha, you're embarrassed about my heritage and your son because he's..."

Jack bit his lip. Max's eyes widened.

"Because he's what?"

"Because he's Puerto Rican too!"

Martha wheeled Max around to face his father.

"Oh, I'm embarrassed alright Jack – embarrassed about you cavorting around town with a harlot, bringing home God knows how many different sexual sicknesses from all your sexcapades at all the sex houses, and sex shops you have sex at with your sexpot sex things."

"Now you are embarrassing yourself."

Martha slowly and deliberately pushed Max aside to face Jack. As Max fell against the counter, she flattened her hand against her chest.

"Me? Me?!" Martha laughed. "I'm not the one who wants to let homosexual gay underwear terrorists get married so they can bring their free Canadian health care and their twelve illegitimate children over the border, let us pay for their adopted crack babies who will eventually rape and murder us in our beds because the communist Democrats took all our guns away and traded them for electric cars that destroyed the oil industry and forced all our innocent children to live in fear of being kidnapped and murdered by escaped convicts who were given a slap on the wrist by a Communist-loving socialist appointed justice system!"

Martha quickly took a swig from her vodka bottle.

Silence, except for Martha's labored breathing, and the radio on the counter, which played 'Guantanomera.' Max's toast popped.

"You're drunk," Jack finally said.

"And you're a screwer Jack. You screw families, and you screw whores!"

Martha plopped the vodka bottle on the counter and wobbled to the kitchen table. She grabbed the table with both hands and humped it with exaggerated thrusts.

"'Give it to me! Give it to me Jack!' Is that what she said? Or did she call you Mr. Molder to keep it professional. 'Give it to me Mr. Molder!' Is that what she said?"

Max stared at his mother, his eyes as big as frisbees. Jack grabbed the vodka bottle. He walked to the sink and poured the contents into the drain. Martha threw her arms in the air and waved emphatically at Jack.

"No! No! No!" she wailed. "It's my life blood, my only escape from this Godless socialist insanity!"

Jack glared at her as the liquor disappeared down the drain. Martha's eyes bulged. She bulldozed her way to the counter and pushed Max aside. She grabbed the jar of strawberry jam, a knife, and quickly spread jam blobs on her palms. She turned around and held her hands out.

"I command you to stop!" Martha announced. "I'm stigmatic!"

Jack cocked an eyebrow to the ceiling.

"Ummmm Mom..." Max said, "that's strawberry jam."

Jack emphatically shook the liquor bottle empty. Martha ran to him and tried to grab it.

"No, no!" she cried. "It's my only friend in this world surrounded by sex-crazed adulterers, and raping and pillaging illegal immigrants!"

Jack set the empty bottle on the counter and grabbed Martha by the shoulders.

"Martha!" he shouted as he peered deep into her eyes. "Stop it! You're acting crazy!"

Martha stared blankly at Jack, then glanced at Max for confirmation. Max vigorously nodded his head. Martha softened her demeanor.

"We'll talk about this later," Jack said, "when you're sober."

Martha gazed at him with a twisted, cartoonish grin.

"If you say so dear," Martha cooed in a controlled, deliberate voice. "I'll make everything better, you'll see."

Jack grimaced at her forced contentment. As he released her shoulders, Martha lurched away from him, and flung her arms out at Max. She awkwardly grabbed his face and squeezed his lips together.

"Oh, my beautiful little Maxie Waxie," she cried, "it's not your fault. It's not your fault your father is controlled by Satan."

She pawed at his face and smeared strawberry jam over his cheeks and lips.

Jack gently pulled her away from Max. "Come on now dear..."

Martha stared at Max with a tortured smile. She relinquished her hold on him and lightly floated her arms in the air as if she were performing a traditional Hawaiian luau dance.

Jack led her to the staircase. "That's it, to the bedroom to beddy bye."

Martha regarded him oddly. "But it's the daytime..."

"But you've had a looooonnnnng day and need some rest."

Martha stepped onto the stairs and thought for a moment. "Oh, okay."

"We'll talk more when I get home tonight."

She regarded him lovingly and caressed his face. "Sure dear, whatever you say."

Max joined his father at the staircase. They watched Martha as she slowly lurched up the stairs. At the top, she spun around with one hand on the banister and faced Max and Jack. She dramatically put a hand over her heart.

"As God is my witness, I'll never eat strawberry jam again!" she announced, before she fluttered along the hallway, disappeared into her bedroom, and closed the door.

Max and Jack eyed each other. Jack glanced at his watch.

"I gotta get outta here," he said as he turned and walked to the table.

Jack grabbed his jacket slung over a chair, lifted his briefcase from the floor, and set it on the table. He put on his jacket.

"Come on Max, I'll give you a ride to school..."

Max stood rooted at the stairs. He repeatedly glanced from Jack to the top of the staircase and motioned helplessly with his arms.

Jack grabbed his briefcase. "Come on Max."

"But Dad," Max finally said, "Mom..."

"Don't worry about her. This is just another outrageous stunt."

"But Dad, I've never seen her like this before – drunk and crazy. I think she needs help."

"I totally agree. Right now, she needs to sleep it off. But later, I'm putting an end to all this nonsense. I can't take anymore."

Max stared at his father and measured his comments.

"Is it me? Is this my fault?"

"What? No."

"Is it because I'm gay?" Max asked. He shuffled into the kitchen and hung his head. "I'm an embarrassment. It sent her over the edge..."

Jack set his briefcase back on the table. "Oh my God, no."

"I'm the problem," Max said as he tried to walk past his father. "I am."

Jack reached out, grabbed Max's arm, and put his hands on his shoulders.

"No!" he shouted. "Look at me Max." Jack took Max's face in his hands. "Look at me."

Max peered at his father. Jack wiped away his son's tears with his thumbs.

"This isn't your fault. Your mother, she's always possessed strong views, but they've become more extreme recently, not because of you, but because the times we're living in have screwed up so many people. And her wanting to get into politics to make people more afraid doesn't help either."

Max tried to smile.

"So, don't think what is going on with her or between me and her is your fault. It's not. And don't you ever think anything is your fault because of who you are. I'm so proud of you Max, and I'm proud you're my son."

They hugged, and Max cried against his father.

"Thanks Dad."

As Max pulled away, he glanced at Jack's shirt. "Sorry, I kinda messed your shirt..."

"It'll dry."

Jack put an arm around Max's shoulder. "So, are you ready to go?"

"Yeah."

Jack grabbed his briefcase from the table, and Max snatched his backpack by the front door. Max opened the door, and they exited the house. Jack shut the door behind him.

When the front door closed, Martha opened her bedroom door and theatrically thrusted her head out. She peered around the corner and smiled deviously. She slowly and exaggeratedly tip toed along the hallway to the stairs. She descended the staircase, histrionically high kicking her legs as if she were in a Broadway musical chorus line.

At the bottom, she dramatically tip toed her way into the kitchen as if the slightest noise would alert a vicious guard dog. In the kitchen, she hurried to the counter where she grabbed the telephone. She deliberately dialed a number, leaned back against the counter, and licked the jam off her hands. She swiped the empty liquor bottle from the counter, tilted her head back, upended the bottle, opened her mouth wide, and tried to get every drop from the bottle.

"Give it to me... uh huh..." Martha mumbled. "I'll bet... I'll give it to you... you haven't seen crazy... uh huh..."

Martha tried to stick her tongue inside the bottle neck to get the last drop and got it stuck as she talked into the phone.

"Thinnnnny Thoe! Ah! Thinnnnny Thoe! Ah!!" she blurted before her tongue popped from the bottle. "Jimmy Joe!... It's Martha Molder... Martha... Your new disciple... No, not popsicle – disciple. Your new follower, and spreader of the great philosophy for your wonderful church... Hi, hi. We need to move on our plan. Now."

Martha smiled deviously, threw her head back, and howled.

"Vengeance is mine sayeth me!"

TWENTY

The decibel level in the school hallways drowned out the announcements from the public address system. A buzz filled the air – as if a massive incident occurred but hadn't been officially announced. Rumours, innuendos and general gossip ruled the hallways.

Students noisily chattered in small groups. Often, one student from the group left, and moved to another pod to relay new information. While they talked to each other, their heads were buried in their cell phones. Text alert notifications continuously sounded in the hallways, in classrooms, and outside the school.

Police officers were stationed at the front door. The food bank donation bin, and the mess surrounding it, were cordoned off with police tape. Officers were stationed outside the biology lab doors.

A short distance away, Miss Tutley's biology class gathered in a circle, and talked quietly amongst themselves. They consulted their cell phones and watched the two police officers.

"What's the latest Jen?" Sarah asked.

Jenny glanced at her phone. "Same. A car crash last night."

"Nothing about what kind of car or if a dumb bleached blond twit drove it?"

"Nope."

"We should have gone to the crash site and got some intel," Robin said.

"Intel? This isn't NCIS," Sarah said. "And you're not Hetty. We want to know if the incompetent tart is gone from our lives," she hissed.

Fiona put a hand on her shoulder. "Okay Sarah, try and keep it together."

"I'm trying," Sarah said through gritted teeth. She left the huddle and pounded the wall with her fist.

"Easy," Alex said. "We don't want to draw any attention to ourselves."

Sarah scowled and leaned against the wall. Blue-tinted, mirrored sunglasses were stuck in her wild, unkempt hair, now streaked with blue highlights. Her jeans were tight and torn. She wore black, knee-high, stiletto boots, and a lime green shirt with the arms cut off. The red X on her forehead displayed an even deeper shade of red.

"No, we don't want that," Robin said as he stared at her.

"Shut up Binster," she spat.

"Did anyone leave anything here last night the cops could find?" Fiona asked.

"I left my dirty gym clothes in my locker..." Elliott said.

"No, I mean at... the scene," Fiona said, and thumbed toward the lab.

They shook their heads.

"And everyone wore gloves, right?"

They nodded.

"Good... good. We'll have to wait and see what's going to happen..."

"But this is torture!" Robin said.

"Binster, you know what was torture? Her," Sarah said as she pointed to the lab. "This here," she said as she spread her arms wide, "is like waiting for the lottery numbers to come in."

"But... but I've never done anything like this before," Robin said. He stared at the officers and hyperventilated.

Alex clamped a hand onto Robin's shoulder. "Keep it together Binster," he whispered.

"I-I don't know if I can..." he wailed.

Sarah rolled her eyes. "Holy crap! This is the time you decide to have a nervous breakdown – in front of the police?!"

"Alex," Fiona said, "take him somewhere, will you?"

Alex nodded. "Come on Binster." Alex put an arm around Robin's shoulder. "Let's go get some water or something..."

"Yeah, or something," Sarah said, "like some lithium."

Alex guided Robin from their small group, and they disappeared around a corner.

"Sheesh, he helps kill his biology teacher, and he goes all to pieces," Sarah said. She dug her sunglasses from her hair and propped them on her nose.

Marc turned the corner at the other end of the hallway, dressed in his practice gear, and an athletic bag slung over his shoulder. He waved to his friends, and Jenny pointed at him.

"Hey, here comes Marc."

He passed the two officers who stood by the biology lab, careful not to make any deliberate or sustained eye contact with them.

"Wow, things have escalated since I got here this morning," he whispered to his friends as he joined their group.

"Have you heard anything?" Jenny asked.

"Rumours... drug addicts broke into the lab... kids broke into the school and made a mess... Tutley was kidnapped... Tutley was in a car accident..."

"Tutley was an incompetent, man-eating idiot who drove her students crazy, so they killed her..." Fiona said.

"No, haven't heard that one yet," Marc said.

"Good," Elliott said, "the heat's off us."

"Hey, where's Alex and Robin?"

"Hmmmppfff," Sarah growled, "Binster experienced a total breakdown in front of the police, so Alex dragged him away."

"Oh man..."

"Where's Max?" Fiona asked. "Last we heard, he was still at home. Something about his mother having a meltdown..."

"Oh no..." Marc said. He pulled his bag off his shoulder, unzipped it, and brought out his cell phone. "Everything was fine before I left..." he said as he scanned his messages.

His friends stared at him.

Marc glanced at them. "What?"

"You stayed at Max's house last night?" Jenny asked.

"Yeah, why?"

"With Max?"

"Yeaahhhh," Marc drawled.

"Holy shit, no wonder his mother had a meltdown," Fiona said.

"She didn't even know I was there..."

"You dirty dog," Sarah said.

"What?"

"Right under his loopy mother's nose. You're lucky she didn't catch you and turn you over to her Nazi friends for sodomizing her son."

Marc shook his head. "Mrs. Molder doesn't know any Nazis..."

Sarah nodded and rolled her eyes. "Uh huh..."

Marc put his phone in his pocket. "Max is on his way. Apparently, his mom found out his dad and Tutley were screwing around."

"Oh, poor Max," Jenny said. "I'm so glad you two are together so you can take him away from all his home craziness."

Jenny put an arm around Marc, and they smiled. "Me too."

"Hey, did anyone study for that Politics test this afternoon?" Elliott asked.

"Test?" Marc asked incredulously.

"Yeah, it's worth a lot..."

Sarah peered at him over her sunglasses. "Are you kidding me Elliott?"

"No... I studied..."

"You mean after you came home from last night's murder and mayhem, you calmly studied for a test?"

"Yeah."

"Elliott," Fiona said, "you're a cold, calculating little monster. We misjudged you."

"But... but my parents know when I have any test or project due," he whined. "My teachers send them my schedule everyday so I won't miss them."

"Elliott!" Sarah snapped, "there's not gonna be any freakin' politics test today! After what happened here, they'll probably cancel classes and send us home... or make us all hold hands and have thoughts and prayers for a brainless twit teacher who ruined all our lives!"

Sarah folded her arms and propped herself against the wall. Elliott stared at her clothes, peered into her hair, and at the red X on her forehead.

"Ummmm Sarah, what's happened to you? Why is the X still on your forehead? And why is it more red now than ever?"

"Oh, come on Elliott!" Sarah implored. "Tutley was an imbecile, but she opened my eyes. What the hell are we all doing here anyway?"

Elliott scanned the corridor. "In the hallway?"

Sarah took off her sunglasses and put them in her hair.

"No! In school. Being a good student. Trying to be the best. Where does it get anyone? When a simpleton like Tutley can make it, why should I even try?"

Jenny stepped forward and put a hand on Sarah's arm. "Elliott's right Sarah. Don't let Tutley get to you. She was the worst teacher ever, but now she's gone... we think..."

"Yeah, Tutley slipped through the cracks," Marc said. "Think about all the great teachers we do have... who care."

"Don't blow it Sarah. You're too smart," Fiona said.

"Pffffft," Sarah said as she waved off her friends' comments.

A scruffily dressed boy sauntered to Sarah.

"Hey Sarah, thanks for getting rid of Tutley for us."

He furtively glanced around, took a joint from his pocket, and stealthily slipped it to her. Sarah's friends stared at her with raised eyebrows, while Elliott's mouth opened so wide, an Airbus could have flown into it.

"Ummmm thanks, thanks a lot," Sarah said quickly.

"Hey, no problem... killer," the boy said. He laughed and walked away.

The bell to start the day rang. Sarah took the sunglasses from her hair and put them on her nose. She linked arms with Elliott.

"Well, come little lambs, time for more scholastic propaganda..."

As she walked away, Elliott remained rooted to the floor. Sarah sprang back into him. She gawked at her friends.

"What?"

"Sarrrrahh," Elliott whined, "that's jerk-off Jeremy! Everyone knows he's a pot head."

"Well duh!"

"And right in front of the cops!" Fiona hissed as she motioned to them.

Sarah dismissively waved a hand at them. "They didn't see nothin'."

"Never mind that," Marc said. "You told someone what we did? Are you nuts?"

"I didn't tell him we did anything," Sarah said. "I might have told a few people how she humiliated me, and it was curtains for her."

"We made a pact we weren't gonna tell anyone about our plan, remember?" Marc said.

"Ohhhh, that bitch!" Elliott spat. "She forced you to make curtains for her?!"

Sarah put an arm around him. "No, Elliott... no."

"Don't mention this to Robin," Jenny said. "He'll have a complete breakdown."

Alex and Robin walked around the corner and returned to their friends.

"How are you, Robin?" Jenny asked.

"Oh, he's fine," Alex said as he punched Robin in the arm.

Robin massaged his arm and glared at Alex.

"The great news," Alex continued, "is the car crash last night..."

"Yeah... yeah, what about it?" Sarah asked excitedly.

"We heard Tutley won't be in today, and the car in the accident matches her car."

Sarah laughed evilly and clasped her hands together. "There is a God!"

Elliott took a deliberate step away from her. "Sarah, you're scaring me..."

"Oh, come off it you guys. Have you forgotten how she treated us? Elliott, you're an overweight elephant. Robin, you're a nerdish virgin. Jenny, you're as plain as vanilla yogurt. Fiona, you're an Irish hothead. Alex, you're a dumb jock. Marc, and Max, you guys are her racial/gay punching bag..."

Sarah stepped toward her friends and jabbed a finger at them.

"So, no matter what's happened to her, she deserved it," she snapped.

The principal, Mr. Douglas, quickly strode along the hallway. He clapped his hands.

"Okay people, please disperse to your first class. I know there's excitement here today, but please move on. Please..."

Students lingered in the hallway and tried to peer into the biology lab where disaster and chaos resided.

"Thank you... keep moving... quickly now..." he said.

Meanwhile, Miss Tutley's students stood in place. He regarded them.

"Are you people Shelley's... I mean Miss Tutley's students?"

"Yes," they groaned.

"Come with me."

He walked to the biology lab. The teens shared looks and slowly shuffled after him.

"Quickly now," he said as he waved at them.

The students stopped with Mr. Douglas at the lab door.

"I need to speak with these children privately," Mr. Douglas said to the officer. "They're her students. May we go inside for a few minutes?"

"Well, there's still quite a mess sir, especially at the front..."

"I know, but what I have to say must be said in private."

The teens eyeballed each other.

"Okay sir, but please don't go beyond the police tape."

"We won't. Thank you."

"These are all Miss Tutley's students?"

"Yes, I believe so."

"We'll need to speak with them individually later..."

Elliott whined. Marc poked him in the ribs. Robin hyperventilated. Alex gripped his arm.

"I'm sure it can be arranged," Mr. Douglas said.

The officer nodded, opened the door, and stood aside.

"Okay people, you heard the officer, please stand at the back of the classroom."

"And don't touch anything..." the officer added.

"And don't touch anything," Mr. Douglas repeated.

The students filed into the classroom filled with the strange feeling of being led to their execution and getting ready to party on New Year's Eve.

TWENTY-ONE

In the lab, police tape divided the class in two. At the front, water from the aquarium still dripped onto the floor, and the killer plant and its cardboard box were a charred, drowned mess. As the students entered, they instantly contorted their faces at the putrid, smoky stench, and murmured amongst themselves.

"Alright, alright, settle everyone," Mr. Douglas said.

The students gathered at the back. Mr. Douglas closed the door, stood behind the last counter, and faced the students.

"As you can see, we had an incident here last night. Now, I don't know what happened, but we'll find out later. Right now, we have..."

Mr. Douglas' voice cracked, and he put a hand to his mouth to stifle the high-pitched squeal that tried to escape.

"...we have," he continued, "a situation..."

Sarah and Fiona reached out simultaneously and grasped each other's hands.

"I have some extremely distressing news..." Mr. Douglas said.

The door opened, and Max fell into the room. He scanned the class, closed the door, and attempted to casually walk toward his classmates who stared at him.

"Molder," Mr. Douglas said, "why are you so late?"

"I-I'm sorry, my parents... we... my mother..."

"Well never mind now. Get in here. I have something important to say."

Max found Marc and stood beside him.

"What's going on?" Max whispered to Marc.

"I think it's about Tutley."

They smirked.

"Now, as I said," Mr. Douglas continued, "I don't know what happened after the parent-teacher interviews, but it may be connected to something the police are... ahhhhhh!"

Mr. Douglas screamed and flailed his arms as he peered to his feet. Mr. Fluffy Puffy had silently sidled to his pants leg and nibbled on his shoelaces. Mr. Douglas bent over, seized the rabbit, and cradled it in his arms.

"Whose hare is this?"

"Mr. Fluffy Puffy, there you are!" Max said.

"Mr. Fluffy... Puff..." Mr. Douglas sputtered. "What a ridiculous name. Why is this rabbit here?"

Elliott thrusted an arm in the air. "Oh! Oh! Because his mother and father were rabbits?!"

"No, no, what is it doing here?" Mr. Douglas said as he pointed to the floor.

"I-I don't know..." Max stammered. "He's supposed to be at home."

Mr. Douglas pushed the rabbit toward him. "Well, put him away Molder!"

Max quickly came forward and took the rabbit from Mr. Douglas. Mr. Fluffy Puffy wiggled his nose. Max walked back to Marc, who took the rabbit and carefully put it in Max's backpack. Mr. Fluffy Puffy poked his head from the backpack.

"Now," Mr. Douglas continued, "as I said before... ahhhhhhhh!"

Mr. Douglas took a step back, slipped, and fell to the floor, screaming. Everyone leaned forward and tried to peer over the lab counter. Mr. Douglas slowly stood. He raised his hand and held the fake eye from the biology dummy between his thumb and forefinger.

"Whose eye is this?"

"It's mine, man," Sarah drawled.

"What? That's ridiculous," Mr. Douglas said. "And take off those sunglasses. This isn't 'Beverley Hills 90210' or whatever you kids watch these days."

Crickets chirped.

Mr. Douglas leaned forward and pointed to a boy with a cardboard box in his hands.

"Put those crickets away son."

"Yes sir," the boy said. He put the box in a cabinet under the counter.

"Now," Mr. Douglas said, irritated, "is that it? Or is there any other bizarre interruption I must deal with? A pizza delivery? Frogs falling from the ceiling tiles? A visit from Santa Claus?"

The students glanced at each other.

"Dude's about to lose it," Alex whispered to Fiona.

"I think he already has."

Mr. Douglas retrieved a handkerchief from his jacket pocket and dabbed at his brow. He took a deep breath and steadied himself.

"Kids, I... I have the most terrible news... terrible..."

He put the handkerchief to his mouth to stifle another high-pitched crack in his voice.

"That wonderful woman... those stately, supple legs... those curvaceous strong hips... those perky ample breasts... the long, flowing golden hair... the child-like laugh... the innocent, not-quite-there look..." He burst into tears. "Oh God, Miss Tutley is dead!"

Shocked silence held the room before the students erupted in a loud cheer. They raised their arms in the air and clenched their fists. They hugged each other. They hooted and hollered. They danced. Some cried in elation. Some thanked whatever deity they believed in.

"Stop it! Stop it!" shouted a horrified Mr. Douglas.

Elliott, Jenny and Robin high-fived each other. Max and Marc, and Alex and Fiona beamed widely, and hugged each other. Sarah did a spaced-out hippy dance.

Max stopped, waved at his friends, and thumbed toward the door. "Guys, guys, remember the police..."

Outside the classroom, the officer turned her head at the ruckus and furrowed her brow.

"What the heck?" she murmured.

She grabbed the doorknob and opened the door. The happy celebration turned into a sorrowful memorial. The students sobbed. Some were inconsolable. Some squatted to their knees and cried. Some hugged each other and cried. A few were slumped on the counter, including Max. He sobbed while he pounded the countertop with his fist.

"Why! Why! Why!" he cried. "She was the best teacher ever!"

Marc patted him on the shoulder. "I know. I know. It's such a loss..."

Sarah, her face twisted in anguish, angrily shook her fists at the ceiling. "Noooooo! Take me instead!"

Elliott put an arm around Jenny's shoulder as she wept. "She was like a sister to me..."

Fiona and Alex hugged. She leaned back and gazed deep into his eyes.

"Why do bad things always happen to good people? Why Alex?"

The officer turned to Mr. Douglas for an explanation.

"I-I... told them their teacher died..." Mr. Douglas stammered.

Sarah faced the officer and amplified her wailing. "What are we going to do without her? What a wonderful woman! We're lost – lost I tells 'ya!"

The officer sympathetically nodded at Mr. Douglas. "The poor kids. I'll let you have some privacy."

The officer closed the door and walked away from the classroom. As soon as she left, the students ceased their staged mourning and instantly resumed their celebration.

"Ughhh, I almost barfed putting on that show... Me too... Alright!... Finally!... I didn't think we'd ever get rid of her!... Do you believe it!... This calls for a celebration!... Let the news be spread, the wicked witch at last is dead!"

Mr. Douglas twisted his face in horror again at the students' vindictiveness.

"Kids! Stop this at once! This isn't right!"

Two students sang the chorus of the song 'Na Na Hey Hey Kiss Him Goodbye', and the entire class joined in.

"Na na na na, Na na na na, Hey hey hey, Goodbye."

Mr. Douglas tried to raise his voice above the chant. "Stop! Stop!" he yelled. He shook his arms and waved his hands at them. As the chant grew louder and with more resonance, the students waved their arms in the air in unison.

"Na na na na, Na na na na, Hey hey hey, Goodbye!"

Mr. Douglas tore at his hair. "Oh my God, you children are horrible!"

He wept uncontrollably, then ran to the door. He flung it open and fled into the hallway. The door banged closed behind him. The students cheered.

"Fucking awesome!" Sarah exclaimed.

"I know," Fiona said. "Everything fell into place. I can't believe it."

"Neither can I," Alex said. "She's actually gone."

"Getting a little misty there Lopez?" Marc asked.

"Fuck off Johnston."

Marc laughed.

"Wow, Mr. Douglas is upset," Robin said.

"You lose a little something on the side, and your whole world goes to pieces," Max said.

"I know, we should have recorded his performance and showed it to his wife," Fiona said. "She'd wonder who this Tutley woman is who made her husband cry."

"Now we have to do something to, you know, celebrate," Jenny said.

"Jenny's right. Party at Max's house tonight!" Alex said.

The students cheered. "Alright! Party at Max's! Sweet! Whoo hoo!"

"What?!" Max exclaimed. "Are you kidding? First, Mom would blow her top if I even suggested such an idea. Second, she'd kill me if we did. And third, she'd kill you all ten times over before she blinked, and your lifeless bodies hit the floor."

"Your dad would be okay with it right Max?" Fiona asked.

"Well yeah, but mom..."

"Come on Max," Alex implored, "this is a celebration! All we gotta do is come up with a plan to get her out of the house."

"But why my house?"

"Because the party should be held at the house of the person who hated her the most."

"Yeah, that's you Max," Jenny said.

"What?! I'd say Fiona hated her the most."

"We all hated her Max," Fiona said, "but your hate was the most sinister, yet subtle. We all admire you for it."

"She's right Max," Marc said. "All those short stories you wrote about her being sucked into airplane engines, chased by giant sewer rats, falling into a bottomless pit, locked in a cellar and forced to solve a defective Rubik's Cube, and so on..."

"And passing them out all over school," Sarah said. "Everyone reading them in class right under her nose... the clueless twit."

"And don't forget, Max gave her one, and asked her to make photocopies for him," Fiona said. "That's beyond clueless."

"Ha! Ha!" Sarah laughed. "I forgot about that. What a twit," she spat.

"Tutley picked at and insulted everyone Max," Robin said, "but you defended us through your words and gave us a voice."

"The things you wrote," Alex said. "Vicious man! Yeah, you hated her the most dude."

"But... but..."

"Don't try and deny it Molder."

"And those nightmares you have about her," Marc said. "She's under your skin more than you think."

"Even more now because Max knows she and his dad have been boinking," Elliott said.

The teens stared at Elliott.

"Boinking?" Alex asked incredulously.

"What?"

"Yeah Max, you hated her the most," Sarah said. She put her hands on his shoulders and shook him. "Admit it. Own it. Be proud."

"Okay, okay!" Max shouted. "You're right, I hated her. But, you guys, a party? Right after Tutley's death? Do you know how it's going to look?"

Jenny grabbed his arm and spun him around to face her. "Look! We all hated her Max. Half the town hated her..."

"And the other half she slept with," Fiona chimed in.

"What are they gonna do, arrest us all for having a party?"

"But... but Mr. Douglas saw us celebrating. This is gonna look bad..."

"Max is right," Robin said. "The optics are bad?"

"Optics? Optics?!" Sarah shouted. "To hell with the optics. We're celebrating the end of the worst teacher in history. Screw the optics!"

Mr. Fluffy Puffy blinked, then wiggled his nose at everyone.

TWENTY-TWO

Martha opened her front door, quickly stepped out onto the doorstep, and adjusted her oversized sunglasses. She was dressed in red, white and blue as if the American flag had vomited on her. Her shoes were ruby red, not unlike Dorothy's. Her navy-blue slacks and blouse showcased different sized white stars on them. Her jacket resembled something a carnival barker would wear, with wide vertical red stripes on a white background. Her pill box hat consisted of the American flag randomly overlaid on top of itself many times.

Martha carried a large box. She bent down and carefully set it on the doorstep. As she stood, she wobbled a bit, then reached out to the railing to steady herself. She put a hand to her forehead and shook her head. She reached into her purse and fished out her keys. She held them close to her eyes to peer at them, examining each key until she found the one she wanted. She locked the front door, but not before missing the keyhole several times.

Martha turned and stood still on the doorstep. She gauged her surroundings, then took in a couple long, deep breaths. She grasped the box and descended the steps. She walked to her car slowly and meticulously as if the biggest hangover in history resided in her head.

Next door, on her front lawn, Connie Frame kneeled at a flower bed and pulled weeds beside her election sign. When she saw Martha, she froze and pretended to be a lawn ornament. The trowel in her hand shook. With nowhere to hide, she became an easy target like a deer in an open field during hunting season. She tried not to blink, fearing the noise would alert Martha. She gulped, then slowly moved like a panther toward a bush near the property line. At the bush, she gradually peered over the greenery, her eyes wide with fear.

Martha set the box on the ground next to her car, then pressed the remote. The hatch opened, Martha grabbed the box and ungracefully plunked it in the trunk. With Martha's back to her, Connie bit her lip and stood. She wavered and waggled like a cat and carefully stepped out from behind the bush.

Unfortunately, the trowel in Connie's hand became ensnared in a metal wind chime that dangled from a low-hanging tree branch. It was as if Connie had rung a ranch house triangle and yelled 'Come and get it!'

Connie slumped her shoulders, shut her eyes, and flopped her head to her chest as she waited to be pounced upon. On cue, Martha turned and lunged a hand at her.

"Oh Connie, yoo hoo."

Martha carefully walked across the driveway as Connie nodded her head, defeated.

"I'm going out campaigning today," Martha said, "and I wondered if you could help me load my car with signs."

Connie's eyes bulged. "Martha, we're running against each other. You want me to help you with your election signs…"

"Oh, thank you for offering Connie. I have a splitting headache this morning. I don't know why…" Martha rubbed her temples with her fingertips. "You're a life saver Connie, especially since you have nothing to do."

"Well actually Martha," Connie said forcefully as she glanced at her watch, "I have to work on my campaign, since I'm a late entry…"

"You are such a brave little working-class girl Connie. I admire you – hiding the fact you work at a communist radio station, come from a broken home, have a tenuous hold on your underage daughter's life, and now you're fighting for the America you think it should be, no matter how twisted and misguided it is. It's what I tell people while I'm out campaigning."

"You talk about me while you're campaigning?" Connie asked.

"Well sure. The voters deserve to know you kill babies, refuse to let our schools be armed to defend themselves against socialist psychopaths, and let atheist homosexuals run around naked in the street. I leave out your messy divorce and money problems of course. I mean, you soiled your sacred wedding vows in the face of God. He'd probably like to spit on you."

Connie almost moved in case Martha spit on her. Instead, Martha quickly reached out and grabbed her hand.

"This will only take a minute dear..."

"But Martha, I have to..."

"Come on girl."

She whistled at Connie and yanked her hand as if she were a disobedient dog. Connie dropped her trowel and crashed into the wind chimes as she stumbled after Martha into her yard. Martha led Connie to the double garage beside the car. Martha's election lawn sign stood propped against the garage.

"They're in the garage Connie dear."

"Martha, I forgot to mention, one of your election signs appeared on my front lawn..."

"It diiiiiid?" Martha asked, way too incredulously. "My my, how did it get there?"

"Well, I..."

"Well, I'll have to have a talk with the election lawn sign guy..."

Martha clicked a button on her key fob, and the garage door opened to reveal stacks upon stacks of campaign signs. Connie's eyes almost dropped from their sockets.

"All those?" she faltered.

"As much as will fit in my well-equipped SUV with oversized storage capacity."

Connie grimaced.

"Here, I'll help you," Martha said. She took a sign and walked toward her car. "Now, if you could grab fifteen or twenty more..."

Connie bit her lip and muttered to herself as she swiped some signs into her arms.

"I'll grab you, you crazy pushy loudmouth..."

Martha slightly turned her head toward Connie. "What did you say dear?"

"I said these signs are so creative, pretty and... you," Connie said as she followed Martha to her car.

"Yes. So much more American than your boring Communist-colored ones."

Connie eyed the back of a sign. At the bottom left corner in small print, it read: MADE IN CHINA. Martha put her one sign in her car. Connie struggled with the heavy bundle in her arms, then fell with the signs into the trunk.

"Oh my, careful dear," Martha cautioned. "Don't crush my professionally designed campaign brochures with the glossy finish."

"I'm sorry Martha, but they're so heavy and awkward..."

"It's okay Connie. I'm sure you'll be more careful with the next few bundles."

Martha patted Connie on the back and steered her toward the garage. A newer-model, shiny Toyota SUV drove along the street, then turned into Martha's driveway. It stopped, and Enrique, Martha's gardener, stepped from the passenger side.

Dressed in clean, sharp-looking, grey overalls, he had a kind face, thick black hair, and a moustache flecked with silver. A twenty-something young man stepped from the backseat. He wore jeans, a black work shirt, a matching ball cap, and work boots. They walked towards Martha and Connie. Martha's eyes grew big, and she hustled Connie from the yard.

"Well Connie, thank you for your help, but I think I can manage this now," she said quickly as she shoved at Connie.

"But your signs..."

"Oh, I'll manage. It's this darn headache this morning... It comes and goes... It's gone now," she said as she pushed Connie forward.

Connie stumbled. Enrique ran forward to help her. He reached out and grabbed her arm.

"Miss Connie, are you okay?"

"Oh, I'm fine Enrique. I must have tripped... or something," she said as she eyed Martha.

"Rick, what are you doing here? The lawn doesn't need mowing" Martha said.

"Ummmm, Mrs. Molder, you asked me to come and fix the irrigation."

"I did?"

"Yes, yesterday. Remember?"

"Well, it's been so crazy around here the past couple days, I must have forgot."

"It's okay Mrs. Molder. We'll get to work right away," Enrique said. He motioned for the younger man to follow him. "Vamos, Jesus."

"Wait!" Martha shouted, as she threw her arms in the air.

Martha leaned into Enrique. She tried not to let the young man hear her, though she whispered loud enough so everyone could hear.

"Is this young man legal?"

"Legal?" Enrique asked. "He's twenty-two."

"No, no, what I mean is..."

Martha leaned in a bit closer.

"Can he work in the United States?"

Enrique smiled and tried not to laugh.

"Mrs. Molder, this is my son Jesus."

"Oh, oh, ha ha!" Martha laughed, then leaned in close again. "So, he's legal, right?"

"Mrs. Molder, Jesus was born here."

"Oh, sure," Martha said, and winked dramatically at Enrique.

Connie rolled her eyes.

"Well, I think it's great your son is tagging along to get spare work so he doesn't lay about and become a drain on the American economy."

"Mrs. Molder, Jesus graduated from college this year with a degree in environmental science."

"Oh."

"Yes," Enrique continued. "Top of his class. Got a job right away. Nice pay, good benefits. This is his day off, so he's helping me out."

"Oh, great..."

"We're so proud."

He waved to the woman who drove the SUV. She sounded the horn a couple times and waved.

"Is that your wife?" Connie asked.

"Yes Miss Connie. Rosalind, the love of my life."

Martha peered at the car. “Is that a new car Rick? You usually come here in a clattering old jalopy that leaks oil on my pristine asphalt.”

“Oh, I only use it to go to job sites. Otherwise, I drive my new BMW.”

Martha regarded him sceptically. “You have a new BMW and a new SUV?”

“Oh, it’s not my car. It’s Rosalind’s.”

Martha gawked at the car. “It is? I thought you told me your wife cleaned houses?”

Enrique and Jesus shared a muted laugh. “No, no, no Mrs. Molder. My wife owns a company that cleans houses.”

“She does?!” Martha blurted as if it were the most outrageous thing she ever heard.

“Perhaps you heard something else Martha,” Connie offered.

Martha stood speechless.

“Well,” Connie announced, satisfied, “I should be going. Nice seeing you again Enrique,” she deliberately pronounced. “And nice to meet you Jesus.”

“And you Connie,” Jesus said.

“Goodbye Miss Connie,” Enrique said, then whispered to her, “my family is behind you one hundred percent.”

Connie nodded and smiled, then strolled along the driveway. As she passed Rosalind in her car, Rosalind leaned from the open window.

“Excuse me,” she said, concerned.

Connie stopped. “Yes?”

Rosalind pointed to Martha. “That woman...”

“Yes,” Connie groaned.

“Esa mujer esta loca.”

Connie nodded. “Si... si...”

Connie walked to her house. Rosalind beeped the horn again, and waved goodbye to Enrique and Jesus. She backed the car from the driveway, and onto the street. Martha barged past Enrique and Jesus, and waved exuberantly to her, almost clocking the men in the head.

“Goodbye Mrs. Rick!” she shouted. “I love your new car!”

Rosalind nodded, offered a muted smile as she desperately closed her window, and quickly drove away. Enrique and Jesus walked onto the lawn to examine the irrigation spigots. Martha turned and animatedly waved at them.

"Wait!" she screamed, and clip-clopped across the driveway in her ruby-red shoes. "I hate to be a bother..."

Jesus glanced at his father, who remained calm, and regarded Martha kindly.

"... but will you help me load my election signs into the car? Connie tried to help me, but she was so weak, clumsy and awkward, like her campaign. You two with your field-labourer background will finish in no time."

Enrique smiled. "Sure, Mrs. Molder. Where are they?"

"In the garage... oh sorry, the shed... the shed."

"Come on Jesus," Enrique said to his son.

The two men walked to the garage while Martha rearranged her signs in the trunk.

"It's so hard to find good help these days," Martha muttered to herself. "I can't do it all by myself. I wish I could, so it would get done properly. But why should I get my hands dirty? I've paid my dues. My family were immigrants to this country too. They started at the bottom, so why shouldn't they start there too? Why oh why is the world always against me?!" she shouted.

Martha ripped open her purse and removed her metal flask. She quickly tipped her head back and took a generous swig. Enrique and Jesus walked behind her with their arms laden with her signs.

"Here are your signs Mrs. Molder," Enrique said.

Martha performed a huge spit take, lurched forward, and fell into her trunk. Enrique set the signs beside the car, and gently patted Martha on the back as she choked and gasped for air.

"Mrs. Molder are you alright?"

"Rick... Rick..." she gasped, "I know you people are good at sneaking up on people, but please don't do it to me..."

"I'm sorry Mrs. Molder" he said sincerely.

"Did she want us to send a mariachi band ahead of us?" Jesus whispered to his father.

Enrique shook his head at his son as he silently scolded him. Martha smoothed the imaginary wrinkles from her Star-Spangled Banner tribute outfit. She tried to discreetly screw the cap back onto her flask. She stood aside as Jesus loaded his signs into her trunk. Enrique grabbed his bundle and carefully placed it beside Jesus'. He stood back and considered the signs.

"I don't think you're going to fit anymore in there Mrs. Molder."

"Ohhhh, too bad," Martha whined. "I'll run out before the day is done. My message resonates with people. That means they like what I have to say," Martha explained to him.

Jesus glared at Martha. She twisted a sign around so Enrique could see it.

"You saw my sign, didn't you?"

"Oh, yes Mrs. Molder," he said. "They are... bold and eye-catching."

"So, are you interested in politics Rick? I mean, are you allowed to vote?"

Jesus glared harder at Martha. Enrique sensed his son's mounting anger and reached out to pat him on the arm.

"Oh sure Mrs. Molder. I have always voted in every election. It is my duty as a citizen to cast a vote for the best possible candidate to represent the people."

"Oh, thank you Rick," Martha gushed. "So, I can count on you and your people to vote for me in the election?"

Enrique glanced away. "Well, actually Mrs. Molder..."

"Actually," Jesus interrupted, "me, my dad and 'our people'" he said as he made air quotations, "are supporting Connie."

Martha regarded them, horrified, and coughed as if she were choking on a fish bone.

"Connie! The Norman Gaines Communist underling?! She'll turn our country into a sex Marxist, anti-freedom, gun-free, gay underwear-wearing, baby killing factory!"

"Mrs. Molder," Enrique said, "Connie is an honorable woman who represents progress, fairness and balance..."

Martha stared at Enrique, then grasped his shoulders as she experienced an epiphany.

"Rick, I'm so glad you came today. I now realize I must try harder to convince people I'm the one who will save this country from pacifist layabouts and terrorist immigrants."

Martha turned to close the trunk, then quickly turned back to the two men.

"No offence."

"None taken," Jesus spat out.

Martha turned again, raced to the driver's side, and opened the door.

"I trust you'll fix the nasty water problem Rick."

"My son and I will fix it no problem Mrs. Molder," Enrique assured her.

Martha sat in the driver's seat. "Good. Oh, I've locked the house so you can't get in."

"No, you wouldn't want us to steal your silverware..." Jesus said under his breath.

Martha shut the door and started the engine. Enrique and Jesus stepped off the pavement, and onto the grass. As she backed from the driveway to the street, she passed them and sneered at their shoes on her precious lawn. Jesus put a hand on his father's shoulder.

"Dad! How can you work for her?! She's a horrible person!"

Martha drove away. Enrique and Jesus stepped onto the pavement, and watched the car disappear around a corner.

"Son, I've always tried to set an example. Be kind, be reasonable, be fair, be honest, and above all, be respectful."

Jesus wildly pointed in Martha's direction. "But Dad, Mama is right. Esta loca!"

Enrique gazed off in the distance and stroked his chin with his fingertips.

"Si... si..."

TWENTY-THREE

Martha parked her car on a residential street. The trunk popped open. Half her signs were gone. She exited her car, skipped to a house, and hopped onto the doorstep. She rang the bell and tapped her shoe on the concrete. She waited, then peered into the window beside the door. She took a brochure from the bundle in her hand and put it in the mailbox.

As Martha walked back to her car, her phone rang. She whipped it from her Star-Spangled Banner outfit and glanced at the screen. She stopped on the sidewalk, put a hand on her hip, and tapped a shoe on the cement.

"Leslie, I'm very busy campaigning right now, after my many, many, many public appearances yesterday..."

Leslie sat on a bench in a public park, ate his lunch, and held his phone to his ear as he watched a group of shirtless men in short shorts play beach volleyball.

"Yes Carlos!" he shouted at a young Latino man who spiked the ball.

"Carlos?!" Martha asked.

"Oh, I'm sorry Mrs. Molder... I'm... I'm at a restaurant and the dumb waiter can't get my order right. So anyway, I have some big news..."

"This better be good Leslie. I have countless socialist heathens to convert today."

"Mrs. Molder, Shelley Tutley is dead."

Martha stopped tapping her shoe. "What?"

"I read it on the internet. A car accident..."

Martha clasped her phone between her hands, then raised it to the heavens.

"Praise be! Thank you, Jesus! Thank you!" she shouted. She brought the phone to her ear again. "This changes everything Leslie. Now, if only I could get rid of that Communist tart..."

"Oh yes! Way to do the splits Garth!" Leslie shouted as a player splayed his legs apart diving for the ball.

"The splits? What restaurant is this Leslie?"

"Ummm it's the dessert I ordered. The waiter wanted to know if I wanted whipped cream on my banana split..."

"Leslie, you don't have time to think about whipped cream right now. We have work to do. Cancel all the plans we made to embarrass Tutley. Get on the phone now and get me appearances everywhere! I'm going to annihilate that Communist mouse and everything she stands for! Everything!" Martha cackled maniacally. "Oh, I'm going to win now. This is only the first step in my plan to make gay socialist pedophile terrorism abortions illegal!!"

As Martha ended the call, Leslie stared at his phone. A wayward volleyball bonked him in the head. A player ran to him, gathered the ball, and stood in front of Leslie.

"Sorry about that. Excuse me for asking, but weren't you at Club le Boeuf the other night?"

Leslie hesitated. "Yes."

The man motioned to the court. "Would you like to play with us?"

Leslie bit his lip, glanced at his phone, turned it off, and tossed it into his backpack.

"Sure."

Martha placed her brochures in the trunk, retrieved a sign and a hammer, and walked to a grassy area four feet wide beside the sidewalk. An election sign for Connie Frame, and a commercial sign for a neighborhood barbershop were posted in the grass.

Martha placed her sign in front of Connie's, then pounded the stake into the ground with her hammer. She stood back with her hands on her hips and admired her effort. She furtively looked around, then wrestled with Connie's sign until it tipped over to one side. She stood beside her sign and gestured to pedestrians and people in cars to look at it as if she were a product model on The Price is Right.

She walked to her car and was about to close the trunk, when a man from the house she had visited stormed out the front door and onto the doorstep. He ripped Martha's brochure from his mailbox, shook his fist, and shouted at her.

"Hey you, lady!"

Martha turned and peered at him. The man shoved Martha's brochure in his pocket. Middle-aged, with thinning black hair, a bushy moustache, and sideburns, the low-cut, white athletic shirt he wore showed off the thick, wiry hair on his chest as he raced along the walkway. The unbuttoned shirt he wore flew behind him like a cape. Shaving cream dotted his face, and he carried a straight razor.

"Yes, you lady! I'm talking to you!" he shouted. He rushed toward Martha and waved his straight razor in the air. "Who do you think you are putting your sign on my property?!"

"Ahhhhh!" Martha screamed. She grabbed an election sign from her trunk and held it against her chest as a shield. "Terrorist! Terrorist! This Middle Eastern terrorist is trying to kill me!" she shouted.

The man stopped, stared at her, and at the razor in his hand. He rolled his eyes, folded the razor, and put it in his pocket.

"Now this terrorist has a concealed weapon! America is under attack! God help us!"

Martha tried to draw attention to the man by wildly pointing at him, but there were no pedestrians nearby. Martha cowered behind her sign as the man stood a few steps away from her. He raised his eyebrows and folded his arms across his chest.

"I am not a terrorist you crazy lady. This is my property." He pointed to the grass. "You can't come along and put anything on my land."

"But... but there are other signs here," Martha protested.

"I put them there!" the man yelled. "And I certainly don't want yours here!"

The man stomped to the grass, put both hands on Martha's sign, and ripped it from the ground. He tossed it on the sidewalk beside her. Martha's mouth fell open.

"Do you know who I am?" Martha announced as if she were a celebrity.

The man stepped toward her and thrusted a finger at her. "I know exactly who you are."

Martha put a hand to her chest, relieved. "Finally."

"You are the cancer killing this great country. You and your fake patriotism. You think if you wrap yourself in the flag, it's okay for you to go around spouting your hate and nobody will care. Well, guess what lady? People do care. They don't confront people like you because if they do, you turn around and call them a terrorist – like you did to me. You know I'm not a terrorist. It's your easy go-to word to describe people who don't look like you because it's what you and people who think like you do to get attention."

Martha's mouth slowly fell open again as the man admonished her.

"You're surprised I speak so well? Don't be. I have two university degrees. I have presented lectures around the world. I am not the uneducated, shifty criminal you always think comes to this country only to terrorize you and make you afraid to leave your home. I have encountered your ignorance and hate many times over, so don't patronize me Mrs. Molder."

Martha almost smiled at his acknowledgement.

"Oh yes, I know who you are Mrs. Molder. You are the bank manager's wife. Your husband is the decent man who gave me a loan to start my own business."

Martha swallowed hard. "He... he did?" she stammered.

"Yes, he did! When my family and I arrived in this country, my credentials were not recognized, so I started a business. My father was a respected barber. I learned from him. This is my barbershop, thanks to your husband." He proudly pointed to the sign on the lawn.

"It is?" Martha asked incredulously.

"Yes! It is! Like most people in this country, your husband didn't see me as a risk, a threat or someone not to be trusted. He didn't try to think of reasons not to do business with me because I wasn't White or where I came from."

"Well, I'll... I'll have to have a talk with him," Martha faltered.

"You do – if he cares to listen to the drunken ramblings from an ignorant fool."

"My husband cares what I think..."

"No one cares what you think Mrs. Molder!" the man thundered.

"But the message I'm spreading through my campaign... people want to hear..."

"Your message is vile, hate-filled and disgusting! Either people are too nice, too shocked or too indifferent to tell you."

"And Connie Frame's message isn't disgusting? Free health care, gay marriage, gun control, birth control. Those aren't American ideals. It is Communism gone crazy!"

The man shook his head. "Once again Mrs. Molder, your ignorance is your weakest link. You call me a terrorist. I am not. You call your opponent a Communist. She is not. You label anyone who disagrees with you. That is not leadership. It is fear. Your entire campaign is about fear, about tearing people apart instead of bringing them together. You want people to live in constant fear so you can control them and how they think – the opposite of reasonable candidates who offer hope and freedom."

"But the Communists are destroying this country! People should be afraid..."

"No, they shouldn't!" the man roared.

The man took Martha's brochure from his pocket and ripped it to pieces.

"Mrs. Molder, I despise everything you stand for. And right now, the only person hurting this... country... is... you."

After the man ripped the brochure into the tiniest possible, confetti-sized pieces, he threw them into the air, and they showered over Martha.

"My beautiful brochure..."

"And some sick fool, probably you," the man pointed at her, "dropped another disgusting flyer in my mailbox the other day about some lunatic fringe, hate-spewing cult. If I wouldn't have given it to the police, I'd rip it to pieces now too."

Martha brushed the fragments of her brochure from her Star-Spangled Banner outfit.

"The Tomorrow People's Liberation Army is doing God's work."

The man turned, walked to Connie's sign, and straightened it.

"God's work? No God anywhere would approve what you or they are doing."

The man pounded the sign back into the ground with his fist, then pointed at Martha.

"Touch this sign or put your hateful propaganda here again, and I'll have you arrested."

Martha put a hand to her chest as he glared at her, walked inside his house, and slammed the door. She stared at her shredded brochure and her sign on the ground as if they were covered with killer bees.

"What have they done to my country?" she moaned as she stared to the sky, lifted her arms, and clasped her hands.

Martha quickly reached in her car and retrieved her flask. Her hand shook as she unscrewed the cap. She tipped her head back with a sudden PEZ-like movement and took a generous swallow. She gulped, then wiped her mouth with her fingers. As she gathered herself, Martha peered around her car. Mrs. Richards walked toward her on the sidewalk as she pushed a baby carriage.

Martha quickly stuffed her flask in her purse. She grabbed some brochures from the trunk, swooped her sign from the ground, and advanced toward Mrs. Richards like a poisonous gas cloud.

"Mrs. Richardsssssss..." Martha twittered.

Mrs. Richards froze. "Oh God..." she muttered, and glanced around for a wormhole she and the carriage could jump into.

"Oh, Mrs. Richards," Martha moaned, "I'm so glad I ran into you. What a day..."

"Oh, hello Mrs. Molder. I can't stop, I..."

Martha latched onto Mrs. Richards' arm like an octopus' tentacle.

"From a trying familial situation to a ghastly run in with immigrants... and now a constituent told me no one wants to hear what I have to say..."

"Well, actually..."

"...and a terrorist destroyed my campaign literature..."

"Well, it is..."

"... what a day. But you're here now Mrs. Richards! My most ardent supporter."

"Well, I'm not ..."

"I passed by your house earlier and noticed my sign you so graciously agreed to display on your lawn isn't there anymore."

"Well, I didn't agree..."

"The wind must have blown it from the ground," Martha said as she flung an arm wide into the air.

"Well, no it didn't..."

"Perhaps if you secured it in concrete..."

"Well, I don't think..."

"I happen to have another one here..."

Martha shoved the sign in her hand at Mrs. Richards who reluctantly took it.

"Well, it's..."

Martha swiped the sign from Mrs. Richards, swept off the imaginary dirt, flattened the non-bent edges, and smoothed the non-existent creases.

"A terrorist attacked this one, but I rescued it, and it is in pristine condition."

Martha slapped the sign on the baby carriage and plopped the brochures on the sign.

"Oh, here are some more beautiful brochures. I remember you said you had no more left from the bundle I gave you. Maybe they blew away too," Martha laughed.

"Well, they..."

"You are too kind Mrs. Richards. When you're out walking with little Danny everyday, perhaps you can distribute them as you go," Martha said as she patted the bundle.

"Well, I don't..."

Martha bent over and peeked into the carriage. Danny's eyes were closed, his head tilted to one side. He held a rattle in his right hand.

"Oh, what a sweetheart, asleep like a little angel," Martha cooed.

She reached in and lightly stroked his face.

"Boo boo dee dee boo boo..." Martha warbled.

Danny slowly opened his eyes, then threw the rattle at Martha. It hit her square in the forehead, bounced off, and onto the ground.

"Oh my," Mrs. Richards exclaimed. She grabbed the rattle and put it in Danny's hands.

Martha rubbed her forehead and backed away. "Oh no, don't arm him again!"

Mrs. Richards lovingly tucked Danny under his blanket and squeezed his hand. "He's only a baby Martha..."

"He's a good shot though. A future candidate for our proud armed forces!"

Martha thrusted a closed fist into the air, stepped closer, and peered at Danny. He made a sudden motion to throw the rattle at Martha again. She flinched and stepped back.

"Ahhhhh!" Martha cried out.

The baby giggled and cooed.

"Well Mrs. Richards," Martha announced as she backed away, "I must be off. I have a million constituents to canvass today. I trust you'll find a good home for my literature..."

Mrs. Richards nodded and smiled. "I sure will."

Martha backed into the street. A car blared its horn at her. She laughed, smiled, and waved at the driver as if she knew them. She turned and quickly skipped to her car. Martha closed the trunk, jumped in the car, and drove away. She offered a royal wave as she passed Mrs. Richards, who reluctantly waved back.

Mrs. Richards pushed the carriage to a new house under construction a short distance away. She stopped beside the chain-link fence that surrounded the site, then tossed Martha's election sign and brochures over the fence into an industrial-sized dumpster. She peeked into the carriage and smiled at Danny.

"Let's go Danny."

She whistled happily as she continued along the sidewalk.

TWENTY-FOUR

Arlene and Jimmy Joe sat in their truck with the windows down. Parked inconspicuously under a leafy tree in the corner of a shopping center's parking lot, they enjoyed an unobstructed view of Jack's bank across the street.

Jimmy Joe sat in the driver's seat. He wore an old ball cap, a bright white athletic shirt, and faded jeans. Arlene, her hair in a loose ponytail, reclined in the passenger seat with her bare feet on the dashboard. She wore ripped jeans, and a cropped pink t-shirt that read 'Hot to the Touch' in flaming red script across the chest.

Jimmy Joe unconsciously popped sunflower seeds into his mouth as he kept an eagle-eye on the bank. After he cracked the seed with his teeth, he spit the shell out his window. On the ground beside his door sat a small mountain of spent shells.

Arlene eyed him and drummed her fingers against the door. "Wud you cut it out."

Jimmy Joe stopped cracking a seed and turned to her. "Wut?"

"Wut?" she emphasized. "Crackin' those seeds 'n spittin' 'em out the window."

"Why?"

Arlene moaned, then counted off the fingers on her left hand.

"First, yer irritatin' the hell outta me. Second, yer makin' a disgustin' mess in here. Third, yer leavin' a trail fer the cops to find. And fourth, yer irritatin' the hell outta me!"

"I'm sorry Leeny, but I'm so nervous," Jimmy Joe wailed. "We got lots on our plate tonight – robbin', kidnappin', hostage takin' – and if it all don't fall in ta place…"

Jimmy Joe moaned and wheezed. Arlene grabbed him by the arm, squeezed until he winced, and pointed a finger in his face.

"Now you listen buster. This here is a big fish fry up tonight, so keep it together. It's not everyday we hit the jackpot.

"Sorry Leeny, but I keep thinkin' bout how many things can go wrong…"

"There ain't nothin' gonna go wrong tonight, ya hear me?"

"But we ain't heard from the sexy 'lil schoolteacher who wants Miss Martha outta the way since yesterday. Where is she?"

Arlene eyed him contemptuously. "Sexy 'lil schoolteacher?"

"Ya know… the crazy, sexy, bouncy 'lil yummy thing with the…"

Arlene slapped him across the head.

"I know who ya mean dummy – the crazy Tutley girl. Who cares where she is! We got her cash for us ta take care a Miss Martha. It's all that counts."

Jimmy Joe frowned and massaged his head.

"I'm sorry for hittin' ya darlin'," Arlene cooed, "but why wud ya want a pile a dumb sillycone like her, when ya have me?"

"Awww Leeny, I don't want her. I's lookin' is all."

"Yeah well, I'm just as crazy, sexy and bouncy as her, but got more brain cells. Those flyers we sent out were a great idea. If I wouldn'ta thought about 'em, we wouldn't be swimmin' in riches right now."

"But I said put 'em in Walmart. 'Member?"

Arlene smiled, then slowly patted his face with her hand. "Yes, you did darlin'. They got great clientele. Like shootin' fish in a barrel."

"Clientele… is that some fancy perfume like Calvin Klein or somethin'?"

Arlene lingered her fingers on his stubbled face. "Yer so sexy when yer dumb."

"Awww thanks." He leaned in for a kiss, then pulled back. "Hey!"

"Hun, I'm givin' ya compliments. I'm the brains and yer the brawn. It's the way it's always been. We're a good team you and me."

Arlene trailed her fingers along his throat, and onto his chest.

"Yeah, we are ain't we?" Jimmy Joe said as he leaned in toward her again.

"Kiss me you crazy dumb fool!"

Arlene put an arm around his neck and forcefully pulled him close to kiss him hard. As they passionately made out, Arlene climbed onto his lap. She untied her ponytail, and let her hair fall loose around her shoulders. She swept Jimmy Joe's ball cap off and rubbed her hands through his short buzz cut.

They moaned and groaned, and their hands were all over each other. Arlene leaned back, turned her head, and spat a sunflower seed out the window. Immediately, she and Jimmy Joe resumed their love making. Arlene bumped against the horn, and it blared.

"Yer makin' the truck do all sorts a crazy things JJ!" she laughed.

"Wasn't it you Leeny...?"

"Oh, shut up and kiss me dum dum."

An elderly couple with a shopping cart passed the truck, and stared at Arlene and Jimmy Joe, who continued their session unaware they had an audience. The elderly couple stopped at their car, parked a few spots away, and unloaded their groceries into the trunk.

"Disgraceful," the woman said loud enough for anyone nearby to hear.

"So why are you watching?" her husband asked.

Arlene casually glanced out the window as she ran her tongue along Jimmy Joe's neck. When she saw the elderly couple staring at them, she purposely sat back on Jimmy Joe's lap and sounded the horn. She leaned out the window.

"Jus wut are you two old raisins starin' at?" she snapped.

"Hmmmpfff," the woman huffed. "The least they could do is keep the window closed."

"The least you cud do granny is mind yer own business. This is a free country and we're not goin' anywhere."

"I can see that. Everyone can see and hear that."

"And yer old man seems more than interested."

Arlene pointed to the woman's husband who stared at Arlene and Jimmy Joe. He quickly put the groceries in the car.

"Ya see, the 'ol man still has fire in the 'ol stove."

"Really?!" the woman said, offended. "We have community standards here you know."

"I know," Arlene drawled. "I seen them community standards posted at city hall. We read 'um... then we ran out back and did it in the alley."

The woman's eyeballs almost popped out. She turned and poked her husband in the ribs.

"Get in the car Harold," she commanded as she got in the passenger seat and slammed the door.

Harold awkwardly waved to Arlene, then jumped in the car. As he drove away, the woman turned her nose in the air and glanced away from Arlene.

Arlene smirked satisfactorily, leaned forward, and kissed Jimmy Joe. He became unresponsive. She leaned back.

"Wut is the problem now?" she snapped.

"I dunno... Maybe them old people catchin' us... Maybe what we have 'ta do tonight... I'm not in the mood anymore Leeny..."

Arlene groaned, climbed off him, and bounced back into her seat.

"Got me all horny toaded, and you turn it off like a frozen water pipe," she groaned.

"Sorry Leeny, but we got a job 'ta do, remember?"

Arlene regarded him, impressed. "Look at y'all, responsible and stuff. Yer right. Let's stick to the program."

Jimmy Joe glanced at his watch. "We got another couple hours before the bank closes."

Arlene laughed. "That old bird remind ya of someone?"

"Miss Martha."

"Yeah, me too."

"No, there she is."

Jimmy Joe pointed across the street. They slumped in their seats as they watched Martha stumble from her car she parked beside the bank. She opened the trunk and removed a sign and a hammer. She strode to the grassy area beside the entrance and proceeded to pound the sign into the ground as if she were chopping wood with an axe.

"Wut in the bloody blue blazes is she wearin'?" Arlene asked.

"Looks like she done sewed herself into a few flags."

"We shoulda came to this town a long, loooooonnng time ago and contacted with Miss Martha. We woulda cleaned out this town with her help."

At the bank, Jack rushed outside, and confronted Martha on the grass.

"Git down!" Arlene hissed at Jimmy Joe.

The pair lowered themselves further into their seats until their eyes peeked over the dashboard. Arlene opened the glove box, removed her phone, and scrolled through it. She landed on a picture of Jack and compared it to the man at the bank having an angry conversation with Martha.

"That's him, her husband, Jack"

"The bank manager?"

"Yup. Too bad we have ta rob his bank and kidnap him. He looks like a fine man."

"Leeny, I'm sittin' right here!"

"Oh, you can lust after some crazy dum dum, but I can't make a simple compliment 'bout a sexy, strong, strappin' hunk."

Jack grabbed the hammer from Martha and held it behind his back. He pointed to the grassy area beside the bank and shook his head. Martha clasped her hands together and raised them to the sky.

"Whaddya think they're talkin' 'bout?" Jimmy Joe asked.

"Talkin'? More like quarrellin' like two pigs over a corn cob."

As Jack ripped Martha's sign from the ground, she grabbed behind his back for the hammer. Jack threw the sign towards her car. She covered her mouth with her hands. Jack stood in one spot and rotated as Martha ran around him trying to get the hammer.

"I dunno this Jack person, but I feel sorry fer 'em," Jimmy Joe said as he shook his head.

Jack lurched away from Martha, walked back inside the bank with the hammer, and closed the door. Martha fell to her knees on the grass, clasped her hands together again, and stared at the sky. People who entered and exited the bank eyed her strangely.

"Yeah, me too," Arlene said wistfully. She turned to Jimmy Joe and pointed at him. "You 'membered ta bring the tear gas 'n grenades, right?"

He thumbed to the truck bed. "In the back."

"Good... good," she said satisfactorily.

Defeated, Martha stood and trudged to her car. She listlessly took her sign and put it in the trunk. She closed the trunk, got in the car, and drove into the parking lot where Arlene and Jimmy Joe were parked.

Max, Marc, Sarah and Robin walked across the same parking lot on their way to a party supply store. They talked amongst themselves as Martha turned into their row and drove straight toward them at a high rate of speed. Sarah casually turned her head.

"Car!" she screamed.

Sarah grabbed Robin and pulled him back. She gave Max a hard push forward. Marc grabbed Max. They fell onto a parked car's hood. Sarah and Robin fell to the ground between two cars.

Martha raced by and did not stop. Inside the car, she wiped at her eyes and sobbed.

"He even took my hammer..."

She veered from the row and blew through a four-way stop. A car blared its horn at her.

"Oh, shut up!" Martha screamed, totally unhinged. "I'm having a crisis here!"

Max and Marc watched as the car continued through the parking lot. It did not stop until it parked near a hardware/liquor/drug/gun store. Marc hauled Max off the car.

"Are you okay?"

Max stared at Martha's car. "Yeah... yeah."

Marc raced to Sarah and Robin as they picked themselves off the ground.

"Are you guys alright?"

"Yeah, I think so..." Sarah said.

"Yeah, except for my arm Sarah nearly pulled from its socket," Robin said as he massaged his shoulder.

"Oh, well, sorry," Sarah drawled. "Let's get the car to come back and try to run us over again. This time, I'll leave you out there to get splattered."

Sarah shook her head and led Robin out from between the cars.

"Who the hell was that anyway?" she asked.

Max joined his friends. They stood and stared at Martha's car.

"Mom."

"What? No way," Sarah said.

"Why would your mom try to run us over?" Robin asked.

"Well, she didn't do it on purpose... I don't think," Max said.

The teens peered across the parking lot as Martha stumbled into the multi-purpose store.

"Holy shit," Marc announced, "she looks like a Fourth of July parade marshal."

"Max, is your mom okay?" Robin asked.

"She's my mom. What do you think?"

Marc put a hand on Max's shoulder. "Do you want to go after her?"

"Fuck no. I've... I've had enough of her crazy shit. She's worse now than before the election. It's sent her over the edge."

"Power, or even the thought of getting some, can make people crazy."

"Well, she can buy a fucking belt sander, a handgun, some Percocet, and some gin, or whatever the fuck she's doing over there. I don't fucking care. We have a party to plan, and it's going to be the party to end all parties."

"Max, what's gotten into you?" Robin asked. "Dropping f-bombs, and a few hours ago, you were scared about having anyone near your house with a noise maker."

"I don't care anymore. Whatever we have to do to get her out of the house, let's do it."

"You mean like, have someone kidnap her?" Sarah asked.

"No..." Max paused and thought for a moment. "Though I do like the idea..."

"Come on guys," Marc said, "let's get our supplies. It's getting late. We can think about what to do with Max's mom on the way."

The teens walked to the party supply store.

"Lock her in the basement?" Robin said randomly.

"What?" Max asked.

"Your mom. Lock her in the basement."

"No, she has to be gone from the house."

"Send her on a wild goose chase?" Sarah said.

Max thought for a moment. "I like it. Though I like the kidnapping idea better." Max eyeballed Martha's car. "I like it a lot better."

TWENTY-FIVE

Sundown, but the looming dark clouds made it appear much later. Max nervously snuck a glance out the kitchen window. Lightning raced across the sky, and thunder boomed in the distance. He tried to peer at the corner of the house where a large bush rustled.

In the dining room, a large candelabra sat on the table. Two place settings were arranged on the table – one at one end, and the other beside it. Fancy dinner plates, cutlery and glassware were perfectly arranged.

Martha stood at the stove in the kitchen. Her flowered apron covered a simple black dress. A garish ornamental brooch resembling a cross adorned her chest. Pearls wrapped around her neck. As she seared steaks on the stove, her knowing grin almost erupted into a sustained giggle. She glanced at Max.

"Max, go sit at the table… and stay there. You've boinged from the table like a yoyo all evening," she said as she bobbed a huge steak fork in the air.

Max peered out the window again. "I'm… I'm watching the sky, Mom. I think we're in for a bad storm tonight. There's thunder and lightning all over…"

"Oh, it's God showing his wrath for all the unrepentant sinners to see honey bunch," Martha said cheerily.

She reached for a full wine glass beside the stove and took a hearty gulp. She poked one steak with her oversized fork.

"Well, mine is done." She jabbed the fork into the steak, lifted it from the pan, and plopped it onto a plate. "And yours, since you don't like God's juices, will have to sit in the pan and become stringy and tough."

Max turned and walked to the dining table. "God's juices? It's blood Mom. Blood. Why would I want to eat a steak dripping with blood? I might as well have a glass with dinner."

"It's Christ's blood!" she squealed. "To deny it is sacrilege."

"Well, I walked into that one," Max muttered as he sat at the table.

Martha set her plate and wine glass on the table, and eyed Max contemptuously. She returned to the kitchen and grabbed bowls of mashed potatoes and green peas. Max stared indifferently at the bloody, oversized steak on her plate.

"I don't know why you cooked two steaks," he said. "I told you I didn't want one."

Martha groaned. "Oh Max, not this again. Meat is filled with vitamins, minerals and other healthy things. You're a growing boy and I will not have you grow weak and malnourished – not on my watch!" she said as she shook the bowls in her hands.

"But what other healthy things are you talking about Mom?"

"Ohhhhh, you know," Martha said, frustrated. "Beef things... iron... protein... hormones... antibiotics... collagen..."

"Yummy."

Martha plopped the bowls on the table. "Max, as long as you're living in this house, you'll eat whatever I give you, and when you're out on your own, you can eat tasteless sawdust burgers for all I care."

"Probably a lot healthier."

Martha glared at him. "I don't know what's gotten into you lately Max. Smart-alecky back talk, disrespecting your elders, spitting in God's face, coveting rabbits..."

She removed her apron and draped it over a chair. She sat at the table, sighed heavily, grabbed the linen napkin beside her plate, and theatrically snapped it in the air. Max flinched as the end almost hit him in the eye. Martha delicately placed the napkin over her lap.

"I mentioned four commandments you've broken," Martha said. "God knows how many more you've soiled I don't know about..."

"Yeah, I'm sure many people break the 'thou shalt not be smart-alecky' one since they don't know about it."

Martha eyed him.

"I'm sorry Mom. When I go to bed tonight, I'll think about someone giving me forty lashes while I'm strapped to a table wearing nothing but a leather harness."

Martha smiled. "Good. Now give me your hand."

She quickly grabbed his hand and pulled it toward her, causing him to fall into the table. Max gawked at his hand as the color quickly drained from it in her vise-like grip. He stifled a high-pitched cry. Martha closed her eyes and bowed her head.

"Dear Lord," she prayed, "help me find guidance for this poor soul. I've tried to raise him in your image, but he continues to spit in your face and mine with his blasphemous ways."

Max scowled.

"He knows not what he says because the liberal media has polluted his mind with crazy leftist ideas like animals roaming free across the land instead of serving us with their tasty goodness. And his father has brainwashed him into being disrespectful as he tiptoes at the lake of fire with harlots. It's not his fault dear Lord..."

"Mom, are you going to say grace, or shall I go out and find a lamb for you to sacrifice?"

Martha opened one eye, glanced at Max, and closed it again.

"It's the way men are – deceitful, unrepentant and ruled by sex... and thank you for this food we are blessed amen," she said quickly.

Martha dropped Max's hand as if it were on fire, and it fell to the table with a thud. Max massaged his hand. Martha grasped her wine glass and glugged another generous slurp.

"You should get your steak from the stove dear. It's going to become even more dried out and tough if you don't."

Martha seized her knife and fork, then sliced into her meat with glee. Max slowly rose from the table and walked to the stove. He turned off the stove and carefully lifted the steak from the pan to his plate.

"You know what," Martha said as she noisily chewed her steak, "we should get a maid."

Max returned to the table. "A maid? There's only three people in this house. And soon there's only going to be two. What do we need a maid for?"

"Oh Max, I'm such a busy woman. Running for office, the PTA, the church, running this house, advocating for the people who live in the gutter, and advocating for the oppressed..."

Max choked on his milk as he took a drink from his glass.

"Then she could do the cooking," Martha waved dismissively at the stove. "And the cleaning, and the laundry, and the shopping..."

"And the child rearing..." Max mumbled under his breath.

"...you know, all the menial things an important woman like me shouldn't have to do."

Max spooned peas from the bowl. "And where exactly would you find this woman... to work for you? Certainly not around here. Everyone knows you."

"Oh no. Maybe the Philippines or Thailand. Those people are good at tedious, boring work. Look at all those efficient sweatshops where they make quality American goods. Fantastic work ethic. But I'll have to keep an eye on all my jewelry..."

The peas from Max's spoon slowly spilled onto his plate.

"But Mom, you'll be taking work away from Americans," he protested as he dug a spoon into the mashed potatoes. "They're immigrants. I thought you didn't want them here."

"Max, Americans don't want to do that work. That's what immigrants are for. Ship them in to do it, and when it's done, ship them back to whatever uncivilized, barbaric country they came from. The least we can do is showcase what a glorious, free life it is on the outside of their brutal Communist dictatorship. It's called capitalism honey bunch."

The potato on his spoon plopped onto Max's plate as Martha finished her quasi-geopolitical lecture. Max put the spoon in the bowl, then played with his potatoes with his fork.

"So, what time is Dad coming home?"

Martha shook her head. "Oh, late... late late late."

"Is he doing more training?"

Martha popped some potato in her mouth. "Oh no. No, there's some silly emergency at the bank. A bomb scare or shooting or something," she said indifferently.

Max dropped his fork on his plate. "What?"

Martha grasped the bowl of peas and casually offered it to Max.

"More peas sweet pea?" she asked gleefully, then giggled.

"A bomb scare? A shooting?" Max asked incredulously.

"Or a roll of pennies went missing, or someone got caught in the ATM... something silly..."

Martha set the bowl on the table. She haphazardly cut her steak like a crazed surgeon performing a reckless amputation. She shovelled the meat into her mouth, chewed it with her mouth open, and spit bits out as she talked.

"Mmmm, this meat is so good. Those crazy liberal veg heads don't know what they're missing." She pointed her knife at Max. "Max, you haven't touched your meat. Now it's tough, dry, and tasteless, like I said, but nooooo you wouldn't listen to me. You're just like your father, stubborn." She stared into space as if in a trance. "Stubborn. Vindictive. Adulterous. Perverse."

She shook herself from her trance, grabbed her wine, and glugged another mouthful.

"Mom, I know what dad did seems bad..."

Martha sputtered and dribbled her wine. She thumped the glass on the table, grabbed her napkin, and dabbed at her chin.

"Seems? Seems?! He soiled our marriage and our vows before God with that scheming tramp... that young plaything."

"It wasn't only dad, Mom. Her claws were in everyone – Mr. Douglas, Fiona's father, my teachers, even my friends."

"Ohhhh, that woman?! At her age? Now I am thoroughly disgusted. The pure, innocent act she put on when all along she was the town harlot."

"And Mom, she killed Fiona's father to get all his money, and left Fiona with nothing." Max leaned back from the table. "She's a conniving killer Mom, so please, don't blame Dad."

Martha considered Max's new information. A lightning flash illuminated the dining room. Martha didn't blink. She calmly finished her wine, then softly set the glass on the table. She gently smoothed imaginary wrinkles from the tablecloth.

"Max, our morally corrupt society has infected your father. I have tried to inoculate him with God's word, but I have been unsuccessful. My God is a loving God, but he also gives me the authority to swing a vengeful axe! I'm sorry, but he and his collection of depraved harlots must be punished!"

Martha slammed a palm on the table. Thunder boomed outside. Max jumped. The phone rang. Max jumped again, then quickly glanced to the phone in the kitchen.

"Who could that be while we're having a nice quiet family dinner?" Martha asked as she rose from her chair. "If it's someone wanting donations for some perverted liberal arts show..."

Martha walked into the kitchen. As she answered the phone, Max slowly gulped.

"Hello?"

Outside, Marc, Alex, Fiona, Sarah, Jenny, Robin, Elliott and the rest of Miss Tutley's biology class were hidden in the shrubbery next to the house. Occasionally, a lightning streak across the sky illuminated them. Loud thunder booms quickly followed.

Jenny, on her cell phone, begged everyone to be quiet.

"Shhhhhhhh!" she hushed, her hand over the microphone.

She cleared her throat, then spoke in a desiccated old woman's voice.

"Hello? Hello?"

"Hello, who is this?" Martha asked.

"Is this Miss Moldy?"

"This is Martha Molder..."

"Ohhhhh!" Jenny shrieked. "Thank the good Lord above! I need your help Miss Moldy."

"Who is this?" Martha insisted again.

Jenny froze, and her eyes grew large. "Uhhhhh, my name is..."

She motioned to her friends and silently asked them for help. She gulped.

"Lawdy... McSinnersin... ston."

Jenny rolled her eyes and shook her head.

"Your name doesn't sound familiar Mrs. McSinnersinston. Are you one of the tireless, invisible volunteers on my election campaign to be a strong authoritative conservative voice in the legislature? Or maybe you want to contribute to my cause?"

Jenny quickly slipped back into her normal voice. "Oh God no."

Sarah gently jabbed her in the ribs.

"I mean, oh no, no," Jenny said in her old woman voice. "My husband already got collared... errr approached by your grifters... errr volunteers. That's not why I'm callin'."

"So, Mrs. McSinnersinston, how may I help you?"

"Aren't you the woman who exorcises the corrupted souls from wayward trespassers?"

"I don't like to brag, but yes, I have been known to vanquish the evil presence the devil has left in the unbelievers, the adulterers, the sinners, the depraved, the perverted, the..."

"Okay, okay, okay," Jenny interrupted. "I only need one of them things fixed, not the whole Bible's worth."

"Yes, Mrs. McSinnersinston. How may I ask did you get this number?"

"From old Mrs. Campbell. She told me you helped fix her grandson real good with his bout of gay."

"Ahhhh yes," Martha said wistfully, "I remember. After our great Republican governor was elected, there were waiting lists for troubled young men... and girls, let's not forget they get it too," she said as she waggled her finger in the air.

Jenny rolled her eyes. "Uh huh..."

"There were long, long lines to get these sick children into the gay deprogramming program because the church referred so many based on recommendations from great Americans like me."

Max closed his eyes, and grimaced.

"Riiiiiight..." Jenny said and quickly motioned to shove a finger down her throat.

"Anyway, this case almost tore the family apart. The damaged young man had a boyfriend and talked about getting married to him in Canada.

Well, that was the final straw. But there wasn't any room at the shock therapy center, and sadly the exorcism I performed didn't take, so we found this place on the internet with whips, chains and restraints..."

"So, you sent him to an M & M camp to have it beaten from him, right?"

"They called it an S & M camp for some strange reason. He came back so much happier..." Martha said reflectively.

"Right..." Jenny said. "So, Miss Moldy, I'm in an awful state here..."

"What's the problem?"

"It's my husband," Jenny fake sobbed. "He's talkin' 'bout votin' Democrat..."

Martha gasped. "Turncoat!"

"And my son... he's thinkin' 'bout buyin' an electric car..."

Martha pulled her hair. "Traitor!"

"And my daughter... I caught her listenin' to k.d. lang..."

Martha bit her hand. "Canadian! Lesbian! Vegetarian!"

She collapsed a bit against the kitchen counter. Max bit his lip. Martha cleared her throat and regained her composure. She authoritatively stood with a hand on her hip and stared out the kitchen window.

"Mrs. McSinnersinston, we must rid this evil from your precious family before it leeches from your house, if it hasn't already, and infects your neighbors, your relatives and your fellow Americans. This is a national security issue! Where are you?"

"I'm on the south side near the abandoned wire coat hanger factory."

"Ahhhh yes, I know it well. I'm the one who picketed to have it closed after our newly stacked Supreme Court forced women to give birth against their will."

"Oh, Miss Moldy, thank you. Thank you!"

"Mrs. McSinnersinston, I will be your saviour tonight. Lock all your doors and windows. Boil some water in case I have to sterilize something. And Mrs. McSinnersinston..."

"Yes?"

"My thoughts and prayers are with you."

"Yes, Miss Moldy. Thank you."

Martha ended the call. She dashed to the door.

"Mom," Max asked calmly, "wherever are you going?"

Martha grabbed her coat from the closet. "To save an American family threatened with socialist liberalism! Oh my, why did this have to happen tonight..."

"Why? What's going on tonight?"

Martha froze, then darted her eyes around the room. "Because... because I wanted to spend the evening with my little Maxie Waxie." She rushed toward him, took his chin in her hand, and wiggled it back and forth.

Max wrenched his face away. "I'll be fine Mom. This sounds much more important."

"Oh, it is." She put on her coat and grabbed her purse. "Our wholesome American society is being torn apart by Godless, sexually deviant international interlopers who want to infect our youth with their liberal socialistic Communism!"

"Again?!" Max exclaimed. "You simply must go Mom. It sounds like an emergency."

Martha dramatically zipped her coat, plopped an oversized fedora on her head, and held her head high as if she were about to go save the world as Martha Molder, P.I.

"It's my duty."

Martha walked toward the door, then turned to Max.

"Now Max, I don't want you throwing any wild parties while I'm on my mission."

"What?!" Max nervously laughed.

"What am I thinking? Of course you wouldn't." She thought for a moment. "Though I wouldn't mind if you invited cute little Sally Frame over for some milk and cookies..."

Max waggled his hands. "Mom, why would I do that?"

"You're a boy. She's a girl. You're at the age when it's time to start thinking of..."

"What? Marriage? Two kids? A detached Cape Cod with a white picket fence? A nine-to-five job as a certified public accountant? Church on Sundays and dinners at the in-laws? Sally at home barefoot and pregnant doin' the washin', the cleanin' and the cookin'?" Max drawled.

Martha clasped her hands together and raised them to the ceiling. "Yes! Yes! Yes! Thank you, sweet Jesus! My prayers have been answered. I thought you'd see it my way!"

She ran to Max again and squished his face between her hands. She quickly turned and ran to the telephone. "Let me phone her..."

"Mom, no!"

"But I may never get another chance like this again to set you on the right path..." she said as she grasped the phone.

"Mom, aren't you afraid what might happen if Sally comes over? I thought you and your cult... I mean church, were against heavy breathing, touching and pre-marital sex?"

"Sex?!" she yelled, then shushed herself. "Shhhhhh! I only want you both to have some milk and cookies and talk about current events."

"Mom, don't you have an exorcism to go to?"

"You're right." Martha set the phone on the counter, then scurried to the door. "Be a good boy til I get back."

"I will."

Martha opened the door. Wind and rain greeted her. Lightning streaked across the sky. She yelped, closed the door, and ran onto the doorstep. Thunder boomed. She cried out, peered to the sky, and ran to her car. She opened the door, jumped in, started the car, and backed from the driveway.

As Martha drove away, the teens popped their heads from the bushes like gophers from their holes after a predator passed. They scrambled from the bushes and ran to the front door. They carried bags of party supplies, food, and drink. Max opened the door.

"Ho-ly Max," Sarah exclaimed. "What the hell took so long for her to leave?"

"You know Mom, once she goes off on a rant, it's hard to get her stopped."

As Sarah flipped the hood of her hoodie back, she revealed the emboldened red X on her forehead. Max peered at it.

"Ummm Sarah, what's going on with your X? Haven't you made your point already?"

"No! I think I'll get it permanently tattooed as a reminder how we're all oppressed by the system."

"Oh no..." Max whispered.

"Stand aside Molder," Alex said, "it's gonna start pissing rain any second."

"Alright, alright..."

Max stood aside, and one by one the teens crammed into the house as a thunderclap quickly followed another lightning flash.

"So, your mom took the bait huh?" Marc asked.

"Took it? She's already digesting it."

Max put an arm around Marc's waist and guided him into the house.

"I knew if we hit on all her stupid prejudices, she'd be out the door in a flash," Marc said.

Max closed the door. "I know. Jenny, how far did you get?"

"Well sonny," Jenny said in her old woman's voice, "I told her my daughter is listenin' to k.d. lang..."

"Sure, that did the trick," Max said.

"And I didn't even get to tell her my son is datin' a brown boy..."

"It's always nice to end with the truth."

"I really wanted her to hear that," Marc said.

"Hmmm, I dunno..." Max mused. "Her head would've exploded, and we'd have a mess on our hands."

The teens laughed as they moved into the kitchen. They put their supplies on the kitchen table and the counter.

"Okay Max, we need bowls, dishes, glasses, cutlery..." Sarah said.

"Guys, guys," Max said as he opened cupboards and retrieved bowls, "let's not get too carried away, okay? If Mom finds a stray crumb anywhere, there'll be a murder here tonight."

The teens laughed.

Outside, it rained hard. Lightning streaked across the sky, and thunder roared. Through the heavy rain, a figure emerged at Max's driveway. Dressed in a dark cloak, the figure stopped at the driveway's entrance and slowly trudged to the house.

TWENTY-SIX

The party turned into a loud, raucous time. Music blasted from the stereo. Colorful streamers draped from lamps, picture frames, bookcases, and door frames. Balloons floated on the ceiling and littered the floor. A large banner strung in the living room said: 'GOOD RIDDANCE!', in large black letters on a gold background.

The teens gathered in the living room, the kitchen, and along the staircase. They danced, sang, ate, drank and talked, even though the loud music mostly drowned out their conversations. At times, the lights in the house flickered, but it only added to the festive atmosphere.

In the kitchen, Robin emptied a bag of chips into a bowl. Fiona put a bag of popcorn into the microwave. Alex poured whiskey into small plastic shot glasses and put them on a tray. Max and Marc stood beside each other next to the stove.

"Max, when's your dad coming home?" Alex asked. "Didn't the bank close hours ago?"

"Yeah, but apparently there's a problem..."

"He's not gonna be pissed when he comes home and finds us here?"

"Are you kidding?" Marc said. "Max's dad is the best."

"Well..." Robin said. "He did have an affair..."

"So, Max's dad is a dirtbag because he screwed around with Tutley?" Alex asked.

"No, I didn't mean..." Robin hesitated. "I know he's a good guy, but he's no saint... you know what I mean? Your dad isn't the only one Max. I heard she had an affair with the guy who drives around cleaning out port-a-potties."

"Ew," Fiona said.

"Robin's right," Max said. "At first, it was only a stupid affair, but dad convinced Tutley to run in the election as a far-out fringe candidate so she and mom would cancel each other out. So, I hate the fact he had an affair, but at the same time, I admire him for using it for good. Still, I can't believe he didn't see through her... maneaterness."

Alex laughed. "Maneaterness. Max, I love how you invent words. They're hilarious."

"Max, would you rather your dad hired a prostitute?" Marc asked.

"He did," Fiona said.

As the teens laughed, lightning lit the sky, closely followed by loud thunder. Robin casually glanced to the door, then screamed.

"Ahhhhh!"

"Holy shit Binster!" Alex said. "It's thunder and lightning, not Armageddon."

Robin pointed at the door. "Something's out there!"

Everyone peered at the door.

"There's nothing there," Marc said.

"But... but I saw it..."

"What was it?" Fiona asked.

"I-I don't know..."

"You saw something, but you don't know what it was?" Alex said. He glanced at the whiskey bottle. "Have you been sneaking swigs Binster?"

"No!"

Max stared out the window. "There's nothing here..."

"But I saw it... some weird mask... like Gritty..."

"Like what?" Marc asked incredulously.

"Gritty."

"What the hell is Gritty?" Fiona asked.

"Gritty, the Philadelphia Flyers mascot."

Fiona shook her head. "Does anyone know what the hell he's talking about?"

"Yeah," Alex said. "Gritty is their mascot. He has wild orange hair and spaced out eyes."

"That's exactly who it looked like!" Robin said

"What would Gritty be doing outside my house?" Max asked.

"Maybe he wants to join the party," Alex said.

"No," Robin insisted, "it was someone in a Gritty mask... wearing a cloak."

"A what?" Alex asked.

"You know, a cloak...with a hood. Something a witch would wear."

"Robin," Fiona said, "there haven't been any witch sightings in this town since... well, since Tutley."

Max opened the door and instantly received a blast of wind and rain. He shielded himself with an arm and peered around the door frame. He quickly shut the door.

"There's nothing out there. Robin, you must have seen a ghost or something."

Fiona made ghost noises and poked Robin in the ribs. "Oooooohhoooooo... scary!"

"Stop it," Robin said as he wriggled away from her.

"Alex, are you done pouring those drinks?" Max asked.

"Yup. I have one for everyone."

"Great. Bring them to the living room so we can all have a toast."

"On it."

Alex lifted the oversized tray, then carried it into the hallway. Fiona followed with a bowl of popcorn, and Robin with a bowl of chips.

"Any regrets having this at your house?" Marc asked Max.

"Not yet."

They smiled and walked into the hallway.

With the kitchen empty, the shrouded figure Robin saw in the window entered the house. They wore a red Handmaid cloak with a white hood, and a bizarre Halloween mask of a white rabbit with wild, spiked orange hair. They moved into the kitchen where they carefully selected, then removed a butcher knife from the knife block on the counter with a gnarled, dirty, blood-spattered hand. Two fingernails were broken.

In the living room, Alex carried the tray to the coffee table.

"Alright," he shouted, "everyone get in here. It's time for a toast. Come on."

The teens on the staircase and in the hallway made their way into the living room.

"Come on, get in here. It's time to say goodbye to Miss Tutley."

After the last few teens entered the living room, the cloaked figure snuck into the hallway. The lights flickered.

"Oh no, not again," Max said.

Thunder cracked outside. The lights in the house briefly went out. The teens screamed, and the shrouded figure quickly moved from the hallway to the staircase. As they climbed the stairs in the dark, they stumbled. The lights came back on. The figure reached the top of the stairs and swiftly made their way to Max's bedroom.

They opened Max's door. The light from the hallway fell on Mr. Fluffy Puffy in his cage. The figure advanced toward the rabbit with the butcher knife raised in the air. As the figure reached out and tried to lift the latch on the cage, they sneezed – repeatedly.

TWENTY-SEVEN

"Okay, everyone grab a glass," Alex said as he grabbed a shot glass from the tray.

The teens in the living room each stepped forward and selected a glass – everyone except Elliott. Alex peered at him.

"Come on Elliott, this is a big moment."

"But it's the hard stuff. Don't you have any Fresca?"

"Fresca?" Fiona said. "I thought they banned that stuff."

Sarah pointed to the only glass on the tray. "Elliott, there's barely enough whiskey in the glass to get a fly drunk. You're not gonna become an alcoholic, trust me man."

"I don't know..."

Max put a hand on his shoulder. "Elliott, don't you remember the 'overripe blueberry incident'?"

Elliott grimaced. "Yes."

"Well, what we're doing is celebrating the fact Tutley will never again be able to call anyone an overripe blueberry, or an elephant, or plain, or ugly, or a dumb jock, or an Oreo..."

"I know..."

"Good," Sarah said. She grabbed the glass and shoved it at him. "Drink."

"But my parents will find out, and they're total tea drinkers."

"I think you mean teetotallers," Marc said.

"Yeah, that too."

"Guys, I don't think we should force Elliott to drink if he doesn't want to," Robin said.

Sarah groaned. “There’s that annoying voice of reason again. Does anyone else hear it?” she asked as she glanced around the room.

“All I’m saying is if Elliott doesn’t want to drink, don’t force him. You’re making him feel like he doesn’t fit in if he doesn’t. Aren’t they?” Robin asked Elliott.

“Well...” Elliott wavered.

“Robin’s right... again,” Max said.

Alex grabbed Elliott’s glass from Sarah. “Alright, I know how to fix this.”

Alex poured the contents into his own glass. “There, now there’s only a drop in it. You can handle a raindrop’s worth can’t you Elliott?”

“I guess...”

“Good,” Alex said, and handed the empty glass to him.

Instantly, Elliott tipped the glass back and drank the single drop of whiskey. Everyone either groaned in disappointment or yelled at him to stop.

“Elliott, what are you doing?!” Sarah asked.

“But you told me to...”

“You were supposed to wait until we all did it together,” Max said.

“I didn’t know. I’ve never done this before...”

“Oh Elliott,” Jenny said.

“But I wanted to fit in,” he said in a small voice.

“I’m surprised his parents let him out on his own after dark,” Fiona whispered to Alex.

“He said they agreed only if he texted them safe words every five minutes.”

Max grabbed a bottle of Sprite from the coffee table and filled Elliott’s glass. “Here Elliott, it’s like Fresca, but with taste.”

“Now don’t drink it until we’re all ready to do it together,” Sarah ordered.

“Okay.”

“Let’s try this again,” Alex said, frustrated. “Okay, everyone raise your glasses, and on three, say whatever you want to say to Tutley.”

The teens raised their glasses.

“Good riddance,” Elliott said.

“Sayonara,” Sarah said.

"Okay, okay, save it for the toast," Alex said. "One... two... three..."

As the teens clanked their glasses together, the lights went out again and stayed out. The music stopped. It became eerily dark and silent, except for the candles on the dining room table, and the heavy rain outside. The teens shrieked and moaned.

"Awwww man..." Max groaned.

"Maybe it's only a temporary flicker," Fiona said.

After a moment in the dark, Alex drank his whiskey. "I don't think so babe."

"Max, do you have any more candles?" Jenny asked.

"Yeah, in the kitchen. I'll be right back."

"And a flashlight," Alex said.

Max stumbled past his friends. He bumped into them and into the furniture.

"Are you sure you live here Max?" Alex asked.

"Shut up."

Lightning flashes streamed through the windows and illuminated the teens.

"This is kinda scary..." Elliott whined.

"Oh Elliott, it is not," Sarah sneered. "The power's out. You're not gonna die."

"But I don't like the dark..."

"It's okay Elliott," Marc said. "Max will be right back with some candles."

"If something didn't happen to him..." Robin said.

Elliott whimpered.

"Knock it off Elliott," Sarah said. "The whiny, fraidy-cat guy always gets it first in horror movies."

Elliott whimpered louder and latched onto Alex. "Hold me!"

"No!" Alex said as he tried to shake him off.

"Sarah," Jenny scolded, "now why did you say that?"

Jenny put an arm around Elliott, and he instantly clung to her.

"It's the truth! Watch any slice 'n dice movie. I'm tryin' to save the kid's life here!"

Elliott grasped Jenny tighter and continued to whimper.

"Hey Alex," Fiona said, "could you hand me my sweater? I'm a little cold."

"Sure babe, if I can find it..."

Alex fumbled in the dark.

"Oh," Fiona exclaimed, "why is it warm and wet?"

"What?"

"My sweater."

"I haven't found it yet."

"So, what the hell is this?" Fiona asked as she peered at the soft mound in her hands.

Max entered the living room with unlit candles, and a flashlight he shone at everyone.

"Let there be light!" he announced.

A woman sneezed.

"Bless you," Jenny said.

"Thank you," the woman said.

A lightning streak illuminated the room. The shrouded figure with the bizarre rabbit mask stood next to Fiona. Max saw them, screamed, and dropped the candles. He shakily pointed the flashlight at the figure, and at Fiona. The lifeless body of what appeared to be Mr. Fluffy Puffy lay in her hands.

"Mr. Fluffy Puffy!" Max screamed.

Fiona glanced at her hands, screamed, and dropped the rabbit. Thunder shook the house. Elliott screamed, then ran and hid in the corner behind a chair.

"What? What?!" Alex screamed.

He stood behind the sofa, Fiona's sweater in his hand, and stared to the flashlight's beam as it shone on Fiona and the shrouded figure beside her. As the figure raised an arm in the air, the glint from the butcher knife in its hand caught the light. Alex leaped toward Fiona.

"Fiona, look out!"

Another lightning streak illuminated the room. Alex pushed Fiona away from the shrouded figure. She fell to the floor. The figure swung the knife. Alex raised an arm to defend himself, and the knife caught him in the chest.

"Alex!" Fiona shrieked.

As thunder shook the house, the teens screamed.

Alex froze, in shock. The figure wrenched the knife from him. Alex's eyes rolled back, and he fell backwards to the floor, hitting his head hard against a chair.

"Alex!" a few teens screamed.

The teens backed away from the figure. Fiona quickly crawled across the floor to Alex. She put a hand under his head and gently raised it off the floor.

"Oh Alex," she cried.

Max pointed the flashlight directly into the shrouded figure's face, revealing the bizarre Halloween mask. He screamed.

"That's it!" Robin said as he pointed at the mask. "That's what I saw in the window!"

"It's Gritty!" Jenny screamed. "He's on a murderous rampage!"

"Go back to Philadelphia, Gritty," Sarah said.

Max shook his head. "It's not Gritty," he moaned. He waved the flashlight at the cloaked figure. "Take off that stupid mask you twit," he demanded.

The figure pulled back the cloak's hood and removed the mask.

"Miss Tutley!" the teens screamed.

TWENTY-EIGHT

Miss Tutley grinned evilly and shook her hair out from the cloak. Her damp and matted hair was soiled with mud and dried blood. Scratches, dirt, and crusted blood covered her face. A gash on her forehead oozed blood. Her lips were red and blistered.

She let her long dark cloak and her mask fall to the floor. She wore the same clothes as the night of her accident. Her nylons were ripped to shreds, her skirt soiled and ripped, her blouse untucked and mud-stained, and her high heels were caked in mud.

"What are you doing here?!" Max asked.

"I think the more appropriate question is, why is she even alive?" Robin asked.

"Isn't it obvious?" Sarah asked. "She came back from the dead because she heard there's a party here tonight. Sorry Tutley, but there aren't any rich old men here for you to sleep with and steal their life savings."

"Oh, shut up Sara Lee!" Miss Tutley snapped. "I came here for this!" she shrieked as she haphazardly chopped the air with the knife.

"Do you believe this woman?" Max asked his friends. "She came here expecting to cut a cake as if it were her birthday or something."

"No..." she tried to interject.

"Sorry," Marc said, "we don't have any cake for you to cut, so turn around..." He twirled a finger in the air. "...and go back to whatever swamp you crawled from."

"But I..."

"Oh man!" Jenny exclaimed as she palmed her forehead, "we forgot to get a cake. Okay guys, who dropped the ball?"

"No, Plain Jane..."

"Fiona's responsible for the food," Robin said. "It's her fault."

Everyone glanced at Fiona. She stared back at them incredulously.

"Are you fucking kidding me?! You're all going on about cake after this psychopath stabbed Alex?!"

As she cradled Alex's head in her lap, Elliott peered from behind the chair and pointed a shaky finger at Miss Tutley.

"Miss Tutley, you're supposed to be dead."

"Does it look like I'm dead, elephant?" she snapped.

She wildly jabbed the knife at him. Elliott squealed and hid behind the chair again.

"As a matter of fact, yes, you do," Robin said.

"But me and Marc killed you," Max said. "We put hydrochloric acid in your water bottle."

"No, I killed you," Jenny said. "I made sure you tripped over another power cord."

"No, I killed you," Robin said. "I sabotaged your shoes."

"No, I killed you," Elliott said as he peeked from behind the chair. "I put a poisonous scorpion in your coat pocket."

"No, I killed you," Sarah said. "I put the biology dummy in your car to scare you."

"No, we killed you," Fiona said as she held Alex. "We tampered with your brakes."

"You..." Miss Tutley slowly said, "you are all horrible, horrible children!"

Max stepped forward and put a hand to his chest. "We're horrible? You killed poor defenceless Mr. Fluffy Puffy!" He pointed the flashlight to the mound of white fluff, motionless on the floor. "You sicko."

"He tried to kill me," Miss Tutley hissed.

She deliberately kicked the mound of fluff away with her pointed, muddy toe.

Max sobbed. "He was my buddy..."

Marc put an arm around him.

"Oh, boo hoo," Miss Tutley heartlessly spat.

"And you killed my father... and Alex!" Fiona screeched at her. "You psychopath!"

"Oh, Fiona dear," Miss Tutley said contemptuously, "the old man killed himself. It's not my fault he had a heart attack."

"You screwed him to death you sick tart!"

"Then you screwed him out of his money," Jenny said.

"Actually, I did that first," Miss Tutley said, and laughed wickedly.

"And Alex..." Fiona wept as she caressed his face.

"Ugghh," Miss Tutley sneered. "He annoyed me. He constantly toyed with me, teased me, turned my thermostat up, and deliberately turned it down. Made me all hot with his man-boy sexiness..."

"Ewww," Sarah said, disgusted. "Someone get a bucket of cold water to throw on this thing."

"She'll melt," Jenny said.

"Do it! Do it!" Elliott shrieked as he peeked from behind the chair again.

"So, you killed Alex because he wouldn't have sex with you?" Marc asked incredulously. "You're nuts lady."

"Alex had more scruples in his big toe than you do in your entire body," Max said.

"Hey," Miss Tutley objected, "I didn't have anything to do with his foot fungus..."

Jenny closed her eyes and palmed her forehead. "Oh, do shut up you idiot..."

"Alex got what he deserved!" Miss Tutley shouted. "No man has ever refused me, and if he ever tried, I'd make sure he regretted it!"

"It's like we've gone through a space-time continuum, and landed in a remake of Fatal Attraction," Max said.

"I would've finally got Alex to submit to my obvious sexiness that night in the lab, but you thoughtless brats all tried to kill me!"

"Ohhhh," Fiona moaned, "you are a conceited cow! Alex was never going to have sex with you in the lab. It was a diversion to get your car keys."

"I don't believe it! He wanted me. I tried to seduce him on the lab counter but..."

"But the decayed fetal pig entrails on it made it hard for him to find you?" Max asked.

Miss Tutley narrowed her eyes at Max. He kept the flashlight's beam on her as he grabbed the candles from the floor. The teens passed them out amongst themselves. Max lit one and passed the flame on until the room brightened.

"I don't understand why you all hate me so much..." Miss Tutley whined.

"Are you flippin' kiddin' me?" Sarah asked. "You're the worst teacher ever!"

Max counted off the fingers on his left hand as he levelled the charges against her.

"You screwed Fiona's father to death. You latched your claws into my father. You treated your students like dirt. You killed my best friend. Tutley, you're a sex-crazed sociopath."

"Now Max," she cooed, "how can you say about your future mother?"

"What?!"

"I've heard you say some pretty dim-witted things in class before Tutley," Sarah said, "but this one's ridiculous."

"That's right Maxie! Once I take care of Mommie Dearest, you, me and your father will all live happily ever after!" Miss Tutley cackled wickedly.

"You're nuts. My father doesn't love you. He's just using you, you moron."

Miss Tutley laughed again, then instantly became serious. "Enough!" she screamed.

She quickly flicked the butcher knife at the teens, stepped forward, put a foot on Alex's torso, and aggressively rolled him away. Fiona stood and stepped back.

"Watch it you stupid cow! It's Alex, not a conquest you've cocooned after you killed them!"

"Shut up Irish Haggis!"

"Haggis is Scottish, you twit!"

Miss Tutley rolled her eyes. "Who cares?"

She stepped toward the teens, raised the knife in the air, and recklessly stabbed it with wild, sudden movements.

"Who's next on the chopping block?" she hissed.

The teens screamed.

The front door blew open as another lightning bolt shot across the sky, and thunder shook the house.

The teens screamed again.

From behind a torrent of rain, Martha rushed into the house. She shook the rain from her coat and slammed the door. She wiped her damp hair from her forehead.

"Whew, it is nasty out there! I made it halfway across town before I realised that I didn't have my bible I use to beat people..."

She stopped and stared into the darkened living room at the teens holding lit candles. She put her hands on her hips.

"Max, what is going on here? A séance? You know my stance on black magic..."

Max emphatically pointed at Miss Tutley. "Mommmm! Miss Tutley!"

Martha stared at Miss Tutley, then put her hands on her hips. "Shelley Tutley, why are you still alive? I thought the car crash that Jimmy Joe and..." She bit her lip.

"Mommmm! She has a knife!" Max exclaimed.

Martha eyed the knife in her hand. "Oh yes. I have one exactly like it. It's from the Henkels Platinum Prestige Collection isn't it? Good quality German stainless steel, nice weight, clean cuts... So, you sell knives in your spare time, do you? How do you manage to do that being a teacher while running for office?"

"No Mom!" Max said, exasperated, "she killed Mr. Fluffy Puffy!"

Max pointed the flashlight's beam at the motionless mound of fluff on the floor.

"Oh, thank God," Martha said as she waved a hand at the white ball. "I hated that beast."

Everyone stared incredulously at Martha.

"What?... Ohhhh, I get it," she said knowingly. "This is a biology class dissection, and you invited your entire class and your favorite teacher over to do the experiment together."

Max silently shook his head.

"I think that deserves bonus points, don't you?" Martha asked Miss Tutley, then winked elaborately at her.

Max rubbed his temples with his fingertips. "No... no Mom. She killed him on purpose."

Martha thought for a moment, and peered at Miss Tutley, who possessed a twisted, cartoonish grin on her face.

"Ohhhh, now I get it," Martha said as she vigorously nodded. "This is a sacrifice – a sacrifice to rid the evil that walks amongst us. A sacrifice to cleanse the sinners who have corrupted our society. A sacrifice only to be performed by a chaste, pure, virginal angel..."

Silence held the room. Everyone, including Miss Tutley, erupted in laughter. As they regained their composure, Miss Tutley reached over, and nudged Max.

"Is she for real?"

"Terrifying, isn't it?"

Fiona impatiently groaned, stepped forward, grabbed the flashlight from Max, and pointed it at Alex, slumped on the floor.

"Mrs. Molder, Miss Tutley murdered Alex. She came here tonight to get revenge because we all tried to kill her. Now do you see?"

Martha gasped and put a hand to her mouth. She peered dubiously at Miss Tutley.

"Shelley? I know we've had our differences in the election, but deep down I thought you were a good person."

"Good?" Max asked. "Tutley? She's a sex-crazed psychopath."

"She killed my father and Alex!" Fiona shouted.

"She's a moron," Sarah said.

Elliott peeked out from behind the chair. "She called me elephant!"

"Mom," Max implored, "you should hate her the most because of what she did with Dad. What's wrong with you?"

"What's your father got to do with..."

The front door burst open again, accompanied by more lightning and thunder.

Everyone screamed.

TWENTY-NINE

Jack, his new assistant Stevie, and Mrs. Horgenstefler were pushed into the living room, their hands tied behind their backs. Jimmy Joe and Arlene followed behind them with handguns drawn. Arlene slammed the door.

Everyone screamed.

"Jack!" Martha shouted.

Arlene scanned the room. "What the bloody blue blazes is goin' on in here?"

Martha inched toward Jimmy Joe and Arlene, then leaned in close to them.

"What are you doing?!" she hissed. "You weren't supposed to bring them here! And Jack wasn't even supposed to be kidnapped."

"Kidnapped?" Max asked.

"Martha, you know these idiots?" Jack asked.

"Idiots? Idiots?!" Arlene said, offended. She shoved the gun's nozzle against Jack's nose. "'Aint no idiots here sweet thang."

"Stop this you horrible child!" Mrs. Horgenstefler shouted.

"Quiet granny!"

Arlene rapped her on the head with the tip of the gun. Mrs. Horgenstefler flinched. Jimmy Joe pulled on Arlene.

"Don't Leeny. Don't hurt 'er!"

"You weren't supposed to hurt them!" Martha hissed.

Miss Tutley quickly stepped forward and chaotically waved the butcher knife back and forth from Jimmy Joe and Arlene to Martha.

"Seize her! Seize her! What are you two stupid hillbillies waiting for?!" she screamed, almost stamping her feet.

Jimmy Joe gawked at her, confused. "My name ain't Cesar. It's Jimmy Joe, remember?"

Marc whispered to Max. "I think a bucket of water would take care of her."

"Or a flying house," Max said.

"Now you keep yer britches on there 'Lil Miss Crazy Pants," Arlene said to Miss Tutley. "We only got two hands. Miss Martha's revenge is first. Besides, we only found out ya'll kicked the bucket in a car crash. It changed our plans and made our 'lil agreement... how they say, null and void," Arlene articulately pronounced. "'Ain't it Jimmy Joe?"

"Right, skull 'n droid."

"But I'm alive! And I paid you to do away with her! So do it!" Miss Tutley hissed.

"Whoa, whoa there Nelly!" Arlene said as she waved her gun at Miss Tutley. "Yer forgettin' who has the upper hand here. We'll get to yer craziness later. We aims to please, but first, Miss Martha's arrangement is a much bigger fish to fry."

"Sheesh Leeny," Jimmy Joe said, "we need one a those high techie 'puter programs ta keep track a all the crazy ladies who hire us."

"I can probably help you out..." Robin offered.

"Thanks kid. Mama said I'd do good in the revenge business," Arlene said.

"But... but we had a deal..." Miss Tutley whined.

Martha scrutinized Miss Tutley. "A deal?" She turned to Arlene. "But we had a deal..."

"Would someone please tell me what the hell is going on here?" Jack yelled. "Martha! Answer me! Who are these two deranged people?"

"Okay, okay!" Martha relented. "This is Arlene and Jimmy Joe Johnson... from the Tomorrow People's Liberation Army. I hired them."

"And I hired them too!" Miss Tutley said proudly.

"Oh, to do what?" Martha asked.

"Oh, you'll find out what, won't she Arlene? Won't she?" Miss Tutley cackled.

Martha leaned into Arlene and pointed at Jack.

"Why is he here?!" she hissed.

"Mr. Big Man decided ta play hero, and tried ta save Miss Oldy Mouldy and 'Lil Boy Blue, so we took him too. This here is a 'lil pit stop ta get yer fancy bits 'n bobs you like displayin' 'round yer... and I'm quotin', 'swan-like neck,'" Arlene deliberately pronounced.

"You hired them?!" Jack asked Martha, astounded. "To rob my bank and kidnap my secretaries?!"

"You robbed the bank too?!" Martha asked Jimmy Joe.

Jimmy Joe sniggered. "That parta tha plan we kinda left ya outta the loop."

He put an arm around Martha's shoulders like an octopus, wiped his mouth with his hand, and leaned close to her face. Martha peered at his arm in disgust and squirmed with revulsion.

"See, we need money, lotsa money, ta fund our 'lil 'ol plan..."

Arlene slapped him in the stomach. "Shut up doofus! They ain't need ta know that."

"Max's family attracts the most interesting people..." Robin whispered to Jenny.

"I know. This is more entertaining than a viral Tik Tok video."

"Terrorist plan?" Martha questioned. "But what about your church?"

Jimmy Joe erupted with laughter. "Church? We ain't got no church Miss Martha."

Arlene grabbed his left ear and pulled him off Martha. "Wut did I tell ya 'bout spillin' yer guts?"

"But... but your pamphlet... the Tomorrow People..." Martha whined.

Arlene moaned. "Oh my Gawd Miss Martha, yer denser than my Grandma's banana bread, which is why we took a likin' to ya. We ain't been to no church in years. We don't care two hoots 'bout all the crazy stuff in them there flyers. It's all honey ta catch some crazy bees – and boy 'o boy did we catch a couple 'a bigguns."

"But... but your message... America needs to hear it."

"All that gobbledegook was done by an ex-member before he experienced an 'unfortunate accident'," Arlene articulately pronounced as she made air quotations.

"Yeah, accident," Jimmy Joe said, then laughed manically.

Arlene frowned, and deliberately patted Jimmy Joe's face. "You never mind hun. You have any a those plastic handcuffs left?"

"Oh yeah. Lots," Jimmy Joe said as he produced a handful of plastic ties from his jacket.

"Good. Tie up those kiddies. Don't want any goin' astray. But first..."

Arlene grabbed an empty chip bowl from the coffee table and held it out in front of the teens. "Put them there candles in here. Be quick now. Don't try any funny stuff there Red," Arlene said to Fiona who hesitated.

The teens put the candles in the bowl. Arlene set the bowl on the coffee table, then grabbed a half-empty bowl of popcorn. She overturned the bowl, and the popcorn scattered over the floor. Martha took in a sudden, sharp breath as she stared at the mess.

"Now yer cell phones," Arlene said.

Arlene thrusted the bowl at each teen, and they dropped their cell phones into the dish. She spied Elliott peeking out from behind the chair and thrust the bowl at him.

"You there, big boy, drop it."

"But... but... my parents..."

"But but but," she mimicked him. "In the bowl."

Elliott dropped his cell phone in the bowl. Arlene set the bowl on the table, and stood guard while Jimmy Joe bound the teens' wrists.

"Don't tie them up," Jack said. "They've nothing to do with your sick plan. Let them go."

"Awww no. Kids are as sneaky as grownups – probably more so."

The doorbell rang the tune Bringing in the Sheaves.

"Git it Miss Martha," Arlene said. "Nice and careful like."

Martha grimaced, then walked to the door. She opened the door to Leslie on the doorstep.

"Leslie? What are you doing here?"

"Ummm, you told me to come here tonight so we could go over your plans now that Shelley Tutley is dead."

Martha frowned, and waved an arm inside to Miss Tutley, who dementedly waved at him. Leslie's eyes grew large as he took in the scene before him.

"What... is going on?"

Arlene waved the gun at him.

"Let the 'lil cutie pie in Miss Martha. He's letttin' in a draft."

Leslie stepped inside, and Martha closed the door.

"So, who do we have here?" Arlene said as she grazed the gun through Leslie's hair.

"I'm... I'm Martha's assistant."

"Assistant?! To all her craziness?"

"Right."

"Well, there ain't gonna be any more craziness, cause Miss Martha is what they say defaultin' from the election."

"Good," Miss Tutley groaned. "I don't have to pretend I'm running anymore."

"I am not defaulting!" Martha exclaimed. "I will defend this country's... wait, what do you mean pretend?"

"Please Martha, how stupid are you? Jack only told me to run and act as crazy as you to split the crazy vote so you wouldn't win," Miss Tutley spat. She pointed at Leslie. "And your assistant gave me your schedule so I'd be wherever you'd be."

Martha opened her mouth so wide she could have swallowed the entire room. Her head shook violently as if she were a malfunctioning robot. She sputtered and stumbled backwards.

"Leslie... Jack..." she whined, "why?"

Leslie lowered his head, and grimaced. "I'm sorry Mrs. Molder, but... your ghoulish hate campaign must be stopped. It goes against everything I stand for... and who I am. It's why I reached out to Jack and asked for his help."

Martha stared at Jack as if she had lost her only friend. "Jack...?" She focussed her anger on Jimmy Joe and Arlene. "You stupid hillbillies! If you would've eliminated this Tutley nitwit like I asked..."

"Ho ho!," Arlene laughed. "You got a pile a wax in yer lug holes Miss Martha? I told ya and 'Lil Miss Crazy Pants here, we got much bigger fish ta fry. We don't care 'bout yer stupid election, besides, we done did yer first request and snatched 'Lil Boy Blue and Miss Oldy Mouldy for ya!" she shouted as she pointed at Stevie and Mrs. Horgenstefler.

Max stared at his mother. "Mom, what have you done?"

"What have I done?" Martha asked as she planted a hand flat against her chest.

"I think he means unintentionally funding a two-bit amateur homegrown terrorist organization, and spreading your ignorant, racist, homophobic hate through what you thought was a radical religious cult," Jack said.

"Wow, you are terrible," Miss Tutley said disparagingly. "At least I'm a respectable schoolteacher..."

"Yeah right, you and Mary Kay Letourneau," Sarah said.

"What I allegedly did is nothing compared to what your father has done," Martha said.

"Oh, sorry Mom," Max said. "Excuse me Dad, but did you commit treason against this country by allowing terrorists to manipulate you?"

"No Max, I did not."

"Excuse me!" Martha yelled as she bobbled her head back and forth. "The most important thing in this country is the family. It must be held together with industrial-strength Crazy Glue," she said as she slapped her palms together, "so the pro-abortionists, homosexuals, atheists, immigrants and adulterers," she explicitly pronounced at Jack, "can't tear it apart."

"Well Max," Marc said, "looks like you and your dad are tied three for five. You're both equally horrible people."

"I'm only trying to preserve the America I deserve..." Martha said sweetly.

"Yeah, from the 1950s," Max said. "You're such an embarrassment..."

"Your father is the one who has embarrassed this country and permanently soiled this family. Soiled it with this..." She gestured repulsively at Stevie and Mrs. Horgenstefler. "... this toy boy and this old harlot!" she spat.

"Mr. Molder," Stevie sobbed, "I'm scared. I know my wife is sick with worry. She's waiting for me at home with our new triplets..."

Jack leaned against Stevie's shoulder.

"It's okay Stevie. I won't let anything happen to you."

Martha contorted her face in disgust. "Ohhhhh! Right in front of me Jack?! How perverted. And you..." Martha said contemptuously to Mrs. Horgenstefler.

Martha slowly circled the elderly woman, regarding her with complete revulsion.

"At your advanced age, you should know better. But I know your kind lady," she hissed close to Mrs. Horgenstefler's ear. "Feigning innocence with your great-grandmotherly façade. Deceptively seductive behind your lavender-scented body butter. Passion bubbling under your girdle. A panther at prey, raging with animal lust. Carnal urges ready to boil over!"

Mrs. Horgenstefler smiled knowingly. "That sounds about right..." she said demurely.

"No Mom! You have it all backwards," Max announced.

"Max..." Jack said slowly.

"Dad's not having an affair with Stevie or Mrs. Horgenstefler!"

"Praise Jesus!" Martha shouted. She clasped her hands together and gazed at the ceiling.

"Max..." Jack said again, slower.

"He's fucking Miss Tutley!"

Everyone turned and stared at Miss Tutley, who smiled and waved with her fingertips. Martha's disgust, which had briefly turned to elation, switched to horror as she instantly lost her direct line to God, and turned to Jack, her eyes as large as communion wafers.

"So, you, Stevie and Mrs. Horgenstefler didn't..." she insinuated as she shook her head.

"No Mom!" Max said, exasperated. "I think we can all agree Stevie is cute, and Mrs. Horgenstefler is a dish, but no!"

"Martha," Jack announced, "let me put it like this so you can understand. Miss Tutley and I fucked at her house. We fucked in her classroom. We fucked in my car. We fucked in our bed. We fucked everywhere! Do you get it?"

"No, she's definitely not getting it," Marc quipped.

Martha quietly pondered Jack's announcement. She stared straight ahead as her eyes glazed over, and she slipped into a semi-conscious coma-like state.

“Mom? Mom?” Max asked as he peered at her.

Martha held her eyes open until a thin layer of filmy crust developed on them. She blinked. She let out a primal scream and lunged at Miss Tutley. She knocked the butcher knife from Miss Tutley’s hand with a quick hack to her wrist with one hand, then delivered a Miss Piggy-esque karate chop to her chest with her other hand, complete with accurate sound effects.

“Hiiii ya!” she screamed.

As Miss Tutley crumpled to the floor, Martha jumped on her. She straddled her, put her hands around Miss Tutley’s throat, and choked her.

“I... trusted... you! Thought... you... were... an... angel! Turns... out... you... are... a... common... tart! You whore! You whore! You whore!”

“Now why didn’t we think of doing that?” Sarah asked.

Elliott quickly poked his head out from behind the chair. “Kill her! Kill her! Kill her!” he screamed, then swiftly hid behind the chair again.

Jimmy Joe finished manacling the kids’ wrists, including Leslie.

“Well, that takes care a her,” he said. “Now we don’t have ta kill ya Miss Mar...”

Arlene elbowed him in the ribs. “Would you can it doofus?”

The doorbell rang Bringing in the Sheaves again.

Martha immediately stopped choking Miss Tutley.

“Could someone answer the door please?” she asked sweetly and instantly continued her Dr. Jekyll and Mr. Hyde interpretation as she violently choked Miss Tutley.

THIRTY

Jack eyed Arlene and Jimmy Joe, then made an awkward move toward the door. Arlene waved her gun at him.

"Oh no ya don't Mr. Happy Pants. Back in line with Miss Oldy Mouldy and Lil Boy Blue. Keep an eye on 'em Jimmy Joe. I don't trust 'em – specially granny there."

Mrs. Horgenstefler stuck her tongue out at her. Arlene walked to the door and opened it to reveal Carter and Christian Riley on the doorstep. She eyed them seductively as she twirled the gun at them.

"Well, helllooo gorgeouses!"

The two men eyed each other.

"Ummm, hi... are the Molders at home?" Carter asked politely.

"Who wants ta know?" Arlene growled.

"Well, I'm Max's teacher, and this is my..."

"Max's teacher? It's a 'lil late for extra-curricularingly, ain't it Max's teacher?"

Carter took a step back and glanced at the house. "This is the Molder's house... right?"

"Oh yes, yes. We have Molders here, and we have olders too," Arlene cackled.

The two men eyed each other again.

"You best come in outta the rain 'fore it soaks them tight shirts through," Arlene said.

As Carter and Christian each took a step forward, Arlene extended an arm and put a hand on Carter's chest – keeping them in the rain.

"Well, a bit more couldn't hurt I guess..."

The two men exchanged nervous glances as Arlene smiled manically at them.

"Okay, git in here," she ordered.

Arlene waved the gun at them and stepped aside. As Carter and Christian entered the house, Arlene ogled them.

"Mmm mmm mmm, my my my, the Lord does fine work, as Miss Martha says."

Arlene closed the door and followed the men.

"Ummm, they're married," Jack said.

"Oh, I'm only flirtin' a 'lil bit Moldy. You should know all 'bout that, seein' as you and 'Lil Miss Crazy Pants got down in the mud."

Arlene grazed the gun's nozzle through Carter's hair.

"I'm sure their wives don't mind a 'lil harmless flirtin'..."

"They're married... to each other," Jack said.

Arlene regarded them. "Figures. Jimmy Joe, shackle these purty boys."

Jimmy Joe stepped forward and bound the new visitors' wrists with cable ties.

"Mr. Riley!" Fiona shouted, "we're being held hostage! Miss Tutley killed Alex!"

Carter and Christian scanned the shackled teens, then stared at Martha on the floor as she choked Miss Tutley.

"What is going on here?" Christian asked, bewildered.

"Miss Tutley came here to kill us, and these crazy yahoos showed up," Jenny said.

"It's alright Jenny," Carter said, "we know all about these crazy yahoos."

"Ya do? Leeny, we're famous!" Jimmy Joe said.

"Yeah," Arlene mused, "it's a blessin' and a curse – like one a those Kardaliens."

Martha stopped choking Miss Tutley unconscious, and let her head fall limply to the floor. She stood, stepped over Miss Tutley's lifeless body, and stood beside Max.

"Well, if it isn't Adam and Steve," she snapped.

"Mrs. Molder, please. Your family is in grave danger," Christian said.

"I'll say it is," Martha said. "Surrounded by adulterers and married homosexuals!"

Martha put an arm around Max and tried to grasp him tight. He squirmed against her.

"Mrs. Molder," Carter said, "Christian showed me that awful brochure..."

"Hey," Jimmy Joe interrupted, "we got us a good deal ta have it done real nice like after we threatened ta blast the print shop..."

"Anyway," Carter continued, "I checked out the Tomorrow People on the internet. They're alienated, unstable, right-wing fanatics who live in their parents' basements."

"Hey!" Jimmy Joe interrupted again, "we're squattin' in our own place thank you very much Mr. Purty Hair."

"Ah yes," Martha nodded knowingly, "the internet. Where all you sex-crazed homosexuals hang out to prey on our innocent children."

Max wrenched himself away from Martha, faced her, and screamed.

"Mom! Shut up! Shut the fuck up! I'm fucking sick of listening to your fucking horse shit! Everyone is! So. Shut. The. Fuck. Up!"

Silence consumed the room. Martha's mouth opened like a drawbridge again. She recoiled and put a hand to her throat. Max let out a huge sigh and turned to face Marc.

"Marc isn't my best friend, or as you like to call him Mom, 'my token Black friend'. He's my boyfriend, and I love him."

Marc stared at Max. "You love me?"

"Yes," Max said softly.

"Max, I love you too."

Unable to put their arms around each other because of their shackled wrists, Marc and Max leaned into each other and shared a tender kiss. The room erupted in oohs and awws.

Arlene wiped away a tear. "This is more movin' than my assault rifle weddin' at the car crushin' place on Hallowe'en."

Martha theatrically hyperventilated. As she heaved, she stumbled backwards and reached for something to grasp to keep from falling over. She found nothing, and continued to awkwardly stumble back to a bookshelf where she could prolong her performance. She grasped the shelf with one hand, while she clunked her other hand to her forehead and moaned.

"Ohhhhhhhh..."

She desperately clutched her pearls. If a couch were nearby, she would have fainted onto it. Instead, she slowly and awkwardly collapsed to the floor. She dragged books by Tucker Carlson, Ann Coulter, Donald Trump and Bill O'Reilly off the shelves, and they fell with her. As she came to rest on the floor, her right leg bent at an awkward angle, and her rear end rested on Donald Trump's book.

"Ow ow ow ow ow," she cried out as she broke her fake-shocked-mother act and quickly straightened her leg.

"Jack," Mrs. Horgenstefler said, "has your wife started drinking again?"

"Again?"

Martha removed Donald Trump's book from her rear end and recklessly tossed it across the room. It bounced into the fireplace where the charred remnants of To Kill a Mockingbird and The Diviners lay. She moaned, gazed to the ceiling, and clasped her hands together so tight, they turned ghostly white, and lost their circulation.

"Why me Lord?" she moaned. "I did everything right. I exposed him to guns at an early age. I made him dress as a cowboy, a policeman, an army man, a construction worker, or a biker on Hallowe'en. I ensured he only watched movies with gladiators and bodybuilders. I made sure all his friends were girls, and his underwear was never too tight or colorful."

"Stop it Mom," Max begged.

"Mrs. Molder, Max isn't a cat that needs de-worming," Christian said.

Robin leaned into Jenny. "I knew Max's life was crazy, but he deserves an award for living with this."

"I know. The worst it gets for me is when my mom politely asks me to clean my room."

Everyone stared at Martha as she sobbed, then crumbled into a fetal position on the floor.

"I'll do anything you say Lord," Martha wept. "I'll have another child and raise him in isolation. I'll change my name to avoid the embarrassment. I'll go into the witness protection program... anything! Give me a sign Lord!"

The doorbell chimed 'Bringing in the Sheaves' again.

"If it's Jesus, tell him I'll be right back," she said as she quickly scrambled from the floor, and ran to the bathroom next to the front door. "I have to fix my makeup."

"Holy moly Jimmy Joe," Arlene said, annoyed, as she walked to the door, "we only came here ta grab some trinkets 'n shiny bits 'n bobs from the Moldys and be on our way again. And here I am doin' maidin' stuff," she grumbled.

Arlene opened the door. Enrique and Jesus, and Connie and Sally stood on the doorstep.

"Well, my word," Arlene announced. "Y'all here for the party?"

"Party?" Connie asked.

Arlene pointed her gun at them. "Yeah," she snarled, "the one with four more hostages."

Arlene waved them inside with the gun. The new visitors eyed each other, and one-by-one entered the house. Arlene slammed the door.

"Alright Jimmy Joe, we got four more stragglers. Cuff 'em."

"But I only got two handcuffy things left..." he said as he held them in the air.

"Shackle the boys," Arlene ordered. "I'll keep a close eye on these here ladies."

Arlene pointed her gun directly at Connie and Sally, who clung to her mother.

"Why hello Carter, Christian," Connie said. "Nice night... isn't it?"

"Never a dull moment with Martha Molder," Carter drawled.

"Mr. Molder," Stevie cried, "this is going to end soon, right?"

"Quiat!" Jimmy Joe shouted.

Arlene turned the gun on Enrique and Jesus as Jimmy Joe bound their wrists. Martha poked her head out from the bathroom and saw her new guests.

"Oh, it is Jesus," she said.

"Mrs. Molder," Enrique said, "my son's name is hey-seuss. Hey-seuss," he pronounced.

Martha exited the bathroom. "Hey-seuss, Dr. Seuss, Canada goose, apple juice," Martha said as she rolled her eyes, and indifferently waved a hand in the air. "It doesn't make any difference Rick."

"Mrs. Molder," Jesus announced, "you're insulting my culture, my family..."

"Oh please! We speak American here. This is America, not the back streets of Santiago!"

"Do you even know what country my father is from?"

"Well sure, one of the poor, disadvantaged ones..."

Jesus fumed and bit his lip. "Mrs. Molder, you know my father was born in Canada..."

"Hmmm, well..." Martha deliberated, "maybe a northern border wall would stop you people from escaping across the frozen tundra into our great country..."

"Of immigrants," Jack added.

Jesus leaned into his father. "Dad, tell her. Tell her now or I will."

As Enrique opened his mouth, Martha's attention turned to Connie and Sally. She latched onto Connie's arm with a falcon-like death grip.

"Connie, I'm so glad you're here. I must tell you it's only you and me now. Shelley Tutley was a fraud out to get me, and my assistant Leslie is a traitorous turncoat..."

Leslie waved hello to Connie, who awkwardly waved back.

"But now with a two-way race between us, it's clear I will emerge victorious!"

"Well, actually..." Connie said.

"As you can see, we have a situation here..." Martha chortled.

Connie scanned the shackled teens, the two bodies on the floor, and Arlene and Jimmy Joe holding everyone at gunpoint.

"Y-yes, I can see," she stammered.

"The Lord knew I needed His help, so he sent your perfect, young, White, heterosexual, virginal daughter to my aid!" Martha cried. She relinquished her hold on Connie and grabbed Sally by the arm. "Come with me child!"

Enrique took a step toward Martha and tried to get her attention. "Mrs. Molder..."

Martha dragged Sally past Enrique to where Max and Marc stood. Arlene followed, while Jimmy Joe stood guard by the door. Sally stumbled after Martha and bumped into her when she abruptly stopped. Martha produced Sally before Max.

"There!" she proclaimed as if Sally were the missing piece in a jigsaw puzzle.

"Hi Sally," Max said.

"Hi Max."

Max shook his head at Martha. "There what?" he asked.

"Well, it's a good start, but do I have to do everything? Compliment her on her clothes and how they accentuate her perfect figure. Tell her how good she looks..."

"Mrs. Molder..." Carter and Christian said in stereo.

Martha glanced back at them. "You keep your gay opinions to yourselves heathens. You're beyond help."

"No, you are," Carter said under his breath.

"Lean in, sniff her hair," Martha continued, "tell her it smells nice, ask for a kiss, offer to lick her fingers..."

"Even that's a bit too kinky even fer me Miss Martha," Arlene said. "'Cept fer the legitimate times me and Jimmy Joe have KFC."

"Mrs. Molder," Sally faltered, "you're... you're kinda creeping me out..."

Marc took a step forward. "Mrs. Molder, you have to accept it..."

Martha quickly stuck an arm out. "You stay out of this Marc the molester!"

Martha deliberately stepped between Max and Sally, and hooked arms with them. She walked them to the staircase as Enrique tried to talk to her again.

"Mrs. Molder..."

Martha walked past him. "Sally dear, you have a mission tonight. I asked God for a favor, and he sent you to drive the perverted evil from my son. So...good luck."

She gave them a push, causing them to stumble on the stairs.

"Max's bedroom is at the top of the stairs and to the right. He'll show you. Now, off you go!" She smiled, nodded, and gleefully clapped her hands.

"Martha… really?" Connie asked.

"She forgot to give them a condom and two cigarettes," Sarah said.

"Max, what is going on?" Sally asked as she helped him stand.

"I told Mom I'm gay, and about me and Marc…"

"Oh, that's great," Sally said as she hugged Max.

"Finally!" Martha exclaimed, "some contact…"

"Mrs. Molder," Enrique interrupted, "we have to talk…"

"Not now Rick, my son is having a heterosexual breakthrough."

"Now she thinks you're going to de-gay me," Max told Sally.

"Mrs. Molder," Sally said, "Max and I are only friends – like we always have been."

"Oh no, she's starting to fade," Martha said in anguish. "That's what I get for sending a girl to do a woman's job."

"Wow," Sarah muttered. "Is Mrs. Molder gonna hire a prostitute for him next?"

"Well, Tutley's unconscious or dead or something, so she's outta luck," Fiona said.

"Oh, for fuck sakes Martha!" Jack shouted. "Cut this bullshit out and leave the kids alone! Everyone knows Max is gay."

"Everyone?" she questioned, shocked.

Everybody murmured and nodded their heads affirmatively.

"Even I did," Arlene said, "by the way he gives his boo those big 'ol googly eyes."

"You mean, I'm the last to know?"

"Oh, can it Martha!" Jack spat. "Even you did. Your ignorance couldn't handle it, so you conveniently didn't want to believe it."

"You're right! I can't handle it!" Martha shouted.

"Mrs. Molder," Carter said, "Max is your son…"

"Yes, thank you Mr. Gay Sex Teacher," Martha shouted.

"I thought Mr. Riley taught English?" Robin whispered to Jenny.

"You don't get it do you Mrs. Molder?" Carter said. "Max needs your unconditional support. What he doesn't need is someone telling him he's somehow a lesser person because of the archaic views in someone's tiny brain."

"Mrs. Molder," Enrique forcefully interjected, "I hate to interfere with your internal family problems, but I must tell you something!"

"What?! What? What? What?!" she screamed at him. "That your son has the hots for my son and wants to marry him, so you came here to ask for my blessing?!"

"What?!" Jesus asked, shocked.

"No, no," Enrique said.

"It might as well be," Martha exclaimed. "Now that Max has made his choice quite clear, there'll be an endless stream of depraved sex maniacs at our door like these gay sex heathens!" she motioned toward Carter and Christian.

"Oh, shut up Martha!" everyone shouted in unison.

"Mom!" Max wailed, "I'm not some man-eating tart like Tutley!"

"Mrs. Molder," Jesus shouted, "my father came here tonight to tell you he quits!"

"Hijo!" Enrique exclaimed.

"Lo siento padre, pero ella tiene que saber."

"What?" Martha asked. "Speak American!"

"Mrs. Molder, I'm sorry but I cannot work for you anymore," Enrique said.

"What? But how will you continue to struggle to lift yourself from the poverty you brought to this country?"

"Mrs. Molder, you are a horrible person!" Jesus announced, then turned to Jack. "I'm so sorry Mr. Molder..."

"No, please, go on," Jack said.

"I have many more clients, and my wife's business is growing Mrs. Molder," Enrique said. "But my son convinced me to stand for my principles and pride."

"In other words, he can no longer work for a racist, ignorant loca!" Jesus shouted, then turned to Jack again. "I apologise..."

"No, no, la mujer esta loca..."

"Why is everyone speaking in a foreign language!" Martha cried. "This is America!"

"This is my language Martha," Jack said. "It always has been – long before you met me, and long before I came to this country. You forced me to change my name and Americanize it, and you passed me off as Italian. Well, I'm not Italian. I'm from Puerto..."

Martha covered her ears with her hands and walked around the room in circles. "La la la la la la la la la la la la..."

"I'm an immigrant from Puerto Rico!" Jack shouted. "And my name is Juan Martinez, not Jack Molder!"

"La la la la la la la la la la la la..." Martha continued.

"And I'm Max Martinez!" Max said.

"La la la la la la la la la la la la..."

"Mrs. Horgenstefler," Stevie cried, "do you want your job back?"

"Helllll no," she drawled.

Martha twirled around the room until she stopped before Connie.

"Oh Connie," she exclaimed, "you're the only one who hasn't metaphorically ripped my heart out tonight and stomped on it. Save me! Save me from all these backstabbers."

Connie awkwardly put a hand on Martha's arm.

"Ummm, well actually Martha, the only reason I came over here is because I wanted to break the news to you in person, so you wouldn't hear it elsewhere, but I now realize it would have been a bonus. Leslie is working for me now."

Martha wheeled around and stared at Leslie. She heaved as if she were an inflatable pool toy quickly losing air. "But you can't!"

"Mrs. Molder, as I said before, you stand for everything I'm not. Your ghoulish, sick hate made me realise that. Working with Connie, I can help stop you."

"I see."

Martha's desperate expression turned to stone. She emitted a high-pitched, hyena-like scream, then walked to the door where she grabbed her purse, rummaged through it, and pulled out her flask. She turned away from everyone and huddled in the corner. She tossed her head back, tipped the flask, and emptied the contents into her mouth.

The doorbell rang 'Bringing in the Sheaves' again.

"Oh Lord," Arlene groaned. "It's fer you Miss Martha. It's the people in the white coats – and they have one with 'lil 'ol buckles fer you."

Martha looked hopefully at the door.

"Get it Martha," Jack said.

THIRTY-ONE

Martha capped her flask, popped it back in her purse, and lurched to the door. She flung it open to find Mrs. Richards on the doorstep.

"Oh, Mrs. Richards," Martha exclaimed. "Thank God you're here! Please come in."

Martha reached out and grabbed the woman's arm.

"Well, I..." she said, and stumbled into the house as Martha yanked on her arm.

Arlene slammed the door. "Now, who's this old bird?" she asked, irritated.

Mrs. Richards jumped back when she saw Arlene with the gun.

Martha grappled onto Mrs. Richards as if she were a long-lost relative. "This is my dear, dear friend Mrs. Richards, a trustworthy, loyal woman of great conviction."

Mrs. Richards gawked at Martha and glanced around the room at the hostages.

"Am I interrupting something?"

"Oh no, just a pesky little family situation."

"Well, I can't stay..."

"Oh no, please, Mrs. Richardsy, stay," Arlene said, and poked the gun into her ribs.

Mrs. Richards reached into her pocket and produced an envelope. "I only stopped by to drop this off..."

"Easy there Mrs. Richardsy," Arlene said as she snatched the envelope from the woman's hand and passed it to Jimmy Joe. "Read it," she ordered.

Jimmy Joe opened the envelope and pulled out a letter. He scanned it carefully.

"Welllllll!?" Arlene moaned.

"Awww, it's nothin'. Jus some blah-de-blah 'bout Miss Martha bein' canned from the PTA..."

"What!?" Martha screeched. She swiped the letter from Jimmy Joe's hand.

Martha's face contorted into several different expressions as she silently read the letter, then sputtered out its general meaning in broken words.

"Terminated... let go... unprofessional... outlandish... conduct... unbecoming... unanimous... well-being... the children... safety... good luck..."

"I'm sorry Mrs. Molder, but you're poisonous," Mrs. Richards said.

"But, but, but the children... We must think of the children!"

"We were thinking of the children," Carter said.

"You!" Martha pointed at Carter. "You were in on this too?"

"That's what unanimous means."

"It's prolly best the PTA canned ya Miss Martha," Jimmy Joe said. "You seems like the kinda person who could make 'lil kiddies cry."

"Oh Lord, why hast thou forsaken me tonight!?" Martha cried. "What have I done to anger thee? I know... I know. I've let the sinners desecrate your earth with their wicked ways. They've taken over – the sex Marxists, the homosexual terrorists, the communist Democrats..."

"Don't forget about the illegal Mexican Canadian immigrants," Jesus said.

"Yes, thank you Hey-Seuss. I won't let them win Lord! Tonight, you sent three prophets of the apocalypse. I'll try to be a better Christian to smash the hold they have on this country!"

"Martha! Would you cut the fucking bullshit and tell your crazy cult leaders to cut these ties off!" Jack shouted as he shook his manacled wrists at her.

"We're no cult leaders," Arlene said.

"No, you're not," Carter said. "You're only franchisees the Tomorrow People use. The real leaders are multi-millionaires from Idaho who sucker unhinged, angry White people into believing the world has done them wrong, and that they're being disenfranchised and left behind after an eternity of privilege..."

"Gosh dang it, Mr. Purty Hair," Jimmy Joe interrupted, "now I'm awful hungry fer some franchise chicken."

"I think you mean fricassee chicken," Mrs. Horgenstefler said. "I used to make it all the time for my late fifth husband."

"How did ya franchise yer chicken granny?" Arlene asked.

"Anyway," Carter continued, "these cult followers create fake news stories, and peddle them to Fox News, you know, like their car tires being slashed when they were just old and cracked..."

"They do grifting," Christian said, "I mean crowdfunding to build a virtual electric fence on the Canadian border, to hold fake Christo Fascist Freedom award galas where they hand out gold foil-covered chocolate medals to those who did the best job in perpetrating treason against their own country, and to fund legal defences for the mentally unstable people they brainwash who threaten presidents and prime ministers."

"And their followers have rotten teeth, a dull, not-quite-there expression, and look like they cut their own hair with dull jack knives," Carter said.

Arlene slapped Jimmy Joe in the stomach. "Stand up straight. He's givin' us flattery!"

"Their brochure was absolute hate, so I called the police," Christian said.

"The police? Leeny, we gotta get outta here! I can't do time again. I'm too purty."

"I know darlin'. When ya got out last time, those new love makin' positions ya learned kinda threw me for a loop."

Carter and Christian eyed each other.

Jimmy Joe grabbed Arlene's arm. "C'mon, let's go! We got the money..."

"Wait, what about Miss Martha's fancy bits 'n bobs?" Arlene asked.

"You said they was ugly anyway."

"Right. And we scared Miss Oldy Mouldy and Lil Boy Blue, like she wanted..."

"No, I wanted you to drive them out into the woods and leave them there or something so their affair with Jack wouldn't ruin my campaign. We had a deal!"

"Seems to me you ruined your campaign all by yourself dear," Mrs. Richards said.

"Miss Martha, where have ya been the last twenty minutes – in cuckoo land?" Arlene asked, perturbed. "You heard your hubby, he ain't been doin' the nasty with Miss Oldy Mouldy or Lil Boy Blue. He did it with Lil Miss Crazy Pants! So, yer beef is with her – and you done conked the life outta her, so our 'lil deal is, I say again, null and voided."

"But you took my money!" Martha bleated.

"What can I say? Thanks. If ya got a problem with that, call one a those Judge Judy shows. I've been lookin' to git on 'em fer awhile now. Come on Jimmy Joe." She yanked on his arm.

"Wait!" Jack shouted. "At least untie us..."

"Oh no, I don't trust ya Moldy. Ya'll can square up after we leave. Miss Connie and Miss Martha can help..."

Arlene glanced at Martha, who silently moved her mouth, and shook her head.

"Well, maybe not Miss Martha, but Mrs. Richardsy has two free hands. Well, sorry for all the commotion Mouldy. We was only doin' business. Come on," Arlene said as she grabbed Jimmy Joe's arm, and they backed toward the door.

"You'll never get away with this you horrible child," Mrs. Horgenstefler said. "We know what you look like, and what you've done."

"You keep forgettin' granny, we already got away with it. You can blabby-de-blab all ya want to yer knittin' circle. We'll be long gone. We popped into yer little 'ol town, scammed some cash outta ya, and popped back out again jus like a Kid Rock concert."

"Yeah, this ain't our first disguise," Jimmy Joe said.

"I knew I recognized those two," Jenny whispered to Robin. "I think they were extras on 'My Big Fat Redneck Wedding'."

Arlene slapped Jimmy Joe in the stomach. "Now looky what ya done. We been celebrity watched."

She put a hand on the doorknob, and hesitated.

"Ya know, Miss Oldy Mouldy's right Jimmy Joe."

"'Bout what?"

"'Bout havin' all these peepers on us and knowin' what we done. Wouldn't hurt ta have some security, ya know, insurance, ta keep all their traps shut..."

Arlene turned, and sauntered to Mrs. Horgenstefler, who put her hands on her hips.

"You lay one more finger on me Squeaky, and I'll drop kick you back to last week."

"Wow!" Arlene said. "Yer a feisty 'ol bird. I like yer style granny. When they make a movie 'bout us, I'll put a word in fer ya ta play Barbara Bush."

Connie nudged Mrs. Richards, and eyed Martha. Mrs. Richards thought for a moment, then nodded. They grabbed Martha's arms and presented her to Arlene and Jimmy Joe.

"Here, take her," Connie said.

"What?!" Martha exclaimed.

"Hmmmm," Arlene pondered. "What'll you give us for her Moldy?"

"Give you? I'm not giving you anything," Jack said. "She'll be a big help to you though when the rapture comes."

"Jack! No! I don't want to go with them. They're nuts!"

"You'll fit right in."

Martha reached out desperately to Max. "Max! Max! Help me my sweet baby!"

Max turned his head and dismissively waved his hand in her general direction.

"Take her away."

"Here," Enrique said as he quickly walked to the door, and fumbled with the handle, his hands still manacled, "let me get the door for you..."

"Miss Martha, do ya need a bag packed or anythin'?" Jimmy Joe asked sincerely.

"I'll do it!" Marc said as he raised a hand.

“Nooooooooo! Don’t take me…” Martha wailed, then pointed at the Rileys. “Take them. Take these sinners. They’re responsible for the destruction of the American family!”

Carter and Christian shook their heads and regarded her pathetically.

“Take anyone else here!” Martha said as she squirmed against Connie and Mrs. Richards. “You’re all sinners,” she announced, and pointed around the room.

“Adulterous fake immigrant sex maniac,” at Jack.

“Flirty kinky closet sex purveyors,” at Mrs. Horgenstefler and Stevie.

“Heartless child endangerer,” at Mrs. Richards.

“Illegal igloo border crossers,” at Enrique and Jesus.

“Terrorist-loving Communist-running backstabber,” at Connie.

“Botched conversion traitor,” at Leslie.

“Failed heterosexual disappointment,” at Sally.

“Son-stealing gay maker,” at Marc.

“Oversexed marriage wrecker,” at Miss Tutley’s body.

“And you,” she pointed at Jenny, “I don’t know who you are, but your shoes are ugly.”

Everyone stared at Jenny’s shoes. Jenny crossed her feet and tried to hide them.

“You’re all responsible for the decay of American society!” Martha thundered.

“Wow,” Marc said, “I’d like to know what wacky bible she got those sins from.”

“They’re from ‘Baby’s First Republican Handbook’,” Max said. “Mom used to read it to me every night when I was a child.”

“I don’t know how you coped Max,” Robin said. “I got scared by ‘The Giving Tree’.”

“Sin! Sin! Sin! Sin!” Martha raged as she wildly pointed at random around the room.

Arlene covered her ears and nodded at Jimmy Joe. “Good Lord, what a racket! Take hold ‘a her will ya!”

Jimmy Joe seized Martha by the shoulders. Connie and Mrs. Richards relinquished their hold on her and stepped back.

"Thank God," Connie said, relieved. "It was like trying to hold onto Regan MacNeil."

"What is going on here?!" Martha exclaimed. "Unhand me you lunatic!"

"You hush up now, ya hear?" Arlene said as she grabbed Martha's hand. "Quit squirmin' 'n bobbin' around like a 'lil fishy danglin' on a line. Yer gonna get all stringy and tired. We need yer energy fer ya ta make pipe bombs and write threatenin' letters to the government."

Arlene and Jimmy Joe turned and led Martha to the door. Enrique swung the door open.

"Why thank you kind sir," Arlene said.

"It's my pleasure," he said.

"This wasn't the plan..." Martha whined as she struggled against them.

"Yer wrong again Miss Martha," Arlene said. "We never got around to Lil Miss Crazy Pants' plan to get rid of ya, so now's our chance to make good on her contract."

"But... but... but she's dead or unconscious or something!" Martha wailed. "Your deal with her is null and void, like mine!"

"But, but, but," Arlene snapped as she imitated Martha. "Miss Martha, weren't ya listenin'? We voided yer contract cause there were... extenuatin' circumstances. The people you wanted revenge on were innocent and the real culprit is..." Arlene searched for the right word.

"Incapacitated?" Carter offered.

"Thank you, Mr. Purty Hair. Any chance you wannabe our PR guy and speech writer?"

"Ummm, no thank you."

"No!" Martha wailed. "I'm too important to my community. I'm a woman standing for public office. This is illegal. This is unconstitutional and will trigger a national crisis!"

"Would you listen to Margaret Thatcher here?" Mrs. Horgenstefler said.

"Okay Miss Martha, let's say we forget our agreement with Lil Miss Crazy Pants..."

"Oh, thank God!" Martha said.

"...and git rid of ya cause it's the decent thang to do fer all these people who can't stand ya."

"For the whole town," Mrs. Richards said.

"For the whole country," Jesus said.

"For the whole world," Carter said.

"But this isn't fair you unhinged, crazy scam artists!" Martha shouted.

"Hey," Jimmy Joe said, "the Tomorra People might be unhinged and crazy, but one thang we ain't is scam artists. We need ta keep our standin' with the Better Business Bureau ya know."

Arlene yanked on Martha. "Come on now, time's a wastin'..."

"Jaaaaaaaack..." Martha wailed as Arlene and Jimmy Joe led her from the house.

"It's Juan to you."

Outside, the storm had passed, and left in its wake a damp, fresh stillness. Martha cried as Arlene and Jimmy Joe led her to their truck. Arlene opened the rear truck door, and they pushed her inside. Arlene slammed the door. Jack stepped outside onto the doorstep. He took in a deep breath and exhaled satisfactorily. Mrs. Horgenstefler joined him.

"Jack, what about the bank's money?"

He pondered her question for a moment. "It's a small price to pay..."

She peered at him, shocked, then nodded in agreement. Jack stepped off the doorstep and stood in the driveway. The truck roared away. He watched as Martha pressed her face and hands on the rear window. Terror covered her face.

Screams filled the house.

THIRTY-TWO

Jack wheeled around, then scampered up the steps. Mrs. Horgenstefler put a hand to her throat and followed him inside the house.

"What's going on?!" Jack shouted as he ran into the living room.

"Miss Tutley's on the loose!" Elliott yelled as he peeked out from behind his chair.

Connie and Mrs. Richards cut the cable tie from Enrique's wrists with scissors. As the hostages were freed, they helped to free others. Fiona grabbed the flashlight from the floor and frantically shone it around the room. She pointed the light to an empty spot on the floor where Miss Tutley had been.

"She was right there!"

"Okay," Jack said, "everyone calm down. Let's all gather in the middle of the room. Has anyone called 9-1-1 yet?"

"I did," Elliott said, "about ten minutes ago when Max's mom went crazy."

"But those two crooks took your phone," Jesus said.

"I gave them my backup phone my parents told me to carry in case I ever got kidnapped. The police and an ambulance should be here soon."

"Oh Elliott, you're brilliant!"

"I've been texting my parents the whole time too. I think my Dad's sending the army..."

Everyone grabbed their cell phones from the bowl on the coffee table, made calls, and texted. Connie spoke into her phone.

"That's right," she said, "former PTA chair, religious zealot, currently running for state rep, and now domestic terrorist Martha Molder..."

Sally touched her arm. "Mom, who are you talking to?"

Connie put a hand over the microphone. "Fox News..."

Elliott scrambled to his feet and clung to Sarah.

"Please don't let Miss Tutley hurt me, I'm an only child."

"No one's going to hurt you Elliott."

Fiona stood by the sofa and carefully searched the room with the flashlight. A hand reached out from behind the sofa and grabbed her ankle. She screamed, then pointed the light to her feet. Alex stared at her.

"Alex!"

Fiona passed the flashlight to Max, and helped Alex sit up.

"Alex! We thought you were dead."

She hugged him and kept an arm around his shoulder to steady him. Alex put a hand to his head and rubbed his skull.

"I-I think I hit my head. I must have passed out... What happened?"

"Tutley attacked you," Elliott said, excited, "and two crazy ex-cons showed up, and Max's mother strangled her, and she tried to get Max and Sally to have sex, and half the town arrived, and..."

"Yes, yes," Jenny said, "we'll fill him in later."

Fiona touched Alex's head, and stared at the large, wet blood stain on his shirt.

"Alex, you know you've been cut, right?"

Alex peered at his chest. He touched the blood with his fingertips, then his eyes bulged as he gawked at them.

"I'm bleeding... I'm dying..." he panicked.

Marc rolled his eyes. "You are not. Lopez, you're such a drama queen."

"But... but that psychopath cut me..."

From across the room, a familiar voice cackled. "And she'll cut you again!"

Everyone screamed, then the front door slammed shut.

Max pointed the flashlight to the door where Miss Tutley stood with the butcher knife in her hand again.

Mrs. Richards peered into the light. "Miss Tutley? You're alive?"

"This cat has ten lives Richards. Rowwrrr!" Miss Tutley snarled as she clawed at her.

"Well, too bad. We already gave away your parking spot, ordered a substitute, removed you from the coffee fund, and gave the personal effects in your locker to the Salvation Army."

"Well, someone somewhere is the proud new owner of kinky sex toys, skanky clothing, and a Biology for Dummies book," Fiona said.

Miss Tutley glared at her, then jabbed the knife at Carter. "Get off your phone Skyler!"

Carter gritted his teeth and reluctantly lowered the phone.

"Get off all your phones!" Miss Tutley yelled at everyone as she swished the knife back and forth at them.

Like Carter, they lowered their phones, but did not end their calls.

"Miss Tutley?" Sally said as she peered at her. "I'm supposed to have her next term..."

"Oh no," Max said, "get out. Get out now before it's too late. Take 'Sock Puppet Making'. Take 'Watching Paint Dry'. Take a year off. Anything."

The lights in the house came back on. Miss Tutley shielded her eyes with her hand, then stumbled forward a step. Closest to her, Carter attempted to advance on her, but she waved him off with a violent, haphazard slash of the knife.

"Stay where you are Arthur!"

"It's Carter, you twit!"

Miss Tutley slowly stepped toward Max and Jack.

"Well, now that Mommie Dearest is gone, I win after all!"

"Win?" Leslie asked. "No one's going to vote for you anymore. You're a hypocritical, psychotic, homewrecking, murdering, sexual degenerate."

"To be fair," Connie said, "it's because of those things Republicans will vote for her."

"No!" Miss Tutley snarled. "Now we can be a family," she said with a twisted grin on her face as she stared psychotically at Jack and Max.

"I think I'd rather have Mom back," Max said. He thought for a moment. "No, that's not an option either."

"After what you pulled here tonight Shelley, you still think you can move in and take Martha's place?" Jack asked. "If only the rabbit would have finished you off..."

Miss Tutley pointed the knife at Jack. "It was you?! Jack, how could you? The times we had... The sex, the more sex, the times you let me win when we played Scrabble..."

"You can actually win Scrabble by spelling dog, cat and it?" Fiona asked.

Sarah gestured at Miss Tutley. "Exhibit A."

"I knew you were allergic to rabbits," Jack continued. "I knew what would happen if I set him loose in the biology lab."

"And I hoped the poisonous killer plant I put in the lab would kill her," Carter said.

Miss Tutley abruptly turned and pointed the knife at Carter. "Parker, how could you? I've been nothing but nice to you."

Carter bit his lip. "You're a horrible, selfish sociopath Shelley! Only the Mother's Love Death Plant from Xtalquepalpalzantengo could stop you."

"Shelley," Jack said, "how psychotic do you have to be to believe that after all the scheming and treachery you've committed against everyone here, you can worm your way into my family? It's not happening. Do you understand me?"

"Hmmmm, I don't know," Sarah said. "It was a long sentence with lots of syllables..."

"You're an ugly, ugly person," Jack continued. "I regret having anything to do with you, like your other victims. You even tried to seduce Carter."

"It was a goal, but oh no, Diego had to be all moral, monogamous and gay."

"Diego?!" Carter said. "Oh, come on! That doesn't even rhyme!"

"At first, you were a little fun on the side," Jack said. "Something to take my mind off my wreck of a marriage. But I discovered I could manipulate you like you manipulated the other married men you sank your claws into, the families you broke apart, and the cruel, unprofessional way you treated your students like they were sticky used gum on the soles of your heels. You had to be stopped, and so did Martha, so I encouraged you to run as crazy a campaign against her. Two birds – one stone."

Mrs. Horgenstefler reached out and gently put a hand on Miss Tutley's arm.

"You do sound like a great big dumpster fire tart dear."

Miss Tutley shook her hand off. "If you people would have minded your own business, and let me have my fun, this would never have happened."

"This woman is nuts," Marc said.

"This woman is a teacher?!" Enrique asked, flabbergasted.

"Yeah," Max said. "Thank you background checks."

"So, it's our fault Tutley?" Jenny asked. "You're a disgrace to the human race."

"No, your shoes are a disgrace Plain Jane!" Miss Tutley retorted.

Jenny stared at her shoes, puzzled.

Miss Tutley shook her hair and gripped the knife. "Now, where was I before I was rudely interrupted by the Jugband Mountain Jamboree?"

She slowly stepped toward Elliott and stabbed the knife in his direction.

"Why won't you die Miss Tutley?" he whimpered.

"Quiet elephant!" she snapped.

Miss Tutley jabbed the knife at Sarah, and at Robin. "Should I knock off Sara Lee, Miss Brains-Before-Beauty? Or should I dissect Gavin the lonely bookworm?"

"Neither," Robin said.

Miss Tutley curiously peered at the enhanced red X on Sarah's forehead.

"Oh, remember this?" Sarah asked. "I call it the Mark of Tutley – a symbol for all students to take a stand against stupidity and incompetence. I'm having it trademarked."

Miss Tutley scoffed, then pointed the knife at Fiona and Alex. "Maybe I should eliminate Fiona the disowned hothead or finish off her dumb jock boyfriend?"

"Fuck off Tutley!" Fiona spat.

Miss Tutley laughed demonically, then waved the knife at Stevie, who wept and held onto Mrs. Horgenstefler.

"I don't even know who you are!" he wailed.

Max leaned toward Jesus. "Do they have teachers like this in Canada?"

"No. Although one time, I heard a teacher got angry and broke some chalk..."

"Or should it be... the Oreo boys!" Miss Tutley exclaimed as she whirled around to face Max and Marc.

"You're sick Tutley," Marc said.

"Miss Tutley, stop torturing these children!" Mrs. Richards shouted.

Miss Tutley weaved the butcher knife back and forth from Max to Marc like a magic wand. "So, who gets it first? I think it should be the person who hates me the most..."

She pointed the knife at Max.

"Yes, I hate you the most!" Max shouted. "You're the worst teacher ever. You insulted and hurt all my friends. You slept with my father. You killed my best friend!"

Miss Tutley smiled deviously. "Then it makes this decision much easier..."

As Miss Tutley took a step toward Max, Jack peeled his way toward him. Marc leapt in front of Max. But Miss Tutley stopped. Her eyes grew big, and her mouth opened wide. She gasped for air. She threw her head back as if she were about to have an exaggerated sneeze.

Everyone took a step back in horror at her wild pre-sneeze. Miss Tutley froze, then stared at her feet in horror. A perfectly healthy and uninjured Mr. Fluffy Puffy snuggled next to her ankles. He wiggled his nose at her.

Miss Tutley screamed and shook as if a circuit blew in her brain. She dropped the knife. It clattered to the floor. As she sneezed continuously, Max grabbed Mr. Fluffy Puffy, Fiona grabbed the knife, and Elliott tackled Miss Tutley, and sat on her.

Max held the rabbit close to his chest. "Mr. Fluffy Puffy, I thought she killed you!"

"There's an elephant sitting on you now bitch!" Elliott shouted at Miss Tutley. "What are you gonna do about it? Huh? Nothing!"

"It's okay Elliott," Max said. "Mr. Fluffy Puffy has her now..."

Max deliberately lowered the rabbit to her face. She sneezed and wheezed continuously.

"Get... that... monster... away... from... me..."

"But she killed him," Robin said. "I saw his body. We all did."

"Wait a minute," Marc said as he walked to the sofa.

A clear liquid pooled on the floor. A fluffy rabbit's ear peeked out from under the sofa. Marc pulled out Max's stuffed toy replica of Mr. Fluffy Puffy.

"This is what she killed," Marc said as the clear gel stuffing leaked over his hands.

"You made these children think you killed a pet rabbit?" Connie exclaimed. "You sicko."

"Si, la mujer es el diablo," Enrique said.

Fists pounded on the front door, and 'Bringing in the Sheaves' rang again.

"That tune is going to haunt me forever Mr. Molder," Stevie wailed.

"Well, I've lived with it for years," Max said.

"This is the police! Open the door!" a man's voice boomed from the doorstep.

Jack swiped Tucker Carlson's book from the floor, marched to the door, wound up like a major league pitcher, and smashed the doorbell apparatus from the wall. He dropped the book and opened the door to two police officers.

"Hello, I'm Officer Greene," the woman said, "and this is Officer Walker," she said as she motioned to her partner.

"Yes, please come in," Jack said. "I'm Jack... I'm Juan Martinez, the homeowner."

The officers stepped into the house.

"Mr. Martinez, what's going on here?" Officer Walker asked. "We received multiple calls from this address about a hostage taking."

Jenny ran forward and gestured wildly at Miss Tutley.

"Our crazy idiot slut teacher Miss Tutley tried to kill us!"

"Hmmmm," Officer Greene said, "another crazy idiot slut teacher..."

"Good grief, how many are there?" Robin asked.

Officer Greene stepped forward and took a closer look at Miss Tutley. "Wait a minute, this looks like the same crazy idiot slut teacher from two towns over who escaped from the women's prison two years ago..."

"Longest... six... months... of... my... life..." Miss Tutley wheezed.

Officer Walker removed handcuffs from his belt. "Alright, we'll handle this..."

"Handcuffs?" Fiona questioned. "You want to lock her up, not turn her on."

"Yeah," Sarah said, "and you need that face mask/straight jacket combo from The Silence of the Lambs."

Max took Mr. Fluffy Puffy away from Miss Tutley's face and gently stroked him.

Officer Greene gestured to Elliott. "Okay, come on now young man, get off her."

"But... but she called me elephant... she killed our history teacher... she tried to make us all stupid... she laughed at Jenny's shoes..." Elliott wailed as he pointed at her shoes.

"Okay, okay," Officer Walker said, "we'll make sure she... oh my God!" he cried out as he stared at Jenny's shoes. "Now those are ugly."

Jenny tried to hide her shoes behind the sofa.

Officer Greene helped Elliott off Miss Tutley. Officer Walker pulled her to her feet, yanked her hands behind her back, and handcuffed her.

"Your reign of terror is over Miss Tutley," he said. "If that's your real name..."

"Yes, it's my real name," she whined. "Why would I lie about that?"

"You lied about being a competent teacher," Carter said.

"Whew," Alex said, "now we don't have to try and kill her anym..."

Fiona jabbed him in the ribs.

"He means with kindness. Kindness," Sarah emphasized. "She was such a selfless, positive influence on all her students... Oh God, I think I'm gonna be sick..."

Sarah wretched and ran into the kitchen.

"You ignorant kids!" Miss Tutley spat. "I made your boring lives more interesting and fun, didn't I?"

"No!" her students chorused.

"I did my best with my fake degree! Who cares if the most I knew about biology was..."

"About the size of a dust mite's heart valve?" Max offered.

Officer Greene peered at the blood on Alex's shirt. "Are you okay young man?"

Marc waved her off. "Awww, it's only a little scratch..."

Fiona thrusted a hand at Miss Tutley. "She tried to kill him!"

Miss Tutley wildly shook her head. "Only because he wouldn't have sex with me!"

"Oh my God," Officer Greene whispered, "this is the same crazy idiot slut teacher..."

Mrs. Richards put a hand on Alex's arm. "I have first aid training dear."

"Oh, thank you," Fiona said.

"Mrs. Richards," Jack said, "while we wait for the ambulance, there are bandages and a first aid kit in the cabinet in the bathroom."

"Right. Let's go dear," Mrs. Richards said as she ushered Alex and Fiona to the bathroom.

"In Canada, a teacher like this would have been fired and publicly shamed," Jesus said.

"Yeah, well here they go to jail, get out, and try to teach again," Max said.

Mrs. Horgenstefler sidled to Miss Tutley and gently put a hand on her arm. "Does your mother know what an embarrassment you are to teaching dear?"

Miss Tutley defiantly shook her head. "I have nothing to be ashamed about! I filled everyone's lives with excitement, joy and happiness."

Connie leaned into Jack. "She's as deluded as Martha."

"What a stretch, but I see your point."

"I'm a good girl I am," Miss Tutley whined like Eliza Doolittle.

Everyone in the room, including the officers, laughed long and hard in unison.

"Man," Carter said through tears, "she does fill our lives with joy and happiness."

"But... but...but..." Miss Tutley tried to explain.

"Well, I've had enough joy and happiness from her..." Max said.

He stepped forward, lifted Mr. Fluffy Puffy to her face, took him away, and repeated the process. Miss Tutley sneezed and wheezed in starts and stops.

"Okay son, you've had your fun," Officer Walker said as he turned and led Miss Tutley to the door.

"But I am a good girl," Miss Tutley said in a trance. "Mommy and Daddy told me so..."

"I'm sure they did," Officer Greene said, nodding as she walked alongside Miss Tutley and her partner. She turned to the group behind her and shook her head. "I'll be back to get your statements," she said, and they led Miss Tutley from the house.

"Ohhhh, woe is me..." Miss Tutley faintly cried.

"Blech," Max retched. "Now that she's gone, I remember there was a party here. Robin, the music."

Max motioned to Robin, who walked to the stereo, and turned on the music.

Max gestured to the snack and drink table. "Would our new guests like to partake? I know it's been quite the night..."

The new guests nodded and joined the teens at the table.

"Enrique, since my wife is no longer with us, would you please stay?" Jack asked. "With a raise. And I'd also like to hire your wife's company to help inside the house."

"Oh, thank you Mr. Molder... err, senor Martinez."

Stevie gripped Jack's arm. "Mr. Molder, I need to phone my wife, but those two crooks stole my phone. Can I borrow yours?"

"Sure Stevie," Jack said as he handed his cell phone to him.

"She'll never believe me when I tell her your wife hired two ex-cons to kidnap me, and your son's psychotic teacher held me hostage – so could you talk to her if she doesn't believe me... or write me a note?"

Jack laughed. "Sure Stevie."

"I sure could use a drink," Mrs. Horgenstefler said. "And I don't mean Fresca either."

"See!" Elliott exclaimed, "someone else likes it too!"

"Right this way ma'am," Jenny said, then she and Elliott guided her to the snack table.

"Well Leslie," Connie said, "we should get to work on my campaign... unless all this has been too traumatising for you..."

"Connie, I worked with Martha for months. Nothing could be more traumatising."

"Max, I'm so sorry all this happened," Carter said.

"Why? It's not your fault Mr. Riley. You didn't know my mother was an unhinged loon."

"Ummm, yeah I did."

"I think what Carter is trying to say is," Christian said, "we should have done more. The second I saw her pamphlet I should have phoned the police. Maybe the sick plans your mother and Miss Tutley concocted never would have gotten off the ground."

"But we'd still be stuck with Tutley and Martha," Carter said. "No offence Max."

"No, I agree. It all worked out in the end."

Jack put a hand on his shoulder and squeezed it.

"Max, you should have told me about this."

"The party?"

"No, about trying to kill Tutley."

"Ummm, it's not something you mention to your parents at the breakfast table. 'Okay, I'm off to school. Oh, and by the way, my friends and I are going to kill our horribly incompetent teacher tonight. 'Bye!'. I don't think so Dad."

"Still, you could get into a lot of trouble for what you guys did..."

"Oh, and you sneaking a killer rabbit into the school after hours is okay?" He wiggled Mr. Fluffy Puffy at Jack. "Smart though Dad, using Mr. Fluffy Puffy as a way to kill her."

Jack patted himself on the back. "Awww thanks. Max, are you okay with what happened to your mom?"

Max shrugged his shoulders. "She's my mom. I'll probably miss her, but..." he shook his head, "the person she turned into... filled with poison."

"I know. It's like the Republican Party switched her with one of their fembots."

Marc returned from the snack and drink table. He carried a glass in each hand, and offered one to Max. “Need a drink?”

Max took the glass from him. “Oh great, thanks.”

“Don’t worry, it’s only ginger ale Mr. Molder… I mean, Mr. Martinez,” Marc said. “Damn, I’m gonna have a hard time with your name.”

Jack laughed. “Everyone will at first.”

Outside, an ambulance siren wailed in the distance.

“There’s the ambulance,” Jack said.

He quickly walked to the door and disappeared outside. Max and Marc slumped to the sofa in a heap. Max put his head on Marc’s shoulder, and Marc put an arm around him.

“Oh man, what a night,” Marc said.

“I am so glad this is over,” Max said.

Marc peered at Max. “Over? Do you really think it’s over? Your mom’s gone off with two unhinged ex-cons, and Tutley’s been arrested. And you have no idea what maniac we’ll get for our next biology teacher.”

“Don’t worry Marc. They’ll be great. No one could possibly be as hopelessly stupid and inept as Tutley…”

THIRTY-THREE

ONE MONTH LATER

The morning sun poured through the biology lab windows. The lab was reconstructed into a modern, neat and tidy classroom. Potted flowers were randomly placed on the counters, and a large vase containing chrysanthemums sat on the teacher's desk at the front. Large, yellow, smiling happy face emoji stickers were pasted on both classroom doors. A large, hand-drawn happy face overwhelmed the whiteboard. A new, neutral expression, eunuched biology dummy stood guard at the back.

The students were seated at their stations. They eyeballed each other as a woman in her mid-fifties with shoulder-length brown hair stood at the first counter. She wore slightly tinted glasses, a neat, red JC Penney pantsuit, and pink elbow-length industrial gloves. She grunted as she frantically scrubbed the counter with a large scouring pad.

"Ummm, Miss Palin..." Jenny said.

"Yes Katie," the woman said cheerily.

"It's Jenny, Miss Palin. You've been scrubbing the counter for ten minutes now..."

"You hold on a sec there Katie," Miss Palin said as she stopped scrubbing to wave a hand at Jenny and point at her. "I knows a thing or two 'bout cleanin' up animal carcasses."

"But it's only a fetal pig," Fiona said.

"You betcha, but you never can trust them little piggies. You gotta disimmigrant them bugs so they won't ever come back – just like Jesus salted the earth..."

"The before teacher didn't like immigrants either," Elliott said.

"Oh, they're horrible, aren't they?" Miss Palin said as she resumed her scrubbing. "Them dirty little bugs are festerin' with disease. Ya gotta build a great big wall to keep 'em out, otherwise they keep breedin' 'n breedin', and everyone pays the piper!"

"Some only want a better life in a new home," Marc said.

"Oh, you kids these days, always wantin' to see the good side of things. That's cute. Where I come from, the woods, it's kill or be killed."

"Oh, is that where you were born?" Alex asked.

"Yes! There's no worryin' 'bout progressive ideas, logical thinkin', reality or people who look and talk different from you. God does all your thinkin' and creatin' for ya!"

"Sounds like a backwoods, irrational, utopian cult," Max said.

"Oh, it is! Ya gotta be on your tippy toes though, or else crazy, liberal, society-clingin' types can swoop in, take your guns away, and let Mr. and Mr. Smith make house together beside an elementary school where innocent kiddies are learnin'."

"Who are they?" Robin asked.

"Oh, two men we ran out of town."

"Miss Palin, the ammonia fumes are making me dizzy..." Elliott said as his eyes crossed.

"Darn tootin'! It's how ya know they're workin'! Now... where's the bleach..."

Miss Palin stopped scrubbing, scanned under the counter, reached in, and plopped a large container marked BLEACH on the counter.

"No Miss Palin!" Sarah warned. "Bleach and ammonia don't mix!"

"You calm yourself there Sarah," Miss Palin said as she dismissively waved a hand at her, then unscrewed the cap on the bleach bottle. "I should know if two liquidy-chemically thingys don't mix – the governor of Alaska and the senator from Arizona for example..."

Miss Palin's elbow bumped the bleach container as she emphasized the difference between the two things by spreading her arms out wide. The container tipped over, and the bleach poured onto the counter. Miss Palin waved a gloved hand in front of her face.

"Whew, those fumes are nasty! I'll just open this air vent and light a match..."

She reached over and turned on the propane valve.

"Everybody down!" Max screamed.

The students ducked under their stations en masse as Miss Palin lit a match.

"Whoopsie doodle..." she said.

Moments later outside the lab, the classroom doors blew off.

#

"Ahhhhhh!" Max screamed as he leaned forward in his bed.

Sweat beaded his forehead. He wildly scanned the room wide-eyed as he heaved and gasped for air. The sun cascaded through the open blinds and caught him in the face as he hyperventilated. He leaned back on his elbows to escape the sun's rays. He pulled his dark navy t-shirt to his brow and wiped his forehead.

In the hallway, footsteps pounded toward his closed bedroom door, followed by a soft, quick knock on the door.

"Max, are you okay?" Martha asked.

"Mom?"

"Yes. Can I come in?"

Max rubbed his eyes, opened them wide, and shook his head. "Yeah..."

The door opened, and Martha entered the room, casually dressed in a grey sweatshirt, jeans, and runners. Her hair was neatly pulled back in a loose ponytail. She wore no jewelry, and no makeup. Her brow furrowed as she stared at him.

"Max?" she asked, legitimately concerned, rather than annoyed.

Max reached out to her, about to burst into tears. "Mom!"

Martha rushed to his bed and sat beside him. Max wrapped his arms around her and held on tight.

"Oh Mom!"

"What's the matter Max – a bad dream?"

"Oh Mom, you're okay!"

"Sure I am."

Max pulled back and stared at her. "And Dad... where's Dad?"

Juan appeared in the doorway. "I'm right here. Are you okay Max?"

Martha stroked Max's cheek with her fingertips. "Awww, he had a bad dream."

Juan sat on the bed next to Martha. "We heard you screaming from the kitchen. That must have been one heck of a nightmare."

"Oh man," Max said, "my biology teacher was a moronic black widow tramp who slept with everybody, killed old men, and made their lives miserable..."

"Miss Tutley?" Juan asked. "The young girl who's the president of both local chapters of Mensa and the Abstinence Society?"

"... and everyone in town tried to kill her, and she kept coming back to life... and Mom was some ghoulish, crazy, religious, right-wing, alcoholic who ran for state representative..."

Martha laughed.

"... and she joined a religious cult that turned out to be a terrorist group, and they robbed the bank, and kidnapped Mom... and Dad was having an affair with Miss Tutley... and he convinced her to run against Mom in the election to stop her... and she wore a Handmaid's outfit and a corset while she burned right-wing books..."

Juan laughed.

"... and Mom thought you were having an affair with your assistant and your secretary..."

Martha and Juan eyeballed each other and laughed.

"Steven?" Juan asked, "the young asthmatic Mormon who's working three jobs to care for his two sets of triplets?"

"And Mrs. Horgenstefler?" Martha asked, "the ninety-year-old retired switchboard operator Social Services placed at the bank to count pennies so she wouldn't play with matches at her retirement home?"

"Oh Max," Juan said as he put a hand on Max's leg and gently shook it.

"And... and Mom called you Jack and said you were Italian, and our last name was Molder, and she forced me to dye my hair blond so no one would know I was Puerto Rican and gay because I'd ruin her election campaign..."

"Martha, how could you?" Juan said playfully.

Martha raised her hands and shook her head.

"...and... and Mom kept trying to marry me off to the girl next door..."

"Sally?" Martha asked. "The girl who changed her name to Arlene, and ran off to join a cult in Idaho?"

"... and Mom had a nervous breakdown when I told her I was gay, and tried to force Sally and me to have sex..."

"Well, that's not how I reacted at all when you told me," Martha said.

"Wow Martha, you don't come off well in this do you?" Juan said.

"... and Dad tried to kill Miss Tutley with Mr... Mr. Fluffy Puffy!" Max screamed as he gripped Martha's arms and stared at her in terror.

Max tore himself from Martha and jumped out of bed. He bounded to the cage on the table and threw the cover off the cage. A fluffy white rabbit inside turned its head, stared at him, and wiggled its nose.

"Mr. Fluffy Puffy..." Max said, relieved. He unlatched the door, reached into the cage, pulled the rabbit out, and cuddled it against him. "You're alive... you're alive."

Juan stood. "Okay, I'm going to continue to eat my breakfast now. Max, no more Xtalquepalpalzantengo hot peppers before bed young man."

Max regarded his father strangely as Juan walked from the room.

"Alright you two," Martha said as she stood, "breakfast time. Today's a big day."

She ruffled Max's hair. Max put the rabbit back in the cage.

"Big day? What's going on?"

Martha walked to the door. "Oh honey, we know you're nervous, but you'll do fine."

"Fine at what?"

"Your speech welcoming the President to town, silly."

"The President?"

Martha turned at the doorway. "Yes, President Sarah Palin."

Max screamed.

ABOUT THE AUTHOR

TC Scott was born and raised in Nova Scotia, Canada. He is a graduate of Acadia University (English Literature) and Toronto Metropolitan University (Broadcasting). A novelist, a screenwriter, and a freelance writer, he also enjoys cycling, tennis, and film. He is also the author of the Mitchell Bay children's mystery/adventure series (writing as Trevor Chittick) that began with *The Boy in Mitchell Bay*, and the young adult thriller/horror *Stanley*. A sequel to *White Rabbit,* a young adult crime thriller, and a political sci-fi thriller are to come. He currently resides in the Canadian Maritimes.

www.ingramcontent.com/pod-product-compliance
Lightning Source LLC
Chambersburg PA
CBHW031255120726
47906CB00003B/753